# ESCAPE FROM EARTH

# ESCAPE
# FROM EARTH
## New Adventures in Space

Edited by

## Jack Dann & Gardner Dozois

SCIENCE
FICTION

# CONTENTS

# INTRODUCTION

## Escaping from Earth

WHEN YOUR EDITORS were young, millennia ago, when dinosaurs walked the Earth, we were introduced to the wonders of science fiction by the "juvenile novels"—today they would be called Young Adult novels—of writers such as Andre Norton and Robert A. Heinlein, by the "Winston juvenile" line of books written by authors such as Lester del Rey, Jack Vance, Poul Anderson, Raymond F. Jones, Donald Wollheim, and Evan Hunter, by the "Lucky Starr" series by Isaac Asimov, the "Tripods" series by John Christopher, and by ostensibly "adult" SF novels that actually functioned very well as defacto "Young Adult" books, such as Hal Clement's *Cycle of Fire* and *Iceworld*. In retrospect, it's clear that the '50s and '60s were the Golden Age of YA SF

Since the '60s, though, although a strong YA tradition remained and remains (can you say, "Harry Potter"?) in the fantasy genre, little Young Adult material has been published in science fiction—meaning that while a "gateway experience" remained in place for fantasy readers, a passageway through which they could progress from Young Adult to adult material, no such passageway was available for science fiction readers. New readers were forced to make the transition to adult SF all in one jump, with no intermediate step—something that may well have proved too difficult a jump for many of them.

Even today, if you want to give someone a good YA SF book,

you're mostly reduced to handing them one of the Heinlein "juveniles" such as *Red Planet* or *The Star Beast* or *Have Space Suit—Will Travel*, all excellent books, but all books that were written and published in the '40s and '50s, and so books that have inevitably dated over the past forty years—perhaps too much so to appeal to modern readers.

Where, we wondered, were the stories that would be as exciting to kids in the Oughts as Heinlein's "juvenile" novels were to kids in the '50s and '60s?

With only a few exceptions, much of the YA SF writing that *has* been done in the past few years has produced only weak imitations of Heinlein juveniles, without the fun—dull, pompous, and condescending stuff, usually stuffed to the gunwales with didactic propaganda. This isn't going to do it for kids raised on MTV, CGI-drenched movies, and computer games.

The launching point for this anthology, then, was to find stories that were *fun* as well as thought-provoking, that dealt with that restless urge to explore, to escape from the humdrum and everyday, to see what's over the next hill, or in the next valley, that is an inextinguishable part of the human spirit in every generation. Stories that help us to escape from the mundane limitations of Earth, stories that open up heretofore unexpected worlds and vistas to new readers, stories that generate that quintessential Sense of Wonder kick that is at the heart of the genre: gorgeously colored, fast-paced, richly detailed, lushly imaginative, widescreen. Exciting, colorful, and fun. The kind of thing that started us all reading science fiction in the first place.

This anthology is our attempt to provide such stories. It's our hope that if SF as a genre can provide stuff that kids are actually *eager* to read, rather than having it prescribed for them medicinally, then that will go a long way to assuring that there are people around who still want to read the stuff even in the middle decades of the new century ahead.

—Jack Dann
Gardner Dozois

# ESCAPE FROM EARTH

# ESCAPE FROM EARTH

## by *Allen M. Steele*

Most kids dream about getting away from home, from their dull little towns and the boring routines of daily life, of striking out into the unknown in search of adventure. *Some*, however, get to go a lot further a lot *faster* than they ever dreamed, and have adventures a lot wilder than any they ever thought possible . . .

Allen M. Steele made his first sale to *Asimov's Science Fiction* magazine in 1988, soon following it up with a long string of other sales to *Asimov's*, as well as to markets such as *The Magazine of Fantasy and Science Fiction* and *Science Fiction Age*. In 1989, he published his critically acclaimed first novel, *Orbital Decay*, which subsequently won the Locus Poll as Best First Novel of the year, and soon Steele was being compared to Golden Age Heinlein by no less an authority than Gregory Benford. His other books include the novels *Clarke County, Space, Lunar Descent, Labyrinth of Night*, the chapbook novella *The Weight, The Tranquility Alternative, A King of Infinite Space, Oceanspace,* and *Chronospace, Coyote,* and *Coyote Rising*. His short work has been gathered in three collections, *Rude Astronauts, All-American Alien Boy,* and *Sex and Violence in Zero-G*. His most recent book is a new novel in the Coyote sequence, *Coyote Frontier*. He won a Hugo Award in 1996 for his novella "The Death of Captain Future," and another Hugo in 1998 for his novella ". . . Where Angels Fear to Tread." Born in Nashville, Tennessee, he has worked for a variety of newspapers and magazines, covering science and business assignments, and is now a full-time writer living in Whately, Massachusetts, with his wife, Linda.

I ALWAYS WANTED to be an astronaut.

I don't remember when the space bug first bit me. Maybe it was when I was six years old, and my dad took me to my first science fiction movie. It was the latest *Star Trek* flick, and maybe not one of the best—Steve, my older brother, fell asleep halfway through it—but when you're a little kid, it's the coolest thing in the world to sit in the Bellingham Theatre, scarfing down popcorn and Milk Duds while watching the *Enterprise* gang take on the Borg. It's also one of my favorite memories of my father, so that may have something to do with it.

Or perhaps it was when Mr. Morton moved away. Mr. Morton wasn't well-liked in our neighborhood; he drank a lot, which was why his wife left him, and once he called the cops on Steve and me when he caught us skate-boarding in his driveway. So when the Narragansett Point nuclear power plant shut down and he—along with a few hundred other people who'd worked there—was forced to look elsewhere for a job, no one was sad to see him go. Mr. Morton packed as much as he could into a U-Haul trailer, and the rest was left on the street for Goodwill to pick up. His taillights had barely vanished when everyone on the block came over to see what they could scavenge.

Amid the battered Wal-Mart furniture and crusty cookware, I found a cardboard box of books, and among all those dog-eared paperbacks I discovered two that interested me: *A Man on the Moon: The Voyages of the Apollo Astronauts* by Andrew Chaikin, and *Rocket Boys: A Memoir* by Homer H. Hickam, Jr. I took them home, and read and reread them so many times that the pages began to fall out. I was twelve years old by then, and those two books whetted my appetite for space. Mr. Morton may have been a nasty old coot, but he inadvertently did one good deed before he split town.

But what really put the lock on things was the first time I saw the space station. My eighth-grade science teacher at Ethan Allen Middle School, Mr. Ciccotelli, was trying to get the class interested in space, so shortly after the first components of the International Space Station were assembled in Earth orbit, he checked the

NASA Web site and found when the ISS could be seen from southern Vermont. He told us when and where it would appear in the evening sky, then as a homework assignment told us to watch for it, and come to class the next day ready to discuss what we'd seen.

So my best friend, Ted Markey, and I got together in my backyard after dinner. The night was cold, with the first snow of the year already on the ground. We huddled within our parkas and stamped our feet to keep warm; through the kitchen window I could see Mom making some hot chocolate for us. We used my Boy Scout compass to get our bearings, and Ted's father had loaned him a pair of binoculars, but for a long time we didn't see anything. I was almost ready to give up when, just as Mr. Ciccotelli predicted, a bright spot of light rose from the northwest.

At first, we thought it was just an A-10 Thunderbolt from Barnes Air National Base down in Massachusetts, perhaps on a night training mission. Dad was in the National Guard, so I'd been to Barnes a couple of times, and we were used to seeing their Warthog squadron over Bellingham. Yet as the light came over the bare branches of the willow tree at the edge of our property, I noticed that it didn't make the dull drone the way Warthogs usually do. It sailed directly above us, moving too fast for Ted to get a fix on it with his binoculars, yet for a brief instant it looked like a tiny *t* moving across the starry sky.

I suddenly realized that there were men aboard that thing, and at that very same moment they were probably looking down at *us*. In that instant, I wanted to be there. Out in space, floating weightless within a space station, gazing upon Earth from hundreds of miles up. I didn't say that to Ted or Mr. Ciccotelli, and especially not to Steve, who had all the imagination of a cucumber, because I thought it would have sounded stupid, but that was when I knew what I was going to do when I grew up.

Some kids want to be pro athletes. They idolize the Red Sox or the Patriots or the Bruins, and spend their afternoons playing baseball or football or ice hockey. In my town, there's a lot of farm kids who follow the family trade, so they join 4-H and bring the roosters, pigs, and calves they've raised to the state fair in hopes of taking home a blue ribbon. Ted read a lot of comic books; he drew pictures of Spider-Man and the Teen Titans in his school notebooks, and dreamed of the day when he'd move to New York and go to work for Marvel or DC. And, of course, there's guys like Steve, who never really figure out what they want to do, and so end up doing nothing.

That night, I decided that I was going to be an astronaut.

But sometimes you get what you want out of life, and sometimes you don't. Maybe it was impossible for Eric Cosby from Bellingham, Vermont, to be an astronaut. A couple of years later, I was beginning to think so. By then my father had been killed in Iraq, my mother was working two jobs, my brother had become a poster child for DARE, and the night I stood out in my back-yard and watched the space station fly over had become a fading memory.

That was before I met the weird kids. After that, nothing would ever be the same again.

It happened early one evening in late October. Just before sun-down, that time of day when the sun is fading and the streetlights are beginning to come on. I was hanging in front of Fat Boy's Music Store on the corner of Main and Birch, wondering what I was going to do that Friday night.

Fat Boy's was a block from the Bellingham Youth Club, where I'd become accustomed to spending my free time until fed-eral cutbacks for after-school programs caused them to shut their doors. One more thing I owe Uncle Sam, along with sending my dad to some hellhole called Falluja. The corner of Main and Birch wasn't so bad, though. It was in the middle of downtown Bellingham, with the Bellingham Theatre just a half-block away. I missed the foosball and pool tables of the BYC, but Fat Boy's had speakers above the door, and if you stood outside you could listen to new CDs. The guys who ran the store didn't mind so long as you didn't make a public nuisance of yourself, and that constituted blocking the door, leaving empty soda cans on the sidewalk, or doing anything that might attract the cops.

Which amounted to doing anything above and beyond breathing, and that was why hanging out at Main and Birch wasn't such a good idea. The leaf-peepers from New York and Connecticut had come up for the fall foliage, and the local constables didn't want ruffians like me loitering on the streets of Ye Olde New England Towne. Once already a cop car had cruised by, with Officer Beauchamp—aka "Bo," as he was not-so-fondly known—giving me the eye. If he'd stopped to ask what I was doing here, I would've told him I was waiting for Mom to pick me up.

Mom was still at the factory, though, and after that she'd only have an hour or so before she started serving drinks at Buster's Pub. Dinner was in the freezer: another microwave entrée, a choice between beef-this or chicken-that. I'd see her late tonight, if I stayed up long enough. And if I stayed up even later, I might catch the reappearance of Smokin' Steve, Bellingham's favorite convenience store clerk and part-time dope dealer.

So ask me why I was propping up a wall on the street corner, watching what passed for rush hour in my town. I'm not sure I knew, either. I told myself that I was waiting for Ted to show up, and after that we'd grab a bite to eat and maybe catch whatever was showing at the theatre—it looked like another horror flick about evil children with butcher knives—but the fact of the matter was that I was trying to avoid going home. The house seemed to have become empty now that Dad was gone, and every minute I spent there only reminded me how much I missed him.

But it wasn't just that. I was sixteen years old, and lately it had occurred to me that I might be stuck in Bellingham for the rest of my life. Only a year ago, my dream had been to follow my heroes—Alan Shepard and John Glenn, Armstrong, Aldrin, and Collins, John Young—and become the first man to set foot on Mars. Heck, I would've settled for a seat on a shuttle flight to deliver a satellite to orbit. But the only person who'd ever encouraged my ambitions was now six feet under, and no matter how many times I'd bicycled out to the cemetery to have a talk with him, he never answered back.

Damn. If only Dad hadn't re-upped with the National Guard. If he was still around, he'd . . .

"Pardon me. Could you give us some directions?"

Wrapped up in my thoughts, I jumped when a voice spoke beside me. Startled, I looked around, saw a guy . . . No. Not a quite a guy. Another teenager, about my own age, give or take a year or two. Average height, dark brown hair, sharp eyes. I'd never seen him before, but that didn't mean anything. Like I said, a lot of tourists came through Bellingham in the fall.

Nor was he alone. To his right was another kid . . . or at least I assumed he was a kid, because his face was young. But only once before I'd met a kid as big as he was, and although Josh Donnigen was the quarterback for the Bellingham Pilgrims, this dude would've smeared Josh all over the scrimmage line.

Yet it was neither the kid who'd spoken nor the giant on his right who attracted my attention, but the girl between them. There were two or three gals at school who interested me; the best of the bunch was Pauline Coullete, who I'd known since the fifth grade, and whom I'd lately been trying to muster enough courage to ask out for a date. Yet this girl—petite and slender, with light brown hair and the most beautiful eyes I'd ever seen— made Pauline look like she'd just finished shoveling out the barn.

"Yeah, sure," I said. "Where do you want to go?"

"Umm . . ." The kid hesitated. "It's difficult to explain, but could you tell us . . . ?"

"We require guidance to the Narragansett Point Nuclear Power Station." This from the big guy, in a voice was that surprisingly mild. "Topographical directions will suffice, but linear coordinates would also . . ."

"Be quiet, Alex." The girl cast him a stern look, and Alex immediately shut up. Which I thought was strange. If Pauline had spoken to me the same way, I would've been embarrassed, yet this guy showed no trace of emotion. Didn't even blink. Just continued to stare at me, like . . .

"We're trying to find the nuclear . . . I mean . . ." The first kid stammered as if English was a foreign language, even though his accent was American. "The Narragansett Point . . ."

"You mean the nuke?" I asked.

"The nuke, yes." He exchanged a glance with the girl. "That's what we . . . I mean, I . . . that is, we . . ." He squared his shoulders. "Can you tell us how to get there?"

That's when I noticed the way they were dressed . . . and I almost laughed out loud.

Go to a flea market, or maybe a vintage clothing store. Select what you're going to wear at random, relying on dumb luck to get the right size. That's what they looked like they'd done. The kid who couldn't speak plain English wore plaid bell-bottoms with a purple disco shirt under a Yankees field jacket. His pal sported a patchwork sweater with camouflage trousers that rose an inch too high above his ankles, revealing a pair of pointed-toe cowboy boots. The girl had the best sense of style, but even then, I've never met anyone who'd matched a tie-dyed Grateful Dead T-shirt with red pants and a faux-fur overcoat.

Their outfits may have been appropriate for a Halloween party, or maybe a rave club in Boston, yet they were as out of place in a small town in Vermont as a clown costume in church. Maybe this was some sort of post-punk, post-grunge, post-whatever fashion statement, yet I had a distinct feeling that they were trying to dress like American teenagers, but couldn't quite get it right.

And I wasn't the only one who noticed. An all-too-familiar police cruiser came to a stop at the traffic light, and I glanced over to see Officer Beauchamp checking us out. He saw me and I saw him, yet for once he was less interested in what I was doing than in my companions. The two guys didn't notice him, but the girl did; she hastily looked away, yet I could tell that Bo made her nervous.

She wasn't alone. We weren't doing anything illegal, but this bunch was awful conspicuous, and the less attention I got from the law, the better. Although my record was clean, nonetheless I was Steve Cosby's kid brother. So far as Bo was concerned, that alone made me a possible accomplice to every sleazy thing my brother did. Time to get rid of these guys, fast.

"Sure." I pointed down Main Street, away from the center of town. "Go that way two blocks to Adams, then hang a right. Follow it five more blocks to Route 10, then cut a left and follow it out of town. Plant's about ten miles that way. Can't miss it."

"Thank you." The girl gave me a smile that would have melted the ice on the school hockey rink. "You've been most kind." She hesitated, then added, "I'm Michaela. My friends call me Mickey."

"Michaela." I savored the name on my tongue. "I'm Eric. Are you from . . . ? I mean, I know you're not from here, but . . ."

"Pleased to meet you, Eric." The big guy extended his hand. "I'm Alex. His name is Tyler. We're . . ."

"Alex, be quiet." Tyler swatted his hand away from mine, and once again Alex went silent. What was it with them? Didn't they want Alex to talk to me?

The light changed. Bo cast one more glance in our direction, then his car slowly glided forward, heading in the direction of the theatre. I knew that he'd just swing around the block and come back for another pass. It would probably be a good idea to be gone by then.

"We must go." Tyler apparently realized this, too, for he took Mickey's arm. "Thank you for the directions . . ."

"Bye, Eric." Again, Mickey turned on her smile. "Nice to meet you."

I was still trying to unstick my tongue from the roof of my mouth when Tyler led her and Alex across the street. He was in so much of a hurry that he didn't notice that they were walking against the light. As it happened, a Ford Explorer was approaching the intersection from Birch. The SUV blared its horn, startling Mickey and Tyler; Alex, though, calmly stepped in front of his friends, raising his hands as if to protect them.

For a second, I thought Alex would bounce off the Explorer's hood. Or maybe—just for an instant—exactly vice versa; Alex was utterly complacent, even as the SUV bore down upon him. Yet as the Explorer skidded to a halt, Tyler grabbed Mickey and yanked her across the street, while Alex lowered his arms and sauntered behind them, ignoring the obscenities yelled at him by the driver.

They continued down Main, heading in the direction I'd given them. Just before they passed Rumke's Department Store, though, Mickey glanced back over her shoulder. I thought she smiled at me, but Tyler dragged her away before I could wave goodbye.

I was still watching them go when Ted showed up. "Let me guess," he said. "You've just met the perfect girl, and now she's gone."

Again, I jumped. It was the second time that evening someone had snuck up on me. Even if it was only Ted, that was one time too many.

"Forget it. They were just asking directions." I looked up Birch; sure enough, I could see Bo's cop car coming our way. "C'mon, let's get out of here. Bo's on my case tonight. Pizza at Louie's?"

"Sure. Why not?" Ted didn't need to ask why Officer Beauchamp might take an interest in me; he knew my recent family history. When the light changed again, we crossed the street, then cut up Birch to an alley that would take us behind the block of buildings along Main, a shortcut to Louie's Pizzeria. "So who were they? And who was the babe?"

"I dunno." I darted a glance behind us as we entered the alley. No sign of Bo. Good. "Just some guys asking how to get to Narragansett."

"Oh, yeah. Right." Ted snickered as he gave me a sidelong look. "The way you were talking to her, I thought maybe you and she . . ."

"Never saw her before in my life." I caught the look in his eye. "She was just asking directions, okay?"

Ted was my best and oldest friend, so I forgave him for a lot

of things, not the least of which was being a total geek. We'd
both recently discovered girls, and were trying to figure out how
to deal with them, yet Ted's interest in the other half of the human race was misinformed by comic books and TV shows. He
didn't want a date that ended with a kiss at the door, but a hot
night with Lana Lang. He was no Clark Kent, though, glasses
aside, and until he learned how to degeekify himself, he had as
much of a chance of getting a steady girl as Brainiac.

"Sure, yeah." But now his expression had become pensive.
"But why would they want to go out there?"

"I dunno." We'd come out of the alley, and were walking
across a parking lot. "Maybe they were part of a school group
taking a tour."

"On a Friday night?" Again, he looked at me askance. "And
since when did the plant let anyone inside?"

He had something there. At one time, New England Energy
allowed local schools to take field trips to the plant. But after
9/11 they closed the plant to the public, and it wasn't long after
that when Narragansett Point was decommissioned. But though
the reactor may have gone out of service, everyone knew that the
spent fuel rods were still being stored on-site until they could be
shipped to the Yucca Mountain nuclear waste facility in Nevada.
So there was no way a school group would be allowed on the
premises.

"Maybe they were looking for a spot to go parking." Even as
I said that, it sounded wrong. Sure, the old visitors' parking lot
had once been a favorite make-out spot, but security patrols
around the plant had put an end to that before I had a chance to
borrow Steve's car for my fantasized date with Pauline.

Besides, how would some out-of-town kids know about the
Point? And come to think of it, how where they going to get out
there in the first place? The plant was ten miles from town, and I
didn't see them get in a car.

"It doesn't make sense," Ted said. "Unless they're . . ."

"You mean they're not interested in the World's Biggest Rock-
ing Chair? Or the Farm Museum?" Despite my own misgivings, I

grinned at him. "Where's your civic pride? Aren't you a proud citizen of Bellingham, Vermont, the greatest town in . . . ?"

I stopped myself. By then we'd come upon another alley, this one leading from behind the Main Street shops to Winchester Street, where the pizza place was located. A Chevy van was blocking our way, though, so we had to go around it. As we started to walk past, I saw that its side doors were open; within the light cast by its ceiling dome, someone was fiddling with something on a fold-down workbench.

A girl just a little older than Ted and me stood in the open back door of one of the shops. She saw us coming, and raised a hand. "Hey, Eric. How'ya doing?"

Sharon Ogilvy, who'd graduated from Bellingham High just last spring. I knew her because she'd gone out with Steve for a short while. Like a lot of my brother's ex-girlfriends, she'd broken up with him because . . . well, because he was Smokin' Steve, and there were better dates you could have than guys who'd make you walk home alone in the rain because you weren't cool enough for him and his crew. But she and I had remained friends, although she never dropped by our house any more. Not that I blamed her; I often wished I lived somewhere else, too.

"Hey, Sharon." I strolled over to her, stepping around the front of the van. The workman barely glanced up at me; now that I was closer, I saw that he was a locksmith, using a portable lathe to make a set of keys. "Just getting some pizza. What are you doing?"

"Working here now." She frowned. "Or at least I hope I'll still have a job tomorrow, after what happened today."

"Break-in?" Ted had noticed the locksmith, too.

"Yeah. Found the door open when I came in this morning. Someone busted the lock . . ."

"Busted, hell." The locksmith didn't look up at us. "Whatever they did to it, they didn't use a crowbar." Before I could ask what he meant, he reached forward to pick up the knob he'd just replaced. "Damnedest thing I ever saw," he went on, handing it to Ted. "Like someone put an acetylene torch to it."

I took a look at it. As he said, the knob itself hadn't been damaged . . . but the bolt looked as if it had been melted. "Whoever did this had a fine touch," the locksmith continued. "No scorch marks on the back plate or the door frame. You'd wonder why they even bothered." An apologetic look at Sharon. "No offense."

"Well, if they thought they'd find enough money . . ." Ted began.

"You kiddin'?" Sharon laughed. "What do you think this is, a jewelry store? We barely make enough to pay the rent."

"What do you . . . ?" I shook my head. "Sorry, but I must be missing something. What is this place?"

"S'okay. You can't tell with the door open like this." Sharon stepped aside to half-shut the door. Now we could see the sign on its outside:

SALVATION ARMY THRIFT SHOP
Deliveries Only—No Dumping
Please Take All Donations To Front Door

"Why'd anyone take the trouble to break into this place . . ." She shrugged. "I mean, we make maybe forty, fifty dollars a day, and it gets deposited at the bank after we close up. If you want to steal something, why bother? Most everything here would cost you less than a Happy Meal at McDonald's . . ."

"So what was stolen?" I asked, feeling a sudden chill.

"Just a few clothes, so far as I can tell. Found the hangers on the floor." She glared at the locksmith. "You could've gotten here earlier, y'know."

"Sorry. Been a long day." He finished with the keys, test-fitted them into the new lock. "Had another break-in just like this at Auto Plaza. Wonder who stole the welding equipment . . . ?"

I was no longer paying much attention. "Gotta go," I said. "Take it easy." Then I nudged Ted and continued heading down the alley.

"You've got something on your mind," Ted said quietly, once we were out of Sharon's earshot. "Want to talk about it?"

"Maybe. I dunno." Clothes stolen from a thrift shop. The

same sort of clothes I'd seen some guys wearing only a few minutes earlier. The same guys who'd asked me the way to the local
nuclear power plant. "Let's talk about it later. I think better when
I've got some food in me."

Louie's didn't have the best pizza in town—that distinction was
held by Le Roma, out near the interstate—but it was the cheap-
est, if you didn't mind a bit of grease. Ted and I ordered our
usual Friday night poison—a large pizza with Italian sausage,
mushrooms, and green peppers—and a pitcher of Pepsi, and
threw a couple of quarters in the pinball machine while we
waited. We'd tucked away about half of the pizza before either of
us brought up the guys I'd met an hour ago.

"What if they're terrorists?" Ted suddenly asked.

I'd just taken a drink from my soda when he said that; it almost came out through my nose. "Aw, man . . ." I forced myself
to swallow, then pulled a paper napkin from the dispenser and
wiped my mouth. "You gotta be jokin'. Terrorists?"

"Seriously. What if they're scoping out the plant?" Ted stared
at me from across the table. "Look at the setup. It's perfect.
Closed-down nuke only about a hundred miles from Boston . . ."

"A hundred and ten miles from Boston. Northwest and up-
wind . . ."

"Whatever. It's still a sitting duck. You break in, set a bomb
near the reactor, blow the thing . . ."

Ted may have been my best friend, but there were times
when his imagination got the better of him. I glanced around to
make sure no one was overhearing us; we were in a corner booth
near the front window, and the waitress was on the other side of
the room. Still, I wasn't taking any chances.

"Keep your voice down, willya?" I murmured. "Dude, the
containment is steel-reinforced concrete, twenty feet thick. It's
built to withstand meltdowns, earthquakes, airplane crashes . . ."

"Yeah, but what if . . . ?"

"Just listen to me, okay?" I peeled off another slice of pizza.
"Even if you had a bomb big enough to crack the dome, how

would you get it in there? You've seen what kind of security they've got around that place. Chain-link fences, vehicle barriers, checkpoints, TV cameras, motion detectors, vault doors with keycard locks . . . not to mention a lot of guys with guns." I smiled. "I pity da fool who try to break inta dat joint."

As always, Ted grinned at my Mr. T impersonation; we'd grown up watching *A-Team* reruns on cable. "Yeah, but still . . ."

"Besides, there isn't any uranium in the reactor." I took a bite, talked around a mouthful of food. "Don't you read the paper? They started removing the fuel rods last spring, storing them in casks outside the building . . . and don't get me started on how big those things are. Not only that, but . . ."

I stopped myself. Until now, I was feeling rather smug, being able to rattle off stuff about the plant that I remembered from the tour we'd taken back in the sixth grade. What I'd been about to say, though, was so dumb that I swallowed it along with the cheese and sausage.

"But what?" Ted asked.

"I dunno." I shrugged. "They just didn't seem like terrorists."

"They didn't *seem* like terrorists?" He laughed out loud. "What do you think they do, wear little stick-on name badges? 'Hello, my name is Osama . . .'"

"You know what I mean." Even as I said this, though, I couldn't help but remember the way Mickey reacted when she spotted Bo. Sure, cops tend to make guys my age a little nervous, even when we've done nothing wrong. If someone was murdered, and the police were to round up five suspects—Al Capone, Charles Manson, Saddam Hussein, Jack the Ripper, and me— and put us all in a lineup, guess which one the eyewitnesses would probably finger?

Still, Mickey had been awful skittish. So was Tyler. And Alex . . . Alex was weird as a three-dollar bill.

Nonetheless, I shook my head. "Look, whatever they are, they're not terrorists. Probably just some guys from out of town who want to see the plant . . ."

"On a Friday night? C'mon . . . this town ain't *that* dead."

Ted started pulling bits of sausage off the pizza. I hated it when he did that. "You saw the way they were dressed . . ."

"Yeah, right." I rescued another slice before he could dissect it. "This from the guy who wears a Fantastic Four T-shirt to gym class."

He glared at me. "Eric, no one dresses like that . . . not even me. And don't tell me it's just a coincidence that the Salvation Army store gets broken into, with nothing taken except some clothes." I started to object, but then he pointed out the window. "Remember what that guy said? About a break-in just like it at Auto Plaza?"

I remembered, all right. What the locksmith had told us sounded odd even then, but I'd pushed it to the back of my mind. Auto Plaza was the biggest car dealership in town; they sold mostly new Fords and GM trucks, but also had a lot full of used cars that they'd acquired as trade-ins. *All makes, all models, best selection in southern Vermont!* the radio ads went. *We've got hot coffee for Mom and Dad, and free balloons for the kiddies!* If you were passing through Bellingham and, just for the hell of it, decided to steal a car, this was the place to go. They even advertised.

"Look . . ." I reached for the pitcher, refilled my glass. "Let's put this together. I run into three guys about our age . . ."

"Whom you or I have never seen before."

"Who dress funny . . ."

"The same day a thrift shop has been broken into."

"And they ask directions to Narragansett Point . . ."

"Uh-huh." Crossing his arms, Ted regarded me with the patience of a priest. "Go on. And they're not quite right, are they?"

I paused. No, they weren't quite right. The way Tyler had spoken, as if English was a foreign language. Mickey getting twitchy when Bo cruised by. Both of them trying to prevent Alex from talking to me. Alex stepping in front of the Explorer that was about to run them down.

"Yeah," I admitted, "they were acting pretty strange . . ."

"And how do you think they intended to get to the plant?" Ted raised an eyebrow. "Walk? Or maybe use a car . . . a stolen car . . . that they'd parked behind a house or in an alley just a few blocks away?"

"Yeah, but . . ." I let out my breath. "C'mon, man . . . terrorists?"

Ted said nothing for a moment. Clasping his hands together, he idly gazed out the window. Night had fallen on downtown Bellingham, all five blocks of it; the stores had closed, and there were only a few cars on the street. Right now, Mom was serving drinks at the local watering hole. At least she behaved like a responsible adult; Ted's parents were probably whooping it up at the same place. With any luck, they'd get home without one of them having to take a roadside test. Neither of us came from happy, wholesome families.

"Yeah. Terrorists." He said this as if it was a matter of fact, not conjecture.

"Get real . . ."

"Okay, then let's get real. Let's head down to the plant, see if they show up."

"Be serious . . ."

"I *am* serious. If I'm wrong, then I'm wrong. But if I'm right . . ."

"If you're so sure, then call the cops." I fished a quarter out of my pocket, slapped it down on the table. "Pay phone's over there. Go do it."

Neither of us had cell phones. Those are for rich kids. Ted gazed at the quarter, a little less certain than he'd been a moment ago. He knew as well as I did how the rest of this would go down. *Hello, Bellingham Police? Yeah, I'm calling to report a terrorist plot to blow up the nuclear power plant. How do I know this? Well, my best friend and I met just some guys who asked directions how to get there. Oh, and they dress funny, too. Who am I? My name's Ted Markey and my friend's name is Eric Cosby, and we're calling from Louie's Pizzeria, and . . .* Five minutes later, Bo shows up to give us a free ride in a police car. Mom would just love that. I'm sure Ted's folks would be similarly amused.

"Yeah, well . . ." He pushed the quarter back across the table. "So what do you want to do tonight? Catch a movie? Or go down to the nuke and see if these guys appear?" He shrugged. "Up to you, man. Whatever you want, I'm game."

Crap. He was throwing this in my lap again. Yet, I had to admit to myself, he had a point. This was a mystery, and a pretty good one at that. And there *had* to be better things to do on a Friday night than doze through another stupid horror movie . . .

"Maybe. But how do we get down there?" I wasn't looking forward to hopping on my ten-speed and peddling all the way out to Narragansett Point. Not at night, and not for ten miles.

"You've got your learner's permit, right?" Ted asked, and I nodded. "Well, then, all we need are the wheels."

It took a second for me to realize what he was implying. "Oh, no," I said. "Not on your life . . ."

But it wasn't his life that he was willing to put on the line. Just mine.

Steve was already home by the time Ted and I got back to my house. I wasn't surprised; my brother called in sick so often, his boss at Speed-E-Mart probably thought he had tuberculosis. Steve's secondhand '92 Mustang was in the driveway; a couple of his buddies had come over, but they'd remembered to leave their cars on the street so Mom would have a place to park. Which was fortunate, because it made what I was about to do that much easier.

Ted and I came in through the kitchen door, careful not to slam it behind us. Not that Steve would have heard the door shut; from the basement, I could hear the sullen backbeat of my brother's stereo thudding against the linoleum. There was a half-finished TV dinner on the kitchen table and Budweiser cans in the garbage; Steve was still underage, but that didn't stop him from swiping a six-pack or two from work. He might get rid of them before Mom came home, or maybe not. Ever since he'd moved into the basement, Steve had come to treat the house where we'd grown up more like a hangout than a home.

Once again, I wondered why Mom hadn't told him to find his own place. Perhaps she was still hoping that he'd eventually clean up his act; more likely, she loved her older son too much to throw him out. Not for the first time, though, I found myself wishing that she would.

Ted said nothing. He'd been over to my house enough times to know that my family had gone seriously downhill since Dad died. And with two overage party animals for parents, his own home life wasn't that much better. So he quietly waited while I looked around. Sure enough, Steve had tossed his black leather jacket on the living room couch. I checked the pockets. Just as I figured, there were his car keys. All I had to do was take them, and . . .

No. I couldn't do that. My brother was a deadbeat, but he was still my brother. Leaving the keys where I found them, I told Ted to wait outside, then I went down to the basement.

The stereo was deafening: Guns N' Roses, with Axl Rose screaming at the top of his lungs. Steve had a thing for '90s head-banger stuff: music by the dumb, for the dumb, so that the dumb wouldn't perish from the face of the earth. The cellar door was shut, but I could smell the pot smoke even before I was halfway down the stairs. Why these idiots couldn't open a window and put a towel against the bottom of the door was beyond me. I knocked twice, waited a second, then let myself in.

Steve sat cross-legged on the mattress he'd hauled down from what used to be his bedroom, a plastic tray he'd swiped from a shopping mall food court in his lap. His two cronies were slumped in the busted-out chairs he'd taken from the junk heap Mr. Morton had left behind; they were watching him clean the seeds and stems from the pound of marijuana he'd just acquired from his supplier, perhaps hoping to snag a joint or two before Steve divided the motherlode into half-ounce Baggies that he'd sell on the street. The old Sony TV my brother had "found" somewhere was on, a rerun of *Jeopardy!* ignored by high school dropouts who couldn't have supplied the question to American History for $200 ("He wrote the Declaration of Independence") if a gun was pointed to their heads. The nude girlfriends of millionaire rock stars glowered at me from posters taped to the cement walls, as beautiful as the distant galaxies and just as untouchable.

Everyone made a nervous jerk when I opened the door, and relaxed when they saw that it was only me. "Oh, it's you," Steve muttered. "What d'ya want?"

"Can I borrow your car?" My voice came as a dry croak; I was trying hard not to inhale. Anything that made Steve the way he was, I didn't want to have in my system.

"No. Get outta here, you little twerp." His friends snickered and passed the bong they'd momentarily hidden from sight.

"Okay." I backed out of the room and shut the door behind me. Then I went back upstairs and took the keys from his jacket.

I felt guilty about doing this . . . but let's be honest, not *too* guilty. Besides, judging from the looks of things, I guessed that he'd be in the basement for two or three more hours. Enough time for Ted and me to make a quick run to Narragansett Point and scope out the situation. With luck, I'd be home before Smokin' Steve and his smokin' crew pried themselves from their hole.

Sometimes it helped that my brother was a loser. I consoled myself with that idea as I backed the 'stang out of the driveway, being careful not to switch on the headlights until I hit the street. But I would've liked it a lot better if he didn't call me a twerp whenever he saw me.

Narragansett Point was located at the east side of town, on a broad spur of land next to the Connecticut River. Built in 1962, it was one of the country's first commercial nuclear power plants, and was thus smaller than the ones that followed it. All the same, the plant once represented the pinnacle of technology, and at one time had supplied Vermont with most of its electricity.

But that was when most Vermonters still said "a-yuh" and Phish was something you pulled out of the river with a 20-test line and a handmade lure. The accident at Three Mile Island scared the beeswax out of a good many people, and it wasn't long before a local anti-nuke group began protesting in front of the main gate. Despite the plant's good safety record, they believed that Narragansett Point was a meltdown waiting to happen, and it helped their cause when NRC inspectors discovered hairline fractures in the reactor's secondary cooling lines.

The plant was shut down for a while and the pipes were replaced, yet that was the first indication that the plant was getting old. Nukes are difficult to run; once billed as being able to supply energy "too cheap to meter," few people truly appreciated how much effort went into maintaining such a complex machine. Shutdowns became more frequent, and after another decade or so the repair work slipped the cost-benefit ratio over to the red end of the scale.

By then, New England Energy realized that it stood to make more money by purchasing power from Canadian hydroelectric plants than from keeping Narragansett Point on the grid. Facing pressure from various environmental and public interest groups, and having failed to find a buyer for the aging plant, the company decided to close it down for good.

Truth be told, I'd never felt one way or another about having a nuclear power plant in my backyard. It was just there, making no more or less difference in my daily life than the occasional nor'easter or the Pats going to the Superbowl again. Dad used to tell me that he'd taken Mom to a protest rally on their first date, but I think it was mostly because Bonnie Raitt was doing a free concert. And like every other guy who got his driver's license before I did, Steve took girls to the visitors' parking lot because it was once the best make-out spot in town.

But that was before 9/11 caused New England Energy to hire more cops to guard the plant, and in the interest of national security they chased away the teenagers and low-riders. I kept that in mind as I got off the state highway and drove down the narrow two-lane blacktop leading to the Point. It wasn't long before I saw signs advising me that trespassing was strictly prohibited, and that possession of firearms, knives, explosive materials, two-way radios, alcoholic beverages, drugs, pets, and just about everything else was punishable under federal law by major prison time and fines that I wouldn't be able to pay off even if I mowed lawns until I was seventy.

Not cool. Not cool at all. I was all too aware of the lingering stench of marijuana in Steve's car, and we'd already found empty beer cans rattling around on the floor of the backseat. No telling what surprises might lie in the ashtray or in the glove compartment. I was half-inclined to do a U-turn and head back, but I didn't want to wuss out in front of my best friend, so I ignored the sign and kept going.

By now we could see the plant: a collection of low buildings illuminated by floodlights, the containment dome that housed its 640-megawatt pressurized water reactor looming over them like an immense pimple. Narragansett Point didn't have one of those big hourglass-shaped cooling towers that typified nukes built later, but instead a long structure from which steam used to rise on cold days when the plant was still in operation. Those days were long gone, though, and now the nuke lay still and silent, like some elaborate toy a giant kid had once played with, then abandoned, but had forgotten to turn off.

It wasn't until we reached the visitors' parking lot that we noticed anything peculiar.

"Look sharp," Ted murmured. "Cop car ahead."

I'd already spotted it: a Jeep Grand Cherokee, painted white and blue, with disco lights mounted on its roof. It was parked near the outer security fence, blue lights flashing against the darkness; beside it was another car, a red Ford Escort, its front left door open. No one in sight; I figured that a security officer had pulled over the driver and was now checking his license and registration.

With any luck, maybe the cop would be too busy to give us more than a passing glance. The way the parking humps were arranged, though, meant that I'd have to make a swing through the lot before I could turn around. I downshifted to third and tried to drive as casually as possible. *No problem here, officer. Just a couple of bored teenagers out for a Friday night cruise to the ol' nuclear power plant . . .*

As we drew closer, though, I saw that the Escort was empty; no one was seated behind the wheel nor in the backseat. I caught a glimpse of the chrome dealer stamp on the trunk above the rear bumper: AUTO PLAZA, BELLINGHAM, VERMONT. The Jeep's driver's side door was open, too, but I couldn't see anyone behind the wheel . . .

"Hey!" Ted pointed at the front of the Jeep. "Look at that!"

I hit the brakes. Caught within the Jeep's headlights was a figure laying facedown on the asphalt, his arms spread out before him. A guy in a dark blue uniform, his ball cap on the ground beside him.

"Holy . . . !" Without thinking twice, I grabbed the parking brake and yanked it up, then opened the door and jumped out.

Ted was right behind me as I rushed over to the fallen security guard. At first I thought he was dead; that caused me to skitter to a halt, but when I looked closer, I didn't see any blood on his uniform or on the pavement. So I kneeled beside him and gently touched the side of his neck. His skin was warm, and I felt a slow pulse beneath my fingertips.

"He's alive," I said. "Just unconscious."

"Oh, man . . ." Ted stood a few yards away, reluctant to come any closer. "Oh man oh man oh man . . ."

"Shut up. Let me think."

The night was cold, with a stiff breeze coming off the Connecticut; I pulled up the hood of my sweatshirt and looked around. Now I saw things I hadn't noticed before. A Glock .45 automatic, only a few inches from the guard. A hand-mike also lay nearby, attached to his belt radio by a spiral cord. The situation became a little more clear; the guard had pulled over the Escort, asked the driver to get out, then seen or heard something that had given him reason to draw his gun while grabbing his mike to call for backup.

Then he was knocked out. Exactly how, I hadn't the foggiest, but nonetheless it happened so fast that he hadn't a chance to sound an alert. Otherwise, where were the other security cops? Why wasn't there . . . ?

"Dude, we gotta get out of here." Ted was inching toward Steve's car. "This is too much. We gotta . . ."

"Yeah. Sure." My own first instinct was to run away. This wasn't our problem. It was something best left to the authorities . . .

Then I took another look at the fallen security guard, and noticed that he was a young guy, no older than forty. About my dad's age when he'd bought a piece of Falluja. His buddies hadn't abandoned him, though; two of his squad-mates had taken bullets hauling his body to the nearest Humvee. The soldier's code: leave no man behind.

How couldn't I do the same? Like it or not, this was my responsibility.

"Go on," I said. "Get outta here."

"What?" Ted stared at me in disbelief. "What are you . . . ?"

"I'm staying." I nodded toward Steve's car. "The keys are in it. Motor's running. Run back to town, find the cops . . ." I stopped myself. Bo knew my brother's car, from all the times he'd pulled Steve over. No telling what'd he'd do if he saw Ted driving my brother's Mustang. "No, scratch that. Find the state troopers instead. Tell 'em what we found."

"But . . ."

"Go on! Get out of here!"

That woke Ted up. He almost tripped over himself as he backpedaled toward the Mustang. He hadn't yet earned his learner's permit, but he'd spent enough time in driver's ed to know how to handle five on the floor. Barely. He slipped the clutch and left some rubber on the asphalt, but in seconds the 'stang's taillights were disappearing up the road.

I watched him go, then I started jogging toward the front gate. There wasn't much I could do for the guard. What I needed to do now was make sure that plant security knew what had just happened here.

Oh, they knew, all right. They found out, just seconds before the same thing happened to them.

☙ ☙ ☙

The front gate was wide open.

The concrete anti-vehicle barriers were still in place, the tire slashers raised from their recessed slots beneath the roadway, yet sprawled all around the gatehouse were unconscious security guards, some with handguns lying nearby. My nose caught the lingering stench of something that smelled like skunk musk mixed with red pepper; someone had lobbed a tear gas grenade. Even though the wind was carrying it away, there was still enough in the air to make my eyes water. But someone had walked through this as if it wasn't there.

I stepped around the fallen sentries, cautiously made my way down the driveway. About twenty yards from the gate, I found a Humvee. Its engine was still running, its doors were open, and on either side of it lay two more security officers. These guys wore military body armor and gas masks; I spotted an Ingram Mac-10 assault rifle resting nearby. There were even a pair of Doberman pinschers, looking for all the world as if they'd suddenly decided to lie down and take a nap.

And above all this, an eerie silence. No sirens, no klaxons, no warning lights. Just a cold autumn breeze, carrying with it the mixed scent of tear gas and fallen leaves.

By now I was really and truly freaked out. Whatever happened here, the guys at the front gate had just enough time to call for backup. Even so, at least a dozen men, along with two attack dogs, had been taken down . . . and yet there was no blood, no gunshot wounds.

Who could do something like this?

*Calm down, man,* I said to myself. *Get a grip. This is no time to panic . . .*

Just ahead lay the employee parking lot. A handful of cars, with no one in sight. Beyond it lay the administration building: lights within a ground-floor window, but no one moving inside. Another ten-foot chain-link fence, this one topped with coils of razor-wire; its gate was still shut. Past that were the turbine building, the control center, and the containment dome. So far as I could tell, though, everything looked peaceful, quiet . . .

No. Not so quiet.

From somewhere to the left, I heard voices.

I couldn't make out what was being said, but nonetheless someone was over there, on the other side of the row of house trailers being used by the decommissioning crew.

For a moment, I considered picking up one of the guns dropped by the guards. They hadn't helped these guys, though, so what good would they do me? Besides, it was only a matter of time before Ted fetched the authorities and led them back here. Did I really want to be caught with a Mac-10 in my hands when a posse of Vermont state troopers stormed the place, along with the National Guard and, for all I knew, the Army, the Air Force, and the Marines?

*No*, I thought. *You're just a kid, not Bruce Willis. Get a little closer, see what you need to see. Then hightail it back to the Jeep and wait for Ted to bring the cavalry.*

(I didn't know it then, but Ted had problems of his own. By then, Smokin' Steve and his buddies had decided to go cruising for burgers. When he'd discovered that his precious Mustang was missing, it'd taken all of five minutes—swift thinking, Sherlock—for him to deduce who'd done the deed. So he and his pals piled into another car and went looking for us, with murder on their minds.)

(As bad luck would have it, they spotted Ted just a couple of miles before he reached the local state police outpost. They whipped their car into the right lane and blocked the Mustang, forcing it into a ditch. Ted knew an ass-kicking when he saw it coming; he abandoned the 'stang and lit out across a pumpkin field. He managed to get away . . . but about the same time I was trying to decide whether to pick up a gun, my friend was making his getaway through next week's Halloween jack-o'-lanterns, praying that he'd survive the night with all his teeth intact. So much for counting on Ted . . . )

Following the sound of the voices, I made my way among the trailers, careful to remain in the shadows. Another ring of flood-lights was just ahead; peering from behind the foreman's shack, I saw that they surrounded a fenced-in enclosure. Within it was a broad concrete pad, slightly elevated above the ground, and upon it were rows of concrete casks.

I'd been paying attention in Mr. Hamm's physics class, so I knew what I was looking at: the temporary repository for the plant's fuel rods. Sixteen casks, each thirteen feet tall and holding thirty-six rods, a half-inch wide and twelve feet long, which in turn contained the uranium-235 pellets that once gave Narragansett Point its oomph. After being used in the reactor, the spent rods—which now contained mainly post-fission U-237, along with trace amounts of plutonium waste and unfissioned U-235—were stored in a pool, twenty feet deep and filled with distilled water, inside the containment dome.

The decommissioning process began when the rods were removed from the pool, one at a time, by robotic cranes, and placed within carbon-steel drums three and a half inches thick. Those in turn were transported by truck to the storage yard, where other cranes lowered them into the casks, which themselves were insulated with twenty-one inches of steel-reinforced concrete. Each cask weighed 110 tons and, as the *Bellingham Times* had said, they were "heavily guarded at all times."

No doubt the last part was true. All the same, a half-dozen or so guys lay on the ground near the storage yard. And standing on top of one of the casks was Alex.

From the distance, it was hard to tell what he was doing. All I could see was that he was bent over, and that a white-hot beam of energy was coming from something within his hands. It lanced straight down into the cask, causing it to spit pieces of concrete, with molten steel drooling down the sides. He should have been wearing welder's goggles and gloves, yet it appeared that he was both bare-handed and bare-faced.

Once again, I found myself wondering what kind of guy he was. The Terminator when he was a teenager, with breaking into nuclear power plants as his idea of a high school prank. And I thought picking up the basketball coach's '69 Volkswagen and carrying it into the gym was a hoot . . .

Tyler and Mickey stood at the base of the cask. Tyler was watching Alex; he seemed nervous, because he restlessly paced back and forth. Mickey was a little more calm, but she had something in her hands that looked like an oversize calculator. She kept it pointed away from the cask, though, toward the plant instead.

A motion detector? I didn't know, but when she moved it in my direction, I held my breath and froze, not daring to twitch a muscle. She paused for a moment, then continued to scan the vicinity.

Okay. Perhaps they weren't your average Islamist terrorists. But neither were they the sort of guys I liked to find at my neighborhood nuclear power plant. Either way, I'd seen enough. I took a couple of steps back . . .

Wrong move. I was still within range of whatever Mickey was using to sweep the area. Shouting something that sounded only vaguely like English, she pointed in my direction. Tyler whipped around, drew something that looked like a weapon . . .

To this day, I don't know why I did what I did. Maybe it was because I didn't want to be just one more guy found unconscious at Narragansett Point. Maybe I was too stupid to be a hero and too brave to be a coward. Or maybe I just didn't know what I was doing.

At any rate, instead of running, I stepped out from behind cover.

"Hold on, guys!" I yelled, throwing up my hands. "It's me!"

Tyler stopped, his gun half-raised. Mickey stared at me in disbelief. Alex paused in whatever he was doing and peered in my direction. For a moment, I don't think they recognized me. Then Mickey said something to Tyler, and he took a step closer to the fence.

"Is that you, Eric?" he called back, using plain English this time.

"Yeah, it's me." I kept my hands in the air. "Don't shoot, okay? I'm harmless. Look . . . no gun, see?"

Tyler didn't seem quite convinced, but since he wasn't aiming his weapon at me, I supposed that I was getting through to him. "What are you doing here?" he demanded. "Did you follow us?"

How to answer that? The truth was too hard to explain, but a lie would have been obvious. So I settled for something in-between. "Just wondered why you guys wanted to come out here," I said, thinking as fast as I could. "Thought . . . y'know, maybe there was a party going on."

Tyler said nothing, but I heard Mickey stifle a laugh. Who-ever these guys were, whatever they were up to, they were still teenagers all the same . . . and every teen who's ever lived knows the attraction of a party. "Look, I'm coming up," I added. "Just don't shoot, all right? I've got nothing."

"You shouldn't be here," Tyler said. "Go away."

I hesitated for a second, then decided to ignore him. His weapon looked like something I could have bought at Toys "R" Us, but he'd managed to use it against a well-armed security force. If he was going to use it on me, too, then fine, so be it. Maybe I'd wake up with a bad headache, but I knew already that its effects weren't fatal. And I was damned if I was going to sim-ply scamper home. Maybe they weren't terrorists—and judging from what I'd seen so far, Ted's theory that they were working for Al Qaeda or Islamic Jihad was highly unlikely—but nobody breaks into a nuclear power plant in my town and gets away with it.

"Eric . . ." Mickey watched as I approached the fence, step-ping around the unconscious guards in my way. "Tyler's right. The less you know what we're doing, the better off you'll be."

"Yeah, well, maybe. But . . ." The gate was half-open, and it looked as if something had melted the lock. Now I knew what. I pushed it open, stepped through. "Y'know, you didn't leave me your phone number, so how else am I going to ask you for a date?"

This from a guy who would've *never* used that line on

Pauline Coullete. Yet fear makes men accomplish impossible things. Mickey's face broke into that incredible smile of hers, and I felt like James Bond sinking Ms. Moneypenny with the best wisecrack of all time.

"You're brave," she said quietly. "I like that."

Tyler scowled at me. For a moment, I thought I'd pushed my luck too far. Perhaps I did, because he glanced down at his pistol, as if remembering that he had it. Before he could do anything, Alex called down from the cask.

"I've penetrated the seal, Lieutenant. Shall I remove the outer cover?"

Tyler forgot about me for a moment. "Go ahead and open it, Alex." Glancing my way, he suddenly became self-conscious. "Resume prior communications protocols," he added. "Use period dialect from now on."

Alex responded in the language I'd heard them use before, something that sounded like a polyglot of English, French, and Spanish. What made me more curious, though, was the formal way Alex had addressed him. Lieutenant? Lieutenant in which service? Whatever it was, it probably wasn't the Coast Guard . . .

"You must leave." Mickey's voice was quiet. "Now, Eric. Please."

"Uh-uh." I folded my arms together. "Not until I . . ."

Whatever I was about to say, I didn't get a chance to finish it. I was too busy watching Alex bend down and grasp the steel handles on either side of the cask cover. It probably weighed two tons, at least; there was the grinding sound of concrete surfaces rasping across each other, then he hoisted the cover with little more effort than it would take for me to pick up an armchair, and tossed it over the side of the cask.

It hit the ground with a solid thump. Alex stood erect, looked down at me, and smiled. I gulped. Whatever high school football team he belonged to, I prayed that I'd never meet them on the fifty-yard line.

Mickey was speaking into her pad, saying something urgent in whatever tongue she and her friends used. By then, I was having second thoughts about being here. This was far too weird for me. When the cops showed up, maybe I could pretend to be unconscious. Play possum, claim that I hadn't seen anything . . .

I'd begun to back away, inching my way toward the gate, when there was a howl from somewhere above us. Wincing, I doubled over, gritting my teeth as I clasped my hands against my ears.

Then I looked up, and saw a spaceship coming down from the sky.

☙ ☙ ☙

The spacecraft was a little larger than a commuter jet, or about half the size of a NASA shuttle. Sleek and streamlined, its broad delta-shaped wings tapered downward at their tips, while twin vertical stabilizers rose from either side of a hump at its aft section that I took to be a drive of some sort; there were no rocket engines so far as I could see. The bow canted slightly forward at the end of a short neck, and wraparound viewports above a beak-like prow lent the ship a vaguely avian appearance, like a giant seagull.

I didn't know whether to laugh, faint, or wet my pants. I did none of the above; instead, I stared at it with open-mouthed wonder, and hoped that I didn't look like some hillbilly who'd never seen technology more advanced than Grandpa's moonshine still.

The ship slowly descended until it hovered twenty feet above the cask on which Alex was standing. A broad hatch on its underside slid open; standing within it was a lone figure, wearing what I took to be a spacesuit. Alex waved his right arm, motioning for the craft to move further to the left. The pilot complied, inching the craft a few degrees port until the hatch was directly above Alex and the cask.

"Seen enough?" Tyler asked. "Good. Time for you to take a nap."

I looked down, saw that he'd raised his weapon again. There was nothing I could do; I stood still, and hoped that being zapped wouldn't hurt . . .

"Stop!" Mickey suddenly put herself between him and me. "You can't do this!"

Tyler quickly pointed the gun toward the ground. "What are you . . . ?"

"You're right . . . he's seen enough. Too much, in fact." Still shielding me from Tyler, she pointed up at the hovering space-craft. "He's the only witness. If you stun him now . . ."

Tyler muttered something I couldn't understand, but that I figured was obscene. "But what else can we do if we don't . . . ?"

"Take me with you," I blurted out.

Tyler's eyes widened, and Mickey glanced back at me in as-tonishment. "Look," I went on, talking as fast as I could, "maybe this is none of my business, but . . . hey, if you just showed me what this is all about, then maybe we can . . . I dunno, work something out."

"Nice try." Tyler raised his weapon again. "Stand down, McGyver. That's an order."

"Don't try pulling rank on me, Tyler." Mickey glared at him. "Remember, Captain Van Owen put *me* in charge of . . ."

She was interrupted by another hatch opening within the spacecraft, this one on the port side. A teenage girl about our age stood within the hatch, her arms braced along its sides; she made an impatient gesture—*c'mon, hurry up!*—and Mickey lifted a hand to her right ear and ducked her head slightly, as if listening to something hidden by her hair. A moment passed, then she looked at me again.

"Do you know anything about the local air defense net-work?" she asked.

"A little." Which was the truth. I knew what everyone else who lived around here knew, plus whatever else Dad had told me. "Why, what do you . . . ?"

Mickey muttered something in her own language, waited a moment, then looked at Tyler. "Hsing says bring him aboard. We'll let the skipper sort it out later."

"But . . ."

"We're running out of time. Shut up and help Alex, or the captain's going to get this in my report. Understood?"

Tyler nodded reluctantly, then put away his gun and turned

toward the cask. From the cargo hatch, two thick cables with hooks at their ends were being lowered; Alex reached up, preparing to grab them once they came within reach. It was obvious what they intended to do, but why . . . ?

"You *do* know what you say you know?" There was apprehension in Mickey's eyes as she turned to look at me. "You're not . . . um, putting us on . . . are you, Eric?"

"I'm no expert, but . . ." I shrugged. "I'll do what I can do."

"Very well. Let's go." She hesitated, then quietly added, "I just hope neither of us regrets this."

Again, she reached beneath her hair to touch something at her ear, and murmured something in her language. A few seconds later, the girl standing in the side hatch tossed something overboard: a rope ladder, uncoiling as it fell. It snapped taut as its weighted end hit the ground; Mickey grasped its rungs and began to climb upward. I waited until she was nearly halfway up, then followed her.

The girl at the top of the ladder was no older than Mickey or me. Perhaps even younger; the baby-blue jumpsuit she wore looked a little too big for someone who would've been a freshman at my local middle school. The compartment was barely large enough for the three of us; while Mickey had a short conversation with her, I got a chance to look around. Recessed storage lockers, a couple of control panels here and there. Obviously an airlock; an interior hatch on one side of the compartment lay open, apparently leading forward to the cockpit, and on the opposite side of the airlock was another hatch. This one was shut. But it had a small window. Figuring that it led to the cargo bay, I was about to peer through the window when something caught my eye.

Hanging within one of the lockers was a spacesuit, although like none I'd ever seen before. Resembling a scuba diver's wet suit, it was made of some fabric that seemed impossibly thin, with a neck-ring around its collar and sockets along its sides. A helmet with an angular face-plate rested on a shelf above the suit, and a small backpack was clamped to the inside of the door.

But that wasn't what got my attention. Above the locker was a small sign; the language was indecipherable, but I know Roman alphabet when I see it. Perhaps that alone should have been a shock—*wow, it's not Klingon!*—yet then I saw the mission patch embroidered on the suit's left shoulder, and I felt my heart skip a beat.

At the center of the patch was an emblem that looked much like a classic diagram of an atom—a nucleus surrounded by electrons—until I realized that it was actually a tiny sun surrounded by eight planets. And wrapped around the emblem was:

SOLAR CONFEDERATION FLEET

S.C.S. VINCENNES

My knees went weak, and I grabbed for something for support. As it happened, it was the girl who'd helped us aboard. She wrapped an arm around my shoulder to keep me on my feet, then said something to Mickey. Following my gaze, she saw what I'd seen. Giving me a sympathetic smile, Mickey pried me loose from her friend.

"There's a lot that needs to be explained," she murmured. "But not now. We have a job to do."

The cockpit was larger on the inside than it appeared from the outside; seats for the pilot and co-pilot up front, with six passenger couches arranged behind it. The pilot was about Steve's age; looking away from his console as we came in, he frowned when he saw me, and said something I couldn't understand yet obviously wasn't warm and friendly. Mickey gave him a curt reply, and he returned his attention to the controls.

His hands were gripped tight around a T-shaped control bar, and he was visibly making an effort to hold the craft in position. No wonder; the wind was causing the deck to pitch back and forth, and we had to hold tight to the seatbacks just to stay on our feet.

"Just a second." Mickey reached up to an overhead storage bin and slid it open. The bin was stuffed with equipment I didn't

recognize; pulling out a small box, Mickey opened it to produce
something that looked like a hearing aid, except that it had a tiny
prong that curved to one side and a miniature wand that went in
the other direction.

"Put it in your right ear," she explained. "Like this, see?"
Pulling back her hair, I saw that she wore an identical unit.
When I fumbled with it, she patiently helped me insert the thing,
with the prong fitting around my upper lobe and the wand nes-
tled against my throat. Once it was in place, she touched a tiny
button.

A double beep, then nothing. "I don't get it," I said. "What's
this supposed to do?"

"Oh, for the love of . . ." The pilot glanced at me in irrita-
tion. "Where'd you find this idiot, Mickey?"

My left ear heard the same weird language he'd been speaking before; my right ear heard plain English. "She found me on
the street corner," I replied. "What's it to you?"

He glared at me, and Mickey hid her smile behind her hand.
An auto-translation device of some sort; now we could under-
stand each other. "It's a long story, Hsing," she said. "His name's
Eric. He says he can help us. Give him a chance."

Hsing hesitated. "Okay, kid. Come here and tell me what I'm
looking at."

Not really believing I was doing this, I stumbled forward until I was just behind his seat. His controls looked like nothing I'd
ever seen before: row upon row of fluorescent touch screens ar-
rayed along a wraparound console, with recessed holograms displaying information I couldn't even begin to comprehend. I'd
been inside cockpits before during air shows at Westfield, but this
one made the most advanced Air Force jet look like something
the Wright brothers had cobbled together from birch wood and
piano wire.

"What do you want to know?" I asked. As if I had anything
to offer. *Me know spaceship, uh-huh. Me want to help . . .*

"This." Hsing tapped a small holographic display midway
between him and the co-pilot's seat. It expanded, revealing a

wire-frame hemisphere with a topographic map at its base. "That's SLIR . . ." he pronounced it as *sleer* ". . . side-looking infrared radar. It works on the principle of . . ."

"I know radar. Go on."

Hsing glanced first at me, then at Mickey. "Got a mouth on him, doesn't he?" he said to her, then he pointed again at the display. "See those? They're coming at us from the south-southwest. Now tell me what they are, smart guy."

I looked closer. Three small red blips, near the outer edge of the hemisphere and one-quarter of the way to its apex, rapidly approaching a blue blip hovering close to the ground at the center of the map. "How far away are they?"

"Sixty-two kilometers and closing. Altitude 6,300 meters, speed . . ."

"Warthogs." I felt something cold at the pit of my stomach,

Hsing looked at me again. "Repeat?"

"A-10 Thunderbolts . . . Warthogs, if you want to call them that. Coming in from Westfield." I pointed to the lowermost right part of the holo, beneath the blips. "They belong to the 104th Fighter Wing, Barnes Air National Guard Base. They probably scrambled as soon as NORAD picked you up on the air-defense grid." I gave him a sidelong look. "Guess they picked you up when you entered the atmosphere. Right?"

Hsing didn't reply, but his face went pale. "Do they pose a threat to us?" Mickey quietly asked.

"Oh, yeah. You definitely have something to worry about." I took a deep breath. "They're built for low-level runs against tanks, anti-aircraft missile launchers, that sort of thing. Gatling guns, air-to-ground missiles . . ."

"Can they operate at night?" Hsing asked, and I threw him a glance he couldn't help but understand. "Oh, boy . . ." he murmured, then he glanced over his shoulder. "Libbie, we have a situation!"

"We've got the canister!" the girl yelled from the airlock. "Alex and Deke are securing it now!"

"Then seal the cargo hatch and get back here!" Hsing

tapped his headset wand. "Tyler, get aboard. We're ready for liftoff."

"Make a hole!" Libbie charged in from the airlock, unapologetically shoving me out of the way. She jumped into the right-hand seat and yanked down a padded harness bar. "Cargo hatch sealed," she snapped, her hands racing across her side of the console. "Initiating main engine sequence . . ."

"Let's get you strapped down." Mickey pushed me into a couch behind Libbie. "We're going to be pulling a few g's until the inertial dampeners kick in, so be prepared for some rough flying."

I had no idea what she meant by inertial dampeners, but I knew all about g's. The harness was much like those on a ride at Six Flags; it came down over my head and shoulders and clicked into place across my chest. I gave Mickey a thumbs-up; she acknowledged it with a brief nod as she secured herself into a seat across the aisle from me.

"MEI green for go." Hsing's voice was tight as a wire. "APU powered up. Main hatch . . . hey, why isn't the hatch secure? Tyler, where are you?" Clasping his right hand over his headset. "What's that? Repeat, please . . ."

I peered over his shoulder at the SLIR. The three red blips were very close to the center of the holo; they couldn't be more than twenty miles away. If we were going to make a clean getaway, the ship would have to launch *now* . . .

"Aw, hell!" Hsing yelled. "Tyler's down!"

"What?" Libbie stared at him. "How did he . . . ?"

"I don't know. He's fallen off the ladder, says his knee's twisted." The pilot glanced at the SLIR again, swore under his breath. "We don't have time for this. Libbie, prepare for liftoff."

"You can't do that!" Mickey grabbed the back of Hsing's seat. "He's . . . !"

"Those jets are almost on top of us." Hsing jabbed a finger at the holo. "We don't have a choice. We're going to have to leave him . . ."

*Leave no man behind . . .*

"Hold the bus!" Before I knew what I was doing, I shoved the harness upward. Mickey stared at me as I leaped from my seat; she raised a hand to stop me, but I was already halfway to the airlock. "Gimme a minute! I'll get him back!"

"No way!" Hsing shouted. "I can't risk . . . !"

"They won't attack! Trust me!" I didn't have time to explain; I could only hope that the pilot would take my word.

The side hatch was open, the ladder still lowered. Through the cargo bay window, I caught a glimpse of Alex and the other crewman, holding tight to bulkhead straps on either side of the fuel-rod canister. They stared at me in mute surprise as I turned around, kneeled down, and carefully put my legs through the airlock hatch. My feet found the top rungs; I grasped the ladder with both hands and began to climb down.

Tyler lay on the concrete pad below me, clutching at his left knee. He shouted something I couldn't understand, so I chose to ignore him. The ladder swayed back and forth; the spacecraft was in motion, and for an instant I thought Hsing was about to lift off. Then I saw that the distance between me and Tyler was getting shorter, and realized the pilot was carefully maneuvering his ship closer to the ground.

I jumped the last five feet, bending my hips and knees to let my legs take the impact. Tyler saw what I intended to do; he struggled to his right knee, wincing as he put weight on his left leg. "Hang on!" I yelled, wrapping my left arm around him. "We're gonna get you out of here!"

"You're out of your . . . !"

He didn't get a chance to finish before the rest was lost in the roar of three Warthogs making a low-level pass over Narragansett Point. Looking up, I saw the amber glow of their jets as they hurtled less than a thousand feet above us. The A-10s howled past us, then peeled apart from one another as they made a steep climb above the Connecticut River.

"C'mon, move!" I hauled Tyler to his feet, carried him to the dangling ladder. "Get your ass up there!"

Tyler didn't argue. He grasped the rungs and began to climb, favoring his left leg but nonetheless using it to balance himself. He didn't have far to travel; Hsing had brought the craft within fifteen feet of the ground, its starboard wingtip nearly grazing the top of the nearest waste cask. Looking up, I saw Mickey crouched within the hatch, reaching down to help Tyler climb aboard.

I didn't wait to make sure he was safe. I grabbed the ladder, scrambled up it like a monkey on a coconut tree. The A-10s were gone, but they'd be back as soon as the hog drivers reported what they'd seen. I had little doubt that whoever was in charge at Barnes would give them permission to open fire upon the strange craft they'd spotted hovering above the local nuclear power plant. Nonetheless, I knew that they wouldn't attack immediately, but instead obey the chain of command. Thank heavens I'd grown up as a soldier's boy. Otherwise I might not have known this.

Yet the clock was ticking, but seriously . . .

Reaching up, I planted my hand against Tyler's butt, gave him a mighty shove. Mickey already had him by the shoulders; she dragged him the rest of the way through the hatch. I scampered up the ladder, then helped Mickey haul it up behind us.

"Clear!" Mickey slammed the hatch shut and twisted a lock-wheel. "Main hatch sealed!"

"Copy that!" Libbie called back. "Hang on!"

Tyler had already limped to the nearest seat. Mickey shoved me into another couch, then planted herself in the one across the aisle. We barely had time to pull down our harnesses before the spacecraft's prow tilted upward . . .

"Go for launch!" Hsing shouted.

"Punch it!" I yelled. Mickey's hand grabbed mine, and then we fell into the sky.

Countless times, I've imagined what it might be like to be aboard a rocket during liftoff. Although the closest I'd ever been to a real spacecraft were the ones at the National Air and Space Museum, where my father had taken Steve and me during a family vacation to Washington, D.C., my fantasies had been fueled by film clips of shuttle launches, movies like *Apollo 13*, and dozens of science fiction novels. So I thought I was ready for the real thing.

I wasn't.

We went up *fast*. As the craft violently shook around me, an invisible hand pressed my body back into the couch. Blood pounded in my ears as I gulped air and fought to keep down the pizza I'd had for dinner.

"They're after us, Van." Libbie's voice was tight. "Range three-fifty meters and closing."

I glanced at the SLIR. Three blips following a blue dot straight up the center of the hemisphere, getting closer every second. On a small screen on Libbie's side of the console, I caught a brief glimpse of three small, angular objects, fuzzy and green-tinted, a phosphorescent glow coming from their aft sections. The Warthogs were right on our tail. If they managed to lock on . . .

"Hang tight, everyone!" Hsing snapped. "I'm going evasive!"

Terrified, I instinctively turned my head away. Bad idea; the same invisible hand caused my neck to twist painfully. Not only that, but it was at this same moment that Hsing rolled the craft 180 degrees. Through a side window, I caught a brief glimpse of my hometown, as seen at night from about 10,000 feet. A small constellation of house lights and street lamps, very pretty . . . except that it was upside down, and rapidly disappearing behind us.

"Easy. Easy." Mickey clutched my hand. "Look straight ahead, take deep, short breaths."

I managed to pull my face forward, concentrated on breathing. For a moment, I saw clouds, backlit by the lights of town. Then we ripped through them, and suddenly there were only stars. Pretty, but I was in no mood to admire them; the invisible hand had become a fat guy who'd just come away from an all-you-can-eat buffet, and decided that my chest was a fine place to sit down.

"They're falling back." Libbie's voice was taut, but no longer alarmed. "Range 400 meters . . . 600 . . . 800 . . ."

"We should be near the limits of their operational ceiling." Hsing held tight to his yoke. "We're almost in the clear, guys."

My guts were beginning to settle down, and it was getting a little easier to breathe; the fat guy got up and went to check out

the dessert bar. By now I could see the stars more clearly; they
didn't glimmer and twinkle, as I'd seen them while standing on
the ground, but instead shined steadily . . . and all of a sudden, I
realized that there were far more than I'd ever seen in my life.

Carefully turning my head, I looked over at Mickey. She met
my gaze, saw that I was doing okay, and gave me a wry smile. I
was about to do the same when dawn broke.

As sunlight streamed through the starboard windows, I
raised a hand against the sudden glare . . . and then stopped myself when I realized what I was seeing. No, not sunrise . . . *sun-
set*, my second one of the day. Or at least it would be if I was still
in Bellingham, Vermont.

Yct I was no longer there, was I? What I was witnessing was
the sun going down somewhere west of the Rockies. Out in California, some guy my age would be strolling the beaches of Mon-
terey, watching the sun paint the waves of the Pacific. And
meanwhile, I was witnessing the same thing, although from a
considerably higher perspective.

It was then—my body floating upward against the seat harness, watching sunlight turn a vast curved horizon into a
crimson-hued scimitar, feeling my ears pop as I swallowed—that
I realized that I was no longer on Earth.

"Holy . . ." I swallowed again. "I'm in space."

Sure, it sounded moronic. It probably was. All the same, I
couldn't get over what I was seeing. It wasn't a movie or a TV
show, it wasn't something I'd read in a science fiction novel, it
wasn't even a particularly vivid dream. This was *real* . . .

Damn. I *was* in space.

"Really? No kidding?" From behind us, Tyler snickered.
"Wow, what a revelation. And here I was, thinking we were . . ."

"Shut up." Mickey looked at him in disgust, then her expression softened. "How's your leg? Want me to break out the
med kit?"

"I'll manage." Tyler reached down to gently massage his
swollen knee. "It'll wait until we're back aboard ship. The doc
will take care of it." He regarded me for a moment, then slowly

let out his breath. "Thanks," he added, albeit reluctantly. "You didn't have to do that."

"No problem." I was having trouble staying focused. "You'd have done the same for me if . . ."

My voice trailed off. No, he would not have, and we both knew it. Yet Tyler wasn't about to let me have the last word. "I was thinking about dropping you off somewhere in China," he muttered, "but I guess we can't do that now, can we?"

My face must have gone red, because Mickey grasped my hand again. "You might try to be a little more grateful," she said, then she turned her attention forward. "How are we doing?"

"Fine. On course for rendezvous and pickup." Hsing didn't look back at us as his hands roamed across the console. "Sorry about the ride. We had to execute some high-g maneuvers to get away from those planes."

"S'okay. Think nothing of it." I was no longer queasy; astonishment had taken care of that problem. Besides, I couldn't help but feel sorry for the A-10 pilots we'd left behind; they were probably on their way back to Westfield, going *hummanahummanahummanna* and trying to figure out how to explain *this* one to the CO.

Yeah, okay. Maybe the Massachusetts Air National Guard had a mystery on their hands, and so did the Narragansett Point security team. Yet I was only slightly less clueless than they were . . .

I looked at Mickey again. "Look, I know it's a lot to ask, but . . . would you mind telling me what's going on here?"

She said nothing for a moment. Libbie gazed back over her shoulder at her. "It's not too late to consider China," she murmured. "Maybe some remote village near the Tibetan border . . . ?"

"No." Mickey's voice was cold. "Set coarse for rendezvous with the *Vincennes*. And re-engage the I-drive . . . I want us there in two and a half standard hours, max."

Libbie and Hsing shared a glance. "On your orders, chief," the pilot said, then he pressed his fingers against his console. "IDE in five . . . four . . . three . . . two . . ."

"Hold on," Mickey said quietly to me. "This may be . . ."

"One . . . zero."

Weight returned, as abruptly as if I was aboard an elevator that had been plummeting down a bottomless shaft, only to have its brakes abruptly kick in. All of a sudden, I went from zero-g to one-g . . . and even if the rest of my body was ready for change, my brain wasn't, and neither was my stomach.

Particularly not my stomach. A Friday night special from Louie's tastes great going down. Coming back up again, it's not so wonderful.

"Aw, for the love of . . . someone get a bag under him!" Tyler snapped, while Mickey held my shoulders and let me heave all over the deck.

Libbie tossed back a folded paper bag from a compartment beneath her seat, but by then the damage was done. "Sorry 'bout that," I apologized to no one in particular, sitting up straight and wiping my mouth with the back of my hand. "If you'll show me where you keep the paper towels, I'll . . ."

I stopped, staring down at where I'd thrown up. The pool of puke was disappearing, as if the deck itself had become a sponge and was rapidly absorbing it. Looking closer, I saw what looked like thousands of tiny maggots eating away at the edges of the vomit. Gross . . .

"Decontamination nanites," Mickey explained. "They automatically activate when a foreign biological substance touches an interior surface and convert it into inert matter. Keeps the shuttle clean." She touched my arm and stood up. "Come with me . . . I've got something to show you."

I followed her only too gladly; the nanites creeped me out. Still feeling a bit rocky, I followed her back to the airlock. Tyler watched us go, and I could feel his eyes at my back. Perhaps I'd saved his bacon, but he still wasn't ready to accept me as anything but a nuisance. Or maybe it was more than that . . . ?

Mickey stopped at the cargo bay hatch. She glanced through the window, then stood aside to let me look inside. The fuel-rod canister was snug within a pair of padded braces; Deke, the third crew member, wore a thick outfit that I took to be anti-radiation armor of some sort, yet Alex was still wearing only the patchwork sweater, cammie trousers, and cowboy boots he'd swiped from the thrift shop. They stood on either side of the canister, patiently waiting for us to get to wherever we were going. Spotting me looking in on him, Alex smiled, then raised his hand to give me a happy, carefree wave.

"Aren't you worried about him?" I asked. "I mean, no telling how many REMs he's taking in there."

"You don't need to worry about him. Alex isn't . . ."

She stopped herself. "He's not human, is he?" I asked.

"No." She shook her head. "Alex isn't human. I suppose you could say that he's an android, although that's an antiquated term. His name is an acronym for Artificial Lifeform Experimental . . ."

"Right. Alex. I get it." It explained a lot about him, but I wasn't about to let her off the hook so easily. "Look, Mickey," I went on, dropping my voice so that the others couldn't hear us, "or whatever your name is, or what it stands for . . ."

"Mickey's my real name." Her face colored a little. "Alex is the only artificial person aboard."

"Great. You had me worried there for a second." I paused. "You might as well tell me the rest. I'm here, right? Either that, or dump me in China or Tibet or wherever. And if you do that, you ought to just hurry up and kill me, because all I have are the clothes on my back, five bucks, my student I.D., and a Blockbuster Video card."

"We're not going to do that." She glanced back at the cockpit. "Don't mind Tyler. He's just sore because . . ."

"Sure. Whatever. Just tell me one thing . . . are you guys from the future?"

Her face went pale, and she stepped back from me. Before she could say anything, though, I went on. "Don't tell me you're from another planet . . ."

"But we are."

"Oh, yeah? Which one?"

"Mars."

"Sure." I tapped the sign above the suit locker I'd spotted earlier. "And I suppose that's Martian, and what you're speaking is . . ."

"Martian." She hesitated. "Or at least the Martian dialect of what you know as English. That's why we need the autotranslators. In my time . . ."

Once more, she stopped herself. "There it is again," I said. " 'My time' . . . like that's different from 'your time.' C'mon, I'm not stupid. Tell me the rest."

She looked down, said nothing. From the corner of my eye, I could see that we were no longer alone. Tyler stood in the hatchway leading to the cockpit, and behind him was Libbie. I had no idea how much they'd overheard, but neither of them looked any more happy with me than Mickey.

Mickey must have noticed them, too. Although she tried not to acknowledge their presence, she was visibly uncomfortable. "I just wanted . . . I just wanted to show you that the fuel-rod canister was intact, and assure you that it wouldn't be used to make an atomic weapon. Since that's your major concern, that is . . ."

"Thanks." She was stating the obvious; the real explanation was still unsaid, but I was in no position to press the issue. "I appreciate it."

She nodded, then silently left the airlock, squeezing between Tyler and Libbie. I let her go, then turned to look at her two companions. "Okay, then," I said, squaring my shoulders, "which one of you Martians wants to tell me where we're going?"

I was trying to be funny, but neither of them were the type to take a joke. Libbie turned to follow Mickey, while Tyler gave me a cold look. "You want the truth?" he asked, and I nodded. "Lunar stationary orbit, on the far side of the Moon. We'll be there in about two hours, twenty minutes, standard."

"Aw, c'mon. That's . . ."

"That's the truth. Take it or leave it." Tyler started to turn away, then stopped. "Thanks for rescuing me," he added. "I appreciate it. So here's my payback . . . 2337."

"Huh?" I shook my head. "What does that . . . ?"

"2337," Tyler repeated. "That's the year we left Mars."

A little less than two hours later, we reached the Moon.

Stop and think about that for a moment. The Moon is approximately 240,000 miles from Earth. The first men to go there were Frank Borman, James Lovell, and William Anders; in 1968, it took three days for them to make the journey—from December 21, 7:51 a.m., when Apollo 8 lifted off from Merritt Island, to December 24, 7:30 a.m., when they transmitted the first close-up TV pictures of the lunar surface—and during that time they established a new world speed record of 24,200 MPH.

I didn't have a watch, so I don't know exactly what time it was when we made our getaway from Narragansett Point, with three A-10s in hot pursuit. All I know is that, when I woke up from a brief nap, I gazed out the window to behold the same awesome sight that Borman, Lovell, and Anders had first seen nearly forty years ago. I didn't ask anyone what time it was, so I have to assume that Hsing had obeyed Mickey's order to get us there in two hours.

How fast had we traveled? Do the math, if you want; I didn't. I was too busy staring out the window beside my seat, watching the barren grey landscape as it rushed past only a few hundred miles below us. Down there were mountains, hills, and craters that only twenty-seven men had ever seen before with their own eyes. A brief glimpse of Mare Tranquillitatis, where Armstrong and Aldrin planted the flag back in '69, then we slingshot around the limb of the Moon and were hurtling toward deep space beyond the lunar farside.

I didn't realize Mickey was standing beside me until she said something. "Beautiful, isn't it?" she asked, keeping her voice low as she gazed past me.

"Yeah," I replied, feeling something pinch my throat. "It's . . . it's awesome."

"Uh-huh." Only then did I notice that her hand lay lightly

upon my arm. "This means something to you." she murmured. "Not just seeing the Moon . . . it's personal, isn't it?"

"Yeah, I . . ." I stopped myself. I didn't want to lay my life story on her; this wasn't the time or place. "I've always wanted to do this," I said. "Y'know, be an astronaut. But I never thought I . . . I mean, I didn't think I . . ."

I halted, looked away. "Never thought what?" Mickey asked. "That you could?"

"Yeah." Then I shook my head. "I mean, no . . . naw, I mean . . ." Tongue-tied, I let out my breath, struggled to articulate myself. "Look, it's something that . . . y'know, I once thought I could do, but . . ."

"You gave up?"

I didn't answer that because I couldn't. Whoever these guys were—Mickey, Tyler, Hsing, Libbie, Deke, even Alex—they'd come from a time and place where the impossible had become easy. You don't tell a girl who's just stolen a few tons of spent fuel rods from a heavily guarded nuclear power plant that you quit believing that you could become an astronaut just because your father's dead, your mother works two lousy jobs, and your brother's a pothead.

Mickey waited a moment for me to answer. When I didn't, her hand left my arm. "Better strap in," she said, returning to her own seat. "We're coming in for rendezvous with the *Vincennes*."

"Rendezvous with the . . . ?" I was about to ask what she meant when I looked forward, and saw something that made the Moon seem like a minor attraction.

Fifty-five thousand miles beyond the far side of the Moon, parked in lunar stationary orbit and concealed from all the telescopes and radar systems of Earth, was a starship.

Nearly four hundred feet long, illuminated by red and green formation lights on either side of its sleek grey hull, the SCS *Vincennes* was a leviathan in space. Streamlined from the slender cone of its bow to the stunted wings of its stern, it retained the same basic design of its shuttlecraft, including the vertical stabilizers that rose on either side of aft-section bulge. Yet there were

significant differences: open-end nacelles, vaguely resembling in-
takes of enormous jet engines, lay on either side of the hull just
forward of the wings, while a superstructure that looked somewhat like a submarine conning tower was elevated above the
cylindrical mid-section leading to the bow.

An enormous hatch yawned open within the upper side of the
vessel's aft section; I didn't need anyone to tell me that this was
the shuttle bay. Yet as we glided closer, I noticed that most of the
portholes along the ship's slender forward section were dark;
only a few were lit, along with those on the forward tower. The
*Vincennes* had gone dark; somehow, it looked less like a starship
than a derelict in space.

"Oh, boy," Tyler murmured from behind us. "They've gone
to low-power mode."

"Roger that." Hsing gently coaxed the shuttle closer, swinging it in a broad arc above the darkened vessel. "Command re-
ports all major systems except life-support and station-keeping
have been shut down. Docking will be manual."

"Copy that." Libbie's hands moved across her console.
"Coming in on manual. All hands, stand by."

"Does that mean we're in trouble?" I asked Mickey.

"Don't worry," She grasped the bars of her harness. "Just
means that *Vincennes* won't be guiding us in on autopilot. Hsing's a good pilot, though. He'll get us down safely."

She knew what she was talking about, of course, but
nonetheless I gripped the armrests of my seat. As the shuttle
glided into position above the hangar, I looked down to see a
broad circle blinking red upon the deck. A moment later, Libbie
cut the inertial dampeners; I felt my guts lurch a bit as we became
weightless once more. There was a thump beneath our feet, signi-
fying that the landing gear had been lowered, then the shuttle began to slowly descend into the mothership.

However, we didn't touch down. Since the *Vincennes'* own
dampeners had been shut down as well, the shuttle was unable to
land in a conventional sense. Instead, Hsing guided the craft until it was just a couple of meters above the deck, then held posi-

tion. Several crewmembers, wearing the same type of skin-tight spacesuits I'd seen earlier, floated toward us, using backpack maneuvering units to haul mooring lines into place. Once the shuttle had been secured, the hangar doors began to close. From my window, I watched while an enclosed gangway telescoped out from the hangar walk. There was a hollow thump against the hull as a crewman mated it with the shuttle's side hatch.

"All right, we're down." Hsing let out his breath; he reached up to push buttons along the overhead console. "Give us a second to match pressure, then we'll pop the hatch. Remember, we're on emergency discipline, so you know what that means."

"What does that mean?" I whispered to Mickey.

"Zero-g," she said softly, raising her seat bar, her hair floating around her. "Just follow me, and try not to bump into anything."

"Mickey, Tyler . . ." Hsing gazed back at us. "Skipper wants to see you both on the bridge, soon as possible." He paused, listening to his headset, then glanced at me. "And bring your guest, too. The old man wants to meet him."

"I bet he does." Tyler had already pushed himself out of his seat. Grasping a rail running along the ceiling, he pulled himself toward the hatch, his feet dangling in midair. "Sorry, but I'm not taking the heat for this."

"I don't expect you to." Mickey's voice was cool, and for a second they shared a look of mutual animosity. Then Tyler twisted the hatch's lockwheel and pulled it open.

Cold air flooded the shuttle, and I felt my ears pop. Mickey waited patiently while I pushed my seat bar upward; still, I found myself reluctant to leave the safety of my seat. "Come on," she said, extending a hand to me while holding onto the ceiling rail with the other. "It's not that hard. You might even like it."

"Sure. Whatever you say." But it wasn't weightlessness that bothered me. It was meeting the captain.

❧ ❧ ❧

Mickey was right: zero-g is *wicked* cool.

I'll admit, I floundered around for the first few minutes, feeling like a little kid in swim class who'd been taken out of the baby pool and tossed into the deep end for the first time. The difference is that you're operating in air, not water, and there's nothing like zero-g to teach you some respect for Newton's third law.

Every action produces an equal and opposite reaction. That means, when you bump into a bulkhead to your left, you bounce to the right, and when you grab a railing above your head, if you're not careful with your feet, they might swing around and kick the guy in front of you.

To make matters worse, the *Vincennes*' passageways were narrow. Even when there was internal gravity, there was barely enough room for two people to pass one another without sucking in your gut; in microgravity, it was like being inside a pinball machine. So I bruised my shoulders and elbows a couple of times, and also put a lump on my head and put my foot against Mickey's behind before I finally got the hang of it.

But I can't lie; it was fun. At some point, words like *up*, *down*, *left*, and *right* lost their meaning; once I got used to that, then everything else was a hoot. Crewmen who passed us in the corridors stared in bafflement at the guy in blue jeans and hooded sweatshirt who was laughing out loud as he performed somersaults that would have put him in the hospital back home. Mickey finally had to grab my shoulders and get me under control; several yards ahead, Tyler regarded me with disgust, as if I was a country bumpkin who'd just used toilet paper for the first time.

Once I got over that, though, I noticed a couple of things.

First, the lighting within the passageways was dim. Much dimmer that it should have been; ceiling panels were dark, leaving only recessed amber lamps here and there to guide our way. Not only that, but as we passed hatches leading to various compartments, I saw through their slot windows that they were without light. Not only that, but the entire ship felt cold; it couldn't have been more than sixty-five degrees. I was born and raised in New England, where temperatures like that mean it's time to put away to put away the snowshoes and start wearing T-shirts and shorts, but everyone I saw wore jackets above their jumpsuits, and some were wearing light gloves. If these guys were from Mars, then Mars in the 24th century must have the climate of Daytona Beach.

And that brings me to the second point: they were young.

By young, I mean that almost no one I saw was older than twenty-one, with the median age somewhere between fifteen and seventeen. I passed one or two crewmen in their mid-thirties, and spotted one geezer with a few threads of white in his mustache and crow's-feet around his eyes. Otherwise, though, the guys looked as if they just learned how to shave, and the girls . . . well, not to be too specific, but most of them weren't exactly women yet.

A starship full of teenagers. Martian teenagers, at that.

"What's so funny?" Mickey saw the expression on my face.

"I dunno. I think I just fell into a Sci-Fi Channel movie." She gave me a puzzled look, not getting the joke. "Never mind," I added. "What I'm trying to say is . . . um, is everyone aboard a kid?"

"No. The captain and senior officers are all adults." She paused to let another crewman slide past us; he couldn't have been more than fifteen, yet was as serious as someone twice his age. "But, yes, most of the crew are between fourteen and twenty. By Earth reckoning, that is . . . about half that if you use the Martian calendar." She smiled. "That makes me eight years old, where I come from."

"Eight. Right . . ." I was having trouble dealing with this. "Look, where *I* come from, you can't even drive a car until you're sixteen . . . eighteen, in some states. So you're telling me . . ."

By now we'd come to a ladder leading up a narrow shaft. Without looking back at us, Tyler was already ascending it, barely touching the rungs as he floated upward. "It's a long story," Mickey said quietly. "I'll tell you the rest later . . . if the captain lets me."

"But . . ."

"Eric . . ." Mickey paused at the bottom of the ladder. "Do me a favor and keep your mouth shut. Don't speak unless the captain speaks to you first . . . and be careful what you say. Understand?"

I made a zipping motion with a finger across my lips. Mickey nodded, then led me up the shaft. We ascended about thirty feet, passing a closed hatch leading to another deck, and emerged through an open manhole. And that's when I found myself on the bridge of the *Vincennes*.

In many ways, it resembled pictures I'd seen of the control rooms of nuclear submarines: a long, narrow compartment, with officers seated at consoles on either side of a central aisle. What appeared to be a plotting table rested in the middle of the compartment, except this one displayed a holographic wire-frame image of the Earth-Moon system, with a tiny replica of the *Vincennes* positioned beyond the lunar farside. On the far side of the compartment, wrapped in a 180-degree arc, were five large portholes; the center one looked out over the ship's bow, and it was in front of this window that I saw the commanding officer of SCS *Vincennes*.

If I was expecting someone more heroic—James T. Kirk, maybe, or even Jean-Luc Picard—then I was disappointed. Captain Van Owen looked no more intimidating than my high school geometry teacher; short and narrow-shouldered, with barely enough brown hair to keep his head from getting cold. He would have looked better if he had glasses and maybe a mustache. One look at his eyes, though, and I knew that this was one guy you didn't throw a spit wad at while his back was turned to you.

"Mr. Ionesco, Ms. McGyver . . ." His voice was low, yet demanding respect. He was standing upright, and it took me a second to realize that the toes of his shoes were tucked into stirrups on the deck. "Welcome back. I see that your mission has been a success . . . for the most part, at least."

"Yes, sir." Tyler grasped the handrail surrounding the plotting table; Mickey and I had to settle for rungs here and there along the low ceiling. "We've retrieved a cache of uranium fuel rods from the objective, and have transported them to . . ."

"Yes, I know. I can see that." The captain gestured to a flatscreen above a console to our left. Looking at it, I saw an image of the hangar deck. Several spacesuited figures were guiding the stolen fuel rod canister from the shuttle, allowing its weight-less condition to do most of the heavy-lifting for them. At the aft end of the hangar, another crewman hovered near an open hatch, apparently waiting for them to pass through. "Well done. But . . ."

He paused, then looked past Tyler at both Mickey and me. "Apparently there were some unforeseen difficulties."

"Yes, sir, there were." Mickey moved a little closer. "Captain, we had problems almost as soon as we entered the vicinity." She glanced back at me. "However, if it hadn't been for . . ."

"Sir, I must protest." Tyler interrupted her. "*Midshipman* McGyver overstates the situation . . ."

"She does, does she?" Van Owen raised an eyebrow; he hadn't missed the way Tyler had emphasized her rank. "She hasn't even told me what that is . . . and as I recall, she was in charge of the retrieval phase, not you."

"Yes, but . . ." Tyler's face colored. "Sir, she allowed an in-digenous native to observe the operation." The way he said *native* made it sound as if I wore a loincloth and had a bone in my nose. "She then brought him aboard, despite my objections . . ."

"Sir, with all due respect, the *native* observed the operation on his own initiative." Mickey spoke as if I wasn't beside her. "There was nothing we could do to prevent his intervention . . ."

"No, sir, that's not true." Tyler jabbed a finger at me. "When I had an opportunity to stun him, she deliberately intervened, and when I insisted that he be left behind . . ."

"Tell him what happened when we almost had to leave *you* behind." Letting go of the ceiling rail, she pushed herself closer to Tyler. "Tell him what he did after you fell off the ladder."

"That's enough, both of you." Although Van Owen's voice remained low, both Mickey and Tyler clammed up. "Lt. Ionesco, I'll remind you that it was my order, relayed to Lt. Wu, that this person be brought aboard. Ms. McGyver was simply following my instructions."

That settled Tyler's hash. "Yes, sir," he murmured. "I didn't understand that, sir."

"Now you do." Ignoring both him and Mickey for a moment, the captain looked straight at me. "What's your name, son?"

"Eric . . . Eric Cosby, sir." My mouth felt dry. "Captain, sir, I didn't mean to . . . I mean, I wasn't trying to . . ."

"Easy, boy. You were just caught up in something you didn't understand." He paused, studying all three of us. "Nonetheless, this is a serious situation . . . and Tyler, you've made some serious charges. I'll speak to you alone."

Tyler nodded, not looking back at Mickey and me. The captain gestured toward the hatch behind us. "Ms. McGyver, please escort Mr. Cosby to the observation lounge. Remain there and keep him company until I summon you."

"Yes, sir."

The captain hesitated. "And while you're at it, tell him whatever he needs to know." A wry smile appeared on his face. "He's come this far . . . might as well let him learn the rest."

The observation lounge was located on the deck below the bridge. Barely wide enough for three people to stand abreast, it had two circular portholes, each six feet in diameter, on either side of the compartment, with chairs anchored to the floor in front of them. Like the rest of the ship, the lounge was almost totally dark, save for a red emergency light glowing above the hatch.

"This is my favorite place on the ship." Grasping a ceiling rail, Mickey led me to the two chairs facing the starboard viewport. "I don't get a chance to come here very often, though . . . usually too busy. Would you like to sit, or . . . ?"

"Uh-uh. I'd just as soon . . . um, float, if it's okay with you." I couldn't take my eyes from the starboard window. Once my eyes became accustomed to the darkness, I saw billions of stars— planets, suns, nebulae, distant galaxies—spread out before us in a broad swath, with the Moon an oval patch of darkness, sunlight forming a slender crescent around its western terminator.

"So would I." Mickey grasped a handrail encircling the porthole, anchoring herself next to the window; I took hold of the rail on the other side. "This is a treat, believe me. No gravity . . . and the place all to ourselves."

Better than the drive-in, that's for sure. But that wasn't what was on my mind. "Mickey . . . what's going on here? Why are you . . . I mean, why did you . . . ?"

"Of course. Questions." She took a deep breath, then released the handrail and folded her legs together in a position that I would've called "sitting" if she wasn't three feet above the floor. "It's like this . . ."

By the year 2337 (she explained), the human race had not only colonized most of Earth's solar system—the Moon, Mars, the asteroid belt and the major satellites of Jupiter and Saturn, along with space stations as close as Venus and as distant as the Kuiper belt—but it had also ventured out to the nearby star systems: Alpha Centauri B, Wolf 359, Epsilon Eridani, and Bernard's Star, among others. The development of nuclear engines had opened the solar system as a frontier during the 21st century; the subsequent invention of hyperspace travel during the 23rd century had carried humankind to the stars.

During this time, Earth's nearby colonies decided to form the Solar System Confederation, a democratic alliance that sought to maintain trade and diplomatic ties among both the near-Earth colonies and the extrasolar settlements. This wasn't an easy task; the colonies often quarreled, and more than once war had threatened to tear the union apart. So in order to keep the peace, as well as facilitate further colonization, the Solar Confederation Fleet was established.

The *Vincennes* was one of three heavy cruisers belonging to Mars, which—next only to Earth itself—was the most populated and politically powerful of the SSC worlds, particularly after it had been terraformed during the 22nd century. The *Vincennes* took its name from the flagship of the United States Exploratory Expedition of 1838, and was the oldest of its class; constructed at the Deimos shipyards in 2278, it remained in service until 2329, when it was retired from active duty and turned over to the Mars campus of the Confederation Fleet Academy as a training vessel.

"Whoa, Wait a minute . . ." Hearing this, I held up a hand. "You mean this . . . ?" I looked around myself, at everything I'd seen so far. "You mean this is . . . this is just a training ship?"

"Sort of a letdown, isn't it?" There was a sad look in her eyes as Mickey glanced up at the ceiling. "Maybe she doesn't look it, but she's obsolete. Range limited to only fifty light-years. Nothing like the . . ."

"Okay, I get it." I shook my head. Only fifty light-years . . . "So I guess that, compared to whatever else you guys have, it's beat to crap . . ."

"Hey, that's my ship you're talking about." Mickey scowled at me, and suddenly I realized that I'd just crossed the line. "Maybe you think this is funny, but here in this century, your people still thought liquid-fuel rockets were . . ."

"Easy. Easy." I held up my hands. "Bad joke, okay? No offense."

Mickey relaxed. Uncurling her legs, she grasped the rail again. "Of course. I forget that irony was a preferred form of humor in your . . . never mind. Let's go on."

When it departed from Phobos Station on Aquarius 47, 2337, the *Vincennes'* crew included sixty-five cadets, ranging from ensigns to junior-grade lieutenants, along with ten senior officers who acted as their instructors. Not to mention Alex, whose full name was Alex Elevendee and who was just as much a part of the *Vincennes* as its lifeboats and life-extinguishing equipment: another piece of hardware, albeit a little more conversational than, say, the toaster. This particular mission was the third one for the Class of '38, and was supposed to be relatively simple: a quick jaunt through hyperspace from Mars to the Moon, a couple of orbits around Earth to test the cadets' knowledge of planetary rendezvous procedures, then another jaunt back through hyperspace to Mars. No one had brought more than the clothes on their backs and their datapads; they'd fully expected to be home by evening mess.

"But it didn't work out that way, did it?" I asked.

"No, it didn't." Mickey shook her head. "The jaygee at the

navigation station laid in the wrong jump coordinates. He accidentally transposed the elements for the $c$-factor for the $t$-factor, which in turn caused . . ." She caught the look on my face. "You haven't had quantum mechanics, have you?"

I snapped my fingers, glanced up at the ceiling. "Gee, y'know, they offered it this year, but I went for trig instead because I heard it was a crib course."

"Never mind." From her expression, I could see that she couldn't tell whether I was putting her on again or not. "Look, plotting a hyperspace jaunt is a very precise business. You've got to get everything right the first time, or . . ."

"Uh-huh. And I take it this guy screwed up."

She nodded. "In a major way, yes. Oh, he got us to the Moon, all right . . . but through a curved timelike loop that opened a wormhole through the space-time continuum. So instead of arriving here in our own year . . ."

"You arrived here in *my* year. Let me guess the rest . . . you can't get back, right?"

"Oh, no. Returning to our time isn't the problem. Once we realized what had happened, all we had to do was sort through the onboard log, detect where the mistake had been made, and figure out how to correct it. If everything had worked out as it should have, we could have been home in less than an hour."

"So what went wrong?" I corrected myself. "I mean, what *else* went wrong?"

"Because the main computer detected a flaw in the flight profile, it automatically tripped the master alarm as soon as we came out of hyperspace. I was on the bridge when it happened, and it was really scary. All the lights went red, and then the horns went off all at once, and then . . ."

Mickey suddenly stopped. Looking away from me, she gazed out the porthole at the far side of the Moon. "It . . . it was my fault," she said quietly. "I was minding the power control station. I was confused, just as they'd warned us might happen when we came out of hyperspace, when I saw the red-alert light on my console, I . . ."

Now I saw a strange thing. Tiny bubbles, like miniature spheres of water, departing from the corners of her eyes, gently floating upward. Tears in the moonlight. A girl crying in zero-g.

"Mickey . . ." I leaned forward, touched her arm. "C'mon . . ."

"I'm sorry. I'm still . . ." She reached up to her face, dried her eyes. "I dumped the reactor," she murmured. "The alarm confused me, and I . . . I mean, we didn't know what had happened. All I knew was . . . that is, I thought the main reactor was about to melt down, so I jettisoned the rods. Which is what they tell us to do in an emergency."

"You use a nuclear reactor?" As soon as I said this, I knew it sounded dumb. What was I expecting, dilithium crystals? Perhaps nuclear fission hadn't worked out so well in my time, but that didn't mean it couldn't be used three hundred years later. "Sorry. Go on . . . so you dumped the reactor, and that meant . . ."

She didn't say anything, only looked at me, and that was when everything came together. Sure, the crew of the *Vincennes* knew how to get home . . . but without fuel for their reactor, there was no way they'd be able to make another jump through space-time. So they did what they had to do: parked the ship in lunar stationary orbit on the far side of the Moon, where it couldn't be seen from Earth, and sent down a team to steal some nuclear fuel rods.

"So how did you . . . ?" I paused. "I mean, how did you know about Narragansett Point?"

"The ship's library system has complete historical records." Mickey snuffled back her tears. "Meant for download into colony computers for educational purposes. Someone did a little research and discovered that, in this time, your nuclear power plant was being decommissioned." She shrugged. "That seemed to be the least dangerous means of getting what we needed. Minimal security . . . or at least nothing that our stun guns and Alex couldn't take down . . ."

"I was wondering about that. All those guards, and the guys inside the plant . . ."

"We used a sleeper. Sort of like a grenade, only it emits an electromagnetic pulse that temporarily disrupts higher brain functions. We hid in the vehicle we'd stolen while Alex penetrated the front gate, then detonated the sleeper to knock out the sentries."

"Right. Got it." But that still left much unexplained. "But if you guys knew about our nuke, then why come into town? Why ask me for directions?"

"We knew there was a plant near Bellingham, but we didn't know exactly where it was located. Also, we needed to take out the security and find the spent fuel before we could bring in the shuttle to take it away. That was my part of the operation. So very early this morning, Hsing dropped us just outside town, then landed the shuttle out in the hills and waited for us to send him a signal. We hiked in, stole an automobile and hid it in an alley, then broke into a shop to steal some clothes . . ."

"I know about that." I tried not to grin as I glanced at her Dead T-shirt and faux-fur overcoat. "Someone should've told you how we dress in my century. You guys stuck out."

"We did?" She looked down at herself, and laughed. "Well, what do I know? Besides, we would've looked even stranger in our academy uniforms." Mickey sighed. "But I think our biggest mistake was asking you for directions."

"Thanks a lot . . ."

"No!" Her eyes widened. "I didn't mean it that way. It's just that our orders were to avoid contact with the inhabitants as much as possible." She frowned. "But Tyler was in charge of that part of the operation, and he became frustrated when we couldn't find a map that would show us exactly where the plant was located. So when he saw you . . ."

"Let me guess. Since I'm your age, he figured that asking me for directions wouldn't be as risky as talking to an adult. Right?"

"Something like that." She gave me a grim smile. "It wasn't the first mistake Tyler made. The first was setting the wrong coordinates for the hyperspace jump."

"He . . . ?" Now it was my turn to be surprised. "I don't get it. If you two were the guys responsible for this mess, why did the captain pick you to . . . ?"

"Because we *were* responsible." She let out her breath. "One of the first things they teach us in the academy is that, if you make a critical error, you're the one who has to make it right."

"You break it, you bought it." She gave me a quizzical look, and I smiled. "Something we say in my time."

"'You break it, you bought it.'" Mickey smiled as she repeated my words. "I like that. Anyway, once we knew how to find the plant, we went out there, and . . . well, you know the rest."

"Yeah, okay." Then I thought about it for a moment. "No, I don't. What good would nuclear waste do you? I mean, what you stole were spent fuel rods. How could you . . . ?"

"Only about three-quarters of the U-235 contained within nuclear fuel rods is actually consumed during fission. The rest gets thrown away along with the U-237 and plutonium waste . . . or at least by the standards by which 20th century nuclear power plants normally operated. But our ships are designed to reprocess spent fuel rods from other ships in the event of an emergency." She nodded in the general direction of the stern. "Right now, nanites are disassembling those uranium-dioxide pellets, molecule by molecule, and recombining the usable U-235 as fuel for our reactor. Believe me, it's a very fast process. We should be back to full power any minute now."

"Oh, I believe you." I remembered how quickly nanites in the floor of the shuttle had cleaned up my vomit. Maybe it wasn't the most savory example of the wonders of the 24th century, but nonetheless it was the one that came to mind. "Then . . . ."

Then? Then nothing. She'd told me everything I needed to know, just as the captain had told her to do. Once again, I gazed out the window. Here I was, aboard a starship lurking above the dark side of the Moon, farther from Earth than anyone had ever been before. I should have been awestruck, or delirious with wonder, or . . . something, I don't know what. Yet instead, I only felt hollow. Something was missing, but I didn't know what it was . . .

"Eric?"

"Yeah?" I didn't look at her. "What?"

For a moment, Mickey said nothing. Then I felt her come closer to me, and as I turned around, she took my face within her hands, looked me straight in the eye, and kissed me.

Exactly three times before, a girl had given me a kiss. I won't go into details about the earlier ones, but take my word for it: this was the best one yet.

And, by the way, did I forget to mention that zero-g is really cool?

It might have lasted longer, but then a shrill alarm came over a ceiling speaker. Hearing this, Mickey reluctantly pulled herself away from me. "Inertial dampeners are coming back online," she murmured. "We're going to get gravity again in about ten seconds." She reached up to grasp the ceiling rail. "Brace yourself."

I had just enough time to grab the rail myself before we went from microgravity to one-g. This time, I was ready for it; no puking in front of my new girlfriend, or at least not for the second time tonight. We waited until the alarms shut off, then dropped to the floor.

"Thanks." I took a deep breath, then took a step closer to her. "So, where were we . . . ?"

Mickey blushed, but she didn't back away as I took her hands. "I think I was thanking you for . . ."

The hatch clicked, and we had a chance to retreat from each other before it swung open. Then the ceiling lights came open; squinting against the abrupt glare, I looked around to see Tyler standing in the hatchway.

He stared at us for a moment, then looked at Mickey. "Skipper wants to talk to you now," he said, with plenty of frost in his voice. Mickey's face went pale, but she said nothing to me. Instead, she silently nodded, and marched out of the observation lounge, taking care not to brush against Tyler on the way to the ladder.

Tyler and I silently regarded one another. For a second, I was afraid that he'd join me in the lounge—there would be no hugging and kissing between the two of us—but instead he turned toward the corridor. I was relieved that he was going to leave me alone, but then a smug grin crept across his face, and he wagged a finger at me.

"See you in China," he said.

"Sure thing, bud," I replied. "Right after you learn quantum math."

His face went red, and then he slammed the hatch shut.

I was alone in the observation lounge for only ten or fifteen minutes. Then an ensign barely old enough to try out for the junior varsity basketball team came to fetch me. Yet I was escorted not to the bridge, as I expected, but to another compartment on the same deck.

The captain's quarters were little larger than the janitor's closet at my high school; just enough room for a small desk, a chair, a locker, a fold-down bunk, and a door leading to what I assumed was a private john. Captain Van Owen was seated at his desk when the ensign led me in; he accepted the kid's salute with a cursory nod, then waited until he shut the hatch behind me.

"Mr. Cosby . . . or may I call you Eric?" I swallowed and nodded, and he gave me a brief smile. "Eric, then . . . please be seated."

There was nowhere else to sit except his bunk. "Thank you, sir," I said, and sat down on the very edge, trying to disturb its drum-tight covers as little as possible.

"You're welcome." His eyes never left mine. "I believe that Midshipman McGyver has fully briefed you about our situation. Correct?"

"Yes, sir. She's told me everything." And a bit more, although the last thing he'd ever learn from me was the exact nature of our briefing.

"Very well." Sitting back in his chair, the captain crossed his arms. "First, let me express my appreciation for the assistance you've given my team. Judging from what both Ms. McGyver and Mr. Ionesco have told me, your performance has been outstanding . . . particularly in regards to the lieutenant's rescue."

"Yes, sir. Thank you, sir." Perhaps I wasn't a member of the crew, but nonetheless I found myself addressing him as if he was my commanding officer. "I did what I had to . . ."

"Of course. And if you were one of my cadets, I'd expect no less." Van Owen hesitated. "Which leads us to our predicament, because you don't belong to *Vincennes*, and I'm at a loss to know what to do with you."

Pushing back his chair, he stood up, walked over to the porthole. "As you now know, this was supposed to be a covert mission. No one on Earth was ever supposed to be aware of our presence. Of course, there'll be an investigation of how spent uranium was stolen from a secure nuclear facility, but I'm gambling that it will be done quietly, with no one in public ever learning what happened tonight."

"Even with Air National Guard jets chasing your shuttle?"

"Yes, even despite that." Van Owen gazed through the porthole, his hands clasped behind his back. "In fact, I'm willing to bet that those pilots have already been thoroughly interrogated by military intelligence. Even if their story is believed . . . and how many unconfirmed UFO sightings were there during your time? . . . chances are that they'll be sworn to silence about what they saw, or thought they saw."

"I . . ."

"Eric, the last thing anyone will suspect is the truth. Think about it for a moment. All eyewitnesses on the ground were rendered unconscious by unknown forces. A single cask of nuclear waste was lifted from the site by an unidentified aircraft that bore no markings and managed to evade military jets. The only clue left behind was a stolen vehicle, and the fingerprints won't match any in law enforcement databases. Now, put yourself in their place. Would you conclude that this was done by men from outer space . . . or by a well-equipped terrorist organization?"

He had a point. Ever since 9/11, the news media had come up with scenarios for future terrorist actions that sounded as if they'd come straight from a bad movie. If you believed everything you read in the magazines or saw on TV, Al Qaeda wasn't a gang of Islamist fanatics led by geek named Osama bin Laden, but SPECTRE itself, with Blofelt in charge. A group of teenage space cadets—from the future, no less—making off with nuclear material to refuel a stranded starship? How absurd could you possibly get?

"I think I see what you mean," I said. "Sir."

"Of course you do." Van Owen gave me a sly wink as he turned back around. "I wouldn't have risked this if I thought otherwise." Then he frowned. "But we still have one loose end . . ."

"That's me, isn't it?"

The captain slowly nodded. "You're the one thing we never expected . . . a witness too valuable to simply knock out and leave behind. You helped my people escape from Earth, and now we have to decide what to do with you."

Leaning against his desk, he raised his fingers one at a time. "First option . . . we kill you." Seeing my expression, he quickly shook his head. "Don't worry, that's out of the question. We're not barbarians." He raised a second finger. "Second option . . . we take you back to Earth, but drop you off in an area so remote that it's unlikely that you'll ever make your way back to civilization."

I had no doubt who'd suggested this one. Before I could object, though, the captain shook his head. 'That's also out of the question, for that's almost as bad as the first option . . . and I'm making it a point to officially reprimand the cadet who made it. He's in enough hot water with me already, so this won't look good on his service record."

Oh, boy. Tyler was in a lot of trouble once he got home. I tried not to smile. "The third option," Van Owen continued, "is that we take you back to where we found you, drop you off, and trust that you'll never, ever breathe a word to anyone about what you've seen. Not now, not tomorrow, not in ten or twenty or fifty years, not ever." He stared at me. "Do you know what I'm asking, Eric? Complete and utter secrecy, for as long as you live."

I swallowed when I heard that. Sure, I can keep a secret . . . but about something like this? It's one thing not to let anyone know that your brother sells dope, or that your best friend wears boxer shorts printed with the Superman logo. It's another to promise that you'll never reveal that you've been to the Moon, or seen the inside of starship from the 24th century . . .

Yet who'd ever believe me? At best, they'd simply think I was making it up, and then I'd be a liar, and a bad one at that. At worst, they'd assume I was delusional; then I'd be sent to a state mental hospital, and spend the next few years playing checkers with all the other guys who'd spent quality time with space aliens.

"I don't have a problem with that," I said.

"All right." Van Owen nodded. "I think I can trust you to keep your word . . . but you still haven't heard the fourth option."

"There's one?"

"Yes, there is," he said, and this time he didn't bother to raise a finger. "You can come with us."

I didn't say anything. I just stared at him, and waited for my heart to start beating again.

"As I said," he went on, "if you were a member of my crew, your conduct would be considered outstanding. You have a quick mind, you're quick to adapt to a crisis situation . . . and most of all, you've displayed true heroism, under circumstances that would've caused ninety-nine out of a hundred men to run for their lives."

The captain paused, then folded his arms together. "Son, you've got what it takes to be a spacer. I don't say that lightly, and neither does Midshipman McGyver. Come with us, and I'll personally recommend you to the academy . . . and I'd be proud to have you aboard the *Vincennes* once you pass basic training."

Not knowing what to say, I didn't say anything. Instead, I walked over to the porthole and looked out at the stars.

I was tempted. Damn, but I was tempted. Everything I'd ever

wanted in my life, within reach of my fingertips. I wouldn't even have to worry about graduating high school; trigonometry would be a thing of the past, because I'd be studying quantum mechanics instead. And not long after that, a berth aboard this very ship, and a chance to see things no one in my time had ever dreamed of seeing . . .

And meanwhile, my mother would be left wondering what had happened to her son, who'd disappeared one October night without a trace. She'd already lost my father; now she'd lose me as well. That would kill her. And did I really want to be the kid brother whose picture Steve would see printed on the side of milk cartons he restocked at Speed-E-Mart? Smokin' Steve was a jerk, but I didn't want to leave him and Mom alone together, trying to put together the pieces after I was gone.

Sometimes, the galaxy can wait. If only just a little while longer . . .

"Thank you, sir." My voice was a dry rasp. "I appreciate the offer, but . . ."

"You'll go for the third option." Captain Van Owen nodded, and smiled. "Somehow, I thought you would."

"You did?"

"Yes, I did." Then he offered his hand. "Because you're that sort of person . . . sir."

I returned to Earth that same night, arriving shortly before dawn. The sun was still below the horizon when the shuttle descended upon a cow pasture about three miles from town. Mickey dropped the ladder overboard; we shared a brief moment in the airlock, then I hastily climbed down the ladder. My feet barely touched ground before she pulled the ladder up behind me. A last wave, then she closed the hatch.

I watched the shuttle as it sprinted into the starlit sky. This time, there were no Warthogs in hot pursuit; I guess the Massachusetts Air National Guard had enough UFO-chasing for one night. In any case, the shuttle vanished within seconds, and then I began the long walk home.

I'd hoped to slip in through the kitchen door without waking anyone, but my luck wasn't with me; Mom had stayed up all night, watching TV in the living room while she waited for me to come home. I couldn't tell whether she was mad or relieved: both, probably. She sniffed my breath, looked closely at my eyes to see if they were bloodshot, then demanded that I tell her where I'd been.

I was too tired to come up with a decent lie, so I told her that I'd been abducted by men from Mars. She stared at me for a long moment, then apparently decided that, since I obviously hadn't been drinking or smoking dope, she'd let me have my little secrets. Maybe she figured that I'd been out with a girl. And that wasn't too far from the truth either . . .

Anyway, she had worse things to think about. As it turned out, Steve had been busted earlier that night. Officer Beauchamp spotted his Mustang tearing down the highway a few miles from Narragansett Point, so he pulled my brother over, and when Steve cranked down his window, Bo caught a strong whiff of reefer smoke. Bo called for backup, and when the cops searched Steve's car, they found all the stuff that had made me so nervous. Mom got the call from the police shortly after she got home from work, but before she went downtown to spring him from jail, she first went downstairs to visit his room.

And that's how my brother lost his car, a pound of marijuana, and his status as Smokin' Steve, all in the same evening. The pot was flushed down the pot, the 'stang was sold to repay Mom for the bail she had to post for him, and Steve spent his free time for the next twelve months picking up roadside trash on behalf of the Honor Court. He didn't call me a twerp after that, either; Mom let him know that he was on probation so far as she was concerned, too, and that if he didn't treat us both with a little more respect, he'd find just how far his Speed-E-Mart paycheck went toward paying for rent, utilities, and groceries.

Not that I got off scot-free. Mom grounded me for a month, which meant that I didn't spend much time that fall hanging out in front of Fat Boy's Music. I didn't mind, though, because now I had a new interest in life.

Just as Captain Van Owen predicted, no one ever learned the truth what really happened at Narragansett Point that night. There was nothing about it in the news media, although a couple of days later Homeland Security escalated the Terror Alert to Code Orange, and Fox News made a squawk about civilian nuclear power plants being put under increased vigilance. As always, no one paid much attention to all this—you've heard one duct-tape alert, you've heard 'em all—although I couldn't help but wonder if my friends hadn't done us a favor, albeit unintentionally.

When I saw Ted at school the next Monday, he didn't want to talk about what he'd seen. In fact, he even denied that we'd done anything after we had pizza at Louie's. It took me a few days to get his part of the story out of him, and then only in hushed tones, under the seats of the football field bleachers during gym class. Once he'd escaped from my brother and his friends, Ted beat it to the nearest gas station, where he used the pay phone to call the state police. But what he didn't get were Vermont smokies, but instead two guys from the FBI field office in Burlington. They put him on the griddle for a couple of hours, then told him that if he ever breathed a word about what he'd seen, he'd find that his ambition to become a comic book writer would be limited to doing funnies for a federal prison newspaper. So, as far as he was concerned, our little adventure together was something that never happened.

I didn't object. Ted was right. Nothing significant happened that night, except that my brother got his comeuppance, my best friend became a little more cautious, and my mother stopped spending so much time away from the house.

And me . . . ?

I hit the books as hard as I could. Every minute I had left in the day, I spent doing my homework, trying to jack up my grades so that I could qualify for a scholarship. The Air Force Academy was my first choice; if not that, then Annapolis. And if those options failed, then MIT, or Stanford, or CalTech. Any school that might lead me, in the long run, to NASA astronaut training, and—if I was lucky—a seat aboard the first ship to Mars.

I'd rediscovered my dreams, sure. I'd also learned that I didn't have to live in Bellingham for the rest of my life. High school is just something you get through, and the corner of Main and Birch is just a temporary resting place along the way. But that's not all. The perfect girl is out there, waiting for me. And when we shared our last kiss aboard the shuttle just before she dropped me off, she told me how to find her again.

I won't tell you how this is going to be done, only to say that we worked it out on the way back from the far side of the Moon. Time isn't an obstacle; it's just an inconvenience. Besides, you wouldn't give out your girlfriend's phone number, would you?

And, like I said, I always wanted to be an astronaut.

☻☻

# WHERE THE GOLDEN APPLES GROW

## by Kage Baker

One of the most prolific new writers to appear in the late '90s, Kage Baker made her first sale in 1997, to *Asimov's Science Fiction*, and has since become one of that magazine's most frequent and popular contributors with her sly and compelling stories of the adventures and misadventures of the time-traveling agents of the Company; of late, she's started two other linked sequences of stories there as well, one of them set in as lush and eccentric a High Fantasy milieu as any we've ever seen. Her stories have also appeared in *Realms of Fantasy*, *Sci Fiction*, *Amazing*, and elsewhere. Her critically acclaimed novels include *In the Garden of Iden*, *Sky Coyote*, *Mendoza in Hollywood*, *The Graveyard Game*, and her first fantasy novel, *The Anvil of the World*. Her short fiction has been collected in *Black Projects, White Knights* and, most recently, *Mother Aegypt and Other Stories*. Her most recent books are a chapbook novella, *The Empress of Mars*, and two new Company novels, *The Life of the World to Come* and *The Children of the Company*. In addition to her writing, Baker has been an artist, actor, and director at the Living History Center, and has taught Elizabethan English as a second language. She lives in Pismo Beach, California.

Here she takes us to a newly colonized frontier Mars, still wild and dangerous, for a taut adventure that demonstrates that the grass is always greener on the other side of the fence—no matter *which* side of the fence you're looking over.

## 1

HE WAS THE third boy born on Mars.

He was twelve years old now, and had spent most of his life in the cab of a freighter. His name was Bill.

Bill lived with his dad, Billy Townsend. Billy Townsend was a Hauler. He made the long runs up and down Mars, to Depot North and Depot South, bringing ice back from the ends of the world. Bill had always gone along on the runs, from the time he'd been packed into the shotgun seat like a little duffel bag to now, when he sat hunched in the far corner of the cab with his Game-buke, ignoring his dad's loud and cheerful conversation.

There was no other place for him to be. The freighter was the only home he had ever known. His dad called her *Beautiful Evelyn*.

As far as Bill knew, his mum had passed on. That was one of the answers his dad had given him, and it might be true; there were a lot of things to die from on Mars, with all the cold and dry and blowing grit, and so little air to breathe. But it was just as likely she had gone back to Earth, to judge from other things his dad had said. Bill tried not to think about her, either way.

He didn't like his life very much. Most of it was either boring— the long, long runs to the Depots, with nothing to look at but the monitor screens showing miles of red rocky plain—or scary, like the times they'd had to run through bad storms, or when *Beautiful Evelyn* had broken down in the middle of nowhere.

Better were the times they'd pull into Mons Olympus. The city on the mountain had a lot to see and do (although Bill's dad usually went straight to the *Empress of Mars Tavern* and stayed there); there were plenty of places to eat, and shops, and a big public data terminal where Bill could download school programs into his Buke. But what Bill liked most about Mons Olympus was that he could look down through its dome and see the Long Acres.

The Long Acres weren't at all like the city, and Bill dreamed of living there. Instead of endless cold red plains, the Long Acres had warm expanses of green life, and actual canals of water for crop irrigation, stretching out for kilometers under vizio tunnels. Bill had heard that from space, it was supposed to look like green lines crossing the lowlands of the planet.

People stayed put in the Long Acres. Families lived down there and worked the land. Bill liked that idea.

His favorite time to look down the mountain was at twilight. Then the lights were just coming on, shining through the vizio panels, and the green fields were empty; Bill liked to imagine families sitting down to dinner together, a dad and a mum and kids in their home, safe in one place from one year to the next. He imagined that they saved their money, instead of going on spending sprees when they hit town, like Bill's dad did. They never forgot things, like birthdays. They never made promises and forgot to keep them.

☙ ☙ ☙

"Payyyydayyyy!" Billy said happily, beating out a rhythm on the console wheel as he drove. "Gonna spend my money free! Yeah! We'll have us a good time, eh, mate?"

"I need to buy socks," said Bill.

"Whatever you want, bookworm. Socks, boots, buy out the whole shop."

"I just need socks," said Bill. They were on the last stretch of the High Road, rocketing along under the glittering stars, and ahead of them he could see the high-up bright lights of Mons Olympus on the monitor. Its main dome was luminous with colors from the neon signs inside; even the outlying Tubes were lit up, from all the psuit-lights of the people going to and fro. It looked like pictures he had seen of circus tents on Earth. Bill shut down his Gamebuke and slid it into the front pocket of his psuit, and carefully zipped the pocket shut.

"Time to put your mask on, Dad," he said. If Billy wasn't reminded, he tended to just take a gulp of air, jump from the cab, and sprint for the Tube airlocks, and one or twice he had tripped and fallen, and nearly killed himself before he'd got his mask on.

"Sure thing," said Billy, fumbling for the mask. He had managed to get it on his face unassisted by the time *Beautiful Evelyn* roared into the freighter barn, and backed into the Unload bay. Father and son climbed from the cab and walked away together toward the Tube, stiff-legged after all those hours on the road.

At this moment, walking side by side, they really did look like father and son. Bill had Billy's shock of wild hair that stuck up above the mask, and though he was small for a Mars-born kid, he was lean and rangy like Billy. Once they stepped through the airlocks and into the Tube, they pushed up their masks, and then they looked different; for Billy had bright crazy eyes in a lean wind-red face, and a lot of wild red beard. Bill's eyes were dark, and there was nothing crazy about him.

"Payday, payday, got money on my mind," sang Billy as they walked up the hill toward the freight office. "Bam! I'm gonna start with a big plate of Scramble with gravy, and then *two* slices of duff, and then it's hello Ares Amber Lager. What'll you do, kiddo?"

"I'm going to buy socks," said Bill patiently. "Then I guess I'll go to the public terminal. I need my next lesson plan, remember?"

"Yeah, right." Billy nodded, but Bill could tell he wasn't paying attention.

Bill went into the freight office with his dad, and waited in the lobby while Billy went in to present their chits. As he waited, he took out his Buke and thumbed it on, and accessed their bank account. He watched the screen until it flashed and updated, and checked the bank balance against what he thought it should be; the amount was correct.

He sighed and relaxed. For a long while last year, the paycheck had been short every month; money taken out by the civil court to pay off a fine Billy had incurred for beating up another guy. Billy was easygoing and never started fights, even when he drank, but he had a long reach and no sense of fear, so he tended to win them. The other Haulers never minded a good fight; this one time, though, the other guy had been a farmer from the MAC, and he had sued Billy.

Billy came out of the office now whistling, with the look in his eyes that meant he wanted to go have fun.

"Come on, bookworm, the night's young!" he said. Bill fell into step beside him as they went on up the Tube, and out to Commerce Square.

Commerce Square was the biggest single structure on the planet. Five square miles of breathable air! The steel beams soared in an unsupported arch, holding up Permavizio panes through which the stars and moons shone down. Beneath it rose the domes of houses and shops, and the spiky towers of the *Edgar Allan Poe Memorial Center for the Performing Arts*. It was built in an Old Earth style called *Gothic*. Bill had learned that just last term.

"Right!" Billy stretched. "I'm off to the *Empress*! Where you going?

"To buy socks, remember?" said Bill.

"Okay," said Billy. "See you round, then." He wandered off into the crowd.

Bill sighed. He went off to the general store.

You could get almost anything at *Prashant's*; this was the only one on Mars and it had been here a whole year now, but Bill still caught his breath when he stepped inside. Row upon row of shiny things in brilliant colors! Cases of fruit juice, electronics, furniture, tools, clothing, tinned delicacies—and all of it imported from Earth. A whole aisle of download stations selling music, movies, books, and games. Bill, packet of cotton socks in hand, approached the aisle furtively.

Should he download more music? It wasn't as though Billy would ever notice or care, but the downloads were expensive. All the same . . .

Bill saw that *Earth Hand* had a new album out, and that decided him. He plugged in his Buke and ordered the album, and twenty minutes later was sneaking out of the store, feeling guilty. He went next to the public terminal and downloaded his lesson plan; that, at least, was free. Then he walked on up the long steep street, under the flashing red and green and blue signs for the posh hotels. His hands were cold, but rather than put his gloves back on he simply jammed his fists in his suit pockets.

At the top of the street was the *Empress of Mars*. It was a big place, a vast echoing tavern with a boarding house and restaurant opening off one side and a bathhouse opening off the other. All the Haulers came here. Mother, who ran the place, didn't mind Haulers. They weren't welcome in the fancy new places, which had rules about noise and gambling and fighting, but they were always welcome at the *Empress*.

Bill stepped through the airlock and looked around. It was dark and noisy in the tavern, with only a muted golden glow over the bar and little colored lights in the booths. It smelled like spilled beer and frying food, and the smell of the food made Bill's mouth water. Haulers sat or stood everywhere, and so did construction workers, and they were all eating and drinking and talking at the top of their lungs.

But where was Billy? Not in his usual place at the bar. Had he decided to go for a bath first? Bill edged his way through the crush to the bathhouse door, which was already so clouded with steam he couldn't see in. He opened the door and peered at the row of psuits hung up behind the attendant, but Billy's psuit wasn't one of them.

"Young Bill?" said someone, touching him on the shoulder. He turned and saw Mother herself, a solid little middle-aged lady who spoke with a thick PanCeltic accent. She wore a lot of jewelry; she was the richest lady on Mars, and owned most of Mons Olympus. "What do you need, my dear?"

"Where's my dad?" Bill shouted, to be heard above the din.

"Hasn't come in yet," Mother replied. "What, was he to meet you here?"

Bill felt the familiar stomachache he got whenever Billy went missing. Mother, looking into his eyes, patted his arm.

"Like as not just stopped to talk to somebody, I'm sure. He's friendly, our Billy, eh? Would start a conversation with any stone in the road, if he thought he recognized it. Now, you come and sit in the warm, my dear, and have some supper. Soygold strip with gravy and sprouts, that's your favorite, yes? And we've barley-sugar duff for afters. Let's get you some tea . . ."

Bill let her settle him in a corner booth and bring him a mug of tea. It was delicious, salty-sweet and spicy, and the warmth of the mug felt good on his hands; but it didn't unclench the knot in his stomach. He sipped tea and watched the airlock opening and closing. He tried raising Billy on the psuit comm, but Billy seemed to have forgotten to turn it on. Where was his dad?

## 2

He was the second boy born on Mars, and he was six years old.

In MAC years, that is.

The Martian year was twenty-four months long, but most of the people in Mons Olympus and the Areco administrative center had simply stuck to reckoning time in twelve-month-long Earth years. That way, every other year, Christmas fell in the Martian summer, and those years were called Australian years. A lot of people on Mars had emigrated from Australia, so it suited them fine.

When the Martian Agricultural Collective had arrived on Mars, though, they'd decided to do things differently. After all (they said), it was a new world; they were breaking with Earth and her traditions forever. So they set up a calendar with twenty-four months. The twelve new months were named Stothart, Engels, Hardie, Bax, Blatchford, Pollitt, Mieville, Attlee, Bentham, Besant, Hobsbawm and Quelch.

When a boy had been born to Mr. and Mrs. Marlon Thur-kettle on the fifth day of the new month of Blatchford, they named their son in honor of the month. His friends, such of them as he had, called him Blatt.

He disliked his name because he thought it sounded stupid, but he *really* disliked Blatt, because it led to another nickname that was even worse: Cockroach.

Martian cockroaches were of the order *Blattidae*, and they had adapted very nicely to all the harsh conditions that had made it such a struggle for humans to settle Mars. In fact, they had mutated, and now averaged six inches in length and could survive outside the Tubes. Fortunately they made good fertilizer when ground up, so the Collective had placed a bounty of three Martian Pence on each insect. MAC children hunted them with hammers and earned pocket money that way. They knew all about cockroaches, and so Blatchford wasn't even two before Hardie Stubbs started calling him Cockroach. All the other children thought it was the funniest thing they'd ever heard.

He called himself Ford.

He lived with his parents and his brothers and sisters, crowded all together in an allotment shelter. He downloaded lesson programs and studied whenever he'd finished his chores for the day, but now that he was as tall as his dad and his brother Sam, his dad had begun to mutter that he'd had all the schooling he needed.

There was a lot of work for an able-bodied young man to do, after all: milking the cows, mucking out their stalls, spreading muck along the rows of sugar beets and soybeans. There was cleaning the canals, repairing the vizio panels that kept out the Martian climate, working in the methane plant. There was work from before the dim sun rose every morning until after the little dim moons rose at night. The work didn't stop for holidays, and it didn't stop if you got sick or got old or had an accident and were hurt.

The work had to be done, because if the MAC worked hard enough, they could turn Mars into another Earth; only one without injustice, corruption, or poverty. Every MAC child was supposed to dream of that wonderful day, and do his or her part to make it arrive.

But Ford liked to steal out of the shelter at night, and look up through the vizio at the foot of Mons Olympus, where its city shone out across the long miles of darkness. That was where he wanted to be! It was full of lights. The high-beam lights of the big freighters rocketed along the High Road toward it, roaring out of the dark and cold, and if you watched you could see them coming and going from the city all night. They came back from the far poles of the world, and went out there again.

The Haulers drove them. The Haulers were the men and women who rode the High Road through the storms, through the harsh dry places nobody else dared to go, but they went because they were brave. Ford had heard lots of stories about them. Ford's dad said Haulers were all scum, and half of them were criminals. They got drunk, they fought, they made huge sums in hazard pay and gambled it away or spent it on rich food. They had adventures. Ford thought he'd like to have an adventure someday.

As he grew up, though, he began to realize that this wasn't very likely to happen.

❧ ❧ ❧

"Will you be taking Blatchford?" asked his mum, as she shaved his head.

Ford nearly jumped up in his seat, he was so startled. But the habit of long years kept him still, and he only peered desperately into the mirror to see his dad's face before the reply. *Yes please, yes please, yes please!*

His dad hesitated a moment, distracted from bad temper.

"I suppose so," he said. "Time he saw for himself what it's like up there."

"I'll pack you another lunch, then," said his mum. She wiped the razor and dried Ford's scalp with the towel. "There you go, dear. Your turn, Baxine."

Ford got up as his little sister slid into his place, and turned to face his dad. He was all on fire with questions he wanted to ask, but he knew it wasn't a good idea to make much noise when his dad was in a bad mood. He sidled up to his older brother Sam, who was sitting by the door looking sullen.

"Never been up there," he said. "What's it like, eh?"

Sam smiled a little.

"You'll see. There's this place called the Blue Room, right? Everything's blue in there, with holos of the Sea of Earth, and lakes too. I remember lakes! And they play sounds from Earth like rain—"

"You shut your face," said his dad. "You ought to be ashamed of yourself, talking like that to a kid."

Sam turned a venomous look on their dad.

"Don't start," said their mum, sounding more tired than angry. "Just go and do what you've got to do."

Ford sat quietly beside Sam until it was time to go, when they all three pulled on their stocking caps and facemasks, slid on their packs, and went skulking up the Tube.

They skulked because visiting Mons Olympus was frowned upon. There was no need to go up there, or so the Council said; everything a good member of the Collective might need could be found in the MAC store, and if it couldn't, then you probably didn't need it, and certainly shouldn't want it.

The problem was that the MAC store didn't carry boots in Sam's size. Ford's dad had tried to order them, but there was endless paperwork to fill out, and the store clerk had looked at Sam as though it was his fault for having such big feet, as though a *good* member of the Collective would have sawed off a few toes to make himself fit the boots the MAC store stocked.

But *Prashant's* up in Mons Olympus carried all sizes, so every time Sam wore out a pair of boots, that was where Ford's dad had to go.

As though to make up for the shame of it, he lectured Ford the whole way up the mountain, while Sam stalked along beside them in resentful silence.

"This'll be an education for you, Blatchford, yes indeed. You'll get to see thieves and drunks and fat cats living off the sweat of others. Everything we left Earth to get away from! Shops full of vanities to make you weak. Eating places full of poisons. It's a right cesspool, that's what it is."

"What'll happen to it when we turn Mars into a paradise?" asked Ford.

"Oh, it'll be gone by then," said his dad. "It'll collapse under its own rotting weight, you mark my words."

"I reckon I'll have to go home to Earth to buy boots then, won't I?" muttered Sam.

"Shut up, you ungrateful lout," said his dad.

They came out under the old Settlement dome, where the Areco offices and the MAC store were, as well as the spaceport and the Ephesian Church. This was the farthest Ford had ever been from home, and up until today the most exotic place he had ever seen. There was a faint sweet incense wafting out from the Church, and the sound of chanting. Ford's dad hurried them past the Ephesian Tea Room with a disdainful sniff, ignoring the signs that invited wayfarers in for a hot meal and edifying brochures about the Goddess.

"Ignorance and superstition, that is," he told Ford. "Another thing we left behind when we came here, but you can see it's still putting out its tentacles, trying to control the minds of the people."

He almost ran them past the MAC store, and they were panting for breath as they ducked up the Tube that led to Mons Olympus.

Ford stared around. The Tube here was much wider, and much better maintained, than where it ran by his parents' allotment. The vizio used was a more expensive kind, for one thing: it was almost as transparent as water. Ford could now see clearly across the mountainside, the wide cinnamon-colored waste of rocks and sand. He gazed up at Mons Olympus, struck with awe at its sheer looming size. He turned and looked back on the lowlands, and for the first time saw the green expanse of the Long Acres that had been his whole world until now, stretching out in domed lines to the horizon. He walked backwards a while, gaping, until he stumbled and his dad caught him.

"It's hard to look away from, isn't it?" said his dad. "Don't worry. We'll be going home soon enough."

"Soon enough," Sam echoed in a melancholy sort of way.

Once past the airlock from the spaceport, the Tube became crowded, with suited strangers pushing past them, dragging baggage, or walking slow and staring as hard as Ford was staring: he realized they must be immigrants from Earth, getting their first glimpse of a new world.

But Ford got his new world when he stepped through the last airlock and looked into Commerce Square.

"Oh . . ." he said.

Even by daylight, it glittered and shone. Along the main street was a double line of actual *trees*, like on Earth; there was a green and park-like place immediately to the left, where real flowers grew. Ford thought he recognized roses, from the images in his lessons. Their scent hung in the air like music. There were other good smells, from spicy foods cooking in a dozen little stalls and wagons along the Square, and big stores breathing out a perfume of expensive wares.

And there were *people*! More people, and more kinds of people, than Ford had even known existed. There were Sherpa contract laborers and Incan construction workers, speaking to one another in languages Ford couldn't understand. There were hawkers selling souvenirs and cheap nanoprocessors from handcarts. There were Ephesian missionaries talking earnestly to thin people in ragged clothes.

There were Haulers—Ford knew them at once, big men and women in their psuits, and their heads were covered in long hair and the men had beards. Some had tattooed faces. All had bloodshot eyes. They talked loudly and laughed a lot, and they looked as though they didn't care what anyone thought of them at all. Ford's dad scowled at them.

"Bloody lunatics," he told Ford. "Most of 'em were in Hospital on Earth, did you know that, Blatchford? Certifiable. The only ones Areco could find who were reckless enough for that kind of work. Exploitation, I call it."

Sam muttered something. Their dad turned on him.

"What did you say, Samuel?" he demanded.

"I said we're at the shop, all right?" said Sam, pointing at the neon sign.

Ford gasped as they went in, as the warmed air and flowery scent wrapped around him. It was nothing like the MAC store, which had rows of empty shelves, and what merchandise was there, was dusty; everything here looked clean and new. He didn't even know what most of it was for. Sleek, pretty people smiled from behind the counters.

He smiled back at them, until he passed a counter and came face to face with three men skulking along—skinny scarecrows with shaven heads, with canal mud on their boots. He blushed scarlet to realize he was looking into a mirror. Was *he* that gawky person between his dad and Sam? Did his ears really stick out like that? Ford pulled his cap down, so mortified he wanted to run all the way back down the mountain.

But he kept his eyes on the back of his dad's coat instead, following until they came to the Footwear Department. There he was diverted by the hundreds and hundreds of shoes on the walls, apparently floating in space, turning so he could see them better. They were every color there was, and they were clearly never designed to be worn while shoveling muck out of the cowsheds.

He came close and peered at them, as his dad and Sam argued with one of the beautiful people, until he saw the big-eyed boy staring back at him from beyond the dancing shoes. Another mirror; did he really have his mouth hanging open like that? And, oh, look at his nose, pinched red by the cold, and look at those watery blue eyes all rimmed in red, and those gangling big hands with the red chapped knuckles!

Ford turned around, wishing he could escape from himself. There were his dad and Sam, and they looked just like him, except his dad was old. Was he, Ford, going to look just like that, when he was somebody's dad? How mean and small his dad looked, trying to sound posh as he talked to the clerk:

"Look, we don't want this fancy trim and we don't want your shiny brass, thank you *very* much, we just want plain decent waders the lad can do a day's honest work in! Now, you can understand that much, can't you?"

"I like the brass buckles, Dad," said Sam.

"Well, you don't need 'em—they're only a vanity," said their dad. Sam shut his mouth like a box.

Ford stood by, cringing inside, as more boots were brought, until at last a pair was found that was plain and cheap enough to suit their dad. More embarrassment followed then, as their dad pulled out a wad of MAC scrip and tried to pay with it, before remembering that scrip could only be used at the MAC store. Worse still, he then pulled out a wrinkly handful of Martian paper money. Both Ford and Sam saw the salesclerks exchange looks; what kind of people didn't have credit accounts? Sam tried to save face by being sarcastic.

"We're all in the Stone Age down the hill, you know," he said loudly, accepting the wrapped boots and tucking them under his arm. "I reckon we'll get around to having banks one of these centuries."

"Banks are corrupt institutions," said their dad like a shot, rounding on him. "How'd you get so tall without learning anything, eh? What have I told—"

"Sam?" A girl's voice stopped him. Ford turned in astonishment and saw one of the beautiful clerks hurrying toward them, smiling as though she meant it. "Sam, where were you last week? We missed you at the party—I wanted to show you my new . . ." She faltered to a stop, looking from Sam to their dad and Ford. Ford felt his heart jump when she looked at him. She had silver-gold hair, and wore makeup, and smelled sweet.

"I . . . er . . . Is this your family? How nice to meet you—" she began lamely, but their dad cut her off.

"Who's *this* painted cobweb, then?" he demanded of Sam. Sam's face turned red.

"Don't you talk that way about her! Her name is Galadriel, and—it so happens we're dating, not that it's any of your business."

"You're *what*?" Outraged, their dad clenched his knobby fists. "So you've been sneaking up here at night to live the high life, have you? No wonder you're no bloody use in the mornings! MAC girls not good enough for you? Fat lot of use a little mannequin like that's going to be when you settle down! Can she drive a tractor, eh?"

Sam threw down the boots. "Got a wire for you, Dad," he shouted. "I'm not settling down on Mars! I *hate* Mars, I've hated it since the day you dragged me up here, and the *minute* I come of age, I'm off back to Earth! Get it?"

Sam leaving? Ford felt a double shock, of sadness and betrayal. Who'd tell him stories if Sam left?

"You self-centered great twerp!" their dad shouted back. "Of all the ungrateful—when the MAC's fed you and clothed you all these years— Just going to walk out on your duty, are you?"

Galadriel was backing away into the crowd, looking as though she wished she were invisible, and Ford wished he could be invisible too. People all over the store had stopped what they were doing to turn and stare.

"I never asked to join the MAC, you know," said Sam. "Nobody's ever given a thought to what *I* wanted at all!"

"That's because there are a few more important things in the world than what one snotty-nosed brat wants for himself!"

"Well, I'm telling you now, Dad—if you think I'm going to live my life doing the same boring thing every day until I get old like you, you're sadly mistaken!"

"Am I then?" Their dad jumped up and grabbed Sam by the ear, wringing tight. "I'll sort you out—"

Sam, grimacing in pain, socked their dad. Ford bit his knuckles, terrified. Their dad staggered back, his eyes wide and furious.

"Right, that's it! You're no son of mine, do you hear me? You're disowned! The Collective doesn't need a lazy, backsliding traitor like you!"

"Don't you call me a traitor!" said Sam. He put his head down and ran at their dad, and their dad jumped up and butted heads with him. Sam's nose gushed blood. They fell to the ground, punching each other. Sam was sobbing in anger.

Ford backed away from them. He was frightened and miserable, but there was a third emotion beginning to float up into his consciousness: a certain sense of wonder. Could Sam really stop being his father's son? Was it really possible just to become somebody else, to drop all the obligations and duties of your old life and step into a new life? Who would he, Ford, be, if he had the chance to be somebody else?

Did he *have* to be that red-nosed farm boy with muddy boots?

People were gathering around, watching the fight with amusement and disgust. Someone shouted, "You can't take the MAC anyplace nice, can you?" Ford's ears burned with humiliation.

Then someone else shouted, "Here come Mother's Boys!"

Startled, Ford looked up and saw several big men in Security uniforms making their way through the crowd. Security!

*The police are a bunch of brutes,* his dad had told him. *They like nothing better than to beat the daylights out of the likes of you and me, son!*

Ford's nerve broke. He turned and fled, weaving and dodging his way through the crowd until he got outside the shop, and then he ran for his life.

He had no idea where he was going, but he soon found himself in a street that wasn't nearly as elegant as the promenade. It was an industrial district, dirty and shabby, with factory workers and energy plant techs hurrying to and fro. If the promenade with its gardens was the fancy case of Mons Olympus, this was its circuit board, where the real works were. Feeling less out of place, Ford slowed to a walk and caught his breath. He wandered on, staring around him.

He watched for a long moment through the open door of a machine shop, where a pair of mechanics were repairing a quaddy. Their welding tools shot out fiery-bright stars that bounced harmlessly to the ground. There were two other men watching too, though as the minutes dragged by they began watching Ford instead. Finally they stepped close to him, smiling.

"Hey, Collective. You play cards?" said one of them.

"No," said Ford.

"That's okay," said the other. "This is an easy game." He opened his coat and Ford saw that he had a kind of box strapped to his chest. It had the word NEBULIZER painted on it, but when the man pressed a button, the front of the box swung down and open like a tray. The other man pulled a handful of cards from his back pocket.

"Here we go," he said. "Just three cards. Ace, deuce, Queen of Diamonds. See 'em? I'm going to shuffle them and lay them out, one, two, three." He laid them out facedown on the tray. "See? Now, which one's the queen? Can you find her?"

Ford couldn't believe what a dumb game this was. Only three cards? He turned over the queen.

"Boy, it's hard to fool *you*," said the man with the tray. "You've got natural luck, kid. Want to go again?" The other man had already swept the three cards up and was shuffling them.

"Okay," said Ford.

"Got any money? Want to place a bet?"

"I don't have any money," said Ford.

"No money? That's too bad," said the man with the tray, closing it up at once. "A lucky guy like you, you could win big. But they don't get rich down there in the Collective, do they? Same dull work every day of your life, and nothing to show for it when it's all over. That's what I hear."

Ford nodded sadly. It wasn't just Sam, he realized; everybody laughed at the MAC.

"What would you say to a chance at something better, eh?" said the man with the cards. In one smooth movement he made the cards vanish and produced instead a text plaquette. Its case was grubby and cracked, but the screen was bright with a lot of very small words.

"Know what I have here? This is a deal that'll set you up as a diamond prospector. Think of that! You could make more with one lucky strike than you'd make working the Long Acres the whole rest of your life. Now, I know what you're going to say— you don't have any tools and you don't have any training. But, you know what you *have* got? You're *young*. You're in good shape, and you can take the weather Outside.

"So here's the deal: Mr. Agar has the tools and the training, but he ain't young. You agree to go to work for him, and he'll provide what you need. You pay him off out of your first big diamond strike, and then you're in business for yourself. Easiest way to get rich there is! And all you have to do is put your thumbprint right there. What do you say?" He held out the plaquette to Ford.

Ford blinked at it. He had heard stories of the people who dug red diamonds out of the clay—why, Mons Olympus had been founded by a lady who'd got rich like that! He was reaching for the plaquette when a voice spoke close to his ear.

"Can you read, kid?"

Ford turned around. A Hauler was looking over his shoulder, smiling.

"Well—I read a little—"

"Get lost!" said the man with the plaquette, looking angry.

"I can't read," the Hauler went on, "but I know these guys. They're with Agar Steelworks. You know what they're trying to get you to thumb? That's a contract that'll legally bind you to work in Agar's iron mines for fifteen years."

"Like you'd know, jackass!" said the man with the plaquette, slipping it out of sight. He brought out a short length of iron bar and waved it at the Hauler meaningfully. The Hauler's red eyes sparkled.

"You want to fight?" he said, smacking his fists together. "Yeah! You think I'm afraid of you? You lousy little street-corner hustler! C'mere!"

The man took a swipe at him with the bar, and the Hauler dodged it and grabbed it out of his hand. The other two broke and ran, vanishing down an alley. The Hauler grinned after them, tossing the bar into the street.

"Freakin' kidnappers," he said to Ford. "You're, what, twelve? I have a kid your age."

"Thank you," Ford stammered.

"That's okay. You want to watch out for Human Resourcers, though, kid. They work that con on a lot of MAC boys like you. Diamond prospectors! Nobody but Mother ever got rich that way." The Hauler yawned and stretched. "You head off to the nearest Security post and report 'em now, okay?"

"I can't," said Ford, and to his horror he felt himself starting to shake. "I—they—there was this fight, and—Security guys came and—I have to hide."

"You in trouble?" The Hauler leaned down and looked at Ford closely. "Fighting? Mother's Boys don't allow no fighting, that's for sure. You need a place to hide? Maybe get out of town until it all blows over?" He gave Ford a conspiratorial wink.

"Yes, please," said Ford.

"You come along with me, then. I got a safe place," said the Hauler. Without looking back to see if Ford was following him, he turned and loped off up the street. Ford ran after him.

"Please, who are you?"

The Hauler glanced over his shoulder. "Billy Townsend," he said. "But don't tell me who *you* are. Safer that way, right?"

"Right," said Ford, falling into step beside him. He looked up at his rescuer. Billy was tall and gangly, and lurched a little when he walked, but he looked as though he wasn't the least bit worried what people thought of him. His face and dreadlocked hair and beard were all red, the funny bricky red that came from years of going Outside and having the red dust get everywhere, until it became so deeply engrained water wouldn't wash it off. There were scars all over his face and hands, too. On the back of his psuit someone had painted white words in a circle.

"What's it say on your back?" Ford asked him.

"Says BIPOLAR BOYS AND GIRLS," said Billy. "On account of we go Up and Down there, see? And because we're nutcases, half of us."

"What's it like in the ice mines?"

"Cold," said Billy, chuckling. "Get your face mask on, now. Here we go! Here's our *Beautiful Evelyn.*"

They stepped out through the airlock, and the cold bit into Ford. He gulped for air and followed Billy into a vast echoing building like a hangar. It was the car barn for the ice processing plant. Just now it was deserted, but over by the loading chute sat a freighter. Ford caught his breath.

He had never seen one up close before, and it was bigger than he had imagined. Seventy-five meters long, set high on big knobbed ball tires. Its steel tank had been scoured to a dull gleam by the wind and sand. At one end was a complication of hatches and lenses and machinery that Ford supposed must be the driver's cab. Billy reached up one long arm and grabbed a lever. The foremost hatch hissed, swung open, and a row of steps clanked down into place.

"There you go," said Billy. "Climb on up! Nobody'll think to look for you in there. I'll be back later. Make yourself at home."

Ford scrambled up eagerly. He looked around as the hatch squeezed shut behind him, and air rushed back in. He pulled down his mask.

He was in a tiny room with a pair of bunks built into one side. The only light came from a dim panel set in the ceiling. There was nothing else in the room, except for a locker under the lower bunk and three doors in the wall opposite. It was disappointingly plain and spotless.

Ford opened the first door and beheld the tiniest lavatory he had ever seen, so compact he couldn't imagine how to use it. He tried the second door and found a kitchen built along similar lines, more a series of shelves than a room. The third door opened into a much larger space. He crawled through and found himself in the driver's cab.

Timidly, he edged his way farther in and sat down at the console. He looked up at the instrument panels, at the big screens that ran all around the inside of the cab. They were blank and blind now, but what would it be like to sit here when the freighter was roaring along the High Road?

On the panel above the console was a little figurine, glued in place. It was a cheap-looking thing, of cast red stone like the souvenirs he had seen for sale on the handcarts in Commerce Square. It represented a lady, leaning forward as though she were running, or perhaps flying. The sculptor had given her hair that streamed back in an imaginary wind. She was grinning crazily, as the Haulers all did. She had only one eye, of red cut glass; Ford guessed the matching one had fallen off. He looked on the floor of the cab, but didn't see it.

Ford grinned too, and, because no one was there to see him,

he put his hands on the wheel. "Brrrrroooom," he whispered, and looked up at the screens as though to check on his location. He felt a little stupid.

But in every one of the screens, his reflection was smiling back at him. Ford couldn't remember when he'd been so happy.

3

Bill's dinner had gone cold, though he stuffed a forkful in his mouth every now and then when he noticed Mother watching him. He couldn't keep his eyes away from the door much. *Where was Billy?*

He might have gotten in a fight, and Mother's Boys might have hauled him off to the Security Station; if that were the case, sooner or later Mother would come over to Bill with an apologetic cough and say something like, "Your dad's just had a bit of an argument, dear, and I think you'd best doss down here tonight until he, er, wakes up. We'll let him out tomorrow." And Bill would feel his face burning with shame, as he always did when that happened.

Or Billy might have met someone he knew, and forgotten about the time . . . or he might have gone for a drink somewhere else . . . or . . .

Bill was so busy imagining all the places Billy might be that he got quite a shock when Billy walked through the airlock. Before Billy had spotted him and started making his way across the room, the cramping worry had turned to anger.

"Where were you?" Bill shouted. "You were supposed to be here!"

"I had stuff to do," said Billy vaguely, sliding into the booth. He waved at Mother, who acknowledged him with a nod and sent one of her daughters over to take his order. Bill looked him over suspiciously. No cuts or bruises on his face, nothing broken on his psuit. Not fighting, then. Maybe he had met a girl. Bill relaxed just a little, but his anger kept smoldering.

When Billy's beer had been brought, Bill said:

"I wondered where you were. How come you had the comm turned off?"

"Is it off?" Billy groped for the switch in his shoulder. "Oh. Wow. Sorry, kiddo. Must have happened when I took my mask off."

He had a sip of beer. Bill gritted his teeth. He could tell that, as far as Billy was concerned, the incident was over. It had just been a mistake, right? What was the point of getting mad about it? Never mind that Bill had been scared and alone . . .

Bill exhaled forcefully and shoveled down his congealing dinner.

"I got my socks," he said loudly.

"That's nice," said Billy. Lifting his glass for another sip, his attention was taken by the holo playing above the bar. He stared across at it. Bill turned around in his seat to look. There was the image of one of Mother's Boys, a sergeant from his uniform, staring into the foremost camera as he made some kind of announcement. His lips moved in silence, though, with whatever he was saying drowned out by the laughter and the shouting in the bar.

Bill looked quickly back at Billy. Why was he watching the police report? Had he been in some kind of incident after all? Billy snorted with laughter, watching, and then pressed his lips shut to hide a smile. Why was he doing that?

Bill looked back at the holo, more certain than ever that Billy was in trouble, but now saw holofootage of two guys fighting. Was either one of them Billy? No; Bill felt his anger damp down again as he realized it was only a couple of MAC colonists, kicking and punching each other as they rolled in the street. Bill was appalled; he hadn't thought the Collective ever did stupid stuff like that.

Then there was a closeup shot of a skinny boy, with a shaven head—MAC, Bill supposed. He shrugged and turned his attention back to his plate.

Billy's food was brought and he dug into it with gusto.

"Think we'll head out again tonight," he said casually.

"But we just got back in!" Bill said, startled.

"Yeah. Well . . ." Billy sliced off a bit of Grilled Strip, put it in his mouth and chewed carefully before going on. "There's . . . mm . . . this big bonus right now for Co2, see? MAC's getting a crop of something or other in the ground and they've placed like this humungous order for it. So we can earn like double what we just deposited if I get a second trip in before the end of the month."

Bill didn't know what to say. It was the sort of thing he nagged at his dad to do, saving more money; usually Billy spent it as fast as he had it. Bill looked at him with narrowed eyes, wondering if he had gotten into trouble after all. But he just shrugged again and said, "Okay."

"Hey, Mona?" Billy waved at the nearest of Mother's daughters. "Takeaway order too, okay, sweetheart? Soygold nuggets and sprouts. And a bottle of batch."

"Why are we getting takeaway?" Bill asked him.

"Er . . ." Billy looked innocent. "I'm just way hungry, is all. Think I'll want a snack later. I'll be driving all night."

"But you drove for twelve hours today!" Bill protested. "Aren't you ever going to sleep?"

"Sleep is for wusses," said Billy. "I'll just pop a Freddie."

Bill scowled. Freddies were little red pills that kept you awake and jittery for days. Haulers took them sometimes when they needed to be on the road for long runs without stopping. It was stupid to take them all the time, because they could kill you, and Bill threw them away whenever he found any in the cab. Billy must have stopped to buy some more. So *that* was where he'd been.

Night had fallen by the time they left the *Empress* and headed back down the hill. Cold penetrated down through the Permavizio; Bill shivered, and his psuit's thermostat turned itself up. There were still people in the streets, though fewer of them, and some of the lights had been turned out. Usually by this time, when they were in off the road, Bill would be soaking in a stone tub full of hot water, and looking forward to a good night's sleep someplace warm for a change. The thought made him grumpy as they came round the corner into the airlock.

"Masks on, Dad," Bill said automatically. Billy nodded, shifting the stoneware bucket of takeaway to his other hand as he reached for his mask. They went out to *Beautiful Evelyn*.

Bill was climbing up to open the cab when Billy grabbed him and pulled him back.

"Hang on," he said, and reached up and knocked on the hatch. "Yo, kid! Mask up, we're coming in!"

"What?" Bill staggered back, staring at Billy. "Who's in there?"

Billy didn't answer, but Bill heard a high-pitched voice calling *Okay* from inside the cab, and Billy swung the hatch open and climbed up. Bill scrambled after him. The hatch sealed behind them and the air whooshed back. Bill pulled off his mask as the lights came on to reveal a boy, pulling off his own mask. They stared at each other, blinking.

Billy held out the bucket of takeaway. "Here you go, kid. Hot dinner!"

"Oh! Thank you," said the other, as Bill recognized him for the MAC boy from the holofootage he'd watched.

"What's *he* doing here?" he demanded.

"Just, you know, sort of laying low," said Billy. "Got in a little trouble and needs to go off someplace until things cool down. Thought we could take him out on the run with us, right? No worries." He stepped sidelong into the cab and threw himself into the console seat, where he proceeded to start up *Beautiful Evelyn*'s drives.

"But—but—" said Bill.

"Er . . . hi," said the other boy, avoiding his eyes. He was taller than Bill but looked younger, with big wide eyes and ears that stuck out. His shaven head made him look even more like a baby.

"Who're you?" said Bill.

"I'm, ah—" said the other boy, just as Billy roared from the cab:

"No names! No names! The less we know, the less they can beat out of us!" And he whooped with laughter. The noise of the drives powering up drowned out anything else he might have said. Bill clenched his fists and stepped close to Ford, glaring up into his eyes.

"What's going on? What'd my dad do?"

"Nothing!" Ford took a step backward.

"Well then, what'd *you* do? You must have done something, because you were on the holo. I saw you! You were fighting, huh?"

Ford gulped. His eyes got even wider and he said, "Er—yeah. Yeah, I punched out these guys. Who were trying to trick me into working into the mines for them. And, uh, I ran because, because the Security Fascists were going to beat the daylights out of me. So Billy let me hide in here. What's your name?"

"Bill," he replied. "You're with the MAC, aren't you? What were you fighting for?"

"Well—the other guys started it," said Ford. He looked with interest at the takeaway. "This smells good. It was really nice of your dad to bring it for me. Is there anywhere I can sit down to eat?"

"In there," said Bill in disgust, pointing into the cab.

"Thank you. You want some?" Ford held out the bucket timidly.

"No," said Bill. "I want to go to sleep. Go on, clear out of here!"

"Okay," said Ford, edging into the cab. "It's nice meeting you, Billy."

"Bill!" said Bill, and slammed the door in his face.

Muttering to himself, he dimmed down the lights and lay down in his bunk. He threw the switch that inflated the mattress, and its contours puffed out around him, cradling him snugly as the freighter began to move. He didn't know why he was so angry, but somehow finding Ford here had been the last straw.

He closed his eyes and tried to send himself to sleep in the way he always had, by imagining he was going down the Tube to the long Acres, step by step, into green, warm, quiet places. Tonight, though, he kept seeing the two MAC colonists from the holo, whaling away at each other like a couple of clowns while the city people looked on and laughed.

❀ ❀ ❀

Ford, clutching his dinner, sat down in the cab and looked around. With all the screens lit up there was plenty of light by which to eat.

"Is it okay if I sit in here?" he asked Billy, who waved expansively.

"Sure, kid. Don't mind li'l Bill. He's cranky sometimes."

Ford opened the bucket and looked inside. "Do you have any forks?"

"Yeah. Somewhere. Try the seat pocket."

Ford groped into the pocket and found a ceramic fork that was, perhaps, clean. He was too hungry to care whether it was or not, and ate quickly. He wasn't sure what he was eating, but it tasted wonderful.

As he ate, he looked up at the screens. Some had just figures on them, data from the drives and external sensors. Four of them had images from the freighter's cameras, mounted front and rear, right and left. There was no windscreen—even Ford knew that an Earth-style glass windscreen would be scoured opaque by even one trip through the storms of sand and grit along the High Road, unless a forcefield was projected in front of it, and big forcefields were expensive, and unlikely to deflect blowing rocks anyhow. Easier and cheaper to fix four little forcefields over the camera lenses.

The foremost screen fascinated him. He saw the High Road itself, rolling out endlessly to the unseen night horizon under the stars. It ran between two lines of big rocks, levered into place over the years by Haulers to make it easier to find the straightest shot to the pole.

Every now and then Ford caught a glimpse of carving on

some of the boulders as they flashed by—words, or figures. Some of them had what looked like tape wrapped around them, streaming out in the night wind.

"Are those . . ." Ford sought to remember his lessons about Earth roads. "Are those road signs? With, er, kilometer numbers and all?"

"What, on the boulders? Nope. They're shrines," said Billy.

"What's a shrine?"

"Place where somebody died," said Billy. "Or where somebody should have died, but didn't, because Marswife saved their butts." He reached out and tapped the little red lady on the console.

Ford thought about that. He looked at the figurine. "So . . . she's like, that Goddess the Ephesians are always on about?"

"No!" Billy grinned. "Not our Marswife. She was just this sheila, see? Somebody from Earth who came up here like the rest of us, and she was crazy. Same as us. She thought Mars, was, like, her husband or something. And there was this big storm and she went out into it, without a mask. And they say she didn't die! Mars got her and changed her into something else so she could live Outside. That's what they say, anyway."

"Like, she mutated?" Ford stared at the little figure.

"I guess so."

"But really she died, huh?"

"Well, you'd think so," Billy said, looking at him sidelong. "Except that there are guys who swear they've seen her. She lives on the wind. She's red like the sand and her eye is a ruby, and if you're lost sometimes you'll see a red light way off, which is her eye, see? And if you follow it, you'll get home again safe. And I *know* that's true, because it happened to me."

"Really?"

Billy held up one hand, palm out. "No lie. It was right out by Two-Fifty-K. There was a storm swept through so big, it was able to pick up the road markers and toss 'em around, see? And *Beautiful Evelyn* got thrown like she was a feather by the gusts, and my nav system went out. It was just me and li'l Bill, and he was only a baby then, and I found myself so far off the road I had no clue, *no clue*, where I was, and I was sure we were going to die out there. But I saw that red light and I figured, that's somebody who knows where they are, anyway. I set off after it. Hour later the light blinks out and there's Two-Fifty-K Station right in front of me on the screen, but there's no red lights anyplace."

"Whoa," said Ford, wondering what Two-Fifty-K station was.

"There's other stories about her, too. Guys who see her riding the storm, and when she's there they know to make for a bunker, because there's a Strawberry coming."

"What's a Strawberry?"

"It's this kind of cyclone. Big *big* storm full of sand and rocks. Big red cone dancing across the ground. One took out that temple the Ephesians built, when they first got up here, and tore open half the Tubes. They don't come up Tharsis way much, but when they do—" Billy shook his head. "People die, man. Some of your people died, that time. You never heard that story?"

"No," said Ford, "But we're not supposed to talk about bad stuff after it happens."

"Really?" Billy looked askance.

"Because we can't afford to be afraid of the past," said Ford, half-quoting what he remembered from every Council Meeting he'd ever been dragged to. "Because fear will make us weak, but working fearlessly for the future will make us strong." He chanted the last line, unconsciously imitating his dad's intonation.

"Huh," said Billy. "I guess that's a good idea. You can't go through life being scared of everything. That's what I tell Bill."

Ford looked into the takeaway bucket, surprised that he had eaten his way to the bottom so quickly.

"It's good to hear stories, though," he said. "Sam, that's my brother, he gets into trouble for telling stories."

"Heh! Little white lies?"

"No," Ford said. "Real stories. Like about Earth. He remembers Earth. He says everything was wonderful there. He wants to go back."

"Back?" Billy looked across at him, startled. "But kids can't go back. I guess if he was old enough when he came up, maybe he might make it. I hear it's tough, though, going back down. The gravity's intense."

"Would you go back?"

Billy shook his head. "All I remember of Earth is the insides of rooms. Who needs that? Nobody up here to tell me what to do, man. I can just point myself at the horizon and go, and *go*, as far and as fast as I want. Zoom! I can think what I want, I can feel what I want, and you know what? The sand and the rocks don't care. The horizon don't care. The wind don't care.

"That's why they call this *space*. No, no way I'd ever go back."

Ford looked up at the screens, and remembered the nights he had watched for the long light-beams coming in from the darkness. It had given him an aching feeling for as long as he could remember, and now he understood why.

He had wanted *space*.


4


They drove all night, and at some point Billy's stories of storms and fights and near-escapes from death turned into confusion, with Sam there somehow, and a room that ran blue with water. Then abruptly Ford was sitting up, staring around at the inside of the cab.

"Where are we?" he asked. The foremost screen showed a spooky gray distance, the High Road rolling ahead between its boulders to . . . what? A pale void full of roaming shadows.

"Almost to Five-Hundred-K Station," said Billy, from where he hunched over the wheel. "Stop pretty soon."

"Can Security follow us out here?"

Billy just laughed and shook his head. "No worries, kiddo. There's no law out here but Mars's."

The door into the living space opened abruptly, and Bill looked in at them.

"Morning, li'l Bill!"

"Good morning," said Bill in a surly voice. "You never stopped once all night. Are you ever going to pull us off somewhere so you can sleep?"

"At Five-Hundred-K," Billy promised. "How about you fix a bite of scran, eh?"

Bill did not reply. He stepped back out of sight and a moment later Ford felt the warmth in the air that meant that water was steaming. He could almost taste it, and realized that he was desperately thirsty. He crawled from his seat and followed the vapor back to where Bill had opened the kitchen and was shoving a block of something under heating coils.

"Are you fixing tea?"

"Yeah," said Bill, with a jerk of his thumb at the tall can that steamed above a heat element.

"Can I have a cup, when it's ready?"

Bill frowned, but he got three mugs from a drawer.

"Do you fight much, in the Collective?" he asked. Ford blinked in surprise.

"No," he said. "It wasn't me fighting, actually. It was just my dad and my brother. They hate each other. But my mum won't let them fight in the house. Sam said he was deserting us and my dad went off on him about it. I ran when the Security came."

"Oh," said Bill. He seemed to become a little less hostile, but he said: "Well, that was pretty bloody stupid. They'd only have taken you to Mother's until your dad sobered up. You'd be safe home by now."

Ford shrugged.

"So, what's your name, really?"

"Ford."

"Like that guy in *The Hitchhiker's Guide to the Galaxy?*" Bill smiled for the first time.

"What's that?"

"It's a book I listen to all the time. Drowns out Billy singing." Bill's smile went away again. The tea can beeped to signal it was hot enough, and Bill turned and pulled it out. He poured dark bubbling stuff into the three mugs, and, reaching in a cold-drawer, took out a slab of something yellow on a dish. He spooned out three lumps of it, one into each mug, and presented one to Ford.

"Whoa." Ford stared into his mug. "That's not sugar."

"It's butter," said Bill, as though that were obvious. He had a gulp of tea, and, not wanting to seem picky, Ford took a gulp too. It wasn't as nasty as he had expected. In fact, it wasn't nasty at all. Bill, watching his face, said:

"You've never had this before?"

Ford shook his head.

"But you guys are the ones who make the butter up here," said Bill. "This is MAC butter. What do you drink, if you don't drink this?"

"Just . . . batch, and tea with sugar sometimes," said Ford, wondering why this should matter. He had another gulp of the tea. It tasted even better this time.

"And the sugar comes from the sugar beets you grow?" Bill persisted.

"I guess so," said Ford. "I never thought about it."

"What's it like, living down there?"

"What's it like?" Ford stared at him. Why in the world would anybody be curious about the Long Acres? "I don't know. I muck out cow sheds. It's boring, mostly."

"How could it be *boring*?" Bill demanded. "It's so beautiful down there! Are you crazy?"

"No," said Ford, taking a step backward. "But if you think a big shovelful of cowshite and mega-roaches is beautiful, *you're* crazy."

Billy shouted something from the front of the cab and a second later *Beautiful Evelyn* swerved around. Both boys staggered a little at the shift in momentum, glaring at each other, and righted themselves as forward motion ceased.

"We're at Five-Hundred-K Station," Bill guessed. There was another beep. He turned automatically to pull the oven drawer open as Billy came staggering back into the living area.

"Mons Olympus to Five-Hundred-K in one night," he chortled. "That is some righteous driving! Where's the tea?"

They crowded together in the cramped space, sipping tea and eating something brown and bubbly that Ford couldn't identify. Afterward Billy climbed into his bunk with a groan, and yanked the cord that inflated his mattress.

"I am so ready for some horizontal. You guys go up front and talk about stuff, okay?"

"Whatever," said Bill, picking up his Gamebuke and stalking out. Billy, utterly failing to notice the withering scorn to which he had just been subjected, smiled and waved sleepily at Ford. Ford smiled back, but his smile faded as he turned, shut the door behind him, and followed Bill, whom he had decided was a nasty little know-it-all.

Bill was sitting in one corner, staring into the screen of his Gamebuke. He had put on a pair of earshells and was listening to something fairly loud. He ignored Ford, who sat and looked up at the screens in puzzlement.

"Is this the station?" he asked, forgetting that Bill couldn't hear him. He had expected a domed settlement, but all he could see was a wide place by the side of the road, circled by boulders that appeared to have been whitewashed.

Bill didn't answer him. Ford looked at him in annoyance. He studied the controls on the inside of the hatch. When he thought he knew which one opened it, he slipped his mask on. Then he leaned over and punched Bill in the shoulder.

"Mask up," he yelled. "I'm going out."

Bill had his mask on before Ford had finished speaking, and Ford saw his eyes going wide with alarm as he activated the hatch. It sprang open; Ford turned and slid into a blast of freezing air.

He hit the ground harder than he expected to, and almost fell. Gasping, hugging himself against a cold so intense it burned, he stared in astonishment at the dawn.

There was no ceiling. There were no walls. There was nothing around the freighter, as far as the limits of his vision, but limitless space, limitless sky of the palest, chilliest blue he had ever seen, stretching down to a limitless red plain of sand and rock. He turned, and kept turning: no domes, no Tubes, nothing but the wide open world in every direction.

And here was a red light appearing on the horizon, red as blood or rubies, so bright a red it dazzled his eyes, and he wondered for a moment if it was the eye of Marswife. Long purple shadows sprang from the boulders and stretched back toward his boots. He realized he was looking at the rising sun.

*So this is where the lights were going to*, he said to himself, *all those nights they were going away into the dark. They were coming out here. This is the most wonderful thing I have ever seen.*

Somehow he had fallen into the place he had always wanted to be.

But the cold was eating into his bones, and he realized that if he kept on standing there he'd freeze solid in his happy dream. He set off toward the nearest boulder, fumbling with the fastening of his pants.

Someone grabbed his shoulder and spun him around.

"You *idiot!*" Bill shouted at him. "Don't you know what happens if you try to pee out here?"

From the horror on Bill's face, even behind the mask, Ford realized that he'd better get back in the cab as fast as he could.

When they were safely inside and the seals had locked, when Bill had finished yelling at him, Ford still sat shivering with more than cold.

"You mean it boils and *then* it explodes?" he said.

"You are such an idiot!" Bill repeated in disbelief.

"How was I supposed to know?" Ford said. "I've never been Outside before! We use the reclamation conduits at home—"

"This isn't the Long Acres, dumbbell. This is the middle of frozen Nowhere and it'll kill you in two seconds, okay?"

"Well, where can you go?"

"In the lavatory!"

"But I didn't want to wake up your dad."

"He'll sleep through anything," said Bill. "Trust me."

Red with humiliation, Ford crawled into the back and after several tries figured out how to operate the toilet, as Billy snored away oblivious. Afterward he crawled back up front, carefully closed the door and said:

"Er . . . so, where does somebody have their bath?"

Bill, who had turned his Gamebuke on again, did not look up as he said:

"At the *Empress.*"

"No, I mean . . . when somebody has a bath *out here*, where do they have it?"

Bill lifted his eyes. He looked perplexed.

"What are you on about? Nobody bathes out here."

"You mean, you only wash when you're at the *Empress?*"

Now it was Bill's turn to flush with embarrassment.

"Yeah."

Ford tried to keep his dismay from showing, but he wasn't very good at hiding his feelings. "You mean I can't have a bath until we get back?"

"No. You can't. I guess people wash themselves every day in the Long Acres, huh?" said Bill angrily.

Ford nodded. "We have to. It stinks too bad if we don't. Because there's, er, manure and algae and, er, the methane plant, and . . . we work hard and sweat a lot. So we shave and wash every day, see?"

"Is *that* why the MAC haven't got any hair?"

"Yeah," said Ford. He added, "Plus my dad says hair is a vanity. Means being a showoff, being flash."

"I know what it means," said Bill. He was silent a moment, and then said:

"Well, you won't be sweating much out here. Freezing is more like it. So you'll have to cope until we get back to the *Empress.* It'll only be two weeks."

Two weeks? Ford thought of what his dad and mum would say to him when he turned up again, after being missing for so long. His mouth dried, his heart pounded. He wondered desperately what kind of lie he might tell to get himself out of trouble.

Maybe that he'd been kidnapped? It had almost really happened. Kidnapped and taken to work in the iron mines, right, and . . . somehow escaped, and . . .

Billy retreated to his Gamebuke again, as Ford sat there trying to imagine what he might say. The stories became wilder, more unbelievable, as they grew more elaborate; and gradually he found himself drifting away from purposeful lies altogether, dreamily wondering what it might be like if he never went back to face the music at all.

After all, Sam was going to do it; Sam was clever and funny and brave, and he was walking away from the Collective to a new life. Why couldn't Ford have a new life too? What if he became a Hauler, like Billy, and lived out the rest of his life up here where there were no limits to the world? Blatchford the MAC boy would vanish and he could be just Ford, himself, not part of anything. *Free.*

5

It took them most of a week to get to Depot South. Ford enjoyed every minute of it, even getting used to the idea of postponing his bath for two weeks. Mostly he rode up front with Billy, as Bill stayed in the back sulking. Billy told him stories as they rocketed along, and taught him the basics of driving the freighter; it was harder than driving a tractor but not by as much as Ford would have thought.

"Look at you, holding our *Evelyn* on the road!" said Billy, chuckling. "You are one strong kid, for your age. Li'l Bill can't drive her at all yet."

"I'm a better navigator than you are!" yelled Bill from the back, in tones of outrage.

"He is, actually," said Billy. "Best navigator I ever saw. Half the time I have to get him to figure coordinates for me. You ever get lost in a storm or anything, you'll wish you had Li'l Bill there with you." He looked carefully into the back to see if Bill was watching, and then unzipped a pouch in his psuit and took out a small bottle. Quickly he shook two tiny red pills into his palm and popped them into his mouth.

"What're those?" Ford asked.

"Freddie Stay-awakes," said Billy in a low voice. "Just getting ready for another night shift. We're going to set a new record for getting to the Depot, man."

"We don't have to hurry or anything," said Ford. "Really."

"Yeah, we do," said Billy, looking uncomfortable for the first time since Ford had known him. "Fun's fun, and everything, but . . . your people must be kind of wondering where you are, you know? I mean, it was a good idea to get you away from Mother's Boys and all, but we don't want people thinking you're dead, huh?"

"I guess not," said Ford. He looked sadly up at the monitor, at the wide open world. The thought of going back into the Tubes, into the reeking dark of the cowsheds and the muddy trenches, made him despair.

◈ ◈ ◈

Depot South loomed ahead of them at last, a low rise of ice above the plain. At first, Ford was disappointed; he had expected a gleaming white mountain, but Billy explained that the glacier was sanded all over with red dust from the windstorms. As the hours went by and they drew closer, Ford saw a low-lying mist of white, from which the glacier rose like an island. Later, two smaller islands seemed to rise from it as well, one on either side of the road.

"There's old Jack and Jim!" cried Billy. "We're almost there, when we see Jack and Jim."

Ford watched them with interest. As they drew near, he laughed; for they looked like a pair of bearded giants hacked out of the red stone. One was sitting up, peering from blind hollow eyes and holding what appeared to be a mug clutched to his stomach. The other reclined, with his big hands folded peacefully on his chest.

"How'd they get there?" he exclaimed, delighted.

"The glacier deposited them," said Bill, who had come out of the back to see.

"No! No! You have to tell him the story," said Billy gleefully. "See, Jack and Jim were these two Haulers, come up from Australia. So they liked their beer cold, see? *Really* cold.

"So they go into the *Empress*, and Mother, she says, *Welcome, my dears, have a drop of good cheer, warm buttery beer won't cost you dear.* But Jack and Jim, both he and him, they liked their beer cold. Really cold!

"Says one to the other, like brother to brother, there must be a place in this here space where a cobber can swill a nice bit of chill, if he likes his beer cold. Really *cold*.

"So they bought them a keg, and off they legged it for the Pole, the pole, where it's nice and cold, and they chopped out a hole in the ice-wall so, and that keg they stowed in the ice, cobber, ever so nice. And it got cold. *Really* cold.

"So they drank it down and another round and another one still and they drank until they set and they sot and they clean forgot, where the white mists creep they fell asleep, and they got cold. Really cold.

"In fact they froze, from nose to toes, and there they are to this very day, and the moral is, don't die that way! 'Cause what's right for Oz ain't right on Moz, 'cause up here it's *cold*. Really cold!"

Billy laughed like a loon, pounding his fist on the console. Bill just rolled his eyes.

"They're only a couple of boulders," he said.

"But you used to love that song," said Billy plaintively.

"When I was three, maybe," said Bill, turning and going into the back. "You'd better get him out one of your extra psuits. He won't fit in any of mine."

"He used to sing it with me," said Billy to Ford, looking crestfallen.

☙ ☙ ☙

They pulled into Depot South, and once again Ford expected to see buildings, but there were none; only a confused impression of tumbled rock on the monitor. He looked up at it as Billy helped him into a psuit.

"Is it colder out there?" he asked.

"Yeah," said Bill, getting down three helmets from a locker. "You're at the South Pole, dummy."

"Aw, now, he's never been there, has he?" said Billy, adjusting the fit of the suit for Ford. "That feel okay?"

"I guess it—whoa!" said Ford, for once the fastenings had been sealed up the suit seemed to flex, like a hand closing around him, and though it felt warm and snug it was still a slightly creepy sensation. "What's it doing?"

"Just kind of programming itself so it gets to know you," Billy explained, accepting a helmet from Bill. "That's how it keeps you alive, see? Just settles in real close and puts a couple of sensors places you don't notice. Anything goes wrong, it'll try to fix you, and if it can't, it'll flash lights at you so you know."

"Like that?" Ford pointed at the little red light flashing on Billy's psuit readout panel. Billy looked down at it.

"Oh. No, that's just a short circuit or glitch or something. It's been doing that all the time lately when nothing's wrong."

"Some people take their suits into the shop when they need repair, you know," said Bill, putting on his own helmet. "Just an idea, Dad. Hope it's not too radical for you."

As Billy helped him seal up his helmet, Ford looked at Bill and thought: *You're a mean little twit. I'd give anything if my dad was like yours.*

But when they stepped Outside, he forgot about Bill and even about Billy. He barely noticed the cold, though it was so intense it took his breath away and the psuit helpfully turned up its thermostat for him. Depot South had all his attention.

They were surrounded on three sides by towering walls, cloudy white swirled through with colors like an Ice Pop, green and blue blue blue and lavender, all scarred and rough, faceted and broken. Underneath his feet was a confusion of crushed and broken rock, pea-sized gravel to cobbles, ice mixed with grit and stone, and a roiling mist swirled about his ankles.

Here and there were carvings in the ice wall, roughly gouged and hacked: HAULERS RULE OK and BARSOOM BRUCE GOT HERE ALIVE, and one that simply said THANKS MARSWIFE, over a niche that had been scraped from the ice where somebody had left a little figurine like the one on *Beautiful Evelyn*'s console. There were figures carved too; on a section of green ice, Ford noticed a four-armed giant with tusks.

Behind him, he became aware of a clatter as Billy and Bill opened a panel in the freighter's side and drew out something between them. He turned to see Billy hoisting a laser-saw, and heard the *hummzap* as it was turned on.

"Okay!" said Billy, his voice coming tinnily over the speaker. "Let's go cut some ice!"

He went up to the nearest wall, hefted the laser, and disappeared in a cloud of white steam. A moment later, a great chunk of ice came hurtling out of the steam, and bounced and rolled to Bill's feet. He picked it up, as another block bounded out.

"Grab that," said Bill. "If we don't start loading this stuff, Dad will be up to his neck in ice."

Ford obeyed, and followed Bill around to the rear of the freighter, where a sort of escalator ramp had been lowered, and watched as Bill dropped the block to the ramp. It traveled swiftly up the ramp to a hopper at the top of *Beautiful Evelyn*'s tank, where it vanished with a grinding roar, throwing up a rainbowed shatter of ice-shards and vapor against the sunlight. Fascinated, Ford set his block on the ramp and watched as the same thing happened.

"What's it doing?"

"Making carbon dioxide snowcones, what do you think?" said Bill. "And we take the whole lot back to Settlement Base, and sell it to the MAC."

"You do?" Ford was astonished. "What do we need it for?"

"Hel-LO, terraforming, remember?" said Bill. "Making Mars green like Earth? What the MAC was brought up here to do?"

He turned and trudged back around the side of the freighter, and Ford walked after him thinking: *I'll bet you wouldn't hold that nose so high up in the air if I bashed it with my forehead.*

But he said nothing, and for the next hour they worked steadily as machines, going back and forth with ice blocks to the ramp. The tank was nearly full when they heard the drone of ice-cutting stop.

"That's not enough, Dad," Bill called, and nobody answered. He turned and ran. Ford walked around the side of the freighter and saw him kneeling beside Billy, who had fallen and lay with the white mist curling over his body.

Ford gasped and ran to them. The whole front of Billy's psuit was lit with blinking colors, dancing over a readout panel that had activated. Bill was bending close, waving away the mist to peer at it. Ford leaned down and saw Billy's face slack within the helmet, his eyes staring and blank.

"What's wrong with him?" said Ford.

"He's had a blowout," said Bill flatly.

"What's a blowout?"

"Blood vessel goes *bang*. Happens sometimes to people who go Outside a lot." Bill rested his hand on his father's chest. He felt something in one of the sealed pouches; he opened it, and drew out the bottle of Freddie Stay-awakes. After staring at it for a long moment, his face contorted. He hurled the bottle at the ice-wall, where it popped open and scattered red pills like beads of blood.

"I knew it! I knew he'd do this! I knew this would happen someday!" he shouted. Ford felt like crying, but he fought it back and said:

"Is he going to die?"

"What do you think?" said Bill. "We're at the bloody South Pole! We're a week away from the infirmary!"

"But—could we maybe keep him alive until we get back?"

Bill turned to him, and a little of the incandescent rage faded from his eyes. "We might," he said. "The psuit's doing what it can. We have some emergency medical stuff. You don't under-stand, though. His brain's turning to goo in there."

"Maybe it isn't," said Ford. "Please! We have to try."

"He'll die anyway," said Bill, but he got Billy under the shoulders and tried to lift him. Ford came around and took his place, lifting Billy easily; Bill grabbed his father's legs, and be-tween them they hoisted Billy up and carried him into the cab.

There they settled him in his bunk, and Bill fumbled in a drawer for a medical kit. He drew out three sealed bags of colored liquid with tubes leading from one end and hooks on the other. The tubes he plugged into ports in the arm of Billy's psuit; the hooks fitted into loops on the underside of the upper bunk, so the bags hung suspended above Billy.

"Should we get his helmet off him?" Ford asked. Bill just shook his head. He turned and stalked out of the compartment. Ford took a last look at Billy, with the glittering lights on his chest and his dead eyes staring, and followed Bill.

"What do we do now?"

"We get the laser," said Bill. "We can't leave it. It cost a month's pay."


## 6

The freighter was a lot harder to handle now, full of ice, than it had been on the way out when Billy had let him drive. It took all Ford's strength to back her around and get her on the road again, and even so the console beeped a warning as they trundled out through Jack and Jim, for he nearly swerved and clipped one of the giants. At last he was able to steer straight between the boulders and get up a little speed.

"We really can't, er, send a distress signal or anything?" he asked Bill. Bill sat hunched at his end of the cab, staring at the monitors.

"Nobody'll hear us," he said bitterly, "There's half a planet between Mons Olympus and us. Did you notice any relay towers on the way out here?"

"No."

"That's because there aren't any. Why should Areco build any? Nobody comes out here except Haulers, and who cares if Haulers die? We do this work because nobody else wants to do it, because it's too dangerous. But Haulers are a bunch of idiots; *they* don't care if they get killed."

"They're not idiots, they're brave!" said Ford. Bill looked at him with contempt. Neither of them said anything for a long while after that.

❧ ❧ ❧

By the time it was beginning to get dark, Ford was aching in every muscle of his body from the sheer effort of keeping the freighter on the road. The approaching darkness was not as fearful as he'd thought it might be, because for several miles now someone had daubed the lines of boulders with photoreflective paint, and they lit up nicely in the freighter's high-beams. But *Beautiful Evelyn* seemed to want to veer to the left, and Ford wondered if there was something wrong with her steering system until he saw drifts of sand flying straight across the road in front of her, like stealthy ghosts.

"I think the wind's rising," he said.

"You think, genius?" Bill pointed to a readout on the console.

"What's it mean?"

"It means we're probably driving right into a storm," said Bill, and then they heard a shrill piping alarm from the back. Bill scrambled aft; Ford held the freighter on the road. *Please don't let that be Billy dying! Please, Marswife, if you're out there, help us!*

Bill returned and crawled into his seat. "The air pressure's dropping in here. The psuit needed somebody to okay turning it up a notch."

"Why's the air pressure dropping?"

Bill sounded weary. "Because this is going to be a really bad storm. You'd better pull over and anchor us."

"But we have to get your dad to an infirmary!"

"Did you think we were going to drive for a whole week without sleeping?" Bill said. "We don't have any Freddies now. We have to sit out the storm no matter what happens. Five-Fifty-K is coming up soon. Maybe we can make it that far."

It was in fact twelve kilometers away, and the light faded steadily as they roared along. Ford could hear the wind howling now. He remembered a story Billy had told him, about people seeing dead Haulers in their high-beams, wraiths signaling for help at the scenes of long-ago breakdowns. The whirling sand looked uncannily like figures with streaming hair, diving in front of the freighter as though waving insubstantial arms. He was grateful when the half-circle of rocks that was Five-Fifty-K Station appeared in her lights at last, and she seemed eager to swerve away from the road.

Bill punched in the anchoring protocol, and *Beautiful Evelyn* gave a lurch and dropped abruptly, as though she were sitting down. Ford cut the power; the drives fell silent. They sat there side by side in the silence that was filled up steadily by the whine of blowing sand, and a patter of blown gravel that might have sounded to them like rain, if they had ever heard rain.

"What do we do now?" said Ford.

"We wait it out," said Bill.

They went into the back to check on Billy—no change—and heated something frozen and ate it, barely registering what it was. Then they went back into the cab and sat, in their opposite corners.

"So we really are on our own?" said Ford at last. "Areco won't send Security looking for us?"

"Areco doesn't send Mother's Boys anyplace," said Bill, staring into the dark. "Mother hired 'em."

"Who's Mother, anyway?"

"The lady who found the diamond and got rich," said Bill. "And bought Mons Olympus, and everybody thought she was crazy, because it was just this big volcano where nobody could grow anything. Only, she had a well drilled into a magma pocket and built a power station. And she leased lots to a bunch of people from Earth and that's why Mons Olympus makes way more money than Areco and the MAC."

"The MAC isn't supposed to make money," said Ford. "We're supposed to turn Mars into a paradise. Our contract says Areco is going to give it to us for our own, once we've done it."

"Well, you can bet Areco isn't going to come rescue us," said Bill. "Nobody looks out for Haulers except other Haulers. And their idea of help would be giving Dad a big funeral and getting stinking drunk afterward."

"Oh," said Ford. Bill gave him an odd look.

"People in the MAC look out for each other, though, don't they?"

"Yeah," said Ford wretchedly. "There's always somebody watching what you do. Always somebody there to tell you why what you want to do is wrong. Council meetings go on for hours because everybody has to say something or it isn't fair, but they all say the same thing anyway. Blah blah blah. I *hate* it there," he said, surprising himself by how intensely he felt.

"What's it supposed to be like, when Mars is a paradise?"

Ford looked at Bill to see if he was being mocking, but he wasn't smiling.

"Well, it'll be like . . . there'll be no corruption or oppression. And stuff. They say water will fall out of the sky, and nobody will ever have to wear a mask again." Ford slumped forward and put his head on his knees. "I used to imagine it'd be . . . I don't know. Full of lights."

"People would be safe, if Mars could be made like that," said Bill in a thoughtful voice. "Terraformed. Another Earth. No more big empty spaces."

"I *like* big empty spaces," said Ford. "Why does Mars have to be just like Earth anyway? Why can't things stay the way they are?"

"You *like* this?" Bill swung his arm up at the monitors, that showed only the howling night and a blur of sand. " 'Cause you can have it. I hate it! Tons of big nothing waiting to kill us, all my whole life! And Dad just laughed at it, but he isn't laughing now, huh? You know what's really sick? If he dies—if we get back alive—I'll be better off."

"Oh, shut up," said Ford.

"But I *will*," said Bill, with a certain wonderment. "Lots better off. I can sell this freighter—and Dad paid into the Hauler's Club, so there'd be some money coming in there—and . . . wow, I could afford a *good* education. Maybe University level. I'll be able to have everything I've always wanted, and I'll never have to come out here again."

"How can you talk like that?" Ford yelled. "You selfish pig! You're talking about your own dad dying! You don't even care, do you? Your dad's the bravest guy I ever met!"

"He got himself killed, after everything I told him. He was stupid," said Bill.

"He isn't even dead yet!" Ford, infuriated, swung at him. Bill ducked backward, away from his flailing fists, and got his legs up on the seat and kicked Ford. Ford fell sideways, but scrambled up on his knees and kept coming, trying to back Bill into the corner. Bill dodged and hit him hard, and then again and again, until Ford got so close he couldn't get his arms up all the way. Ford, sobbing with anger, punched as hard as he could in the cramped space, but Bill was a much better fighter for all that he was so small.

By the time they had hurt each other enough to stop, both of them had bloody noses and Ford had the beginning of a black eye. Swearing, they retreated into their separate corners of the cab, and glared at each other until the droning hiss of the wind and the pattering of gravel on the tank lulled them to sleep.

7

When they woke, hours later, it was dead quiet.

Ford woke groaning, partly because his face was so sore and partly because he had a stiff neck from sleeping curled up on the seat. He sat up and looked around blearily.

He realized that he couldn't hear anything. He looked up at the monitors and realized that he couldn't see anything, either; the screens were black. Frightened, he leaned over and shook Bill awake. Bill woke instantly, staring around.

"The power's gone out!" Ford said.

"No, it hasn't. We'd be dead," said Bill. He punched a few buttons on the console and peered intently at figures that appeared on the readout. Then he looked up at the monitors. "What's that?" He pointed at the monitor for the rear of the freighter, where there was a sliver of image along the top. Just a grayish triangle of light, shifting a little along its lower edge, just like . . .

"Sand," said Bill. "We're buried. The storm blew a dune over us."

"What do we do now?" said Ford, shivering, and the psuit thought he was cold and warmed up comfortingly.

"Maybe we can blow it away," said Bill. "Some, anyway." He switched on the drives and there was a shudder and a jolt that ran the whole length of the freighter. With a *whoosh, Beautiful Evelyn* rose a few inches. The rear monitor lit up with an image of sand cascading past it; some light showed on her left-hand monitor too.

"Okay!" said Bill, shutting her down again. "We're not going to die. Not here, anyway. We can dig out. Get a helmet on."

They went aft to get helmets—Billy still stared at nothing, though his psuit blinked at them reassuringly—and, when they had helmeted up, Bill reached past Ford to activate the hatch. It made a dull muffled sound, but would not open. He had to try three more times before it consented to open out about a hand's width. Sand spilled into the cab, followed by daylight.

Bill swore and climbed up on the seat, pushing the hatch outward. "Get up here and help me!"

Ford scrambled up beside him and set his shoulder to the hatch. A lot more sand fell in, but they were able to push it open far enough for Bill to grab the edge and pull himself up, and worm his way out. Ford climbed after, and in a moment was standing with Bill on the top of the dune that covered the freighter.

Bill swore quietly. Ford didn't blame him.

They stood on a mountain of red sand and looked out on a plain of red sand, endless, smooth to the wide horizon, and the low early sun threw their shadows far out behind them. The sky had a flat metallic glare; the wind wailed high and mournful.

"Where's the road?" cried Ford.

"Buried under there," said Bill, pointing down the slope in

front of them. "It happens sometimes. Come on." He turned and started down the slope. Ford stumbled after him, slipped, and fell, rolling ignominiously to the bottom. He picked himself up, feeling stupid, but Bill hadn't noticed; he was digging with his hands, scooping away sand from the freighter.

Ford waded in to help him. He reached up to brush sand from the tank, but at his touch the sand puckered out in a funny starred pattern. Startled, he drew his hand back. Cautiously he reached out a fingertip to the tank; the instant he touched it, a rayed star of sand formed once again.

"Hey, look at this!" Giggling, he drew his finger along the tank, and the star spread and followed it.

"It's magnetic," said Bill. "Happens sometimes, when the wind's been bad. My dad said it's all the iron in the sand. It fries electronics. Hard to clean off, too."

Ford brushed experimentally at the tank, but the sand stuck as though it were a dense syrup.

"This'll take us forever," he said.

"Not if we get to the tool chest," said Bill. "We can scrape off most of it."

They worked together and after ten minutes had cleared a panel in the freighter's undercarriage; Bill pried it open and pulled out a couple of big shovels, and after that the work went more quickly.

"Wowie. Sand spades. All we need is buckets and we could make sand castles, huh?" said Ford, grinning sheepishly.

"What's that mean?"

"It's something kids do on Earth. Sam says, before we emigrated, our dad and mum took him to this place called Blackpool. There was all this blue water, see, washing in over the sand. He had a bucket and spade and he made sand castles. So here we are in the biggest Blackpool in the universe, with the biggest sand spades, yeah? Only there's no water."

"How could you make castles out of sand?" Bill said, scowling as he worked. "They'd just fall in on you."

"I don't know. I think you'd have to get the sand wet."

"But why would anybody get sand wet?"

"I don't know. I don't think people do it on purpose; I think it just happens. There's all this water on Earth, see, and it gets on things. That's what Sam says."

Bill shook his head grimly and kept digging. They cleared the freighter's rear wheels, and Ford said:

"Why do you reckon the water's blue on Earth? It's only green or brown up here."

"It's not blue," said Bill.

"Yes, it is," said Ford. "Sam has holos of it. I've seen 'em. It's bluer than the sky. Blue as blue paint."

"Water isn't any color really," said Bill. "It just looks blue. Something about the air."

Ford scowled and went around to the other side of the freighter, where he dug out great shovelfuls of sand and muttered, "It *is* blue. They wouldn't have that Blue Room if it wasn't blue. All the songs and stories say it's blue. So there, you little know-it-all."

He had forgotten that Bill could hear him on the psuit comm, so he was quite startled when Bill's voice sounded inside his helmet:

"Songs and stories? Right. Go stick your head in a dune, moron."

Ford just gritted his teeth and kept shoveling.

It took them a long while to clear the freighter, because they only made real progress once the wind fell a little. Eventually, though, they were able to climb back into the cab and start up *Beautiful Evelyn*'s drives. She blasted her way free of the dune and Ford strained to steer her up, over and down across the rippled slope below.

"Okay! Where's the road?" he said.

"There," said Bill, pointing. "Don't you even know directions? We anchored at right angles to the road. It's still there, even if we can't see it. Just take her straight that way."

Ford obeyed. They rumbled off.

They drove for five hours, over sand and then over rocky sand

and at last over a cobbled plain, and there was no sign of the double row of boulders that should have been there if they had been on the High Road.

Bill, who had been watching the readouts, grew more and more pale and silent.

"We need to stop," he said at last. "Something's wrong."

"We aren't on the High Road anymore, are we?" said Ford sadly.

"No. We're lost."

"What happened?"

"The storm must have screwed up the nav system," said Bill. "All that magnetic crap spraying around."

"Can we fix it?"

"I can reset it," said Bill. "But I can't recalibrate it, because I don't know where we are. So it wouldn't do us any good."

"But your dad said you were this great navigator!" said Ford.

Bill looked at his boots. "I'm not. He just thought I was."

"Well, isn't that great?" said Ford. "And here you thought *I* was such an idiot. What do we do now, Professor?"

"Shut up," said Bill. "Just shut up. We're supposed to go north, okay? And the sun rises in the east and sets in the west. So as long as we keep the setting sun on our left, we're going mostly in the right direction."

"What happens at night?"

"If the sky's clear of dust clouds, maybe we can steer by the stars."

Ford brightened up at that. "I used to watch the stars a lot," he said. "And we ought to be able to see the mountain after a while, right?"

"Mons Olympus? Yeah."

"Okay then!" Ford accelerated again, and *Beautiful Evelyn* plunged forward. "We can do this! Billy wouldn't be scared if he was lost, would he?"

"No," admitted Bill.

"No, because he'd just point himself at the horizon and he'd just *go*, zoom, and he wouldn't worry about it."

"He never worried about anything," said Bill, though not as though he thought that was especially smart.

"Well, it's dumb to worry," said Ford, with a slightly rising note of hysteria in his voice. "You live or you die, right? The main thing, is . . . is . . . to be really *alive* before you die. I could have lived my whole life walking around in the Tubes and never, ever seen stuff like I've seen since I ran away. All this sky. All that sand. The ice and the mist and the different colors and everything! So maybe I don't get to be old like Hardie Stubbs's granddad. Who wants to be all shriveled up and coughing anyway?"

"Don't be stupid," said Bill. "I'd give anything to be down in the Long Acres right now, and I wouldn't care what work I had to do. And you wish you were there too."

"No, I don't!" Ford shouted. "You know what I'm going to do? As soon as we get back, I'll go see my dad and I'll say: 'Dad, I'm leaving the MAC.' Sam did it and so can I. Only I'm not going back to Earth. Mars is *my* place! And I'm going to be a Hauler, and stay Outside all the rest of my life!"

Bill stared at him.

"You're crazy," he said. "You think your dad will just let you go?"

"No," said Ford. "He'll grab my ear and about pull it off. It doesn't matter. Once I'm nine, the MAC says I have a right to pick whatever job I want."

"Once you're *nine?*"

Ford turned red. "In MAC years. We have one for every two Earth years."

"So . . . you're how old now?" Bill began to grin. "Six?"

"Yeah," said Ford. "And you can just shut up, okay?"

"Okay," said Bill, but his grin widened.


8


They drove all the rest of that day, but when night fell they were so tired they agreed to pull over to sleep. Ford stretched out in the cab and Bill went back to crawl into the bunk above Billy, who lay there still, staring and unresponsive as a waxwork.

☙ ☙ ☙

He was still alive when morning came. Bill was changing his tube-bags when Ford came edging in, yawning.

"You wait and see," said Ford, in an attempt to be comforting. "He'll be fine if we can get him to the infirmary. Eric Chetwynd's dad fell off a tractor and fractured his skull, and *he* was in this coma, see, for days, but then they did surgery on him and he was opening his eyes and talking and everything. And your dad hasn't even got any broken bones."

"It's not the same," said Bill morosely. "Never mind. Let's get going. Sun's on our right until noon, got it?"

They drove on. Ford's muscles ached less now; he was beginning to feel more confident with *Beautiful Evelyn*. He watched the horizon and imagined Mons Olympus rising there, inevitable, the red queen on the vast chessboard of the plain. She *would* come into view soon. She had to. And someday, when he had a freighter of his own and drove this route all the time, a little thing like going off course wouldn't bother him at all. He'd know every sand hill and rock outcropping like the palm of his hand.

He thought about getting a tattoo on his face. Deciding what it ought to look like occupied his thoughts for the next couple of hours, as Bill sat silent across from him, staring at the monitors and twisting his hands together in his lap.

Then:

"Something's moving!" said Bill, pointing at the backup cam monitor.

Ford spotted it: something gleaming, sunlight striking off a vehicle far back in their dust-wake.

"Yowie! It's another Hauler!" he said. "Billy's saved!"

He slowed *Beautiful Evelyn* and turned her around, so the plume of dust whirled away and they could see the other vehicle more clearly.

"It's not a Hauler," said Bill. "It's just a cab. Who is that? That's nobody I know."

"Who cares?" said Ford, pounding on the console in his glee. "They'll know how to get back to the road!"

"Not if they're lost too," said Bill. The stranger was barreling toward them quite deliberately and they could see it clearly now: a freighter's cab with no tank attached, just the tang of the hookup sticking out behind, looking strange as some tiny insect with an immense head. It pulled up alongside them. Bill hit the comm switch and cried, "Who's that?"

There was a silence. Then a voice crackled through the speakers, distorted and harsh: "Who's that crying 'who's that?' Sounds like a youngster."

Ford leaned over and shouted, "Please, we're lost! Can you show us how to get back to the road?"

Another silence, and then:

"Two little boys? What're you doing out here, then? Daddy had a mishap, did he?"

Bill gave Ford a furious look. Ford wondered why, but said:

"Yes, sir! We need to get him to the infirmary, and our nav system went out in the storm! Can you help us?"

"Why, sure I can," said the voice, and it sounded as though the speaker were smiling. "Mask up now, kids, and step Outside. Let's talk close-up, eh?"

"You jackass," muttered Bill, but he pulled on his mask.

When they slid down out of the cab they saw that the stranger had painted his cab with the logo CELTIC POWER and pictures of what had been celtic knots and four-leaved clovers, though they were half scoured away. The hatch swung up and a man climbed out, a big man in a psuit also painted in green and yellow patterns. He looked them over and grinned within his mask.

"Well, hello there, kids," he said. "Gwill Griffin, at your service. Diamond prospector by trade. What's the story?"

"Bill's dad had a blowout," said Ford. "And we were trying to get him back, but we've lost the road. Can you help us, please?"

"A blowout?" The man raised his eyebrows. "Now, that's an awful thing. Let's have a look at him."

"You don't need—" began Bill, but Mr. Griffin had already vaulted up into *Beautiful Evelyn*'s cab. Bill and Ford scrambled after him. By the time they had got in he was already in the back, leaning down to peer at Billy.

"Dear, dear, he's certainly in trouble," he said. "Yes, you'd better get him back to Mons Olympus, and no mistake." He looked around the inside of the cab. "Nice rig he's got here, though, isn't it? And a nice full tank of $CO_2$, I take it?"

"Yeah," said Ford. "It happened right as we were finishing up. Do you know how to, er, recalibrate nav systems?"

"No trouble at all," said Mr. Griffin, shoving past them and into the seat at the console. Bill watched him closely as he punched it up and set in new figures. "Poor little lads, lost on your own Outside. You're lucky I found you, you know. The road's just five kilometers east of here, but you might have wandered around forever without finding it."

"I knew we had to be close," said Ford, though he did not feel quite the sense of relief he might have, and wondered why.

"Yes; terrible things can happen out here. I saw your rig in the middle of nowhere, zigzagging along, and I said to myself: 'Goddess save me, that must be Freeze-Dried Dave!' I've seen some strange things out here in my time, I can tell you."

"Who's Freeze-Dried Dave?" asked Ford.

"Him? The Demon Hauler of Mare Cimmerium?" Mr. Griffin turned to him, pushing his mask up. He was beardless and freckled, though he wore a wide mustache, and was not as old as Ford had thought him to be at first.

"Nobody knows who Freeze-Dried Dave was; just some poor soul who was up here in the early days, and they say he died at the console whilst on a run, see? And his cab's system took over and went on Autopilot. They think it veered off the road in a storm and just kept rovering on, and every time the battery'd wear out it'd sit somewhere until another storm scoured the dust off the solar cells. Then it'd just start itself up again."

Ford realized what was making him uneasy. The man

sounded like an actor in a holo, like somebody who was speaking lines for an effect.

"Some prospectors found it clean out in the middle of nowhere, and went up to it and got the hatch to open. There was Freeze-Dried Dave still sitting inside her, shriveled up like; but no sooner had they set foot to the ladder than she roared to life and took off, scattering 'em like bowling pins. And what do you think she did then? Only swerved around and came back at 'em, that's what she did, and mashed one into the sand while the others ran for their lives.

"*They* made it home to tell the tale. There's many a Hauler since then who's seen her, thundering along on her own business off the road, with that dead man rattling around inside. Some say it's Dave's ghost driving her, trying to find his way back to Settlement Base. Some say it's the freighter herself, that her system's gone mad with sorrow and wants to kill anyone gets close enough, so they don't take her Dave away. You'll never find a prospector like me who'll go anywhere near her. Why, it's bad luck even to see her." He winked broadly at Ford.

"We need to get my dad to the infirmary," said Bill, clearing his throat. "Thanks for helping us. Let's go, okay?"

"Right," said Mr. Griffin, masking up again. "Only you'd best let me do a point-check on your freighter first, don't you think? That was quite a storm; could be all sorts of things gummed up you don't know about. Wouldn't want to have a breakdown out here, eh?"

"No, sir," said Ford. Mr. Griffin jumped down from the cab. Bill was preparing to jump after him, but he held up his hand.

"Now, I'll tell you what we'll do," he said. "You lads sit in there and watch the console. I'm going to test the tread relays; that's the surest thing will go wrong after a storm, with all those little magnetic particles getting everywhere and persuading the relays to do things they shouldn't. Could cause all your wheels to lock on one side, and you don't want that to happen at speed! You'd roll and kill yourselves for sure. I'll just open the panel and run a quick diagnostic; you can give me a shout when the green lights go on."

"Okay," said Bill, and climbed back in and closed the hatch. As soon as it was closed, he swore, and kept swearing. Ford stared at him.

"What are you on about?" he demanded. "We're safe now."

"No, we bloody aren't," said Bill. "Gwill Griffin, my butt. I know who that guy is. His name's Art Finlay. He was one of Mother's Boys. She fired him last year. He liked to go into the holding cell and slap guys around. He thought nobody was look-ing, but the cameras caught him. So all that old-diamond-prospector-with-his-tall-tales stuff was so much crap. So's the PanCeltic accent; he emigrated up here from some place in the Americans on Earth."

"So he's a phony?" Ford thought of the inexplicably creepy feeling the stranger had given him.

"Yeah. He's a phony," said Bill, and reached over to switch on the comm unit. "How are those relays?" he said.

"Look fine," was the crackly answer. "Your daddy took care of this rig, sure enough. Look at the console, now, lads; tell me when the green lights go on."

They stared at the panel, and in a moment: "They're on," chorused Bill and Ford.

"Then you're home and dry."

"Thanks! We're going to go on now, okay?" said Bill.

"You do that. I'll just follow along behind to be sure you get home safe, eh?"

"Okay," said Bill, and shut off the comm. "Get going!" he told Ford. "Five kilometers due east. We ought to be able to see it once we get over that rise. Let's leave this guy way behind us."

Ford started her up again, and *Beautiful Evelyn* rolled for-ward. She picked up speed and he charged her at the hill, feeling a wonderful sense of freedom as she zoomed upward. Bill cut into his reverie by yelling:

"The camera's been changed!"

"Huh?"

"Look," said Bill, pointing up at the left-hand monitor. It was no longer showing *Beautiful Evelyn*'s port side and a slice of ground, as it had been; now there was only a view of the northern horizon. "He moved the lens. Move it back!"

"I don't know how!" Ford leaned in, flustered, as Bill jumped up and reached past him to stab at the controls that would align the camera lenses. *Beautiful Evelyn*'s side came back into view.

"She looks all right," said Ford. "And, hey! There's the High Road! Hooray!"

"No, she doesn't look all right!" said Bill. "Look! He left the relay panel open! How come the telltale warning isn't lit?"

"I don't know," said Ford.

"Of course *you* don't know, you flaming idiot," said Bill, shrill with anger. "And here he comes!"

Ford looked up at the backup cam and saw Mr. Griffin's cab advancing behind the freighter; then the image switched to the left-hand camera, as it moved up on *Beautiful Evelyn*'s port side. It drew level with the open panel. They watched in horror as the cab's hatch swung down. They saw Mr. Griffin, masked up, leaning out.

"He's going to do something to the panel!" shrieked Bill.

"Oh, no, he won't," said Ford, more angry than he had ever been in his life. Without a second's hesitation, he steered *Beautiful Evelyn* sharply to the left. She more than sideswiped Mr. Griffin; with a terrific crash, she sent his cab spinning away, rolling over and over, and they saw him go flying out of it. *Beautiful Evelyn* lurched and sagged. They rumbled to a stop. They sat for a moment, shaking.

"We have to go see," said Bill. "Something's wrong."

They masked up and went Outside.


9


*Beautiful Evelyn*'s foremost left tire had exploded. There was a thick crust of polyceramic around the wheel, but nothing else. It must have sent pieces flying in all directions when it burst. Ford gaped at it while Bill ran down to the open panel. Ford heard a lot of swearing. He turned and saw Bill tearing something loose, and holding it up.

"Duct tape," said Bill. "He put a piece of duct tape over the warning sensor."

"Did he damage the, whatzis, the relays?" Ford looked in concern at the open panel, with no idea what he was seeing inside.

"No. You nailed him in time. But if he'd bashed them with something once we'd come up to speed, we'd have flipped over, just like he said. Then all he'd have had to do was move in and pick over the wreck. Help himself to the tank. Tell anybody who asked questions a story about some 'poor little dead lads' he'd found out here." Bill looked over at the dust rising from the wreck of Griffin's cab.

He bent and picked up a good-sized rock.

Ford followed his gaze.

"You think he's still alive?" he said, shuddering.

"Maybe," said Bill. "Get a rock. Let's go find out."

But he wasn't alive. They found him where he'd fallen, nine meters from his cab.

His mask had come off.

"Oh," said Ford, backing away. "Oh—"

He turned hastily and doubled up, vomiting into his mask. Turning, he ran for the freighter. Scrambling in and closing the hatch, he groped his way to the lavatory and pulled his mask off. He vomited again, under Billy's blank gaze.

He had cleaned himself up a little and stopped crying by the time he heard Bill coming back.

"Can you mask up?" Bill asked him, over the commlink.

"Yeah—" said Ford, his voice breaking on another sob. Hating himself, he pulled the mask on and heard the hatch open. Bill climbed in.

"We might be okay," said Bill. "I had a look at his rig. Same size tires as ours. Maybe we can change one out."

"Okay," said Ford. Bill looked at him.

"Are you going to be all right? You're green."

"I killed a guy," said Ford.

"He was trying to kill us," said Bill. "He deserved what he got."

"I know," said Ford, beginning to shiver again. "It's just— the way it *looked*. The face. Oh, man. I'm going to see it when I close my eyes at night, for the rest of my life."

"I know," said Bill, sounding tired. "That was how I felt, the first time I saw somebody die like that."

"Does it happen a lot?"

"To Haulers? Yeah. Mostly to new guys." Bill stood up. "Come on. Blow your nose and let's go see if we can change the tire."

Walking out to the wreck, Ford began to giggle weakly.

"We really blew *his* nose for him, huh?"

❀ ❀ ❀

The cab had come to rest upright. Its hatch had been torn away, and the inside was a litter of tumbled trash and spilled coffee that had already frozen. Ford made a step of his hands so Bill could climb up and in.

"I don't see any lug nuts," Ford said, looking at the nearest tire. "How do we get them off?"

"They're not like tractor tires," said Bill crossly, punching buttons on the console. "Crap. All the electronics are fried. There's supposed to be an emergency release, though. Ours is under the console, because it's a Mitsubishi. This is a Toutatis. Let me look around in here . . ."

Ford glanced over his shoulder in the direction in which the dead man lay. He looked back hurriedly and gave an experimental tug at the tire. It felt as immovable as a ten-ton boulder. He reached in and got his arms around it, and pulled as hard as he could.

"I think maybe this is it," said Bill, from inside the cab. "Stand clear, okay?"

Ford let go hastily and tried to scramble away, but the tire shot off the axle as though it had been fired from a cannon.

It caught him in the stomach. He was thrown backward two meters, and fell sprawling on the ground, too winded to groan.

"Dumbass," said Bill, looking down. He jumped from the cab and pushed the tire off Ford. "I *said* stand clear. Why doesn't anybody ever listen to me?"

Ford rolled over, thinking he might have to throw up again. He got painfully to his hands and knees. Bill was already rolling the tire toward *Beautiful Evelyn*, so Ford struggled to his feet and followed.

He held the tire upright, standing well clear of the axle when Bill fired off the burst one. It shot all the way over to the wreck. Then Bill got back down, and, together, they lifted the tire up and slammed it into place. They drove down to the road, between two boulders, and turned north again.

๑ ๑ ๑

"Look, you need to get over it," said Bill, who had been watching Ford. "It's not like you meant to kill him."

"It's not that," said Ford, who was gray-faced and sweating. "My stomach really hurts, is all."

Bill leaned close and looked at him.

"Your psuit says something's wrong," he said.

"It does?" Ford looked down at himself. How had he missed that flashing yellow light? "It's like it's shrinking or something. It's so tight I can almost not breathe."

"We have to stop," said Bill.

"Okay," said Ford. *Beautiful Evelyn* coasted to a stop and sat there in the middle of the road, as Bill climbed over and stared intently at the diagnostic panel on the front of Ford's psuit. He went pale, but all he said was:

"Let's trade places."

"But you can't drive her," Ford protested.

"If we're on the straightaway and there's no wind, I can sort of drive," said Bill. He dove into the back, as Ford crawled sideways into his seat, and came out a moment later with one of the little tube-bags. "Stick your arm up like *this*, okay?"

Ford obeyed, and watched as Bill plugged the tube into the psuit's port. "So that'll make me feel better?"

"Yeah, it ought to." Bill swung himself into the console seat and sent *Beautiful Evelyn* trundling on.

"Good." Ford sighed. "What's wrong with me?"

"Psuit says you've ruptured something," said Bill, staring at the monitor. He accelerated.

"Oh. Well, that's not too bad," said Ford, blinking. "Jimmy Linton got a rupture and he's okay. Better than okay, actually. The medic said he couldn't work with a shovel anymore. So . . . they made him official secretary for the Council, see? All he has to do is record stuff at meetings and post notices."

"Really."

"So if I have a rupture, maybe my dad won't take it so hard that I want to be a Hauler. Since that way I get out of working in the methane plant and the cow sheds. Maybe."

Bill gave him an incredulous look.

"All this, and you still want to be a Hauler?"

"Of course I do!"

Bill just shook his head.

☙ ☙ ☙

They drove in a dead calm, at least compared to the weather before. Far off across the plains they saw dust devils here and there, twirling lazily. The farther north they drove, the clearer the air was, the brighter the light of the sun, shining on standing out-croppings of rock the color of rust, or milk chocolate, or tangerines, or new pennies.

"This is so great," said Ford, slurring his words as he spoke. "This is more beautiful than anything. Isn't the world a big place?"

"I guess so," said Bill.

"It's *our* place," said Ford. "They can all go back to Earth, but we never will. We're Martians."

"Yeah."

"Did you see, I have hair growing in?" Ford swung his hand up to pat his scalp. "Red like Mars."

"Don't move your arm around, okay? You'll rip the tube out."

"Sorry."

"That's all right. Maybe you should mask up, you know? You could probably use the oxygen."

"Sure . . ." Ford dragged his mask into place

After a while, he smiled and said: "I know who I am."

He murmured to himself for a while, muffled behind the mask. The next time Bill glanced over at him, he was unconscious.

And Bill was all alone.

Billy wasn't there to be yelled at, or blamed for anything. He might never be there again. He couldn't be argued with, he couldn't be shamed or ignored or made to feel anything Bill wanted him to feel. Not if he was dead.

But he'd been like that when he'd been alive, too, hadn't he?

The cold straight road stretched out across the cold flat plain, and there was no mercy out here, no right or wrong, no lies. There was only this giant machine hurtling along, that took all Bill's strength to keep on the road.

If he couldn't do it, he'd die.

Bill realized, with a certain shock, how much of his life he'd wanted an audience. Someone else to be a witness to how scared and angry he was, to agree with him on how bad a father Billy had been.

What had he thought? That someday he'd stand up in some kind of giant courtroom, letting the whole world know how unfair everything had been from the day he'd been born?

Out here, he knew the truth.

There was no vast cosmic court of justice that would turn Billy into the kind of father Bill had wanted him to be. There was no Marswife to swoop down from the dust clouds and guide a lost boy home. The red world didn't care if he sulked; it would casually kill him, if it caught him Outside.

And he had always known it.

*Then what was the point of being angry about it all the time?*

What was the point of white-knuckled fists and a knotted-up stomach if things would never change?

His anger would never force anybody to fix the world for him. But . . .

There were people who tried to fix the world for themselves. Maybe he could fix his world, just the narrow slice of it that was his.

He watched the monitors, watched the wind driving sand across the barren stony plain, the emptiness that he had hated ever since he could remember. What would it take to make him love it, the way Billy or Ford loved it?

He imagined water falling from the sky, bubbling up from under the frozen rock. Maybe it would be blue water. It would splash and steam, the way it did in the bathhouse. Running, gurgling water to drown the dust and irrigate the red sand.

And green would come. He couldn't get a mental image of vizio acres over the whole world, tenting in greenness even up here; that was crazy. But the green might creep out on its own, if there was enough water. Wiry little desert plants at first, maybe, and then . . . Bill tried to remember the names of plants from his lesson plans. Sagebrush, right. Sequoias. Clover. Edelweiss. Apples. A memory came back to him, a nursery rhyme he'd had on his Buke once: *I should like to rise and go, where the golden apples grow* . . .

He blurred his vision a little and saw himself soaring past green rows that went out forever, that arched over and made warm shade and shelter from the wind. Another memory floated up, a picture from a lesson plan, and his dream caught it and slapped it into place: cows grazing in a green meadow, out under a sky full of white clouds, clouds of water, not dust.

And, in the most sheltered places, there would be people. Families. Houses lit warm at night, with the lights winking through the green leaves. Just as he had always imagined. One of them would be his house. He'd live there with his family.

Nobody would give him a house, or a family, or a safe world to live in, of course. Ever. They didn't exist. But . . .

Bill wrapped it all around himself anyway, to keep out the cold and the fear, and he drove on.

At some point—hours or days later, he never knew—his strength gave out and he couldn't hold *Beautiful Evelyn* on the road anymore. She drifted gently to the side, clipping the boulders as she came, and rumbled to a halt just inside Thousand-K Station.

Bill lay along the seat where he had fallen, too tired and in too much pain to move. Ford still sat, propped up in his corner, most of his face hidden by his mask. Bill couldn't tell if he was still alive.

He closed his eyes and went down, and down, into the green rows.

☙ ☙ ☙

He was awakened by thumping on the cab, and shouting, and was bolt upright with his mask on before he had time to realize that he wasn't dreaming. He crawled across the seat and threw the release switches. The hatch swung down, and red light streamed in out of a black night. There stood Old Brick, granddaddy of the Haulers, with his long beard streaming sideways in the gale and at least three other Haulers behind him. His eyes widened behind his mask as he took in Bill and Ford. He reached up and turned up the volume on his psuit.

"CONVOY! WE GOT KIDS HERE! LOOKS LIKE TOWNSEND'S RIG!"

10

Bill was all right after a couple of days, even though he had to have stuff fed into his arm while he slept. He was still foggy-headed when Mother came and sat by his bed, and very gently told him about Billy.

Bill mustn't worry, she said; she would find Billy a warm corner in the *Empress*, with all the food and drink he wanted the rest of his days, and surely Bill would come talk to him sometimes? For Billy was ever so proud of Young Bill, as everyone knew. And perhaps take him on little walks round the Tubes, so he could see Outside now and again? For Billy had so loved the High Road.

❦ ❦ ❦

Ford wasn't all right. He had to have surgery for a ruptured spleen, and almost bled to death once they'd cut his psuit off him.

He still hadn't regained consciousness when Bill, wrapped in an outsize bathrobe, shuffled down to the infirmary's intensive care unit to see him. *See him* was all Bill could do; pale as an egg, Ford lay in the center of a mass of tubes and plastic tenting. The only parts of him that weren't white were his hair, which was growing in red as Martian sand, and the greenish bruise where Bill had punched him in the eye.

Bill sat there staring at the floor tiles, until he became aware that someone else had entered the room. He looked up.

He knew the man in front of him must be Ford's father; his eyes were the same watery blue, and his ears stuck out the same way. He wore patched denim and muddy boots, and a stocking cap pulled down almost low enough to hide the bandage over his left eyebrow. There was a little white stubble along the line of his jaw, like a light frost.

He looked at Ford, and the watery eyes brimmed over with tears. He glanced uncertainly at Bill. He looked down, lined up the toes of his boots against a seam in the tile.

"You'd be that Hauler's boy, then?" he said. "I have to thank you, on behalf of my Blatchford."

"Blatchford," repeated Bill, dumfounded until he realized whom the old man meant. "Oh."

"That woman explained everything to me," said Ford's dad. "Wasn't my Blatchford's fault. Poor boy. Don't blame him for running off scared. Your dad did a good thing, taking him in like that. I'm sorry about your dad."

"Me, too," said Bill. "But For— Blatchford'll be all right."

"I know he will," said Ford's dad, looking yearningly at his son. "He's a strong boy, my Blatchford. Not like his brother. You can raise somebody up his whole life and do your best to teach him what's right, and—and overnight, he can just turn into a stranger on you.

"My Sam did that. I should have seen it coming, him walking out on us. He never was any good, really. A weakling.

"Not like my little Blatchford. Never a word of complaint out of *him*, or whining after vanities. *He* knows who he is. He'll make the Collective proud one day."

Bill swallowed hard. He knew that Ford would never make the Collective proud; Ford would be off on the High Road as soon as he could, in love with the wide horizon, and the old man's angry heart would break again.

The weight of everything that had happened seemed to come crashing down on Bill at once. He couldn't remember when he'd felt so miserable.

"Would you tell me something, sir?" he said. "What does it take to join the MAC?"

"Hm?" Ford's dad turned.

"What do you have to do?"

Ford's dad looked at him speculatively. He cleared his throat. "It isn't what you do. It's what you *are*, young man."

He came and sat down beside Bill, and threw back his shoulders.

"You have to be the kind of person who believes a better world is worth working for. You can't be weak, or afraid, or greedy for things for yourself. You have to know that the only thing that matters is making that better world, and making it for everyone, not just for you.

"You may not even get to see it come into existence, because making the world right is hard work. It'll take all your strength and all your bravery, and maybe you'll be left at the end with nothing but knowing that you did your duty.

"But that'll be enough for you."

His voice was thin and harsh; he sounded as though he was reciting a lecture he'd memorized. But his eyes shone like Ford's had, when Ford had looked out on the open sky for the first time.

"Well—I'm going to study agriculture," said Bill. "And I thought, maybe, when I pass my levels, I'd like to join the MAC. I want that world you talk about. It's all I've ever wanted."

"Good on you, son," said Ford's dad, nodding solemnly. "You study hard, and I'm sure you'd be welcome to join us. You're the sort of young man we need in the MAC. And it does my heart good to know my Blatchford's got a friend like you. Gives me hope for the future, to think we'll have two heroes like you working in our cause!"

He shook Bill's hand, and then the nurse looked in at them and said that visiting hours were over. Ford's dad went away, down the hill. Bill walked slowly back to his room.

He didn't climb back into bed. He sat down in a chair in the corner, and looked out through Settlement Dome at the cold red desert, at the far double line of boulders where the High Road ran off into places Billy would never see again. He began to cry, silently, tears burning as they ran down his face.

He didn't know whether he was crying for Billy, or for Ford's dad.

The world was ending. The world was beginning.

# DERELICT

## by Geoffrey A. Landis

At one time or another, every kid has been told to stay away from dangerous places, from that rotting old pier on the lake to that spooky old abandoned house to the high railroad trestle over the river—and generations of kids have ignored those stern admonishments and headed *right for* the danger spot, drawn like iron filings to a magnet by the lure of the forbidden. The kids who live in the orbital space-colonies of the future, though, will have to go a lot further for an illicit thrill, and face dangers considerably worse than a railroad bridge when they get there.

A physicist who works for NASA, and who has recently been working on the Martian Lander program, Geoffrey A. Landis is a frequent contributor to *Analog* and to *Asimov's Science Fiction*, and has also sold stories to markets such as *Interzone*, *Amazing*, and *Pulphouse*. Landis is not a prolific writer—by the high-production standards of the genre—but he *is* popular. His story "A Walk in the Sun," won him a Hugo Award in 1992, his story "Ripples in the Dirac Sea" won him a Nebula Award in 1990, and his story "Elemental" was on the Final Hugo Ballot in 1985. His first book was the collection *Myths, Legends, and True History* and in 2002 he published his first novel, *Mars Crossing*. He lives with his wife, writer Mary Turzillo, in Brook Park, Ohio.

WHEN IT WAS built, it had been the largest object ever made by human beings, a small city in space. They named it for a hero, the son of a god: Hercules. It was a wheel a kilometer across, with mirrors angling sunlight through enormous transparent panes set in the bright aluminum.

Hercules had been a bubble of Earth floating in space, only

better—utopia, or as close to utopia as human beings had ever dared approach. Fifty thousand people lived inside it. A handful of them had a secret, and perhaps that secret made them a little smug, a little self-satisfied and swaggering. But most of the people living in Hercules knew nothing about secrets.

The end came with, perhaps, a few seconds warning. The first impact, a particle no larger than a coin, hit at nearly orbital velocity, seventeen thousand miles an hour. At that speed a particle does not impact so much as it explodes. The noise was like a grenade going off, a blue-white fireball that was too bright to look at.

On the kilometer-wide colony, such an impact was like a gnat attacking an elephant. The hole was the size of a fist: a minor leak, which would be patched in a day or two. A few people, in the wide parks down at the outermost spin levels, looked across the wheel toward the impact, a trail of fire piercing upwards toward the metal sky.

And then, all at once, the real firestorm started. A thousand impacts. A million, all at once.

In five minutes, fifty thousand people died.

That was long ago.

۞ ۞ ۞

On the wheels and the loops and grape-clusters that swarm in thousands of orbits around the Earth, lives are regulated, and the kids—us—have strict limits on freedom. Space is hard, cold, and unforgiving.

But Malina colony had been founded on principles of freedom and intellectual daring, and it was the guiding ethos of our founders that everyone should have as much liberty as they could handle, even children. So we kids learned to take as much advantage of that as we dared. It was, after all, a way to learn common sense—the hard way to learn, the adults told us. But the teachers always said that nobody really learns how to do something right until they've learned it by trying all the wrong ways first. Each of us has to learn things our own way. So they gave us a certain amount of freedom, to allow us to learn.

Oh, we had rules, of course, rules and rules on rules, all to be memorized and quizzed on at any moment without warning. Every time you put on a space suit, each and every item in the fifty-three point vacuum safety check had to be acknowledged aloud by your buddy, for example. And if one of the grown-ups catches you trying to slide by some item on the list without checking it! Well! That would lose you a bit of freedom, for sure. Get you iced—earn you a month of staying inside, minimum, and another six months of only going outside under supervision, and being watched pretty darn closely every time, too. And when you protest, "Hey, I know what I'm doing," you would only get a reply of "Evidently not, young man. I think you'd best be watched, until you prove you do." And your back talk would probably get you a snap quiz on safety regulations.

You can ask me, I've tried it.

But to a moderate extent, we were trusted; at least, trusted up to as far as we could push it.

All of which is a roundabout way to explain how it was that me and Kibbie came to be floating in vac, spinning lazily around each other (we were connected to each other by a tether, of course—freedom doesn't extend as far as ignoring safety rules), not doing anything but gazing out at the immensity of it all, the Earth and the habitat and the black velvet sky, with the moon a crescent way off in the distance, clear and cold and gray.

Me and Kibbie, whenever we could steal some free time, would always use it to go vac, even if there was no reason for it, just because we could. That day we had a couple of hours free from chores, and since the rest of the gang wasn't free, I grabbed Kibbie aside, and said, "Hey, Kib man, nobody will miss us, let's go vac a while, spend some time with the stars."

"I'm with ya, Dylan."

So we did, because we could.

I loved to go vac. I don't think Kibbie or Barb really did, at least, not like I did. It was a way to get away from the others, and just stare at the universe.

Our cluster was Kibbie and Barb and me, Dylan. The two

Teniman kids, Nipper and Gray, tagged along with us as well most days, although they were a year younger, but the real cluster was the three of us, me and Kibbie and Barb. We were a constellation of three, and we tramped around and poked into every corner of the habitat, and, as a general rule, got into about as much trouble as we could get, without actually getting locked away or kicked off the habitat.

Have I told you about our habitat yet?

Malina habitat was circular, more or less, an immense ring of irregular bubbles strung out along a hexagonal aluminum truss that formed its external skeleton. Each bubble along the circular spine was a different size and shape, forty-seven of them, some neat spheres, some elongated like sausages, some complicated bulging shapes like half-melted glass beads. Each double-walled bubble interconnected with two on either side. Two long tubes, like hoses, circling the habitat. One was on the inside— "above"—which we called the infinite corridor. The infinite corridor threaded through the center of the structural truss like a spinal cord through vertebrae. That one was for humans. The second one was on the outside—below. It was a backup corridor for mechanical transport, in case of a problem, but was mostly unused, except for storage of minor equipment, and maintenance.

All that, and I haven't yet mentioned the solar arrays, sticking out like dark purple blades in all directions, or that in the middle, the exact center of the ring, is a fuzzy white puffball, to all appearances like an Earth cloud (not that I've ever seen an Earth cloud—not from below, anyway), so white as to be almost too dazzling to look at. The puffball collected and diffused and reflected the sun, so that no matter what the orientation of the habitat, light gets evenly reflected to the habitats and greenhouses, so the people and the plants alike had sunlight to enjoy.

It all sounds tiny and claustrophobic when I describe it, but if it does, that's only because I haven't described it very well. If you're from down below, I don't think you've ever quite caught on just how huge the habitats are. Malina was three kilometers in diameter; that makes the circumference just over ten kilometers—

six miles. You can walk the whole way around, on the infinite corridor, but it would take hours, and the largest of the individual bubbles were each nearly a kilometer in diameter themselves. You may not be able to comprehend just how big a one-kilometer bubble is, but it is amazingly huge; well over a hundred thousand people lived in it, and it wasn't crowded at all.

Malina has parks and open space too; it wasn't just people packed in warrens like the cages we use to raise rabbits or cuy for protein. But on the outside, it looked like a lumpy necklace of glass beads.

We had hooked a tether onto the station and swung it around until we could get enough of a swing to let go with exactly enough speed to kill Malina's spin.

That might need some explaining. Malina colony spins to give us the feeling of gravity. Not very fast—one revolution in a hundred seconds exactly, you can use it for a chronometer if you like—but that gives us enough gravity to keep our bones from dissolving away from lack of gee. So if we just dropped off into vac, we'd still be moving at a hundred meters a second, right? So to just float, we have to kill that speed.

After coasting away, we killed our spinward momentum with a quick burst from our suit-thrusters, and then just drifted slowly away.

The Earth is ever changing, and fascinating in its way, with its brilliant blues and browns and greens and its swirling spirals of clouds, but Malina was mostly what we were looking at, Kibbie and me, when we floated vac. A trillion trillion miles of infinite space in all directions, and yet we always look first toward our home. Malina was a thrown-together string of mismatched parts, and yet, in its complexity and unexpected details, Malina habitat was a staggering work of sculpture, a human artifact of stunning beauty.

As Malina rotates, it constantly shifts its aspect, always showing a new face, something new to see. The sunward side was dazzlingly brilliant, with bits of metal and facets and windows intermittently catching the sun and glinting sparks. The shadowed side, illuminated only by Earthlight, was lit a spooky, ghostly blue, so dim that it was almost just the memory of color. Crossing from rim to rim were the tension wires, so thin as to be invisible, but strung with strobe lights and radar reflectors to keep them from having a taxi or a transport accidentally try to cross the gap. As it slowly rotated, the perspective would constantly shift, the shadows moving around the habitat bubbles and revealing and then concealing details, conduits, airlocks, antennas, transport tubes, radiators.

So we stared, Kibbie and I, just staring at the ever-altering aspects of the miniature world we lived in.

I had the earphones in my helmet playing me some background music. I like something deep and mysterious while I float, and I'd messed around with the settings that the computer used to construct music for me until I found something that made deep and mysterious rumbles, like voices chanting a language nobody had ever heard before. It flowed around and through my brain, in a tone so low you could feel it more than you heard it.

The computer making my music isn't an artificial intelligence, only a routine just smart enough to compose tunes in real-time. We don't trust AIs here, not very much, not since the disaster of 2093. Never allow a machine to make a life-or-death decision for you, that's what Mr. Cubertou says.

In the distance, we could see other orbital habitats, mostly just points of light that moved quickly across the sky, with occasional bright flashes as the sunlight catches on a mirrored facet or a solar array. Space traffic control kept them all carefully choreographed. One degree behind us in orbit, von Kármán habitat was stationary, a point of light; Tsien habitat, a degree ahead of us was invisible. Tsien and von Kármán habitats were always there, in the same place, but it was a game to spot the others, and guess which ones they were. "Ankara and Adara," I said, pointing cross-orbit at two speckles of slowly drifting light.

"Ah, those are easy," Kibbie said. The Turkish habitats were nearly co-orbital with us, at a slightly different eccentricity to keep them away from a collision. He pointed toward the limb of the Earth. "New Trenton. That's one you don't see very often."

The speck of light was small, but moving fast. I checked the time in my heads-up display and quickly calculated to myself. Yes, New Trenton indeed. The computer could have identified it for me, of course, but that would be cheating. I was silent for a few minutes, looking intently for something to top him with, and caught a lucky glimpse of a speck of dark against a cloud, directly between us and the Earth. I had to look twice to make sure I'd really seen it.

"Look. Devi Station. There, see it?"

"No, where?" Kibbie said, then, "Shoot, yes, got it. Wow, how'd you spot that one? Can't be Devi, though. Devi's over the horizon by now."

"The hell you say. If it's not Devi, who do you say it is?" I'd said Devi too quickly; not thinking—it was almost in the right place—but Kibbie was right, curse him. Devi wouldn't be visible now. Exactly 1,123 functioning habitats orbited the Earth in hundreds of different orbits, each one with ten thousand or more inhabitants, and I ran through the list in my mind, trying to think of which this one could be, if it wasn't Devi colony.

Kibbie was silent for a minute, and we watched the little dark speck move across the globe. It was only visible when it was in front of clouds. It was just slightly lower than us, and hence moving a little bit faster. In a minute of traverse it moved across the full width of the Earth, and then, entering the shadow, suddenly winked out.

We both stared, trying to spot the docking strobes, staring until darkness floated in front of darkness in our eyes, but we saw nothing.

"Gotcha," Kibbie said. "Hercules. It has to be Hercules."

Hercules. The ghost colony. Of course it was. No wonder I hadn't thought of it; I'd been running through the list of functioning colonies, and nobody lived on Hercules colony. Nobody had lived there for a very long time.

Without thinking, I said. "We're going there, you know."

"Yeah?" Kibbie said. "We are?"

And, right then, I knew it. It would take some planning, but we were going. Oh yes, oh yes, of course we were. "We are," I said.

❦ ❦ ❦

"Absolutely we're going," Barb said, when Kibbie and I got back. She got that blank look for a moment. "Best time will be in six weeks."

You could never beat Barb in the game of spotting habitats; she always knew exactly where to look. Kibbie was my best friend—we'd been almost like brothers when we were kids—but Barb was more than a friend; she was the orbital calculation goddess.

We were sitting in the crow's nest. This was the place we met, a spot in the big bubble that Kibbie and I had found back when we were kids; an inside corner where two odd-shaped buildings came together. It was completely hidden out of view and yet right next to anywhere you wanted to go.

It was a little awkward that Barb wanted to go. One of the reasons I wanted to go to an abandoned habitat was one I didn't quite want to share with a girl. But, hell! I never thought of Barb as a girl anyway; she was just in my cluster. We hovered around everywhere together. Of course she'd be going, how could it be any way else?

And anyway, she was the orbital mechanics goddess.

So Barb drew orbits on a plan for us, to show us what she'd already worked out in her head. "Orbits precess," Barb said. "An orbit is a living thing, varying slowly with time." It was all review material. We'd plotted orbits in class a year ago, and I already knew about precession. The orbital plane of a habitat precesses around the Earth's pole in a slow cycle, like the spin axis of an electron precessing in a magnetic field. So the orbit is always changing.

But I knew I had to let Barb explain it her way, to get to the part where we planned trajectories, so I decided not to daydream too much, and tried to pay attention.

The Malina colony maintenance crew corrects our orbit from time to time, of course—space traffic control makes sure of that—but the Hercules orbit is unmaintained, so it's been drifting for a long time. As Barb explained, the eccentricity and even the orbital inclination mutate slowly, distorted by the gravitational perturbations of the sun and moon.

"In a very slow cycle—four years, more or less—the apogee of the Hercules orbit stretches out enough that the Hercules orbit nearly touches the orbit of Malina habitat," Barb said, drawing the orbit. "So, for a period of a few weeks, it would be easy to transfer from the one habitat's orbit to the other. Not much delta-V needed."

"You could do it by just jumping?" I said.

Barb looked at me, smiled, and nodded.

"Man," Kibbie said, "what do you think's gonna happen to us if we get caught?"

Barb and I looked at each other.

"We'll lose vac privilege," I said. "Grounded for sure."

"Lose vac privileges?" Barb said. "That'll be the least of it. We won't even be allowed to *look* at a suit for, like, a thousand years."

"Look at a suit?" I said. "We won't be allowed in the same *room* as a suit for like, at least a million years."

"Decommissioned," Barb said.

"The big D," I said. "We'll be iced."

"Lucky if we're not dropped right down to Earth," she said.

We looked at each other, and then said, in perfect chorus, "So we're not going to get caught."

And then we laughed like idiots. After a while, Kibbie joined in.

Me and Barb and Kibbie worked at putting the plan together over the next few weeks. We had to keep it secret from the adults, of course. They'd never explicitly told us that we couldn't go explore an abandoned colony, but there are some things that you just already know the answer would be no. And we didn't want the whole cohort going along as a field trip, with proctors and lectures and one kid in every five designated to be the safety-warden. This was going to be just us. There was one thing I wanted to collect that the adults would definitely just have an embolism if I mentioned; something that had to do with some future plans of mine I wasn't quite ready to share yet. A little sample of something we called weed.

It was Barb who did the calculations, mostly. She only used the computer to confirm what she'd already worked out in her head.

Six weeks. We would have plenty of time for planning.

But, in the meantime, we had school.

۞  ۞  ۞

Kibbie and Barb and I were all in the same cohort, a group of four hundred kids all about the same age, who did schooling and work assignments as a group. Whenever we could, we tried to arrange it so that when the cohort broke up into teams for projects, we were on the same team, but the teachers were on to us, and it was getting to be almost impossible to do that. We were in the middle of a project to build a robotic inspection drone (which may sound easy to you, but we had to do it from scratch), and I'd been assigned to the vision team, while Barb and Kibbie were together on the propulsion team.

I was building the little imaging array, programming a micromanipulator to paint dots of phosphorus onto a silicon wafer, when a teacher came up to watch. I was swaying to some music while I worked. The computer system aimed the music in a narrow beam directly to my ears, so only I could hear it.

It was old man Cubertou. I liked him. He was cool, as teachers go, but it made me nervous to have him looking at me. "Why do we have to build these by hand, anyway?" I asked him.

The routine automatically fades down the music whenever somebody talks, sliding the music into background so that the voice is clear, and it's like the music is a perfectly natural accompaniment to the voice.

"They mass-produce focal-plane arrays, like, a million at a time," I said. "And billion-pixel arrays too, not a lousy two hundred like the ones you're having me make."

"You are going to spend your next hundred years, if you are lucky and cautious, trusting your life to technology," Cubertou said. "I'd think you would want to know how it works."

"Well, yeah, but I can read up on how it works, if I want to know. I don't have to build one."

Cubertou shook his head. "You learn with your hands, not with your head." He rubbed my hair. "Certainly, not with a thick skull like yours."

I was intensely annoyed at his treating me like a child, but didn't want to admit it. "Well, since when am I going to trust my life to a focal plane array?"

He didn't answer the question, just said, "Have you thought about your selection yet?"

"Not yet." Which was a lie, of course, since I was thinking about it all the time. We all were. Next year our cohort would be done with the general knowledge, and we each had to pick three specialties to study. It was possible to change specialties, if you decided you didn't like what you'd picked—but it would be pretty unusual. Our lives were about to be narrowed down from a million million possibilities to just three, and I wasn't sure I liked that.

"If you need to talk . . ." Cubertou said, and then, after a moment, he wandered off.

Kibbie came up and watched Cubertou's back. "What was he on about?" he asked.

"Pushing on me about my selection."

"Oh." Kibbie said. "You have any good ideas yet?"

"Nope."

"Me neither." He squeezed his eye shut. "One thing I know; I'm not going to be a fish nanny." Kibbie's mother and father both were fish farmers—aquaculturalists, as the official word was. Real life, that meant they worked in dirty water, raising carp and tilapia that lived in waste water and turned refuse into protein. It was a slimy job. There were always openings in aquaculture, but I could see that he might want anything else but.

I'd better think of something, or else somebody else would decide for me, and I could end up in aquaculture myself.

"But forget about that," he said. "I don't want to think about it for a while. How about our other project? Hercules?"

We agreed to meet at the library after classes, do some more work on the Hercules venture.

Kibbie was the crazy one. He was the one who'd figured that if you ran down the infinite corridor counter-spinwise, as fast as you could go, you would get noticeably lighter. If you could run fast enough, you ought to actually float, we thought, but for all that we tried, we never managed. Much later, I figured that we would have had to run about two hundred miles an hour to cancel out the habitat's rotation and the centrifugal gravity, but Kibbie and me certainly raced ourselves dizzy trying.

Before we went to the library, I saw Leeila talking with a couple of her friends, and I wandered away from Kibbie to go bother her for a while. I walked up behind her and put a hand lightly on her shoulder.

"Hey, Leeila," I said.

She leaned back slightly against my hand. "Hey, Dylan," she said. Sina, Darty, and Nan, the friends she was hovering around with, acknowledged me with slight nods.

I stood there with my hand on her shoulder, feeling the warmth of her flesh though the jumper, not really knowing what to say. The girls she was with had suddenly become silent, which didn't help any. "What are you up to?" I asked.

"Not much," Leeila said. "Talking."

"Oh," I said. "Guess I shouldn't disturb you."

"You're not disturbing us," she said.

"Well, I'm heading for the library."

"Sure," she said. "With your cluster."

"Yeah," I said. I'd never really introduced her to Kibbie and Barb and the two Teniman kids who sometimes stuck around with us, but she knew well enough who my cluster was; I guess everybody in the cohort pretty much knew, just like I knew that Sina, Darty, and Nan, and a couple of other girls I didn't know very well were hers. Everybody has their cluster. Clusters grow and shrink and change, but me and Barb and Kibbie had always been a cluster, as long as I could remember. It was hard to imagine that we would grow up and drift apart, making new clusters based on our work and our families.

I knew that eight pairs of eyes were watching me as I walked away. I focused on walking gracefully, swinging my arms a little, and was concentrating on walking so hard I almost ran right into a structural column. I tried to ignore the giggling. It was too far away for me to actually hear, but I knew it was there.

I always liked the library. I liked it even if I just closed my eyes and smelled.

Visitors have remarked with distaste on the closed atmosphere of our habitat, where every molecule of air has circulated a thousand times. But it seems to me that it would be very disconcerting to be in a place where you couldn't smell the air. You could blindfold any one of us and put us down anywhere on Malina, and we could tell right where we were on the habitat by how it smelled. The greenhouse modules had their smells of chemicals and water and chlorophyll, the machine bays the more subtle scents of ozone and silicone oil, the dormitories the odors of humanity. The library had a complicated smell mixed of paper and people and electronics and recirculated air. It actually did have some books—real, physical books; words printed on sheets of paper—but mostly it was a quiet place for students to study, with fast-bandwidth connections to the electronic databases. Barb was already waiting there for Kibbie and me.

Barb, as usual, went directly to the point. "It's really weird," she said. "There's kilotons of information about the Hercules disaster here, but no details. Nothing ever quite says just exactly what happened."

"So?" Kibbie said. "I know what happened. It was an impact event, right? I mean, that was before space traffic control, right? All the habitats and construction bots and trailers and ore-freighters and old fuel tanks, and who knows what all stuff. Nobody was shepherding all that junk."

"That's why we have space traffic control now," I said. "We learned that in class. One chunk of steel at twenty thousand miles per hour can ruin your whole day." That was an expression Mr. Cubertou had used in the unit we did on hazards of orbital environments. It showed how old-fashioned he was, talking about miles per hour instead of meters per second.

"Yeah," said Barb, slowly. "But exactly what hit it? Nobody quite mentions it."

"What kind of habitat was it, anyway?" Kibbie asked. "Any of your sources say? Refugees?"

"Or idealists, I'll bet," I said. Many of the habitats from way back then had housed refugees. Earth had a lot of wars, and people were always kicking other people off of one chunk of desert or another. That's a problem with planets; you can't just build more land when you want to. It's hard to see how anybody would want to live on a planet. Back in those days, a lot of the old habitats were full of idealists and dissidents, people who didn't like the governments and rules of Earth, thinking that—hah!—space would be a place of fewer rules, instead of more. A few were even prison habitats. Today, the new habitats were capitalist—places for people going into the space mining, manufacturing, and service economy, staging areas for asteroid mining, and manufacturing and transport nodes for industrial production. But not back then—it took a while for the mining economy to take off.

"Oh, I did find that out," Barb said. "It was an old nation-state habitat. You know, patriotism? We learned about that in school."

"Wow, weird," I said. I knew about nations; they still even had them on Earth, although I couldn't see why. The idea sounded so strange to me that I just couldn't imagine it. Millions of people—sometimes billions—so many that most people didn't know people who knew each other? How odd.

"Which nation was it?" Kibbie asked.

"One of the old books said, but I don't remember," Barb

said. "Austrians. Or Australians. Armenians, maybe? I think it was something with an A. Does it matter?"

"Nah, doesn't make any real difference," Kibbie said. "One nation is just like another. It hardly matters—they're dead now anyway." Kibbie bounced in his seat as he spoke.

Did I describe us yet? I don't think so. Kibbie was squat and powerfully built, with hair so dark and curly his head looked like a sponge. He was sitting there, constantly moving, one moment his legs up over the chair in front of him, the next moment bouncing to internal music.

Unlike Kibbie, I'm perfectly average—average height, average weight, average-looking face and hair. So boring that nobody could even pick me out in a crowd of two.

I hate being average.

Barb has long legs and an awkward way of moving that seems as if she hasn't quite grown into her body and is about to trip over her own feet. But when she gets into low gravity, she moves like a dancer. She has hair that's some undetermined color, right on that dividing line where some people say it's brown, and others are certain it's blonde. It's straight, and she keeps it cut to a length where, when she goes into micro-gee, it flies straight out from her head, like a sea anemone, waving in each puff from the circulation fans. I want to go up and run my hands through it, just to feel the way it moves under my fingers, but of course I don't.

Barb's my best friend, not my girlfriend. I don't have a girlfriend.

I'd like to change that.

⊕ ⊕ ⊕

We were studying antique technologies in science the next day, and the teacher—Mr. Cubertou again—had just gotten to explaining Otto cycle engines before the class got released. We would be building them the next week, I bet. "I got it," Kibbie said, as we headed out. "Suck, squeeze, bang, blow." He counted it out on his fingers. "That's not a technology, Dylan, that's my new philosophy of life."

I cracked up. "I'm with you," I said, although, to be truthful, my knowledge of the subtleties of human relations was mostly theoretical. So was his, I'm pretty sure.

We met Barb coming out of her last lecture, and I decided I'd better change the subject.

"Which way are you thinking to go next year?" I asked Barb. "What do you figure you'll select?" I didn't need to ask; I just wanted some reassurance.

"I've got a couple of ideas," she said, "but haven't picked one."

"Really? I thought you were in for pilot." It surprised me that she was still uncertain. With her lightning ability to calculate orbits, being a pilot was the obvious choice. And she'd be great at it.

"I don't know, don't know," she sang. "Maybe, maybe not. There are so many choices. You?"

I scuffed the deck with a foot. "Dunno either."

Kibbie said, "Anything but fish nanny for me."

"Anything?" I asked. "Sure. How about oxygen plant monitor." That was the lowest job I could think of, overseeing the algae that turn carbon dioxide into oxygen in their endless transparent spaghetti tubes. A job for somebody with no ambition.

Kibbie shrugged. "Suits me," he said. "Easy work, not a lot of tension. Might be nice."

I stared at him. "You're joking. Algae monitor? You?"

He cracked a grin. "Of course I'm joking. I don't know, I'm still thinking about it. I like vacuum welding. Building stuff."

Yeah, that was something Kibbie was good at. I could see him as a vacuum welder.

"But that could get boring too, I guess," he said. "I want some adventure, you know it? Maybe I'll pick planetary geophysics as a specialty, so I can go be an ammonia prospector for the outer moon expeditions. That would be cool."

"You gotta like being lonely if you want to do icy moon expeditions," Barb said. "I don't think I could take the outer moons."

"Yeah," I said. "It's way out there."

"Maybe I should go for medicine," Barb said, as if she hadn't heard Kibbie. "You can use that anywhere."

"Anywhere?" I said. "You thinking of emigrating to another hab?"

Barb looked at the deck. "I don't know. Maybe," she said.

"I couldn't even think of leaving Malina," I said.

I was suddenly sucking vacuum at the thought of Barb and Kibbie leaving. I didn't know what I wanted. Sometimes Malina seemed so tiny, so claustrophobic; I hated all the adults and their endless rules. But I couldn't think of leaving it, and everybody I knew.

I guess that didn't matter to Barb, though. Barb was heartless. It was good that I learned that about her. She was the ice princess, ruthless and unsentimental.

"I want to be an explorer," I blurted. It didn't make any sense, even to me. Hadn't I just said I never wanted to leave Malina? But suddenly Malina seemed so tiny. So, I don't know, *safe*.

I didn't know what I wanted.

"Yeah? An explorer?" Barb said. "You just said you weren't going to leave Malina. What are you going to explore?"

"We're starting with Hercules," Kibbie said. "You coming?"

"You bet your oxygen I am," Barb said, and suddenly everything was cool, and it was clear we were a cluster again.

☙ ☙ ☙

Hercules haunted my dreams, my nightmares.

Hercules had been a stressed-shell colony, one of the first, interior tension cables holding it together like a suspension bridge, with parks and tiny groves of forest on an outermost level, and habitats and offices and manufacturing levels suspended above, in the lower gravity regions. I could see it vividly. All at once the air inside the colony must have come alive with lines of fire. Cables pinged and then snapped, and the broken cables whizzed through the air, singing like whips, slashing aluminum structures into ribbons of twisted metal. Stressed panels ripped, releasing air that froze as it boiled off into vacuum. The lakes in the outermost park levels rose up in waterspouts as the pressure suddenly dropped, serpents of water writhing in crazy agony, and then there was fire, real fire, as million-liter tanks of rocket propellant were ripped open and the spilled fuel burst into flame, ignited by sparks from meteor trails.

The fire didn't last long. With the outer panels breached, the shell blew apart, exploding into shards like a punctured balloon.

Fifty thousand people had lived in Hercules.

I will skip past our weeks of planning, not that it wasn't important, but without showing all the diagrams and calculations, which would certainly bore you, it wouldn't make much sense. Space suits have rocket packs, but they are only designed for jetting around the outside of the habitat, and if we used up a kilometer per second of backpack fuel going out to Hercules and getting back, it would have been noticed. Our first plan had been to do a Tarzan-style swing over to the colony, using a super-strength tether as a whip to give us the velocity to change orbits. That was a dangerous move, one that would certainly get us iced if we got caught, no matter what our target might be. But the problem was that the ruined colony of Hercules was on the radar watch—nothing that big was allowed to go unwatched, and the swing trajectory was too long; there was no way space traffic wouldn't see us going, and ask who we were, and alert our parents.

"There's no way to do it in our suits alone," Barb said, frustrated. "I've looked and looked for a way, but it doesn't work, not without too high a risk of getting caught."

"So how do we do it," I asked her.

"We have to sneak a ride on an oat-boat."

Oat-boat was the nickname everybody used for orbital transfer boats, the small spaceships used for ship-to-colony transfers. They were "oat-boats" partly because that was easier to say than orbital transfer ship, and partly because what they shipped from one colony to another was very often food. The orbit-to-orbit run, Barb pointed out, dropped in to a slightly lower orbit—one that, if we picked it right, would just kiss the Hercules habitat's orbit. On the right boat, we could drop free with almost zero velocity relative to Hercules. The delta-V we'd need would be small enough that we could use our suits to do the final maneuvering, and we could swing back according to our original idea.

"An oat-boat?" said Kibbie. "Not a problem. I know a guy."

The guy Kibbie knew was a friend of his older brother, a guy named Rip. Rip, as Kibbie told us, was apprenticed as a hand on an inter-colony freighter, and didn't have a problem if we decided to sneak on board right before a colony-to-colony run. We all agreed that this would be a better plan.

And when we met him to check the plan, Rip mentioned that he'd been to Hercules.

"Really?" I asked, suddenly interested. "When?"

"Oh, years ago. When we were kids."

"You've been there? Yourself?" I'd known that some of the more daredevil kids in previous cohorts had gone over to the abandoned habitats, but I hadn't met somebody who'd done it.

"Oh, yeah." At my look of astonishment, he said, "See, in our cohort—we were what, four years ahead of you? That was the thing to do. Hit the old wrecked hab, paint it up a little. It was macho, you know that word? And there's a certain thing there, you know of it, right? Weed. We used to call it chinga weed." He laughed. "It grows in vacuum, anywhere that there's enough contamination for it to scavenge."

A thrill ran through me. Yeah, I knew about the weed.

"So what's it like? Hercules, I mean."

He paused. "You'll see."

"And—do you know? What happened to it, anyway? We couldn't figure that out from the records."

Rip shook his head. "Look around. Maybe you'll find out."

The weed was my other objective, the one I'd told Kibbie about but not Barb. Going to the ruined habitat and seeing it close up, understanding firsthand what had happened, that was the main part of it. The adults always said that you can never understand something just by reading or being told about it, and we had been told about disasters that could happen to orbital habitats for the last fourteen years. I wanted to see it. Hercules had been an old habitat, a first-generation colony, but I wanted to see it for myself, feel the bent and shattered metal under my gloved fingers, maybe even find something that might explain the mystery of exactly what had happened to it.

But weed was my second goal. It had an official name, *salvia vacui*—literally sage that grows in the void—but the kids had a cruder name for it.

If you chewed on it, it made you relaxed, happy. Or so the gossip went; I'd never had any. I'd never even seen it. It had some kind of drug in it, I guess, but mild enough that you wouldn't lose your judgment and open a valve to vacuum or forget to do your suit check. The older kids called it chinga weed, because the story was that if you shared some of the weed with a girl you liked, and you both chewed some, then she'd be so relaxed and happy that you'd be able to get some time in. It was—or I'd heard the older kids say it was—a surefire way to score.

I couldn't quite picture how it went. What did you do, come up to a girl and say, let's go away alone somewhere, see, I have some of this weed, let's chew it? Surely they'd know what you were thinking about, they must know the same stories. I couldn't ever see Barb doing that. When I tried to picture Leeila, it was a little easier, but the picture was still a little fuzzy in the details.

But I wanted to find some of the weed anyway.

So that was it, my dirty secret. Exploration, sure, that's mostly why I wanted to go.

But the weed, well, that was part of it, too.

☙ ☙ ☙

We did our planning in bits and chunks of time, between our schooling and our work rotations. Schooling had finished lectures for the term and was a series of overlapping projects. Form teams and build a closed life-support pod. List five economic factors that caused the Anteros asteroid rebellion to fail. Form teams and debate your reasons. Could the rebels have known that it would fail? Form teams to debate both sides of the question.

A lot of team building.

Outside the formal schooling, we had our jobs, and that was schooling, too. They rotated us kids through every position in colony maintenance and life support. This was partly so we would have some experience in different roles, to help us when we made our selections, and partly so that we would all have the knowledge and training to be able to fill in a position without warning in an emergency. But mostly, though, we were rotated through the crud jobs, the icky work nobody else wanted to do, and we kids were all a hundred percent certain that the main reason we rotated through was because the adults had the power to force us to do the crud work so that they wouldn't have to.

That was our big worry, the X-for-unknown factor in our planning. Assignments hadn't been announced for the next work cycle yet. I might be assigned, say, to external maintenance. That was a job that was just like breadfruit pudding to me, one I'd grovel and beg to get in any other cycle, but one where the work crew had to be on call 24 hours, available on twenty minutes notice to fix a problem for the whole duration of the twenty-day shift. No way I'd be able to sneak away until after Hercules was receding far into the distance.

So Barb, Kibbie, and I were all watching the postings nervously.

Waiting for assignments was sort of a social ritual. All the kids hung around, waiting to hear what they drew, ready to swap jobs with their friends. You could trade off your assignments with another kid as long as the authorities were willing to believe that you were still getting a full education in all the jobs. If you found somebody else willing to take your assignment, that is. But there was always a lot of swapping, as kids tried to get jobs they liked better, or to switch to work alongside some other kids in whatever cluster they hovered around with.

I saw Leeila off in the distance, waiting with Sina and Darty for the assignments to be announced, and I resolved that I would go over and talk to her, just as soon as we found out what assignments the three of us were going to get. I wasn't sure, but I thought maybe she had smiled when she saw me looking in her direction. Had she really smiled at me? I convinced myself she did.

Barb got her assignment first.

"Crud!" she said. "I got put on slime patrol! I can't believe it! I did that last year! I can't believe I got it again!"

A moment later, "No!" Kibbie said. "I got slime, too! I don't get it! Is this punishment, you think?"

That was unlikely, I knew. The jobs were assigned at random, and if there was any hint that jobs went to certain people for any reason, there would be a general rebellion in the whole colony. When you got a crud job, the only thing that kept you at it was the thought that it was nothing personal, and you would be off the list for that particular job for a year. Next rotation you'd be at something else.

Slime patrol meant inspecting the niches and inside corners and pipe-bays of the colony, looking for the slime that accumulates in all of the cooler areas where atmospheric water might condense out. It was a never-ending task. Green slime, brown slime, biofilm—all sorts of nasty stuff would grow, if you didn't keep everything inspected and cleaned regularly. The worst of the stuff looked like drips of half-congealed snot, and you had to wear a mask and take a sample of it to bio, so they could check it and verify that it wasn't a biohazard.

"Water filtration duty," I said, a moment later, when I got my assignment. "That's not so bad." And then I thought for a moment, and said, "Wait a minute—you're on slime patrol? That's perfect!"

"What do you mean, perfect?" Kibbie said. "If you think it's perfect, you're welcome to swap with me. I'll take water filtration over slime any day."

"No, I'm going to swap with somebody else," I said. "Look. Here's the way it is. With slime patrol, you have the whole twenty-day shift to cover the territory. As long as you inspect everything on the list, you're fine. You don't have a schedule, and they don't care when you do it, just as long as it gets done."

"So it's perfect for us," Barb said. "Of course. It gives us the free time to do the Hercules jaunt, just as long as we make up the inspection time sometime." She paused for a moment. "So, you going to swap?"

"I'm not thrilled about it," I said. Water filtration was a job that kept pretty strict hours. "But, unless you have another idea?" I was looking at the listings. I couldn't believe I was about to swap a perfectly okay job for a crud job like slime patrol. "Jaime Ibarra," I said. "Looks like he got slime, too. He'll trade me, I'll bet."

☙ ☙ ☙

And then the day came. We had all the stuff we'd gathered, our suits had full air packs and emergency packs, we had checked and double-checked and triple-checked everything.

Old Chris, the outside-safety warden for B-4 (the bubble in Malina I lived in—did I mention it?) walked in as I was checking my gear. "What are you up to, young man?"

"Just giving my suit a safety check. Looks like it might need refurb."

"Guess I can't fault you for good safety habits. Could save your life someday. Any particular reason?" He paused. "I couldn't help but notice that your friend Kibbie logged his suit out for refurbishment just half an hour ago."

"Yeah," I said, "well, yeah, we both use them a lot, you know? I bet his needs it too."

"You wouldn't be, say, thinking about going over to the old Hercules colony, would you? No, don't answer that—I'd hate to have you start lying. I guess every kid has to do it once. We tell 'em it's dangerous, but they don't care. Makes it seem more exciting, hah. Not much excitement to waiting for your air to bleed out, I can tell you. Had it happen once. Not quite fun, no sir, not at all."

I had heard the warnings a dozen times already. "You wouldn't, ah, tell Dad you saw me here, would you?"

"Talk to your father? Why should I? What do you think I'd have to say, that you were checking out and refurbishing your suit? Nothing wrong with that."

"Thanks."

"Nothing. Hah. Yes, Hercules may be out of bounds, but I know darn well the fool kids go over there anyway. Test of manhood or some such. I suppose kids have to get such idiocy out of their systems. Now, if you somehow *were* jaunting over to old Hercules, be careful now, hear? Maybe so it's not as dangerous as some of us adults make out like it is, but not all of us are old fools, and there are still things left in there that could get a kid who wasn't alert. Hah."

And, to my astonishment, he let me go.

Barb and Kibbie met me with their suits in the oat-boat, and there we did something that would get Old Chris to suspend our vac privileges immediately, if we got caught: we tampered with our finder beacons. They weren't ever supposed to be turned off—if we were outside, and the suit's finder beacon wasn't sending its regular blip every thirty seconds, a search party would be sent out without a moment's delay. But that would let everybody know where we were, and so we turned them off. We logged all three of our suits into the system as having been taken in for refurbishment and repair.

It was about time for that anyway, I realized; mine was getting filthy. I had over a hundred hours of vac since the last refurb; I resolved to clean it for real after we got back.

So we were out in vac without logging the exit, wearing suits that were tagged as under repair, and without working finder beacons. Any one of these would get our vac privilege yanked. All three together would certainly get us the big D.

We still had our emergency locator beacons, of course, and if we got in deep enough trouble we could yank the pull-tab and a high-power scream would go out across every emergency band with our exact locations. But they were to be activated only in emergencies, and if we needed that, we were in deep trouble already.

Once we exited the airlock, we were committed.

The oat-boat silently made its way on a standard run, ferrying supplies from Malina over to Parsons habitat, three degrees ahead. The orbit dropped down to nearly kiss the Hercules orbit, and we were hidden away inside.

Ready to eject. One by one, we exited the airlock, me in my

tiger-striped yellow suit, Kibbie's suit striped in orange, Barb's suit an eye-popping shade of electric blue.

"Radio check," I said, speaking on the encrypted spread-spectrum channel. I found myself whispering, although that made no sense. The spread-spectrum signal should be undetectable to anybody who wasn't tuned specifically into it, and if it wasn't, whispering wouldn't make any difference.

"Check two," "Check three," Barb and Kibbie's voices came back, also whispering.

I flicked the radio off, and switched to the backup radio on my belt. "Radio two check."

"Radio two, got it," and "Radio two, check," Barb and Kibbie's voices came back.

"Radios go," I said. "Ready for suit check. Kibbie, I'm checking for you; Barb, you're on me; and Kibbie, you're checking Barb."

I was nervous, but the familiar ritual of suit check-outs calmed me down. Kibbie had two quik-seals that were tight, but not tight enough; I cinched him down and gave him a quick scolding, the same one that I'd received myself a dozen times when I'd been lax suiting up, and then pronounced him safe. He must have been even more nervous than I'd been when we suited up, I realized. Barb found only a minor problem on me—one equipment pocket not fully zipped. Barb herself, of course, had done everything perfectly by the book. We each checked each other's oxygen levels again, looked at our radiation monitors to verify that they were working, and checked the life-support tell-tales. Green, green, and green. We were go.

I'd been playing music on the trip over, but reluctantly decided not to play once we were over in Hercules. I wanted to be completely in the moment, so I selected only a mild percussion rhythm to accompany me.

Kibbie was bopping to his own music, clearly something pretty energetic. Barb was, as always, unnaturally calm.

I paused, floating next to the oat-boat, and looked across the void at the approach of Hercules, a twisted jungle of mirror-bright aluminum. The remains of Hercules colony no longer even slightly resembled the smoothly curved, squat cylinder of the active colony it had been. It looked like an old-style beer can somebody had tossed up and hit with a couple of shotgun blasts. Here and there, names and logos boldly spray-painted across the surface showed the record of various clandestine visitors who had journeyed there over the years since depressurization. I had my own spray can tucked away in the jack-pack of my yellow tiger-striped skin-suit. Kibbie would have brought one for himself as well; I wasn't sure about Barb. I looked out across the structure, trying to make a mental note of a good place to leave my mark without getting caught off-limits and sent back in humiliation to my parents.

The wreckage had long since been stripped of anything valuable. Nobody ever talked about the decades-old disaster, and I wondered once again what had caused it. Strut failure? Collision?

Barb elbowed me in the ribs. "So, what are you guys waiting for? O'Neill's birthday? Get to it."

"We're going, we're going," I said. "Give us a minute, willya? Lemme check my stuff."

"You checked it three times," Barb said. "So go already. You remember the evasion pattern? In fast when the wide-range radar's over the horizon, hide in the radar-shadow of the big spike, then skim in through the dead spot in the proximity radar. Got it?"

"Got it."

"Then go!" Barb gave me a shove. Well, now was as good a time as any. I killed the spin I'd picked up from Barb's shove and took off. In the corner of my vision I could see Kibbie push off from the oat-boat and follow. In my earphones I heard Rip, sending us off.

"Remember, next conjunction with Malina is in six orbits; seven hundred minutes. Don't miss it or you'll be stranded, got it? And bring us back a chunk of weed for me, hear? A *big* chunk."

I turned down my radio gain to squelch him. The wrecked

colony loomed before us, rotating imperceptibly, almost glued to the sky. In a moment it ceased being an object and turned into a landscape of jagged metal girders and twisted aluminum skin. I felt a thrill compounded of both anticipation and fear. As the spike came around I turned my suit-jet sideways, curved around toward the spin-axis, and hovered in the radar shadow for a moment to catch my breath, waiting for Kibbie and Barb to catch up and for the pounding of my heart to slow back to normal. I floated over a vast blue plain, an old, rigid array of solar cells, too old and too badly damaged to be worth the delta-V to salvage. The glass of the solar cells was frosted and pitted by almost a century's exposure to micrometeoroid dust.

It was a risk to be here, sure, but the element of risk was half the excitement. Parents all had the same horror stories, about some kid who jetted over to a derelict habitat on a dare, got trapped inside, and ran out of air. Or got lost in the maze inside. Or ran short of reaction mass, and ended up in an eternal orbit around the wreckage. The details varied (nobody seems to have personally known the kid it happened to) but the moral was always the same.

In a moment there was a bump as Kibbie arrived, and then Barb, twisting around to kill her relative momentum, landed without a bump, graceful in low-gravity as she always was. "Awesome, isn't it?" she said.

I nodded silently.

"Can you imagine it?" Kibbie said. "Fifty thousand people used to live here."

"Yeah, I know," I said. "You told me already, like, a hundred times."

We floated slowly across the outside of the structure, gawking. Neither of us had ever seen it close up. Its desolation held a peculiar form of beauty. Here was one place where aluminum skin had peeled up in a graceful spiral; there a girder bent into a pretzel-arc. Everywhere it was painted with splotches of color; mostly initials and dates. An enormous, purple and black sprayed mural of a coiled snake dominated one nearly intact panel. I got out my spray can and looked around.

"Hey! Get out of there! Out! Now!"

Yow, a watchman! I twisted and scooted, looking for an opening. I didn't have the slightest notion that there would be a guard. Man, what would people *think* if we got caught and I hadn't even been *inside*? What was I doing, getting caught up in a daze right out there in the open? I jetted across the blue plain of the solar arrays, twisted, rebounded off a girder, and dodged into the interior of the structure through a vast ragged-edged tear. The voice abruptly cut off as I was radio-shielded by the aluminum. I was in what had once been one of the agricultural tubes. I coasted across the chamber and passed through a ripped panel into the next.

I had lost the watchman, but where were Kibbie and Barb? Better not use the radio, not yet. Spread-spectrum was hard to detect, but this close to the watchman, I couldn't risk it. I looked around.

This had apparently once been part of the outermost level of residential sections of the habitat, underneath the parks. I floated past doors, furniture, a broken toilet. I took a couple of turns at random. Maybe I was far enough from the watchman. I turned my transmission power down low and was about to transmit when I saw Kibbie's bright orange suit floating down the corridor.

"Kibbie?"

Kibbie turned. "Dylan. I *knew* I saw you dodge off this way."

"Where's Barb?"

"Right behind. You take a look around this place yet? We're talking, like, massive destruction here."

"Yeah. What *did* all this?"

"Meteoroid strike?" Kibbie guessed. "Debris?"

"I dunno. Nobody ever says anything 'bout it. Look up there." I pointed.

Something had pierced the structure, hard. Rather, many things had perforated it. Holes the size of my fist speckled the tattered shards of the aluminum skin. The colony been a stressed-shell structure with internal wire bracing, and when enough of the tension members had been broken, it ripped apart of its own internal stress. In places, snapped tension lines had buzz-sawed across the structure, carving through aluminum beams like a knife blade. Other places, beams had twisted and broken, forming shapes like avant-garde sculpture. There was nothing loose; probably anything that could be easily carried off had been taken long ago for a souvenir.

I looked around to see if I could find a piece of what had hit the habitat. But there were only the fist-sized holes, hundreds of them. The colony must have rammed it at near orbital velocity, and whatever it was had been vaporized on impact.

Kibbie was far down the corridor already, putting the finishing touches to an elaborate signature on the wall.

"Hey, Kibbie," I said.

He looked up. "I think we better get moving, or we're likely to get caught."

"Okay." I pushed off a bulkhead and came up abreast of him, and then Barb came up to coast along next to us. I was still thinking. The colony had, quite literally, been hit by a shotgun blast. How? Why?

The spot we were seeking was inward, toward the center, where the low-gravity greenhouse had been. I'd been so caught up in thinking about why somebody would want to destroy a peaceful space colony, I'd almost forgotten about the ostensible object of our quest.

We moved inward, still looking around wide-eyed. As we passed one sleep chamber, Kibbie nudged me. "Look." Somebody had patched up the chamber to hold pressure. I looked inside. Padding and sex restraints. "Ooh-ooh. I know what somebody's been doing in there." Kibbie snickered.

I looked around to see if Barb was watching, but she was way ahead of us, gazing into another chamber.

We continued on. Through the gaping holes in the skin, we could see the blackness of space and occasionally flashes of the Earth below.

We passed the park levels, cavernous empty space. There was nothing of the park left, only blackened debris and the barren truss-work of the construction stripped bare.

We drifted across the levels. When we reached a stratum that must have been residential, we stopped momentarily to rest and get oriented. This level had originally been suspended by cables stretching directly from the hub, large rooms with the shattered remains of windows that allowed them to look out over the park levels below.

Something tapped on my suit from behind. "What?"

But Barb and Kibbie were both ahead of me.

"I didn't say anything." Kibbie twisted around to look at me. "Yow!"

I twisted around and found myself staring into the empty eye sockets of a skull. Floating up behind us were silent ghosts that had been dead for most of a century.

They had been in shadow; we would never have noticed them as we passed, but the exhaust blast from our cold-gas suit-thrusters had disturbed them. Eighty years of exposure to hard vacuum and radiation had desiccated the flesh away, leaving nothing but brown skulls, staring blankly out of jumpsuits from which the vacuum had leeched all traces of color. The skeletons drifted aimlessly. The one that had touched me was spinning slightly from the force of its own touch.

Kibbie pushed toward me, fascinated. "Let me see." He raised all his suit illuminators up to full power, and in the sudden blaze of light, the skeletons were pale and dusty, no more scary than old sticks poking out of a bundle of rags.

Barb floated, looking back at us without saying anything.

Kibbie put out a hand and pushed gently against the jumpsuit of the skeleton behind me. The body folded up and drifted backwards, the skull separating and floating free. Kibbie reached out. With one gloved finger into each of the eye sockets and his thumb in the mouth, he grabbed it out of the vacuum. "Gotcha."

He held the skull at arm's length, inspecting it with a show of reverence.

"Don't," I said. "That's gross. Leave them be."

"Fine with me." Kibbie opened his fingers and released the skull, letting it hover in the space before him, and touched it with one finger to steady it. "Bye-bye, dead guy."

"Let's move on," Barb said.

The skull rotated with a slow wobble, as if it were turning its head to look around at what had become of its little world, nodding at what it saw. When it had turned to face away from us, we moved out.

"Rest in peace," Barb said.

After that, now that we knew what to look for, we flashed our illuminators more carefully into the shadows, and could see bones everywhere. Tidal forces had gathered the bodies into clusters of bones in the corners of rooms, or wedged behind equipment. For the first time, the magnitude of the destruction impressed itself on me. For a while, even Kibbie was silent.

☙ ☙ ☙

We emerged into the sunlight of a vast open space. "How's our time?"

"Five hundred seventy minutes."

"Plenty of time to explore."

"Right." Barb turned around—

And suddenly we were surrounded by silent figures in purple-and-gray-striped suits. For a crazy second I thought it was more skeletons, a whole army of skeletons, but then I realized it was something rather more dangerous than that. It was Adders.

I had never run into them before, but I knew the Adders were a cluster from the Parsons habitat, and had a bad reputation. They carried bolos and whips, potent weapons for zero-gee fighting. I gulped.

"So, what have we here?" A figure slightly bigger than the rest drifted out. The voice was on the common channel, unencrypted. "A couple of little lost school boys. A bit far from home, aren't we, children?" His skin-suit had an elaborate decoration across the front, an embroidery of a snake coiling around his chest and up his neck to his cheek.

I killed my background music and switched over to broad-cast, keeping the encrypted link to Barb and Kibbie open as listen-only. "What do you want?" I said. I tried to keep my voice firm.

"Want? That's a good question. I notice you've got a really spiffy suit there, all dolled up in yellow stripes like a tiger. Maybe I might decide to be wanting that, huh?"

"Well, I'm using it right now."

"Now, isn't that too bad. Too bad for you, that is."

"Look, we're not bothering you. We don't want trouble. Why don't you just let us go on with our business?"

I could see his face through the glass of his helmet. He was older than we were, perhaps nineteen or twenty years old. His head was shaven, and he had tattoos of snakes running around his face and eyes. Parsons habitat was known for having lax rules (and, the adults always told us, a high death rate). Tattoos like that would never have been permitted in Malina habitat. The Snake, I thought. The name seemed to fit.

"We've decided that this is our private place, see. We don't like children coming here to play. When they do, we like to teach them a lesson they won't forget real soon."

Barb was suddenly a blur in the corner of my vision, kicking off a wall and launching herself ahead. She cartwheeled as she shot forward, and when she came past the leader, she was in-verted. She reached down and opened the dump-valve on her suit's urine-collection pouch.

The liquid sprayed out in the Snake's face, freezing and boil-ing at the same time, a cotton-fog of glistening white crystals. She bounced off of him, kicking off his shoulder as she passed, timing her move so perfectly that she rebounded directly through a nar-row rift in the wall without touching either side. Her voice in my earphones lingered behind her: "Run, you idiot!"

The Snake spun lazily around, the faceplate of his helmet momentarily covered with white frost. As the ice sublimated away into the vacuum of space, I took advantage of the distrac-tion and headed through the same rent Barb had taken, hoping that Kibbie was smart enough to vanish as well. I caught a glimpse of her blue suit disappearing through an opening that looked too narrow to pass through, and I squeezed through after her. It was evidently once a ventilation duct, intact save for half a dozen holes, and she shot through it like an ore pellet down a railgun. I followed.

At the end of the tube, she dodged into a tiny cubicle, an ancient control room. I came up behind her. She was peering through a rip in the wall.

I started to giggle. She turned to look at me.

"Urine dump?" I managed to say. "Where'd you learn that trick?"

She started giggling as well. "You gotta use what you got."

We looked out in all directions, but there was no sign of chase. "What now?" I asked.

"Back for Kibbie," she said, and without a moment's hesitation pushed off down a different corridor. How in the universe does she know where she's going, I wondered, but there was no time to sit and ponder. I pushed off behind her.

The big main chamber was empty; the Adders all off chasing us. We found Kibbie hiding in a utility corridor, not more than five meters from where we'd been when the Adders confronted us.

"Yow!" I said. "How in the universe did you know where he was?"

"Oh, I saw him slide into the hiding spot when all the attention was focused on you," Barb said. "It was you I was worried about. What's wrong, were you frozen or something? Why didn't you slide away the moment you saw them?"

"I don't think they ever saw me," Kibbie said. "I was behind, and in pretty dark shadow when I heard the voices. I figured it would be best to hide where I was, and not get further lost trying to find you."

The big room was clearly the Adders' assembly area, I saw. The walls had been covered with bold swatches of graffiti. Even more unnerving, near where the leader had been, dozens of skulls had been lined up, each one garishly spray-painted in gray and purple—Adder colors—and with names and crude slogans scrawled across the foreheads. KENNYS HO. KNUCKLE BOY. FIVE HOLES NO WAITING. AWESOME HEAD. SPINNER EATS FECAL WASTE. NO FEAR-DIE YOUNG.

If this was their gathering place, they would be back soon enough when they didn't find us, I realized. "We shouldn't stick around here."

"We're not lost," Barb said.

"What?" I said, and then realized she'd been responding to Kibbie's comment, not mine. "What do you mean?"

"It's pretty twisted up and distorted by the impact," she said, "but you can still see how it used to be laid out. This is the common room outside the D-level dormitories. That's the intersection of C and D corridors there, see it? And over there is the air-filtration substation."

I digested this. Had Barb memorized the whole plan of the habitat? I had the electronic version of the engineering diagram of the habitat, but once I'd seen how twisted up everything was, I'd assumed it was useless. "Which way?" I asked.

"Here, I think." Barb pointed. "Around through the manufacturing levels. We'll stay off the main corridors for the moment. And keep an eye out for more trouble."

"Good idea," I said.

"We shouldn't maybe go home?" Kibbie asked. "We came, we saw."

"And we didn't conquer," I said. "We have as much right to be here as they do. We're not going to let them chase us off."

And anyway, it was a huge colony, a city in the sky. As long as we got out of the territory the Adders knew, there was little chance they would find us again. "But still, we better get some movement on. Rockets, everybody. Go."

Up to now we had been moving by kick-and-coast, pushing off walls and girders with our legs and sometimes our arms, using the suit jets only for occasional fine control. Now, for speed, we used our rocket thrusters. That was dangerous in the cluttered chaos of the interior, since rocket thrusters let you build up speed scary fast, but it moved us out quickly. We moved in toward the center, rocketing along the twisted remains of what had once been a secondary corridor, zig-zagging at intersections to break the line of sight in case any Adders spotted us.

The corridor opened up into a huge area, a sphere a hundred meters in diameter, capped by shattered glass that let in cold blue Earthlight that bathed the area in a spectral glow. Barb moved toward a central fixture, some kind of electronics switching center. "Look!"

On all of the wires of the switching center, sending hair-thin spikes off in every direction, was a green fuzz.

"Weed," I whispered.

Barb approached, and brushed her hand against it. Thin green needles broke off, drifting and spinning slowly away. Barb looked at me. "That's odd. I thought it was weed—what else could it be? But—"

She brushed her hand against it again, more gently this time, and broke off a single delicate long needle. She plucked it out of the vacuum and brought it to her helmet, examining it. Then she looked up and tossed it to me. "Look."

I caught it and held it up to my faceplate, triggering one of my wrist illuminators to shine some light on it to look it over. Seen closer up, it branched away, intricate as a snowflake. "What is it?"

"Inorganic, that's for sure," Barb said. "I think I've got it. That green—that's copper oxide. Some kind of electromigration, I'd say—it's growing dendritic crystals, forming on the copper."

"Oxide?" I passed the crystal to Kibbie, who examined it casually and then tossed it aside. "We're in vacuum."

"Atomic oxygen," Barb said. "Must be. There's not much oxygen here, but a little is leaking out, and what is there is very energetic. Weird."

"Weird," I agreed. What was really disturbing was that Barb had on her mind the same thing that I did: weed. I could feel the air in my lungs with each breath. I didn't want to do it, but I had to ask.

"Barb?"

"Yeah?"

"Weed?"

"Yeah." She stayed silent for a long heartbeat, and then said, "You think I couldn't guess? Come on, Dylan, I'm not dumb; I can figure out what you're looking for out here."

"Look," I said. "It's not like—"

She waited silently, looking at me calmly, waiting for me to finish a sentence which I had no real idea of how to complete. I was able to look anywhere but toward her eyes.

"I do know what the stories about chinga weed are, Dylan," she said softly.

"Well, yeah."

"You know what?" she said. Kibbie had silently vanished somewhere else. Barb was floating in front of me. She pushed off with one hand, doing a slow backwards tumble while continuing to talk. "The stories are overrated. It's a mild euphoric, that's all. At least, that's what my sister says." She stopped her rotation with one hand on a bulkhead, and then tapped it with one finger, floating in a slow spin in front of me. Then she said, "It's that girl Leeila you're thinking about, I expect? The one you're always slipping off to say hi to?"

"Leeila?" I protested. "No, no, you got it wrong. Look, she's nothing to me, just—"

"She's nice enough," Barb said. "I approve. You'll like her. Have you talked to her? Her little sister and my little sister are best friends." She stopped her spin, bent her knees, and then shoved hard off of the electronics enclosure, arrowing across the center of the cavity, receding into the distance, dappled with blue light.

In my headphones, on a suit-to-suit private channel, Kibbie's voice said, "Score one for Barb, Dylan. Looks like she nailed you good." To my right, he jumped to follow her, tumbling as he flew.

I hung there, paralyzed for a moment, as they both drifted into the shadows on the other side. Then I jumped, too.

I was in free fall for thirty seconds. My own illuminators were off—no sense making a target of myself. Just before hitting the far side I flipped over and absorbed the impact with bent knees, steadying myself with a brief burst from my thruster and looking around as I hit.

A pair of small red eyes glowing out of the shadows. I stopped myself against an I-beam, fascinated. In an alcove that had been ripped open, two light-emitting diodes, ancient technology, glowed from an electronic read-out panel. That brought the age of the station out to me immediately; I'd never seen such things except in old videos of the history of space colonization. Nobody had used diodes for indicator lights for a century.

The old wrecked solar panels, still attached to the station only because they were too heavy and too ancient to salvage, were still generating power! Only a trickle of power, a tiny fraction of the megawatts that had once lit and powered the colony, but there was still a tiny bit of life left in it.

They were error indicator lights, I saw. Light-emitting diodes were a robust technology. These had been glowing for eighty years, a mute cry for help to reset one of the thousands of circuit failures that would never be fixed.

"Check this out!" I said. "Power!"

But Kibbie and Barb were otherwise engaged. I saw their illuminators suddenly go on, and I heard Kibbie on the radio: "Take a look at this."

I pushed off, and coasted over, using a burst of my jet to stop and hover immediately over them. Kibbie had hooked one foot under a cable to keep himself from drifting. Barb was holding onto a beam. I triggered my illuminator to look down.

The first thing I saw was a dark-colored streak, like paint that had spurted out onto the aluminum. I swung my illuminators over the area. The streaks were a dark, dusty rust. I followed the streak backwards with my eyes to see what Kibbie and Barb were floating over.

We'd seen a lot of skeletons, but so far none of them had been in space suits. This was a body in an expensive late-model skin-suit, decorated with purple and gray stripes.

A dead Adder.

Kibbie pulled loose the arm that had tangled into a knot of electrical cord, and the body floated free to face us. Centered in his throat, protruding just above the suit environment controls, was a slender metal rod.

His eyes were wide and looked dull, almost dusty, bulging slightly from the lack of pressure in his helmet. Frothy bubbles of blood had come out of his nose and dried on the wisps of a beard and mustache around his mouth. He was only a year or two older than us. But old enough to be dead.

I didn't want to touch him. Kibbie silently turned him around, and I saw where the rod protruded slightly from his back. The rod was hollow, I saw, a short length of conduit, scavenged from the station, the end cut at an angle to give it a wicked point. The surface of the rod was roughened with marks that spiraled around it.

"Gang war, maybe?" Kibbie asked.

"His suit's been stripped," Barb pointed out. "Look. Where's his pack, his emergency kit, his propellant?"

She was right. Everything that could be snatched away quickly had been taken. "Whoever it is, they play rough," I said. "Lights out, you guys. If there's anybody here, we want to see them before they see us."

Barb and Kibbie flicked their lights out at the same instant I did. My eyes took a moment to adjust to the dim. While they were adjusting, I scanned through the radio bands, but found nothing. "Barb? Best way out?"

"From here, it's just as easy to continue on toward the center, and out the hub," she said. "I don't think we want to go back through Adder territory."

We crossed the empty area, and were in a corridor that was twenty meters or so wide. The Hercules habitat was much more cluttered than Malina. Malina colony was spacious, with enormous empty bubbles holding parks a kilometer or more in diameter. On Malina, the habitat levels were a ring around an empty hub, but Hercules was a much older habitat concept—what they called a "beer can design" in the old days. The solar illumination came upward through windows on the lowest levels, and there was no opening in the central axis. The designers had seemed afraid to let any bit of pressurized volume go to waste.

We followed the corridor past cryogenic tanks that must have once stored supplies of liquid oxygen and other gasses, toward what had once been the center of the colony.

All the way in, I had been looking at the holes, trying to understand what it could have been that hit the colony. Here the holes were all around us, and at last I found a spot where a chunk had happened to pass lengthwise through the vacuum-foam insulation of a cryotank. The tenuous vacuum foam, barely more dense than soap bubbles, had slowed the impacting object without vaporizing it. I followed the furrow through two meters of foam, and found the impacting object embedded into a shard of machinery, where it had welded itself into place.

"Look at this," I whispered.

Barb and Kibbie clustered around to see what I had found. It was a steel ball the size of a marble, deformed by impact from a once-spherical shape.

I saw Kibbie raise his eyes, looking around him at the skin of the section. Dozens of holes. Extrapolating to the size of the colony, there must have been millions of balls, exactly placed in the orbital path of the colony.

"It wasn't an accident," I said. "That's not a micrometeoroid, and it's not a chunk of space debris, either. It was deliberate." An involuntary shudder rippled across my body. Why?

You may ask why we lived up here, floating in orbit, instead of down below. What is the economic purpose? Well, why does anybody live anywhere? We live here, because this is where we live. To be sure, we had to build the very ground we stood on, and the bubbles that held our air. But that's not so different from cities down below, if you think about it, where people also build the ground they live on—they call them "skyscrapers" and "highways" and "office buildings." An orbital habitat is only a skyscraper, really, just a little bit higher up. And what do we do? Well, about the same thing as anybody in any city anywhere else, I'd say—a little of everything.

I guess, the answer is, if there's a place people can live, they will live there. And love it, too.

But the thing is, we don't have wars. Wars are something they do down there on Earth, not up here. There are disagreements, sure, but you never find one colony fighting another. Space is hard, and cold, and there are a thousand ways to die.

Who would murder a colony?

◈ ◈ ◈

Further in.

"Look at this," Barb said.

It was a tank, but it had been refitted with an airlock, crudely welded on, so that the tank could hold pressure and serve as a habitat.

I examined it. "There's people living here," Kibbie said.

"You think?" I said.

"The Adders?" Barb said, and then, "No, couldn't be—not unless they've been here for a few decades. Some of the welds here look like they've been here a long time."

"Maybe other gangs have been coming here," Kibbie said.

Barb's voice was low in my headphones, on the private band. "Don't move, guys," she said. "I see something."

"Adders?"

"I think so. My right, your left. See it?"

A flash of motion, purple and gray. "Shoot. Yeah."

"He see us?" And then there was a flash of suit illuminators, swinging in our direction and then stopping, glaring directly in my eyes. Three of them.

"Yeah," I said. "Move!"

All three of us hit our jets. Barb was fastest, and Kibbie right behind her. They were both ahead of me and gaining ground when Barb collided right into three more of the Adders, coming the opposite direction.

All three of them tumbled into a crazy ball, and Kibbie, firing his suit jets frantically to stop, careened straight into the whole mess. Barb reacted immediately, but there were two more of them right behind, and they weren't slow. One grabbed her arm. She kicked free, but it put her into a tumble, and before she could correct and get free, the other two had grabbed her.

Kibbie was still free, but the Adder with the suit that had the snake coiled around it drifted forward to confront them. The Snake. He had a short spear in one hand, and gestured with it for Kibbie to move over next to Barb.

"Better do it," I whispered. "No telling what would make him use that thing."

I had been far enough behind that I didn't think they had seen me, so when the three that had been behind us floated up, I drifted back into the shadows, trying to move slowly so as to not attract notice. Their attention was focused on Barb and Kibbie, not on me. I flicked my radio over to the common band.

"Found you," the Snake said. "You know, I was just playing with you before. You shoulda known that." He rotated around until his helmet was almost up against Barb's. "I was just going to scare you a bit, make you run back home. But you shouldn't have attacked me, you know? I can't allow you to get away with that."

"You can't do anything to us," Barb said. "You wouldn't dare."

"Sure, I can," the Snake said. "Nobody knows you're here. Nobody's going to help you. Nobody's even going to find you. We can do anything we want. And we will."

Not quite nobody, I thought. Rip would know we were here, since he knew we'd hitched a ride on his oat-boat. He—

But I cut that thought off abruptly. Rip knew we were here, sure, but he wasn't waiting for us—we'd told him we would make our way home ourselves. It would be days before he realized we hadn't come back. When it turned out we were missing, would he even tell anybody he'd let us ride over to Hercules? Or would he be afraid to reveal how he'd broken safety rules? And, even if he did, it would be far too late by then anyway.

We needed help now.

"This place is dangerous," the Snake said. "You knew that when you came here, didn't you? Well, now you two children are going to see just how dangerous it can be."

The rest of the Adders had arrived and clustered around. I counted eight, and all of them were watching Kibbie and Barb. Nobody was looking for me, but why should they? They didn't seem to realize that there were more than two of us. In the poor light, Kibbie's orange-striped suit could easily be mistaken for my yellow-striped one—they'd only seen it once, after all.

So it was up to me to rescue them! That was the wrong way around—Barb was the clever one, not me. So, what would Barb do?

That had been a neat trick she'd done with the urine dump. I doubted that it would work twice, though. I looked around. The shadowed area I had been drifting into was once a power-switching sub-station. Voltage busses and circuit breakers surrounded me.

I took a sip from my water bottle, and then closed the valve and detached it from my suit. I could see another power-switching sub-station next to the Snake; he was holding onto a panel of aluminum that had peeled away from it. I tried to see if there were any of the red light-emitting diodes glowing in the darkness. I could imagine I saw one, but with the Adders' illuminators glaring in all directions, it was hard to tell.

I hefted the water bottle, waited until none of the Adders were looking in my direction, then cracked the valve and tossed it.

The water squirting out the opening acted like a feeble rocket. I'd tried to make it spin when I threw it, but it wobbled as it spun, and so it flew with an odd, erratic motion, wavering in a scribbled line across the vacuum, going only vaguely in the direction I aimed it.

The water bottle rebounded off a wall next to one of the Adders, and bounced up, spinning. As it tumbled, it sprayed out a jet of water that instantly turned into snow as it boiled into the vacuum.

I heard a shout over the radio. "What the crap is that?"

The ones holding Barb were ready for that trick, though, and weren't distracted this time. "Where did that come from?" Two of the Adders shone their illuminators back in the direction that they thought it had come from, but the trajectory had been so wobbly that they were peering in the wrong direction. One of the Adders reached out to grab at the bottle as it wobbled past. He missed, and in process he batted it away. It tumbled off, bouncing and spinning and squirting the remains of the water into the power sub-station next to the Snake.

Which is where I had aimed it in the first place.

It wasn't my imagination; there really *was* a red glow from a light-emitting diode. The bottle sprayed water and ice across the exposed high-voltage conductors.

Vacuum is an excellent electrical insulator. Water vapor and tiny particles of ice, sprayed into vacuum, is not. There was a purple-red flash as a high-voltage arc discharged, accompanied by a spangle of electrical noise in my headphones. Tiny droplets of molten aluminum sprayed away from the power bus, and a ball of glowing purple mist blossomed out in a lumpy sphere, crackling and snapping. The Snake jumped backward, tumbling through the vacuum. Gotcha! I thought. It didn't look like he was seriously damaged, but I was ready to bet that the electrical arc must have taken out his radio, and that would slow him down a bit.

And it was the distraction Barb had been waiting for. "Go!" I shouted.

Barb sprang away first, not down the corridor in the direction I'd expected, but through a gap between two of the tanks.

Kibbie was already springing down the corridor. I sailed out after him, and I managed to grab his foot as he coasted by. We spun around in a crazy tumble. "Kibbie!" I shouted, as I frantically used my suit-thruster to kill our momentum. "Not that way. Follow Barb!"

We straightened out, and I pushed off through the gap, dragging Kibbie behind me. A bolo thrown by the closest of the Adders ricocheted off the tank behind him, just missing tangling in Kibbie's feet. We'd only taken a couple of seconds, but we had blown our advantage of surprise, and now they were right behind us. I grabbed Kibbie around the waist, and turned his and my main thrusters on full, accelerating to follow the dwindling figure of Barb down a narrow space between the tanks and a bulkhead. "Hold on," I said. Barb made an abrupt turn through a gap in the bulkhead. I reversed our thrust for three seconds, and reached out a hand to snag the edge of the bulkhead as we sailed past, swinging both of us around.

It was a long corridor, perfectly circular, with hundreds of tiny openings leading off from every side. For a moment, I couldn't imagine what it had been, but after a moment it clicked in: a sewer pipe. It opened up at the end to a wide space that once might have been a waste-water reservoir, but now had been ripped open. I released Kibbie—now that we were clear, it would be easier for us to maneuver separately, and pushed off down the tube, adding a little rocket thrust to increase my speed.

I looked back. Kibbie was right behind me. Behind him, the Adders had made the turn, but they had stopped at the end of the pipe. They were watching us flee without making any move to follow. As I looked, one of the Adders extinguished his suit illuminator, and then the other two followed, leaving them in darkness.

I could smell the stink of my own sweat; the recycler wasn't keeping up with my exertion. I tweaked up the cooling-unit power to lower my suit temperature a few degrees.

Barb got to the end of the corridor first, and swung around out of sight. Kibbie and I followed a moment later.

Barb was just hanging there, one toe hooked under a handhold.

I fired a burst from my attitude thruster to bring me to a stop and rotate myself around so that I was oriented in the same direction as Barb. The space we were in had a dozen tanks, probably a water-processing facility, with every one of the tanks ripped open by the ancient disaster. "Barb?" I said. I wasn't looking at her, but was watching the pipe, watching for Adders to start coming out of it. But they hadn't seemed to be following. Maybe they decided they had scared us enough, and it was time to let us go. Or maybe they went back for reinforcements. I started to look for something I might be able to use as a weapon.

"Dylan?" Barb said. "Turn around."

I rotated and looked up. While I had been staring at the end of the pipe, people had come up to us. These weren't the Adders. These were people in dented and patched-up hard-suits, ancient space-suit designs that I had seen before only in history lessons.

The man in the front of the group held a crossbow.

The metal of his suit was scratched and abraded. You could still see the places where it had once been painted red—a good color, often used for easy visibility—but the paint had long ago rubbed away in most of the places, leaving dull, bare metal. The glass of his helmet was so scratched and pitted that it was hard to guess how he could see through it.

I couldn't help staring at the crossbow. It was loaded with a length of hollowed rod, electrical conduit, sharpened at the end. He had another half dozen in a belt-loop, ready to reload. A crossbow is a rotten weapon to use in free-fall: when you fired it, the reaction force would send you spinning backward, and the bolt would almost certainly go anywhere except where you aimed it. But he held the crossbow down low, the butt against his belly. It was exactly at his center of gravity, I would guess, so he wouldn't spin when it fired. He would still recoil backward, but if he were adept enough in low gravity to avoid spinning even the least bit? It would have to take an awful lot of practice to use it.

From the confidence with which he held it, I guessed he'd had a lot of practice. And some of it had come from shooting Adders.

I scrolled frantically through the radio channels until I found one where he was talking.

"—are you," he said, in a voice strained by years of sucking oxygen at too low a pressure. "What are you doing in our home?"

I started to answer, and Barb moved in front of me.

"Hello," she said. "Good afternoon. How are you? We're really pleased to meet you. This is my friend Dylan—" She waved at me—"And here is my friend Kibbie. I'm Barb." She did something that approached a bow, and I hurriedly tried to copy her.

"Ah, very pleased to meet you," I said. "Sir."

To my astonishment, the old man in the red suit returned the bow. His low-gravity movement put even Barb's grace to shame. At no time did the crossbow waver in its aim. It was pointed just exactly halfway between Barb and me, not a threat exactly, more of a threat of a threat.

"What do you want?" he repeated.

"We're just looking around?" I said.

"We don't mean you any harm," Barb added.

I could see his lips moving, apparently talking to some of the others on a private channel. They adjusted their positions, closing around us in a globe. They moved with precise economy of motion, showing years or maybe decades of microgravity experience. They were carrying things that might or might not be weapons—staffs, tethers that might be used as whips. At least none of the others had a crossbow.

None that I could see, anyway.

"You should go back where you came from," he said. "We don't like you hoodlums coming in here, busting everything up."

It took me a moment to even understand what he was saying. I don't think anybody had used the word "hoodlum" in a century. When I understood what he said, I realized he took us for members of the Adders, or some other cluster.

"We were just ready to leave, sir," Kibbie said, at the same time that Barb said, "We're not going to destroy anything. We're not like that."

His eyes flicked from Barb to Kibbie and back, and his crossbow shifted slightly. It was aimed right at Barb now. He allowed himself to drift closer to her.

"You're a girl," he said. "I don't like that. Girl gangs, they're bad business, bad bad business."

"We're not a gang!" Barb said. "I told you."

"Only three," he said, musing. "Where's the rest of ya?"

Without moving his eyes, he said something on the private channel, and in the edges of my vision I could see some of the people
surrounding us slip into the shadows and away.

"We're it," Barb said. "There are only three of us."

"Three ain't a gang," he said. Then, not bothering to switch
to the private channel, he said, "Whatta they got?"

I felt a touch, and twisted around. While I had been distracted, my pack and pockets were being ransacked, so expertly
that I'd only just noticed. The contents floated spread out, sorted
into neat categories—batteries, lights, ration packs, utility knife,
suit-repair kit, mesh nets to carry things in, list after list of lami-
nated safety checklists (all of which I'd long ago memorized),
navigation aids, emergency beacon, low vapor-pressure fluid for
de-gunking a fogged visor, several pencils, first-aid kit, instruc-
tion manuals, zero-torque tools including a small welding torch
(not that I'd been planning on needing tools, but they were the
usual suit pack and I didn't see any reason to leave them out),
reels of utility tape, thermal gloves, spare hose connectors and
three sizes of O-rings, restraints and tethers and quick-clips to
use to keep from drifting away while working, two paint spray-
cans, and a pocket full of other useless clutter. Some of it was
stuff I hadn't even realized I'd had with me, including for no particular reason, three small plastic dinosaurs. They had even detached my urine collection pouch (half full), my fecal collection
bags (still empty), and the spares.

The man sorting through it separated out three things; the
welding torch from the tool kit, the utility knife, and the long
tether. Most important of this was the long tether, which we
would need for the swing back to Malina. Except for the bag of
urine, the rest he scooped up into one of the mesh sacks and
pushed toward me. The welding torch, knife, and long tether—
the three things that could be taken as possible weapons, I
thought—he held up to show the red-suited man.

My mouth was dry, and I wished that I still had the water
bottle that I'd tossed at the Adders.

While the man had been rummaging through my stuff, others checked over Barb and Kibbie's possessions. They found pretty much the same things, except that the one looking over Barb's stuff had found a fine gold chain with a locket in one of her pockets, and was looking at it with curiosity.

"That's not a weapon," Barb said indignantly. "That's mine." She reached out carefully, plucked it out of the man's hand, and put it back into a pocket at her breast. I was intensely curious about what it was—she'd never shown any hint of interest in jewelry before—but decided that now was the wrong time to ask.

The inspection complete, they made a quick consultation with the leader—again on the private band—and then, much to my surprise, the tools, knives, and tether were politely returned. Apparently they'd decided they would take Barb at her word, and we were no threat.

The only items they kept were the bags of urine, two of them half-filled, the third nearly empty.

As suddenly as they had appeared, the people surrounding us melted away. Only the leader in the once-red suit remained. "Look around?" he said, as if thinking it over. "Okay," he said. "Don't stay," and he bent to push off.

"Wait," Barb said, and he turned for a moment. "Who are you? How long have you lived here?"

"How long?" he asked. "We've always lived here."

"But, where did you come from?"

"Come from? We didn't come from anywhere. This is where we come from."

The Hercules disaster had been seventy-eight years ago. Could it be true, that some people had survived, and that they had lived here, in the wreckage, for nearly eighty years? It seemed impossible. How did they survive? What did they live on? Surely one of the other colonies would have taken in survivors.

No, I thought, it was impossible. These must be refugees, rejects from other colonies, people who had come here fleeing some political system. Out of the ten thousand colonies it would be unlikely that they couldn't find one that would choose to take them in, but perhaps they preferred their independence over their comfort.

"But what happened?" Barb continued. She gestured around her at the wrecked colony. "What did this?"

"That was a long time ago," the leader said. He had unstrung his crossbow, and without the weapon aimed at us, he seemed no more than a tired old man. "A long, long time."

"But what *did* this?" she pressed. "How could it happen? Who was it?"

"How?" the man said, as if it had never occurred to him to ask. "God was angry."

And with that, he kicked the wall and twisted down a corridor, expertly adding speed with a push off of the wall on each rebound, too deftly and quickly to follow, leaving us alone.

☙ ☙ ☙

We floated onward, for the most part, in silence. As we got closer to the center of the colony, the spaces got larger and more empty, and it was easier to see how the colony had been savaged. We floated across emptiness, toward the wreckage of what had once been the central hub.

But it was looking like we would have to cut our voyage short. After all this, I was getting worried. My radio was beginning to hiss and chatter, although nobody was broadcasting. Radiation levels were rising. It seemed impossible that there could be a solar storm with no warnings, but my radiation monitor was slowly counting upwards. My fingers unconsciously fondled the pull-tab that activated the emergency beacon, but I didn't tug on it yet. If I had to, I would use it—better to be iced than to be fried—but we weren't in trouble, not yet, not as long as the radiation level didn't continue to rise.

"Barb?" I said. "You watching the radiation?"

"Yeah," she said. "Pretty weird, isn't it?"

"Yeah," I said. "The sun was supposed to be calm." We had been watching the solar alert predictions for the entire last week, and no solar events, not even little ones, were predicted.

"The sun?" Barb said, as if something entirely different had been on her mind. "That's not it—look at the breakdown. We're seeing neutrons here. What in the universe could be emitting neutrons?"

"Neutrons?" I said, baffled, but then I toggled over to a breakdown display, and saw that she was right. The rising radiation was entirely neutrons and neutron-decay electrons. That couldn't be right, I thought. Neutrons don't have enough lifetime to make it from the sun.

And then we were inside the hub. "Yow," Kibbie said. "I don't believe it."

I grabbed onto a strut and stopped, amazed. There was nothing to say.

In the center of the habitat we had expected mostly empty space, perhaps the wreckage of a few transfer ships that had been too damaged to bother to salvage.

We entered a huge chamber with racks upon racks of warhead-tipped missiles. Weapons. The colony had wielded weapons.

In its high-inclination orbit, it had flown over every part of the Earth—well, all of the inhabited parts—twice a day.

At last, I understood everything.

Hercules had been a threat.

All around us, plutonium from hundreds of shattered nuclear warheads leaked neutrons into space. In and around the weapons grew the weeds. They had adapted to the vacuum perfectly and were spreading out, seeking the light, scavenging whatever organic material they could find. Could they actually be living off the radiation? The leaves had a tough, waxy surface to hold in water. When I pulled on a leaf, it was tough, and would not tear loose. I cut it, and a viscous sap welled out of the stem, drying almost instantly to a hard resin that sealed the wound against the vacuum.

Barb pried out a single plant and placed it into a collector's bag. Me and Kibbie filled our bags, ignoring the wreckage of weapons around us.

"We can't stay," Barb said. "Too much radiation." She looked at us. "Finish up, you guys, we're getting out of here."

Our suit waste bags were almost empty—we'd replaced the urine pouches the Hercules dwellers had taken, but the new ones had barely been used. We used them now, and then, in tribute to the plants' tenacity, we opened our waste bags into space. The liquid contents foamed out, boiling and freezing, and a fine white frost glittered for a moment in the sunlight. Most of it would be lost to the vacuum, but the plants would scavenge some of it, getting back a little fraction of what they'd lost to our harvesting.

We headed out straight along what had once been the spin axis of the habitat, and saw neither the squatters nor the Adders as we went. From the center of the hub we jetted across to the rim, tethered ourselves together for safety, and swung off into the long transfer orbit that would take us back to Malina.

We coasted in silence, and I was alone with my thoughts.

We were fragile. That was the meaning of Hercules habitat. I had always thought that, in the orbital colonies, we did not have wars because we were better than the people left behind on Earth, but that was not it at all. We had no wars because we *couldn't*, because we were so fragile that our first battle would also be our last.

For Hercules, it had been. They had weapons, lots of them, but a cargo-load of ball-bearings ejected into place for them to run into at orbital velocity had destroyed them.

We entered eclipse, and, for a moment, all the sunsets of Earth painted us in rusty orange. The stars came out. I turned my gloves' heater on.

Barb broke into my silence, speaking on the suit-to-suit channel. "You know you don't really need it, Dylan."

It took me a moment to come back from my thoughts and realize she was talking to me. "What?"

"The weed. You know you don't need it."

The mesh bag was at my belt, filled with the *salvia vacui* I'd collected. "Don't I?"

Her voice was infinitely soft, with a gentleness I'd never heard her use before. "Of course not. Didn't you know that?"

Far ahead of us, I could see flashing strobe beacons that marked the docking ports of Malina, where a hundred thousand people went about their daily lives in a habitat that was as fragile as a glass ornament, ignoring the vacuum that surrounded them.

Home.

I toggled my radio. "Yes," I said to her. "Yes, I know."

# SPACE BOY

## by Orson Scott Card

Orson Scott Card began publishing in 1977, and by 1978 had won the John W. Campbell Award as best new writer of the year. In 1986, his famous novel *Ender's Game*, one of the best-known and best-selling SF novels of the '80s, won both the Hugo and the Nebula awards; the next year, his novel *Speaker for the Dead*, a sequel to *Ender's Game*, also won both awards, the only time in SF history that a book and its sequel have taken both the Hugo and Nebula awards in sequential years. He won a World Fantasy Award in 1987 for his story "Hatrack River," the start of his long "Prentice Alvin" series, and another Hugo in 1988 for his novella "Eye for Eye." His many short stories have been collected in *Cardography*, *Tales from the Mormon Sea*, *Unaccompanied Sonata and Other Stories*, *The Folk of the Fringe*, *The Elephants of Posnan and Other Stories*, *First Meetings: Three Stories from the Enderverse*, and the massive *Maps in a Mirror: The Short Fiction of Orson Scott Card*. His many novels include *Ender's Shadow*, *Shadow of the Hegemon*, *Shadow Puppets*, *Hot Sleep*, *A Planet Called Treason*, *Songmaster*, *Hart's Hope*, *Wyrms*, *Seventh Son*, *Red Prophet*, *Prentice Alvin*, *Heartfire*, *The Call of Earth*, *Earthborn*, *Earthfall*, *Homebody*, *The Memory of Earth*, *Treason*, *Xenocide*, and *Children of the Mind*. As editor, he has produced *Dragons of Light*, *Dragons of Darkness*, *Future on Ice*, *Future on Fire*, and *Masterpieces: The Best Science Fiction of the Twentieth Century*. His most recent books are the novels *Magic Street* and *Shadow of the Giant*. Card lives in Greensboro, North Carolina, with his family.

In the deceptively simple story that follows, he shows
us that sometimes if you can't go to space, space will come
to *you* . . .

TODD MEMORIZED THE Solar System at the age of four. By
seven, he knew the distance of every planet from the sun, including the perigee and apogee of Pluto's eccentric orbit, and its degree of declension from the ecliptic. By ten, he had all the
constellations and the names of the major stars.

Mostly, though, he had the astronauts and cosmonauts, every
one of them, the vehicles they rode in, the missions they accomplished, what years they flew and their ages at the time they went.
He knew every kind of satellite in orbit and the distances and orbits
that weren't classified and, using the telescope Dad and Mom had
given him for his sixth birthday, he was pretty sure he knew twenty-
two separate satellites that were probably some nation's little secret.

He kept a shrine to all the men and women who had died in
the space programs, on the launching pad, on landing, or beyond
the atmosphere. His noblest heroes were the three Chinese voy-
agers who had set foot on Mars, but never made it home. He envied them, death and all.

Todd was going into space. He was going to set foot on another planet.

The only problem was that by the time he turned thirteen he
knew was never going to be particularly good at math. Or even
*average*. Nor was he the kind of athletic kid who looked like an
astronaut. He wasn't skinny, he wasn't fat, he was just kind of
soft-bodied with slackish arms no matter how much he exercised.
He ran to school every day, his backpack bumping on his back.
He got bruises on his butt, but he didn't get any faster.

When he ran competitively in P.E. he was always one of the
last kids back to the coach, and he couldn't ever tell where the
ball was coming when they threw to him, or, when it left his own
hand, where it was likely to go. He wasn't the last kid chosen for
teams—not while Sol and Vawn were in his P.E. class. But no one
thought of him as much of a prize, either.

But he didn't give up. He spent an hour a day in the backyard throwing a baseball against the pitchback net. A lot of the time, the ball missed the frame altogether, and sometimes it didn't reach the thing at all, dribbling across the lawn.

"If I had been responsible for the evolution of the human race," he said to his father once, "all the rabbits would have been safe from my thrown stones and we would have starved. And the sabertooth tigers would have outrun whoever didn't starve."

Father only laughed and said, "Evolution needs every kind of body. No one kind is best."

Todd wouldn't be assuaged so easily. "If the human race was like *me*, then launching rockets and going into space would have to wait for the possums to do it."

"Well," said Father, "that would mean smaller spaceships and less fuel. But where in a spacesuit would they stow that tail?"

Really funny, Dad. Downright amusing. He actually thought about smiling.

He couldn't tell anybody how desperate and sad he was about the fact that he would probably have to become a high school drama teacher like his Dad. Because if he *did* say how he felt, they'd make him go to a shrink again to deal with his "depression" or his "resentment of his father" the way they did after his mother disappeared when he was nine and Dad gave up on searching for her.

The shrink just wouldn't accept it when he screamed at him and said, "My mother's gone and we don't know where she went and everybody's stopped looking! I'm not depressed, you moron, I'm *sad*. I'm *pissed off*!"

To which the shrink replied with questions like, "Do you feel better when you get to call a grown-up a 'moron' and say words like 'pissed'?" Or, worse yet, "I think we're beginning to make progress." Yeah, I didn't choke you for saying that, so I guess that's progress.

Nobody even remembered these days that sometimes people were just plain miserable because something really bad was going on in their lives and they didn't need a drug, they needed somebody to say, "Let's go get your mother now, she's ready to come home," or, "That was a great throw—look, after all these years, Todd's become a *terrific* pitcher and he's great at math so let's make him an astronaut!"

Ha ha, like that would ever happen.

Instead, he took a kitchen timer with him out to the backyard every afternoon, and when it went off he'd drop what he was doing and go inside and fix dinner. Jared kept trying to help, which was okay because Jared wasn't a complete idiot even though he was only seven and certifiably insane. Todd's arm was usually pretty sore from misthrowing the ball, so Jared would take his turn stirring things.

There was a lot of stirring, because when Todd cooked, he *cooked*. Okay, he mostly opened soup cans or cans of beans or made mac and cheese, but he didn't nuke them, he made them on the stove. He told Dad that it was because he liked the taste better when it was cooked that way, but one day when Jared said, "Mom always cooked on the stove," Todd realized that's why he liked to do it that way. Because Mom knew what was right.

It wasn't *all* soup or beans or macaroni. He'd make spaghetti starting with dry noodles and plain tomato sauce and hamburger in a frying pan, and Dad said it was great. Todd even made the birthday cakes for all their birthdays, including his own, and for the last few years he made them from recipes, not from mixes. Ditto with his chocolate chip cookies.

Why was it he could calculate a half recipe involving thirds of a cup, and couldn't find $n$ in the equation $n = 5$?

He took a kind of weird pleasure from the way Dad's face got when he bit into one of Todd's cookies, because Todd had finally remembered or figured out all the things Mom used to do to make her cookies different from other people's. So when Dad got all melancholy and looked out the window or closed his eyes while he chewed, Todd knew he was thinking about her and missing her even though Dad *never* talked about her. I made you remember her, Todd said silently. I win.

Jared didn't talk about Mom, but that was for a different reason. For a year after Mom left, Jared talked about her all the time. He would tell everybody that the monster in his closet ate her. At first people looked at him with fond indulgence. Later, they recoiled and changed the subject.

He only stopped after Dad finally yelled at him. "There's no monster in your closet!" It sounded like somebody had torn the words from him like pulling off a finger.

Todd had been doing the dishes while Dad put Jared to bed, and by the time Todd got to the back of the house, Jared was in his room crying and Dad was sitting on the edge of his and Mom's bed and *he* was crying and then Todd, like a complete fool, said, "And you send *me* to a shrink?"

Dad looked up at Todd with his face so twisted with pain that Todd could hardly recognize him, and then he buried his face in his hands again, and so Todd went in to Jared and put his arm around him and said, "You've got to stop saying that, Jared."

"But it's true," Jared said. "I saw her go. I warned her but she did the very exact thing I told her *not* to do because it almost got my arm the time I did it, and—"

Todd hugged him closer, "Right, I know, Jared. I know. But stop saying it, okay? Because nobody's ever going to believe it."

"You believe me, don't you, Todd?"

Todd said, "Of course I do. Where else could she have gone?" Why not agree with the crazy kid? Todd was already seeing a shrink. He had nothing to lose. "But if we talk about it, they'll just think we're insane. And it made Dad cry."

"Well he made *me* cry too!"

"So you're even. But don't do it anymore, Jared. It's a secret."

"Same thing with the monster's elf?"

"The monster itself? What do you mean?"

"The elf. Of the monster. I can't talk about the elf?"

Geeze louise, doesn't he let up? "Same thing with the monster's elf and his fairies and his dentist, too."

Jared looked at him like he was insane. "The monster doesn't have a dentist. And there's no such thing as fairies."

Oh, right, lecture *me* on what's real and what's not!

So it went on, days and weeks and months, Todd fixing dinner and Dad getting home from after-school play practices and they'd sit down and eat and Dad would tell funny things that happened that day, doing all the voices. Sometimes he *sang* the stories, even when he had to have thirty words on the same note till he came up with a rhyme. They'd all laugh and it was great, they had a great life . . .

Except Mom wasn't there to sing harmony. The way they *used* to do it was they'd take turns singing a line and the other one would rhyme to it. Mom could always make a great rhyme that was exactly in rhythm with the song. Dad was funny about it, but Mom was actually *good*.

Grief is like that. You live on, day to day, happy sometimes, but you can always think of something that makes you sad all over again.

Everybody had their secrets, even though everybody else knew them. Jared had his closet monster *and* its elf. Dad had his memory of Mom, which he never discussed with anyone. Todd had his secret dreams of going to other worlds.

Then on a cool Saturday morning in September, a few weeks after his thirteenth birthday, he was out in the side yard, screwing the spare hose onto the faucet so he could water Mom's roses, when he heard a hissing sound behind him and turned around in time to see a weird kind of shimmering appear in midair just a few feet out from the wall.

Then a bare child-size foot slid from nowhere into existence right in the middle of the shimmering.

If it had been a hairy claw or some slime-covered talon or the mandibles of some enormous insect, Todd might have been more alarmed. Instead, his fear at the strangeness of a midair arrival was trumped by his curiosity. All at once Jared's talk about mother disappearing in the closet because she did the same thing *he* did when the monster "caught his arm" didn't sound quite as crazy.

The foot was followed, in the natural course of things, by a leg, with another foot snaking out beside it. The legs were bare and kept on being bare right up to the top, where Todd was vaguely disgusted to see that whoever was coming was *not* a child. It was a man as hairy as the most apelike of the guys in gym class, and as sweaty and naked as they were when they headed for the showers. Except that he was about half their size.

"Eew, get some pants on," said Todd, more by reflex than anything. Since the little man's head had not yet emerged, Todd didn't feel like he was being rude to a person—personhood really seemed to require a head, in Todd's opinion—but apparently the dwarf—no, the *elf*, it was pretty obvious that Jared must have been referring to something like this—must have heard him somehow because he stopped wriggling further out, and instead a hand snaked out of the opening and covered the naked crotch.

The elf must have been holding on to something on the other side of that opening, because all of a sudden, instead of wriggling further out, he simply dropped the rest of the way, hit the ground, and rolled. It reminded Todd of the way a pooping dog will strain and strain, making very little progress, and then all of a sudden the poop breaks off and drops. He knew it was a disgusting thought, which made him regret that there was no one there to say it to. Still, he couldn't help laughing, especially because this particular dropping was a stark-naked man about half Todd's size.

At the sound of Todd's laughter, the man rolled over and, now making no attempt at modesty, said, "Oh, it's you."

"Why, have we met?" asked Todd. "What are you doing naked in my backyard? I think that's illegal."

"In case you weren't watching," said the man, "I just squeezed through the worm, so it's not like any clothes I was wearing would have made it anyway. And what are you doing out here? You're never out here."

"I'm out here all the time," said Todd.

The elf pointed to the backyard, around the corner of the house. "You're always over there, throwing a ball at a fishnet. I admit I wondered why you haven't figured out that the net will *never* catch the ball."

"Who are you, and what are you doing here, and why did Jared know about you and the rest of us didn't, and where is my mother, what happened to her?"

"Do you mind if I get dressed first?"

"Yes, I do mind." If this was Todd's only chance to get his questions answered, he wasn't going to be put off. If the stories about elves and leprechauns were true—and now he had to figure they must have *some* basis in fact—they were tricky and dishonest and you couldn't take any of them at their word. Which meant that they would fit right into eighth grade. Todd was experienced at being suspicious.

"Too bad," said the elf.

The elf started walking toward the fence that separated the side yard from the front yard. Todd got in front of him to block his way.

The elf swatted him away. It *looked* like a swat, anyway—but it felt like the back of his hand sank two inches into Todd's shoulder and shoved him out of the way with all the force of a bulldozer. He smacked into the bricks of the side of the house, and slid sharply enough that his arm was scraped raw. His head also rang from the impact, and when he reached up his sore arm to touch his face, the right side of his forehead up near the hairline was bleeding.

"Hey!" Todd yelled at him. "You got no right to do that! That *hurt!*"

"Boo-hoo, poor baby," said the elf. He was kneeling now. It seemed he counted boards in the fence and then plunged his hand right down into the dirt in front of a certain board.

Todd had dug in this hard-clay soil. It was hard enough to dig when the soil was wet; when it was dry, it was like trying to dig a hole in the bottom of a dish using only a spoon. But the little man's hand plunged in as if the dirt were nothing but Jell-O and Todd began to realize that just because somebody was little didn't mean he wasn't strong.

The elf's hand came up with a metal strongbox. He punched

buttons to do the combination of the lock, and then lifted it open. Inside were clothes in a plastic bag. Within a minute, the man had pants and a shirt on. They looked like they had been bought at Gap Kids—new enough but way too cute for a guy as hairy as this.

"Where did you get those shoes?" asked Todd. They were like clown shoes, much wider and longer than his feet. Almost like snowshoes.

"I had them specially made," the elf said irritably.

For the first time, Todd realized that despite the elf's fluency, he had an accent—English wasn't his native language. "Where are you from?" he asked.

"Oh, right, like you'd recognize the name," said the elf.

"I mean is it another country? Or . . ." Todd looked at the shimmering in the air, which was now *way* less visible and fading fast. "Like, another dimension?"

"Another planet," said the elf. "And your mouth can't make the sounds necessary to pronounce the real name. But your mother calls it 'Lilliput.' "

"My mother?" said Todd. All at once it felt like his heart was in his throat. "She's alive, like Jared said?"

"Of course she's alive, why wouldn't she be alive? I warned Jared about the worm and he warned your mother, but did she *believe* him? No, he was just a child, so now she's stuck there and she's starting to get annoyed about it."

"Starting? She's been gone four years."

"Time doesn't work the same way back home. Your mother's only been gone for about a week."

"Four years!" shouted Todd. "She's been gone four years and why hasn't she come home? If *you* can get here, why can't she?"

"Because she's too big to get where she needs to go," said the elf. "You think I'm small, but I'm a tall man in my world. Your mother—she's a giant. Only she's a big *weak* giant. A big weak naked giant because clothes don't do so well coming through the worm—"

"What worm? Where's the worm?"

The elf waved toward the shimmering in the air. "That's the worm's anus. The mouth is in the closet in Jared's bedroom."

"So there really is a monster there."

"Not a monster," said the elf. "A worm. It's not out to get anybody. It just sucks stuff in at one end of a connection between worlds. You'd be surprised how much energy is released where worlds connect, if you can bridge them, and worms can do it, so they attach the two worlds together and process things through. Like earthworms. Only worldworms don't move, they just sit there and suck."

"Suck *what*?" said Todd.

"I told you, Energy. They suck a star's worth of energy in a year."

"Out of Jared's *closet*?"

"No." The elf sounded scornful. "Out of the friction between universes. The differing time flows—they rub up against each other because they aren't synchronized. Four years for you, a week for your mother—you think that timeflow difference doesn't *burn*?"

"Don't talk to me like I'm an idiot," said Todd. "How exactly was I supposed to know any of this? I didn't even know your universe existed."

"Your mother disappears and you don't *suspect* something?"

"Yeah, we suspected that somebody pointed a gun at her and made her go with them. Or she maybe ran away from us because she stopped loving Dad. Or she died in some freak accident and her body simply hasn't been found. But no, the idea of her disappearing into another universe with a different timeflow didn't come up much."

"I *heard* Jared tell your father."

"Jared told Dad about a monster in the closet! For pete's sake, if I hadn't seen you come out of midair myself I wouldn't believe it. What, are little kids taught all about the friction between timeflows in *your* world?"

The elf looked a little abashed. "Actually, no," he said. "In fact, I'm the scientist who finally figured out what's going on. I've been coming back and forth between worlds, riding the worm for years. Not just here, either, this is the fourth worm I've ridden."

"So you're like—what, the Einstein of the elves?"

"More like Galileo. Nobody believes me on my end of the worm, either. In fact, most of my science and math come from your world. Which is why I expected it to be obvious to *you*."

"Just because I'm from planet Earth I'm supposed to be a math genius? I guess that means that since you're an elf, you make great shoes. You probably made those stupid clown shoes yourself."

The elf glowered at him. "I'm not an elf. And I don't make shoes. I don't *wear* shoes back home. I wear them here because unless I wear shoes with wide soles to spread my weight, I sink too far into the ground, which slows me down and leaves tracks everywhere."

"They make you look stupid."

"I'd look a lot stupider up to my ankles in asphalt."

While they'd been talking, Todd had also been thinking. "You said Mom's been gone for only a week."

"The timeflow difference fluctuates, but that's about right."

"So she hasn't even begun to miss me yet. Us. Yet."

"She's a big baby about it. Cries all the time. Worse than your father."

Todd remembered hearing his father cry, how private that had been. "You spy on us?"

"The worm I'm riding comes out here, and to get home I have to go into your brother's bedroom. I'm not spying, I'm traveling. With my eyes and ears open." The elf sighed. "OK, so I stop and gather data. I'm a scientist. You're an interesting people. And you'll notice I called you *people*, not some insulting diminutive derogatory name like 'elves.' "

"Why doesn't Mom come home? If you can get through, why can't she?"

The elf—for lack of a better name—did a weird move with his fingers. He'd done it a couple of times before, and Todd finally realized that where he came from, it must be the equivalent of rolling his eyes. "Because like I said, in my world she's huge. And very . . . light. Insubstantial. She can't *do* anything. She can barely make her voice heard."

Todd tried to imagine what that might mean. "She's some kind of mist?"

The elf chuckled. "Yes, she has some fog-like properties."

Todd took a threatening step toward him. "Don't laugh at my mother!"

"If you'd seen her during a windstorm, trying to hold on to trees, *anything* to keep from blowing away—"

"It's not funny!" Todd tried to shove him, but it was like hitting a brick wall. It hurt his hands, and the elf didn't even budge.

"You still don't get it," said the elf. "I'm very dense."

It took a moment for Todd to realize he meant *dense* like in physics instead of *dense* as in "kind of dumb."

"I want my mother back. And you're a lousy sack of crap to make fun of her when she's stuck in your world."

"Oh, and you didn't make fun of *me* at *all*, I take it," said the elf. "When I popped through naked, that wasn't funny to you?"

"It was disgusting. And if mother could fit through the wormhole in the closet, she must have fit through the worm's . . . whatever, on *your* side. So she *can* fit."

"Anus," said the elf. "The worm's mouth is in your closet. Its anus, in my world, is on a lovely wooded hillside behind my house. And yes, it has a mouth and an anus on both worlds. It's a single organism, but its digestive systems are bidirectional. It eats both worlds at once."

"Eats *what*?" Now Jared's childhood fears of being eaten by the monster in the closet seemed too literally true.

"Eats time. Eats dark matter. Eats dust. I have no idea. Why does gravity suck? I'm just starting to try to figure out a whole branch of science that neither your world nor mine knows anything about."

Todd's mind jumped back to the real question. "My mother lives with you?"

"Your mother is living in the woods because there's more room for her there and she can avoid being seen. She can avoid having someone maliciously dissipate her."

"What?"

"Throw rocks at her, for instance, until she's so full of holes she can't stick together and the bits of her just drift away."

"What kind of sick people *are* you in that world!"

"She's a huge woman who looks as translucent as mist! The few who have met her don't think she's alive! *They* haven't been to this world. They're ignorant peasants, most of them. It's all very awkward." The elf leaned in close to Todd. "I'm doing everything I can to set things right. But please remember that I didn't take her to my world. She did that herself in spite of being warned. And I didn't put that stupid worm's mouth in your closet."

Then he got a strange look on his face. "Well, actually, I did, but not deliberately."

"You *put* it there?"

"The worm is apparently drawn to inhabited places. I don't know what it thinks we are, or if it thinks at all, but I've never seen a worm that wasn't close to the dwelling place of a sentient being. It may even be drawn to people who might want to use it to travel from world to world. It might have been aware of my passion for exploration, which is why the anus showed up in my front garden." Then, almost to himself: "Though it would have been much more convenient to have the *mouth* within easy reach."

"My mother didn't want to travel anywhere," said Todd. As he was saying it, he realized that maybe it wasn't mother or even Jared who had drawn the worm to Jared's closet. There *was* someone in their family who had a passionate desire to travel to other planets.

"Your brother kept putting things through the worm," said the elf. "I'd find them in my garden. Wooden blocks. Socks. Underwear. A baseball cap. Little model cars. Plastic soldiers. A coat hanger. Money. And once a huge, misty, terrified cat."

Todd thought back to all the times things had disappeared. His favorite plastic soldiers. His baseball cap. His socks. His underwear. His Hot Wheels cars. Jared must have been stealing them to make them disappear down the wormhole. He had no idea where Jared got the cat, but it would have been just like him.

Of course, maybe Jared thought he was *feeding* the monster in the closet. Placating it, so it wouldn't come out of the closet and eat him. Was this how the worship of idols began? You put things in a certain place and they disappear into thin air—what could you imagine, except it was a hungry god?

And the kid was smart enough to figure out that if he needed to make stuff disappear, it might as well be something of Todd's. Amoral little dork.

"The first time I saw something appear in midair," said the elf, "it was broad daylight. I knew what it was—I'd been investigating worms for some time. It was a . . . hobby of mine. But I also knew that if people found out I had one in our neighborhood, I'd either be inundated with curiosity seekers, or plagued by pious people determined to sit around and see what the gods would give them, or I'd be arrested for witchcraft."

"Witchcraft? That's just superstition."

"Don't get superior with me. I've been studying your culture for years. On television you marry witches, but in real life you burn them. And if somebody in your world saw *me* plop out of the sky . . ."

"Which I just did."

". . . then what do you think would happen *here*?"

"Scientists would come and study the worm and—"

"You really are naive. No self-respecting scientist would come anywhere near something like this, because it would sound like pure tabloid journalism. They could lose their careers!"

"Is that what happened to you?" asked Todd. "Have you lost your career?"

"I don't have a career, exactly."

"You're not a scientist?"

"In our world, scientists are rare and they work alone."

Todd gave that the worst possible spin. "People think you're crazy and pay no attention to you."

"They'd think I was crazy and pay a *lot* of attention to me if I hadn't moved the anus."

It occurred to Todd that "moving the anus" could be rendered as "hauling ass," which he found amusing.

"Now look who's laughing," said the elf.

Todd got back to business. "You can *move* this thing."

"With enormous difficulty and great risk."

"So you could move it out of our closet. You didn't have to put it there!"

"I didn't put it in your closet. I moved it a hundred yards to a dense woods behind my house. I had no idea where it would go in *your* world. It moved a thousand miles. I couldn't plan its location here, and I'm not going to change it now. It happens to be well-hidden and convenient to a town with a decent library. It's perfect."

"Perfect for you. Really lousy for my mother and our whole family."

"I told you, that was not my fault." The elf sounded bored, which made Todd mad.

"Listen, you little runt, you get my mother back and then you get your worm out of our house and out of my yard!"

The elf was just as furious. "Listen yourself, you bug of a boy, don't give orders to a 'runt' who happens to be dense enough that I could reach into your chest with my bare hand and pull out your beating heart and stuff it into the worm's anus! You have 'suppository' written all over you."

There was a moment of silence while Todd realized that the elf was right. There was nothing Todd could do to threaten him; so it did no good to get angry or make demands. If he was going to get any help from the elf, he'd have to keep the conversation calm. So he said the first nonthreatening thing he could think of. "That's like what they did in *Temple of Doom*."

Exasperated, the elf said, "*What* is what *who* did? And where is the temple of doom?"

"It's a movie. An Indiana Jones movie. They pulled the beating heart out of their sacrificial victims."

"I don't have time to go to movies," said the elf. "I don't have time to talk to ignorant, pugnacious boys."

"What does pugnacious even mean?"

"It means that I apparently have become much more fluent in your ridiculously misspelled and underinflected language than you will ever be."

"Well, you're a scientist and I'm not." And then something else dawned on Todd. If the worm had been attracted to Todd, then it must also have been attracted to this guy and for maybe the same reason. "You're a space traveler."

"No I'm not."

"You travel between worlds."

"But not through space. My world doesn't exist in your space. No light from our sun can ever possibly reach this planet. You cannot board any kind of imaginable spacecraft and get from there to here no matter how long you flew. I am not a space traveler."

"You get from one planet to another. And you didn't have to build anything or get good grades in any subject or anything at all. It was just dumb luck, but you got to visit an alien world!"

"From your tone of voice, I suspect you're about to say, 'No fair'!"

"Well, why should *you* get to do it, and I can't!"

"Oh, you can—if you're stupid enough to reach into the throat of the worm and get sucked through and pooped out into a world where you're like a kind of atmospheric diarrhea."

"So what does that make you, interplanetary constipation or something?"

"It makes me sick of talking to you. I've got work to accomplish." The elf started walking away.

"Hey!" called Todd.

The elf didn't pause.

"What's your name!" Todd yelled.

The elf turned around. "You don't need my name!"

Why not? Did it give Todd some kind of magical power? Todd remembered a fairy tale about secret names that his mother used to read to them. "Then I'll call you Rumpelstiltskin!"

To his surprise, the elf came back, looking very angry. "What did you call me?"

"Rumpelstiltskin?" said Todd, remembering the heart-grabbing threat.

"Don't you ever call me that again."

Which almost made Todd call him that twenty times in a row. But no, he had to have this guy's cooperation if he was going to get his mother back. "Then tell me your name."

The elf stood there, irritably considering. "Eggo," he finally said.

Of all things. "Like the waffles?"

"Like *me*. My *name* is Eggo. And yes, your mother already explained about frozen toaster waffles. In my language it doesn't mean anything of the kind."

"What *does* it mean?"

"It means me, I told you! Just like Todd means you. It's a name, not a word."

The elf—Eggo—turned around and headed out across the backyard. Todd almost laughed, his gait was so ducklike as he swung those big shoes around each other so he didn't trip on his own feet. But it wasn't funny. Eggo was doing what he had to in order not to sink into the Earth; what was mother doing, to keep from dissolving into mist on the other side?

Todd went back into the house, determined to do something. He didn't know what, yet, but he had to act, stir things up, change things so that somehow Mom would come back and life would get back to normal. Or maybe it would get even worse, maybe people would die, but isn't that what they already believed happened to Mom? They'd already been through a death and now there was a chance to undo it.

And Todd knew that it was going to be him who did the undoing. Not because he was the smartest or strongest one in the family but because he had decided to. Because he was going to go through the worm and get Mom home. He was going to travel to another world. It's what he was born for.

He couldn't say that to anybody or they'd think he was crazy. Not like seeing elves materialize in the backyard . . .

Dad was still asleep, as usual on a Saturday morning. Jared was up, but he hadn't left his room yet. Todd went in and sat beside the little sorted-out piles of LEGOs that Todd was drawing from to build his . . . what?

"It's like an amusement park ride," said Jared.

"It looks like a skyscraper."

"I put little LEGO guys into this hole at the top and they bounce around inside and pop out here."

"That's not an amusement park, it's a machine for killing people."

"It's not for killing people," Jared said vehemently—but quietly, so Dad wouldn't wake up. "People are perfectly OK when they come through the other side. They are *alive*."

He's building the stupid worm, thought Todd. "You're right," said Todd. "They're perfectly all right when they come out the other end."

Jared looked up at him suspiciously.

"I met your elf," said Todd.

"There's no elf," said Jared.

"All my stuff you put through the mouth in the closet," said Todd. "By the way, thanks for stealing my Hot Wheels and all my other crap."

"I didn't steal anything."

"Mother's alive," said Todd. "I know it now."

But Jared didn't look relieved or happy or anything. In fact, he looked panicky. Only when he felt a strong hand on his shoulder did he realize that Dad must have come into the room and heard him.

Dad had never handled Todd roughly before, not like this. The grip on his shoulder was harsh—it hurt. And he dragged Todd so quickly out of the room that he could barely keep his feet under him. "Hey!" Todd yelled. "Hey, hey, what're you—"

But by then they were in Dad's room and the door slammed shut behind them. "What the *hell* do you think you're doing?" said Dad. He practically threw Todd onto the bed. Then he leaned over him, one hand on either side of him, his face angry and only about a foot away from Todd's. "Do you think it's funny to try to make your brother believe that all his childhood fantasies are true?"

"Dad," said Todd.

"It's all a joke to you, is that it?" Dad said, his voice a harsh whisper. "All that I've done, trying to make life normal again, you think it's really clever to undo it and make your brother think that your mother is still alive somewhere. Do you know what that would mean? That your mother *wants* to be away from us, that she *chose* to leave us like that. You think that's *better* than believing she's dead? Well you're wrong."

"It's not about believing anything," said Todd quietly, reasonably, trying to calm Father down.

And it worked, at least a little. Dad stopped looming over him and sat on the bed beside him. "What is it, then, Todd? Why are you telling your brother that he should believe his mother is alive?"

"Because she is, Dad," said Todd.

Dad turned away from him, slumped over, leaning on his knees. "It never ends."

"Dad," said Todd, "I didn't believe it either. I thought she was dead until this very exact morning when I found out the truth. Something I saw with my own eyes. Dad, I'm not crazy and I'm not joking."

Dad was now leaning his forehead on his hands. "What do you think crazy people say, Todd?"

"They say there's a worm that passes between two worlds, and the mouth of it is in Jared's closet and it sucks things out of our world and drops them into another. And mother's there, only she can't get back because the rules of physics are different in that place, and she's not as dense as we are here, so she can't hold onto things and she doesn't know how to find the mouth on the other side and the jerk who's studying the thing, the guy who moved the mouth of the worm into Jared's closet, he doesn't care about anything except his stupid science. And I can't go there myself and get Mom back if you don't help."

By the time Todd was through, Dad had sat up and was staring at him. "Yes, Todd," he finally said. "That's exactly what crazy people say."

"But I can prove it," said Todd.

Dad buried his face in his hands again. "God help us," he murmured.

"Dad, what if there's one chance in a million that I'm not crazy. Do you love me enough to give me that chance? Will you come and *look*?"

Dad nodded behind his hands. "Yeah, I'll look." He stood up. "Show me whatever you've got to show me, Todd."

Todd knew perfectly well that Dad still thought he was crazy. But he was at least willing to give him a chance. So Todd led the way back into Jared's room.

Jared was sitting on his bed, pressed into the corner of the room, holding a little LEGO guy in one hand and gnawing on a finger. Not the nail, the whole finger in his mouth, chewing on it like it was gum.

"Get your hand out of your mouth, Jared, and come over here and help me," said Todd.

Jared didn't move.

"I've got to show Dad the worm's mouth," said Todd. "And you're the one who knows exactly where it is."

Jared didn't move.

"I can't believe you'd do this, Todd," said Dad. His voice was full of grief. "Jared's made so much progress, and now look."

"Listen to me, both of you! Mom's still alive on the other end of this thing! Stop trying to solve things, Dad, stop trying to make sense of it and just *watch*."

Todd picked up Jared's LEGO thing, his representation of the worm, and took it to the closet and flung open the door.

He couldn't see anything at all like that slice of air out in the

backyard. He walked back and forth in front of the closet, trying
to get the right angle. Then he went to the drapes and opened
them, letting sunlight flood in. It didn't help.

"Todd," said Dad.

"Jared," said Todd angrily, "if you don't help me, Dad's going to think we're both crazy and we'll *never* get Mom back.
Now get off your butt and help me find it!"

Jared didn't move.

Todd took the LEGO thing and stepped right into the closet
and began waving his hand around, thrusting here and there, trying to accidentally find the hole in the air.

"Stop it," said Jared.

"What do you care whether I fall in or not?" said Todd. "Of
course, if you guys aren't helping, I'll fall through just like Mom
did, and I'll be just as helpless as she is on the other side, and then
you'll lose us both, but at least Dad will know I'm not crazy!"
Todd stopped and looked at his father. "Only now things will get
really ugly, because the cops will want to know what happened
to your son Todd, and they'll begin to get curious about how *two*
people from the same family both disappeared under mysterious
circumstances. I watch *Law & Order*, Dad. You'll be the prime
suspect. And then they'll think *you're* crazy, unless *you* fall
through the hole to prove it to them. And then Jared will be an
orphan and there'll be some cops who are thrown out of the police force because they insist that they saw this man—this mass
murder suspect—disappear into thin air in his son's closet. Is that
how you want this to go?"

Father was looking halfway between grief-stricken and terrified. But Jared had gotten off his bed and was padding across the
floor, stepping over LEGO piles. He took the LEGO structure
out of Todd's hands. Todd let him.

"Give me something," said Jared.

"Like what?"

"Your shoe."

"Why can't you use something of your own for once?" said
Todd.

"I can't use my own stuff, because then it grabs hold of my hand and sucks me in."

"You mean it knows who *owns* things?"

"When I throw your crap in, it doesn't grab my hand," said Jared.

"Then let *me* throw *your* crap in."

"Do you want Dad to see this or not?" demanded Jared.

Todd peeled his shoe off, but he didn't give it to Jared. "Shoes are expensive, in case you didn't know," he said. He rolled his dirty white sock off. "Socks are cheap."

"They also stink," said Jared. "You're such a pig, you never wash your clothes, you just wear them forever." But he took the sock and ducked into the closet—ducked *under* something—and then shoved Todd out. "Both of you watch," he said.

Then he held the sock out between his fingers and began swinging it back and forth like a floppy pendulum.

And then, on one of the outward swings, it stopped and didn't come back. It just hung there in the air, Jared holding onto the top of the sock, and something else holding onto the toe end.

"Now it's got it," said Jared. "Watch close because it's quick."

Jared let go. The sock disappeared.

But Todd had indeed been watching closely, and even though it happened fast, he saw that the sock was sucked into something by the toe.

Jared was pressed up against the closet door frame. He was still scared of the thing. Smart kid.

"Get out of the closet, Jared," said Dad. His voice was soft. He was scared, too.

Jared sidled out.

Dad looked from Jared to Todd, back and forth. Then he settled on Todd. "Why didn't you tell me before?"

"Because up till this morning I thought the kid was wacked-out."

"Thanks," said Jared.

"You mean you never saw him do this?" said Dad.

"Did it look like I knew where the thing was?" asked Todd.

"I've put things in that closet hundreds of times," said Dad.

"You have to come at it from the side," said Jared. "And kind of slow."

"And Mother did that?"

"She was trying to prove to me that there was nothing there. I told her how it worked, and so she was going to prove to me that it was just a nightmare. I begged her not to do it. I cried, I screamed at her, I threw things at her to get her to stop."

"Jared," said Dad, "that would just convince her that it was all the more important to prove it to you."

"It got her," said Jared. "I tried to pull her back but it got her whole arm and shoulder and her head so she couldn't even talk to me and then it just grabbed the rest of her, all at once, and ripped her leg right out of my hands." Jared was crying now. "I told you and told you but you didn't believe me and Todd finally said to stop talking about it because you'd think I was crazy."

Dad held Jared against him, patting his shoulder, letting him have his cry. He looked at Todd. "What happened this morning? What convinced you that it was real?"

So Todd told Dad all about Eggo the superdense scientist elf with duckfoot shoes, which sounded crazier the more he talked. He had to keep stopping and reminding Dad about the sock that disappeared, and half the time he was really reminding himself that this insane thing was real.

"I don't know what to make of all this," said Dad. "I don't know what to do. We can't tell this to the cops."

"We *could*," said Todd. "We could demonstrate it just like Jared did. I've got a lot of socks. But I don't think it would help. They'd just take over, they'd throw us out of the house and bring in a bunch of scientists but then *we'd* never get Mom back. 'Cause I don't care about studying this thing, I just want to go through it and get Mom."

"Not a chance," said Dad. "If anyone goes, I go."

"Dad," said Todd. "Think about it a minute. If *you* go, then there's no adult here in the house. Just me and Jared. Somebody's going to notice when you don't show up at work. They'll come here and find out you're gone."

"I'll come right back."

"Did *Mom* come right back?" said Todd. "No, because time flows differently there, it's only been a *week* for her, the guy said. So if you're gone even a few hours, that's days and weeks for us. So you're just as stuck as Mom is, and Jared and I are in foster homes somewhere far away from here while the cops try to figure out who murdered you and Mom because there's no chance they'll listen to two crazy kids, right?"

"So there's nothing we can do."

"I can go," said Todd.

"Not a chance," said Dad. "What can you do that I *can't* do?"

"You can cover up my absence," said Todd. "You can say I'm visiting Aunt Heather and Uncle Peace on their hippie commune which doesn't have a phone. You can say it's therapy because I'm still so messed up about Mom's death."

"That still doesn't get you *or* Mom back from . . . that other place."

"Right," said Todd. "But as long as you're *here*, at the house, you can help us. Because what is Mom's problem? She can't find the mouth on the other side so she can come through it. Eggo knows where it is, he comes through it all the time. So maybe it's in some place where she can't go. Maybe it's inside some building or in a public street where Eggo doesn't want her to be seen. Or maybe he *wants* to keep her captive so he just won't tell her."

"And you think *you* can find it?" asked Dad.

"No," said Todd. "I think you can move it and then show us where it's at."

"Move it?"

"Eggo moved the worm's anus on his side, and it moved the mouth of it into Jared's closet. So if you move the anus on *this* side, the mouth on *that* side should move, too."

"Then neither you nor Mom nor this Eggo person will know where it is," said Dad. "I can't believe I'm talking about moving some interstellar worm's ass."

"It's right out there by the garden hose," said Todd. "You give the thing an enema."

"What?" asked Dad.

"You stick the garden hose in and turn it on full blast."

"What makes you think that will work? It only digests in one direction."

"Eggo threatened to stuff my heart into the anus," said Todd. "You must be able to jam things through that way."

"Unless he was just making a stupid threat that wasn't actually possible."

"Then let's test it," said Todd.

A few minutes later, Dad was in his gym clothes instead of his pajamas and they stood in the backyard. Todd was afraid that he wouldn't be able to find the spot again, but by standing exactly where he had been when Eggo came through, he could see the very, very slight shimmering in the air. He made both Dad and Jared stand in that spot so they could find it. Then he went and got the garden hose and turned it on, just a trickle, and held the hose up so the water was running back down the green shaft of it.

He took it to the shimmering slice of air and tried to push it through. But it was just like waving it around in the air. It met no resistance, it found no aperture. He was just watering the lawn.

Then he remembered that Jared said you had to approach it from exactly the right angle. He tried to remember which direction Eggo's naked body had come through, and moved so he was standing at exactly the same angle from the hole. Then, very slowly, he extended the hose, holding it just behind the metal end where the water came out.

He felt just a little resistance, just *there*, but when he pushed harder, the hose slid aside and it was just air again.

Exact angle of approach. How much was Eggo's body tilted when it came through?

Todd brought his hand down and pushed the hose upward toward the spot where he had met resistance before. Now it felt solid. Real resistance. "I'm there," he said.

He tried to push the hose in. It went a little way, and to his surprise the water started squirting back at him, like when some-body covers the end of the hose with his thumb.

"Yow!" shouted Jared. "Cool!"

"You got it," said Dad.

"I can't push it through," said Todd. "I'm not strong enough."

"Or it only goes one way," said Jared.

"Help me!" Todd said to Dad.

A moment later, Dad was beside him, gripping Todd's hands over the hose. With his strength added on—or maybe entirely be-cause of his strength, because Todd was certainly no strongman—the end of the hose suddenly moved and . . . disappeared.

So did the water. Nothing trickled back down the hose. The water was flowing somewhere else.

"Enema," said Jared. "Cool."

Dad let go.

"No!" said Todd. "We've got to move it."

"Where?" said Dad. "How?"

"We've got the hose jammed into it, don't we? Let's use it like a handle and shove it somewhere else."

"Where to?"

"I don't know," said Todd. "I don't think it matters. Eggo couldn't predict where it would move on *our* side, he could only move it where he wanted on *his* side. So let's move it where we want it and let the other side go wherever it goes."

"Maybe thousands of miles."

"What else can we do?" said Todd. "Wherever it is on that side, Dad, Mom hasn't been able to get to it. So we have to move it, and then when I get there, Mom and I have to find it."

"But how?" asked Dad. "If you and Mom are . . . misty or whatever . . ."

"Dad," said Todd. "It's probably going to be pretty easy to find. There's water coming out of it."

"Or fog," said Dad. "If things are mistier there."

"Water, fog—*something*'s coming out of it right now. So let's move the thing, if we can."

It was only hard because the hose was so flexible. Twice when they tried to move the thing sideways, the hose slipped out, squirting them for a moment before it settled back to being just a trickle. Finally Dad had the idea of using the handle of the rake from the tool shed, and that worked. He shoved it in beside the hose. It was rigid, and they were able to move the thing ten yards across the yard to the shed. The hose slid out as they went, spurting water for a moment when it did.

The shed door was still open, so they easily slid the worm's anus inside.

"Don't pull the rake out yet," said Dad. "Hold it in place."

He ran to the house and came back out with the digital camera. He took pictures of the hose from several angles. "I don't want to run the risk of not being able to get the hose back into it."

It was ten more minutes after that, but Dad got the printouts taped up on the inside walls of the shed. "OK," he said. "Pull out the rake."

It was a lot easier in that direction. *Out* was the direction that the anus wanted things to go.

Dad was all for putting the hose right back in, but Todd said no. "Think about it," said Todd. "I'm not even there yet. And time moves a lot slower there. If we start pumping water, somebody over there is going to notice it. Because it *better* be noticeable in a big way, or Mom and I will never find it."

"They've probably already noticed it," said Dad. "Even that trickle of water wasn't nothing. And what if somebody saw the rake handle?"

"It wasn't all that much water and it wasn't all that long," said Todd. "So give me time to get through and find Mom. Give me time to explain things to her. Eggo said it was hard to talk. Even if it only takes me ten minutes, how long is that *here*, where time goes so much quicker?"

"I see," said Dad. "Can we figure it out?"

"Eggo said maybe it fluctuates. I don't know. We don't want to wait too long, because what if a storm comes up and blows

Mom and me to smithereens? So I think maybe . . . tomorrow? It's a Sunday."

"Too soon," said Jared. "Take your time. What if Mom isn't right there? What if it takes you a long time even to find her?"

"Then when?"

"Next week," said Dad. "A week from now. I can tell the school you're visiting your aunt and uncle, though we'll skip the hippie commune part. And next Saturday morning, we come out and give this thing a full-blast enema."

"Four years," said Jared. "Well, four years and four months. So that's two hundred and . . . twenty-five weeks. Two-twenty-five to one."

"You're doing all this math in your head?" said Todd. If *Todd* could've done that, he might've been able to become an astronaut.

"Sh," said Jared. "One week is 168 hours. Divide that by 225. That's about three-quarters of an hour. Forty-five minutes."

"I don't think it's that precise," said Todd.

"Even if I'm off by double," said Jared, "that gives you somewhere between twenty minutes and an hour and a half."

"You did that in your head?" asked Dad. "Why do your arithmetic grades suck so badly?"

Jared shrugged. "They make me do all these stupid problems and 'show my work.' What do I put down? 'Think think think'?"

"I don't know if that's enough time," said Todd. "I don't know how long it will take."

"It also means," said Dad, "if we run the water for 225 minutes, it will only be *one* minute on the other side."

"Yeah," said Todd, "but it'll mean that in one minute, 225 minutes' worth of water will come through."

"Man," said Jared. "That worm's gonna be doing some serious puking."

"What I'm saying," said Todd, "is that it'll be noticeable."

"And what I'm saying," said Dad, "is that if it takes you half an hour to get to the worm's mouth, we've got to be running that hose for nearly a week."

"Are you worried about the water bill?" said Todd.

"No," said Dad. "Just thinking that in a week, a lot of things might go wrong on our end."

"Dad," said Todd, "so many things can go wrong on both ends that it'll be a miracle if this works at all. But we can't leave Mom there without even trying, can we?"

A few minutes later, Todd was standing in Jared's closet. Stark naked. No point in having his clothes just disappear or whatever they did if you tried to go through the worm wearing them.

"Just make sure you have clothes waiting for Mom and me when we come through in the shed," said Todd.

"You're going to see Mom naked?" said Jared, like it was too weird to imagine.

"It's that or never see her again as long as any of us live," said Todd.

"Mom won't mind," said Dad. "She's in great shape, she kind of likes to show off." He laughed, but it was also kind of a sob.

"Here goes nothing," said Todd.

He reached out his hand.

"Higher," said Jared.

And then the mouth had him. It wasn't like something grabbing him. It was more like getting sucked up against the vacuum cleaner hose. Only instead of sticking to it, he got sucked right in.

He thought he'd come right out the other end, but he didn't. There was time. Like Jonah being stuck in the belly of the whale long enough to call on God to get him out. Only it wasn't a whale, was it, or a big fish, or whatever. It was a worm, like this one. Jonah gets tossed overboard right into the worm's mouth and then it takes him a while to find the mouth on the other side and then he comes through and he's on the beach. He's got to make sense of it somehow, right? So he tells people he was swallowed by a big fish and then God made the fish throw him up on the shore.

That thought took him only a minute. Or a second. Or an hour. And then Todd got distracted by what he was seeing. Stars. All of them distant, but shifting rapidly. As if he were moving through them at an incredible speed. Faster than light. No space-

ship around him, no spacesuit, no way to breathe, only he realized that he didn't need to breathe, he could just look and see
space all around him until a particular star up ahead didn't move
off to the side, it came right at him, getting bigger and brighter,
and then he dodged toward a planet and rushed toward the
planet's surface, going way too fast, reentry was going to burn
him up.

He didn't burn up. He didn't slow down, either. One moment
he was plunging toward the planet's surface and the next moment, without any sensation of stopping, he was being squeezed
headfirst out of a tight space with waves of peristaltic action.
Like a bunch of crap. He could see the ground below him. He
couldn't get his arms free. He was going to drop down and land
on his face.

And with one last spasm of the worm's colon, that's exactly
what happened.

It didn't hurt. He barely felt it. He barely felt anything.

He gathered his legs under him and got his hands in place,
like a push-up, only the grassy ground felt like it was hardly
there. Or maybe like his fingers weren't there. Then he realized
that the bushes around him weren't bushes, they were trees. He
was a giant here. A stark-naked, insubstantial giant.

He felt a breeze blowing. And on the breeze, a distant voice.
Calling his name. "Todd," it was saying. And "no, no," it said.

He looked around, hoping it was mother, hoping she was off
in the distance somewhere. It *was* mother, but she was not distant. She was entangled in the branches of some trees, not touching the ground at all.

"Hold on, Todd!" she called. It looked like she was shouting
with all her strength, but the sound was barely audible. She
couldn't be more than twenty feet away. Well, twenty feet compared to their body size—a lot farther compared to the size of the
trees.

Hold on, she had said, and now he realized that the breeze
was tugging at him, making him drift. He was still in kneeling
position, but he was sliding across the ground.

Mother had the right idea, obviously. Get entangled in the branches. Get *caught* so the wind couldn't carry him like a stray balloon.

It took a while to get the knack of it. To move *through* the branches, heedless of how they poked into his skin. It didn't hurt, really. More like tickling sometimes, and sometimes a vague pressure. He figured the tickling was twigs and leaves, the pressure the heavier, more substantial, less-yielding branches.

Carefully, slowly, he made his way among the interlacing branches of the trees until he was close enough to Mother that neither of them had to shout, though their voices were still breathy and soft. "Don't eat anything," she warned him.

"How could I anyway?" he said.

"You can," she said. "And you can drink. But don't do it. It starts to change you. It makes you more solid."

"But isn't that good?"

"We could never go home," said Mother. "That's what *he* says, anyway. If I ever want to get home, I can't eat or drink."

"You haven't eaten or drunk anything in a week?" asked Todd.

"What are you doing here?" she said. "Why did you come through the hole in the closet?"

"Why did *you*?" he said. "Jared warned you."

"How could I believe him?" She started to cry. "Now we're both trapped here."

"Mom," said Todd. "Two things. First, we have a plan. Dad and Jared are going to help us find the worm's mouth."

"Worm's mouth?" she asked.

"And the second thing. It's been four years."

"No," she said. "A week. It's been a week."

"Four years," repeated Todd. "Look at me. I'm older. I'm bigger. Jared is, too. Four years we thought you were dead."

"A week," she murmured. "Oh, my poor children. My poor husband."

"Mom, you've got to be thirsty. You can't last a week without any water."

"I don't get as thirsty as I thought I would. But yes, I'm getting very weak now. I expected—I thought that pretty soon I'll just let go and blow away."

"Don't let go," said Todd. "Just hold on until they turn on the hose." Then he told her about the plan.

❀ ❀ ❀

It was the longest week of Jared's life. He kept wanting to go out and check the worm's butt to make sure it was there in the shed. Or sit and stare at the mouth in the closet. But he knew if he did that, he'd start wanting to throw things in it. Or go through it himself so he could see Mom. It wasn't fair that Todd got to see her first, when Jared was the one who knew about it all along. But I saw her last, Jared told himself. That wasn't fair either. And if I accidentally or on purpose go through the mouth, who'll help Dad? Who'll turn the hose on?

Who'll keep watch in case the elf comes back?

Because what Jared knew about the elf was this: He wasn't nice. He didn't want Mom to come back. Hadn't Jared begged him to bring her back, the first time he saw him after Mom went through? And the elf just shoved him away. It hurt so bad. The elf was so *strong*.

What if the elf came back and went through the mouth and saw Todd and Mom and realized what was happening and . . . and *killed* them? He might. He was selfish and cruel, Jared knew that about him. He didn't care about anybody. Oh, he asked questions, all the time, but he never answered any, he wouldn't tell anything. "You wouldn't understand anyway, you're just a child," he said. Well, children understand things, Jared wanted to scream at him. But he never did. Because if he got too demanding, if he got *mad*, the elf just left. And what if the elf shoved him again? He didn't want the elf to shove him. It hurt, deep inside, when he did that.

So Jared went through the days with Dad. Without Todd there, Jared and Dad had to do all kinds of jobs. He hadn't realized how hard Todd worked, all the things he did. Or how lonely it got without Todd there to gripe at and play with and yell at and fight over the television remote with.

He had thought all these years that it would be so nice if anyone would just believe him. But he hadn't thought through what that might mean. Believe him and then what? Well, then they would *do* something about it. But he thought it would be like the government would do it, the police, the fire department. Somebody official who already knew all about everything and they could just say, Oh, lost your mother in one of *those* things, of course, happens all the time, give us a minute . . . there! There's your mom!

But of course it couldn't work that way. Nobody knew anything about this. Nobody could just fix it. They had to do it themselves. So now the question was: Would Mom come back? Or had they just lost Todd, too? And if Todd couldn't come back, either, would the cops think Dad had killed him and Mom both and lock him up and put Jared in foster care? A part of him wished they had just left things alone. Losing Mom was bad. But losing everybody else, too, wouldn't exactly make anything better. If he had just kept it to himself. If he had just refused to put that sock into the monster's mouth when Todd told him to.

If . . .

Then it would be Jared's fault if Mom never came back. Even thinking like this, wasn't that the same is wishing Mom would never come home? I'm selfish and evil, Jared thought. I don't even deserve to have a mother.

And then, underneath all the wondering and worrying and blaming, there was this, like a constant drumbeat: Hope. Mom was coming home. Todd would get her and Jared and Dad would show them where the mouth was on the other side by hosing the worm's butt, and they'd all be together again and it would be partly because Jared knew and showed them and helped make it happen.

He nearly flunked three different tests that week and the teachers were quite concerned at his sudden lapse in performance. It was hard to concentrate on anything. Hard to think that their stupid baby easy meaningless tests were worth taking. Hard even to listen to their sympathetic blabbing. "Is everything all right at home?" My brother just got swallowed up by the same monster that ate my mom, but we've got a plan, so, "Everything's fine." "Has anyone *done* anything to you?" Jared knew what they were asking, but apart from the worm in the closet eating his mom and his brother, Jared had to say that nobody had done anything to *him* at all.

And then it was Friday and he got to go home from school and fix himself some food and stay away from the closet because that would make him crazy, to sit and stare at the thing. Nothing was ever coming out of it, and nobody except the stupid elf was ever going into it again. There was nothing to see.

Except there he was when Dad got home, the closet door open and Jared sitting on the floor just looking at it, remembering Mom's look of panic as the thing caught hold of her and then how she looked, just her left shoulder and the rest of her body still in the closet, but not her head, not her right shoulder or arm, because they were going, and how Jared lunged and caught her but then she was torn right out of his arms. Like the thing had to get her in two swallows.

In two *bites*.

"Whatcha lookin' at?" Dad asked. Softly, which meant he didn't think anything was really funny.

"It didn't take Mom all at once," said Jared. "What if it bit her in half? What if she's dead and Todd can't ever bring her home?"

Dad took a slow breath. "Then Todd will tell us that when he gets back."

"And if he never comes back?"

"Then we'll move away from here."

"And leave somebody else to find it?"

"Jared, what can we do? Nuke the house? We didn't make this problem. Especially not you. It was done *to* us. And we're doing our best to undo it." He came and sat beside Jared.

"Things can get a lot worse. Or they can get a lot better. But at least we're doing something, and we're doing the best thing we could think of, and what more can anybody do?"

Jared didn't answer. There wasn't an answer.

"Let's have dinner and watch a DVD tonight," said Dad. "What about a Harry Potter movie? What about all of them?"

"No magic," said Jared, shuddering in spite of himself. "No crap about people turning invisible or going back in time or three-headed dogs or vines that choke you or chessmen that try to kill you or teachers with a face on the back of their head."

"*Charlotte's Web?*"

"Dad, that's for kids."

So they watched *The Dirty Dozen* and when they threw those grenades down the shafts and the German officers in the bomb shelter were panicking and screaming, Jared felt a moment of breathless panic himself, but then he thought: At least the good guys were *doing* something, even though some of them were going to get killed in the process, even though some of them would never get home.

They were saving the world, maybe. Or helping to. We're just saving Mom.

But to Jared, that was better than saving the world. He didn't care about the world.

Saturday morning, Jared was up before the sun. He wanted to wake Dad, but he waited. And not long. Dad usually slept in on Saturday, but today he joined Jared at the breakfast table, pouring out Cheerios and stirring a couple of spoonfuls of brown sugar into the bowl and eating them, all without milk.

"That's so gross," said Jared.

"Better than watching the milk turn grey with sugar," said Dad.

"Do we have to wait till, like, noon or something?" asked Jared.

"There's a lot of oat bran in this stuff," said Dad. "I think I'll need to use the bathroom before I can go anywhere or do anything."

"Yeah, and you'll read a whole book in there."

"Reading, the best laxative." Dad said it in his Lee Marvin voice, which was a pretty good imitation.

"You might as well stick a plug in it," said Jared. "When you're reading, you never let fly."

"I can't believe you're speaking of the bodily functions of your father." This time Dad was doing Charles Bronson. It was nothing like Charles Bronson, actually, but somehow Jared knew that was who he was doing.

"We're giving an interstellar worm an enema today, Dad. I got rectums on my mind."

And Dad went into Groucho Marx. "I don't let anybody say my kid's got poop for brains."

"Poop?" said Jared.

"Got to get used to saying 'poop,' now that Mom's coming back."

"Is she, Dad?"

Dad's Groucho Marx grin didn't fade, but his voice came out like W. C. Fields. "I'll never lie to you, my boy. Now finish your breakfast, you bother me."

"That's all you got? Lee Marvin, a half-assed Charles Bronson, Groucho Marx, and W. C. Fields?"

"I did three others that you didn't catch," said Dad. "And besides, I had Cheerios in my mouth."

"Oh!" said Jared, doing the old family joke associated with Cheerios. "O-o-o-o-oh."

Which would have been the cue for Dad to launch into singing "We're off to see the wizard, the wonderful Wizard of Oh's," but instead he reached across the table and covered Jared's hand with his own. "I can't really eat much this morning, can you?"

"You see anything in my mouth?" said Jared.

Dad pushed back from the table. "I've gotta see a man about a hose."

Jared followed him out into the backyard. Dad unlocked the back shed and set down the clothes he had brought for Todd and

Mom, while Jared unspooled the hose and dragged it across the lawn. Of course it got heavier the farther he pulled it, but it didn't slow him down. Quite the contrary—by the time he reached the shed, he was running.

"Careful," said Dad. "Let's do this methodically and get it right."

Jared watched as Dad found the gap in the air, following the pictures taped to the wall. Then he pushed it in, and kept pushing, and pushing. "Get me more slack, Jared."

Jared went back to the hose reel and pulled it until it was stretched tight. He could see Dad back in the shed, pushing more and more of it into the hole in the air, so it looked for all the world as if it were disappearing.

"It's pushing back," said Dad. "It wants to get it out."

"Wouldn't *you*?" asked Jared.

"Turn the water on. Full blast. Every bit of pressure the city can give us."

Jared turned the handle, turned and turned until it couldn't open any more. He could see Dad bracing his back against the shelves, pushing forward against the worm's efforts to expel the enema.

Jared walked closer to the shed, to ask whether any water was coming back or whether it was all getting through, when he saw the elf walking toward him across the back lawn.

Careful not to speed up, Jared continued toward the shed, but instead of talking or even letting himself look at what Dad was doing, he closed the door, loudly saying as he did so, "Hello, Eggo. Why didn't you tell me that was your name?" With any luck, Dad would realize that they didn't exactly want the elf to know what they were doing.

"You never asked," said Eggo. He headed toward the side-yard fence beyond where the worm's anus used to be and started stripping off his clothes in order to stow them back in the box. Only when he was down to his pants did he turn around and look at Jared, who was now leaning against the corner of the house, looking as nonchalant as he could.

"What are you watching?" he asked.

"All these years I see you, you never tell me anything. One time you talk to Todd, and suddenly you're full of information."

"You were a baby."

"I was, but I'm not now."

"So . . . what do you want to know?" Eggo returned to stripping off his pants. He was buck naked now, stuffing everything into a plastic bag before putting it into the box.

"When are you going to get Mom back to us?"

"I didn't take your mommy away from you," said Eggo. "It's none of my business."

"You're like half a worm," said Jared. "All asshole, no heart."

Eggo reburied the box and stood back up. By Jared's rough guess, it had been about five minutes since he started the water running. That was three hundred seconds. So in the other place, it wouldn't even have been running for two full seconds yet.

Eggo was looking at him. "What are you doing?"

"Math in my head," said Jared.

"I mean with the hose. The water's on, I can hear it, but you've got it flowing into the shed."

"Through the shed and out the back window," said Jared. "It's the only way to reach the very back of the yard without buying a longer hose."

But Eggo wasn't buying it. He was striding toward the shed now.

"It's none of your business!" cried Jared. "Haven't you done enough? Why don't you leave us alone!"

Eggo turned back to face Jared. "Everything's my business if I decide it is," he said. "What are you hiding in there?"

The elf glanced toward the place where there had once been a shimmering slit in the air. He walked toward it, searching. He waved his hand. "What have you done?" he said. He whirled and faced Jared. "You moved it, you little moron! Do you know what you've done? I'll never find it! It'll take months!"

"Good!" shouted Jared. "I hope it takes you *years*, because that'll be *centuries* here, and I won't ever have to see your ugly face and your ugly butt again!"

The elf's face was turning red as he strode toward Jared. His hand rose up as if to smack at him—to swat him into oblivion, as if he were a fly. But then the elf looked at the hose again and then at the shed and then he took off running straight toward it.

"Dad!" shouted Jared. "Don't try to fight him! He'll kill you!"

Eggo flung the door of the shed open—flung it so hard that it ripped from the hinges and sailed like a Frisbee halfway across the lawn. Jared saw that Dad must have understood what was happening, because instead of holding on to the hose, he was gripping the chain saw and pulling the cord. It roared to life just as Eggo reached for the hose.

"Just how dense do you think you are!" shouted Dad.

Eggo backed off a little, but he was holding the hose now, pulling it out. "You moved it! You can't move it!"

"We already did," yelled Jared, "and you'll never get it back exactly where it was!"

"You're drowning my city!" shouted the elf.

"You kept my mother there when you could have brought her home!"

By now Dad had stepped out of the shed and was approaching Eggo. "Drop the hose!" he yelled. "I don't want to see how much damage this can do!"

Eggo roared and smacked at the chain saw with his left hand. It flew out of Dad's grasp, staggering him; but the elf came away from the encounter with his hand bleeding. No, spurting blood.

The deadman switch on the chain saw shut it down, now that nobody was gripping the handle. The sudden silence was deafening.

"What have you done to me!" wailed Eggo.

"You want me to call 911?" asked Jared.

"Drop the hose," said Dad.

"I'll bleed to death!"

"Drop the hose." Dad was picking up the chain saw again.

Eggo stamped his left foot repeatedly, spinning him in a circle as he howled and gripped his bleeding hand. It was as if he was screwing his right foot into the ground, and indeed it was already in the lawn up to the knee.

"You *are* Rumpelstiltskin, you little jerk," Jared said. "You told Todd that you weren't!"

"We're going to get them home, and you're not going to stop us," said Dad. The chain saw roared to life.

With a final howl, Eggo pulled his right foot out of the ground and ran into the house. Not through any of the doors—he leapt for the wall and his body hurtled through, leaving torn vinyl siding and broken studs and peeled-back drywall behind him. Jared ran to the gap in the wall in time to see Eggo dive through the worm's mouth.

He turned around to see Dad already back at the shed, pushing the hose back up into the worm's anus.

"What if he hurts them?" asked Jared. "He's gone back and he'll find them."

"We can only hope they're already on their way."

"The water only started a couple of seconds ago, in that world."

"Then I hope they aren't wasting any time," said Dad. "What else can we do?"

❧ ❧ ❧

Once Mom understood what Todd was talking about, he began to ask her questions. She didn't know any answers. "If I try to go anywhere, either the wind starts lifting me or people see me and start throwing rocks or . . . screaming, or calling for other people to come and look and . . . I'm naked."

Todd knew perfectly well she was naked. But to his surprise, it didn't *feel* like she was naked. She was so misty that it was as if she were wearing the leaves behind her—he saw them better than he saw her.

"But you have to know where he comes from."

"He comes from the same hole in the air that we came through," said Mom.

"Then where does he *go?*"

"How can I tell, from here in the leaves?"

"I mean where does he *head?* Which way? Uphill? Downhill?"

"I'm sorry," she said. "Downhill. I just didn't—I can't think. It's like my mind is fading along with my body. I think bits of me have been blowing away. I'm being shredded. I'm leaving pieces of me in the tree. Todd, I don't even know if I *can* go home. Maybe if I get back there I'll die."

"You'll have a better chance there than here. Can you hold my hand?"

"I can't hold anything," she said.

But when he held out his hand to her, she took it. And he felt her hand in his. He could hold on to her. Better than he could hold on to the branches, because she wasn't so hard and unyielding; he didn't feel as if his body would tear itself apart if he held her too tightly. "Stay with me," he said. "We'll try to get closer to the mouth of the worm. If *he* goes this way, the mouth has got to be down here, too."

The faster they moved, the more control they had, or so it felt. Their feet touched the ground very lightly, but they didn't bounce up and into the air. With the wind coming from their right side, they had to keep correcting in order to move in the direction they intended. But soon enough they emerged from the trees and there was a town.

It looked vaguely oriental, mostly because of the shape of the roofs on the nearest houses. The colors of the walls had once been garish, but they were faded, the paint peeling. But there wasn't time to study the architecture. People were milling around in the streets, jabbering at each other. They didn't speak a language Todd had ever heard before. How could they? Only Eggo had had a chance to learn English. There'd be no talking with these people. No asking them for directions.

Then again, maybe it wouldn't be necessary. Because now he

could see what they were all excited about. The street was covered with a drift of water. Not puddles, a drift—thicker than a mist or a fog, but not rushing anywhere, just hovering.

It was the trickle of water they had sent through the hose when they first tested it up the worm's anus. Only here, it was a lot of water.

Which meant that the original position of the worm's mouth wasn't far from here.

"Come on," he said to Mom, dragging her around the crowd.

"Wait," she said. "It's water from *our* world, isn't it? Todd, I'm so thirsty."

He couldn't force her to stay with him, though he thought it was a bad idea for her to head toward the people. He needn't have worried, though. They were apparently so freaked out by the water that it made them jumpy. When Mom started drifting through the crowd, they parted for her, and some of them screamed and ran away. She knelt in the pool of water and drank.

Todd could watch her gain solidity as she did. Apparently the lack of water had desiccated her, faded her. Now she was more solid, and more naked, but still it didn't bother him. It was like seeing a baby naked. There was a job to do, no time to worry about embarrassment.

He drifted toward her; but the moment he touched the water, it felt familiar and real—and cold and wet. He slogged through the water to where she knelt. "Let's go now, Mom, before they start figuring out just how solid we aren't."

She drank just a little more, then took his hand. They made better progress now that she could find a little better purchase for her feet, more strength in her legs. At the same time, being more solid made her more vulnerable to the wind.

They found the source of the water—a house. The people had broken down the door, apparently to find out what was causing the mini-flood, or perhaps to make sure no one was inside, drowning.

Todd also saw that the water trailed off in another direction.

"When we moved it, the hose stayed with it for a few steps. I think the new location must be in that direction."

He pulled her along. She stopped and drank again. "I need that water," she said. "Don't leave it behind."

"There's plenty of water where we're going," he said.

"But you don't *know* where we're going. Just . . . this direction."

"Mom, we only took a few steps before the hose fell out, and here it's hundreds of yards. So the final location could be a mile farther on. We've got to keep moving."

A crowd of people, many of them children, were following them as they drifted out of the water and on up the streets. Todd tried to figure what a straight line would be, extending in the direction that the thick low fog had trailed off, but the streets weren't cooperating. He kept trying to double back to get in the line, but nothing led in the right direction.

Until finally they reached a street with a high fence enclosing a park, with green lawns and stately trees. He wasn't sure exactly where the line from the hose-water would have intersected with the park, but he knew it was bound to reach it somewhere. Quite possibly the real flood, when it came, would pour out in this park, which would make it much easier to see.

As if on command, there was a loud crashing sound not very far off, and when Todd looked in that direction, he saw a wall of water rushing toward them—toward the whole length of the fence.

There was no point in trying to face it head-on. They had to get around the flood, behind it. And for now, the only way to do that without having to slog through water was to get above it.

He led his mother up into one of the trees. But in this wide open park, they couldn't climb hand over hand, tree to tree. There were wide gaps, and all they could do was leap, hoping they wouldn't get taken by the wind and drift away.

It was slow going, but they made steady progress, and Todd did a fair job of estimating how the breeze would influence their flight. It was kind of exhilarating, to leap out into the air and drift only slowly downward, over the rushing water.

And as they moved around the water, they found that it was flowing out of a huge house. The crashing sound had been the stone front wall of the house giving way, crumbling from the pressure of the thick fog. Which seemed absurd. Except that the water would be coming so hard and fast out of the hose on this end that it wasn't *water* pressure that knocked down the wall, it was the explosive force of air pressure.

He heard shouting behind him, which wasn't a surprise; but it was growing closer, which was. Most of the people had fled from the flood when they saw it coming at them through the wrought-iron fence. But now there was someone plunging ahead through the water. It was easier for him than it would have been for Todd or Mom—the water was only fog to him, though it was a very thick one.

It was Eggo. And he was aiming something at them.

A gun. He had a gun.

Eggo fired. The bullet passed through Todd. He felt it, but not as pain. More like a belch, a rumbling. But that didn't mean the damage wasn't real.

"Why are you doing this!" shouted Todd.

He could see that Eggo didn't hear him. "Keep going toward that house, Mother." He let go of her hand. "Go! Don't make all this a wasted effort!"

She went, looking at him once in anguish but plunging ahead.

Todd headed straight toward Eggo, who was reloading the thing. It was a muzzle-loader. He only had a musket. Thank heaven he hadn't figured out how to make an AK-47.

"Don't be stupid!" shouted Todd. "Stop it!"

Now the elf heard him. "No!" he shouted. "You wrecked everything!"

"The sooner we get back home, the sooner this flood will stop!"

"I don't care!" shouted Eggo. "That's the king's house, you fool! You destroyed the king's house!"

"And you can save it by driving us out of here! Let us go, and be the hero who ended the flood!"

Eggo's gun was loaded and he was pointing it right at Todd, who was close enough now that he thought this time it would probably hurt.

But Eggo didn't fire the thing. "All right!" he said. "Go! I'll shoot *past* you. Just get out of here. And act like you're afraid of me!"

"I won't be acting," murmured Todd.

But he couldn't change direction in midair, and he knew if he once got into that water, he'd never be able to take off again.

"Give me a push!" he shouted at Eggo.

Eggo ran at him and held up the barrel of his musket. Todd grabbed it, barely clung to it with his attenuated fingers, and then hung on for dear life as the elf swung him and threw him toward the palace, where Mom was just reaching the huge gap through which water was flowing.

Soon they were inside, grabbing sconces and chandeliers and furniture to keep them moving forward through the air over the flood. And finally they found it, the place where a huge, thick hose-end was spewing out an incredible volume of icy, jet-speed water. Todd made the mistake of being in the path of the blast and it felt like it had broken half his ribs. He dropped down into the water. Mom screamed and pulled herself down to help him, which saved *her* from getting blasted by another whiplike pass from the hose.

"We've got to get under it," he said. "Look for where the hose comes out of nothing. We have to climb the hose into the worm's mouth!"

Now it was Mom's turn to drag Todd, through the water, barely raising their heads above the surface to breathe. Finally they got behind the hose-end, and even though it was whipping around, the base of it, the place where it came out of nowhere, was fairly solidly in place.

The hose was exactly the right size for Todd to grip it. "You first!" he shouted to Mom. "Climb up the hose! When you get to the end, tell them to turn it off, but don't pull it out till I climb down after you!"

Mom gripped the hose and when her hand inched up past the place where the hose disappeared, it also vanished. "Keep climbing," Todd urged her. "Don't stop no matter what you see. Don't let go!"

As Mom disappeared, he turned around to avoid watching her, and to take one last look around the room. There were soldiers in flamboyantly colored uniforms gathered in the doorways, aiming arrows at him. Oh, good, he thought. They don't have guns.

❧ ❧ ❧

The chain saw lay discarded on the lawn. Jared stood near it, straddling the hose, watching as Dad wrestled with it like a python. He couldn't keep it from being thrust back at him, no matter how tightly he held it against the spot where it became invisible. Suddenly a loop of it would extrude and Dad would have to grasp it again, at the new endpoint. Already several coils were on the floor. What if Mom and Todd weren't anywhere near the point where it emerged on the other side? What if all of this was for nothing?

And then, along with a coil of hose, a hand emerged out of nothingness in the shed.

Dad let go of the hose and took the hand, dragged at it.

Mother's head emerged from the wormhole. "Turn off the water!" she croaked. "Turn it off, but keep the hose—"

Jared was already rushing for the faucet. He turned it off, turned back to face her, and . . .

The hose lay completely on the ground, Mom tangled up in it. Nothing was poking into the worm's anus now. How would Todd get back?

Mom and Dad were hugging while at the same time Dad was trying to wrap a shirt around her, to cover her.

"What about Todd!" Jared shouted.

"He's coming," said Mom. "He's right behind me."

"The hose is out of the worm!"

Apparently they hadn't realized it until now. Father lunged for the hose-end, still dripping, and tried frantically to reinsert it. Mother, half-wearing the shirt now, tried to help him, but she was panting heavily and then she collapsed onto the hose.

Dad cried out and dropped the hose-end. "He's right behind me," Mom whispered.

Jared helped him get Mom up. She wasn't unconscious; once Dad was holding her, she could shuffle along. Dad led her toward the house.

Jared took up the hose again and started trying to feed it through. Finding the hole was hard; pushing the hose was harder.

Until he realized: It doesn't have to be the hose any more. We aren't trying to pump water any more.

He found the rake and fed the handle of it into the gap in the air. Rigid, the handle went in much more easily—which was to say, it took all of Jared's strength, but he could do it. He jammed the handle in all the way up to the metal of the rake and then held it there, gripping it tightly and bracing his feet against the lowest shelf on the wall of the shed.

The rake kept lunging toward him, pressing at him, shoving him backward, but he'd push it in again. It went on until he was too tired to hold it any longer and his belly and hips hurt where the rake had jabbed him, but still he held.

And then a hand came out of the hole along with a shove of the rake, and this time Jared shoved back only long enough to get out from behind the rake. It was practically shot out of the wormhole, and along with it came Todd.

Todd was bleeding all over from vicious-looking puncture wounds. "They shot me," he said, and then he fell into unconsciousness.

❀ ❀ ❀

Mother spent two days in the hospital, rehydrating and recovering. They pumped her with questions about what had happened, where she was for four years and four months, but she told them over and over that she couldn't remember, that one minute she was putting Jared to bed, and the next minute she was lying out in the shed, gasping for breath, feeling as if someone had stretched her so thin that a gust of wind could blow her away.

They questioned Jared, too. And Dad. What did you see? How did you find them? Did you see who hurt your brother? And all they could say, either of them, was, "Mom was just there in the shed. And after we helped her back into the house, we came out and Todd was there, too, bleeding, and we called 911."

Because Dad had told Mom and Jared, "No lies. Tell the truth. Up to Mom going and after Mom and Todd reappeared. No explanations. No guesses. Nothing. We don't know anything, we don't remember anything."

Jared didn't bother telling him that "I don't remember" was a huge lie. He knew enough to realize that telling the truth would convince everybody that they were liars, and only lies would convince anybody they were telling the truth.

Todd didn't recover consciousness after the surgery for three days, and then he was in and out as his body fought off a devastating fever and an infection that antibiotics didn't seem to help. So delirious that nothing he said made sense—to the cops and the doctors, anyway. Men with arrows. Elves. Eggo waffles. Worms with mouths and anuses. Flying through space. Floods and flying and . . . definitely delirium.

The cops found what looked like bloodstains on the chain saw, but since Todd's wounds were punctures and the stains turned out not to react properly to any of the tests for blood, the evidence led them nowhere. It might end up in somebody's X file, but what the whole event would not do is end up in court.

When Todd woke up for real, Dad and Jared were there by his bed. Dad only had time to say, "It's a shame if you don't remember anything at all," before the detective and the doctor were both all over him, asking how it happened, who did it, where the injuries were inflicted.

"On another planet," said Todd. "I flew through space to get there and I never let go of the hose but then it got sucked away from me and I was lost until I got jabbed in the shoulder with the rake and I held on and rode it home."

That was even better than amnesia, since the doctor assumed he was still delirious and they left Todd and Dad and Jared alone. Later, when Todd was clearly *not* delirious, he was ready with his own amnesia story, along with tales of weird dreams he had while in a coma.

The doctor's report finally said that Todd's injuries were consistent with old-fashioned arrows, the kind with barbs, only there were no removal injuries. It was as if the arrows had entered his body and dissolved somehow. And as to where Mom had been all those years, they hadn't a clue, and except for dehydration and some serious but generalized weight loss, she seemed to be in good health.

And when at last they were home together, they didn't talk about it much. One time through the story so everybody would know what happened to everybody else, but then it was done.

Mom couldn't get over how many years she had missed, how much bigger and older Todd and Jared had become. She started blaming herself for being gone that whole time, but Dad wouldn't let her. "We all did what made sense to us at the time," he said. "The best we could. And we're back together *now*. Todd has some interesting scars. You have to take calcium pills to recover from bone loss. There's only one thing left to take care of."

The mouth of the worm in the closet. The anus of the worm in the shed.

The solution wasn't elegant, but it worked. First they hooked the anus with the rake one last time, covered the top with a tarpaulin, and dragged it to the car. They drove to the lake and dragged the thing up to the edge of a steep cliff overlooking the water, then shoved it as far as they could over the edge, with Dad and Mom gripping Todd tightly so he wouldn't fall.

Let Eggo come back if he wanted. Given how tough he was, it probably wouldn't hurt him much, but it would be a very inconvenient location.

The mouth in the closet was harder, because they couldn't move it from their end. But a truckload of manure dumped on the front lawn allowed them to bring wheelbarrows full of it into the house and on into the bedroom, where they took turns shoveling it into the maw.

On the other side, they knew, it would be a fine mist of manure, spreading with the wind out across the town. Huge volumes of it, coming thick and fast.

And sure enough, by the time the manure pile was half gone, the mouth disappeared. Eggo must have moved it from his end. Which was all they wanted.

Of course, then they had to get the smell out of the house and spread a huge amount of leftover manure over the lawn and across the garden, and the neighbors were really annoyed with the stench in the neighborhood until a couple of rains had settled it down. But they had a great lawn the next spring.

Only one thing that Todd had to know. He asked Mom when they were alone one night, watching the last installment of the BBC miniseries of *Pride and Prejudice* after Dad and Jared had fallen asleep.

"What did you see?" he asked. "During the passage?" When she seemed baffled, he added, "Between worlds."

"See?" asked Mom. "What did *you* see?"

"It was like I was in space," said Todd, "only I could breathe. Faster than light I was going, stars everywhere, and then I zoomed down to the planet and . . . there I was."

She shook her head. "I guess we each saw what we wanted to see. Needed to see, maybe. No outer space for me. No stars. Just you and Jared and your dad, waiting for me. Beckoning to me. Telling me to come home."

"And the hose?"

"Never saw it," she said. "During the whole passage. I could *feel* it, hold tightly to it, but all I saw was . . . home."

Todd nodded. "OK," he said. "But it *was* another planet, just the same. Even if I didn't really see my passage through space. It was a real place, and I was there."

"You were there," said Mom.

"And you know what?" said Todd.

"I hope you're not telling me you ever want to go back."

"Are you kidding?" said Todd. "I've had my fill of space travel. I'm done."

"There's no place like home," said Mom, clicking her heels together.

# INCARNATION DAY

## by Walter Jon Williams

In every society, in every age, the transition from child to adult, the time of Coming of Age, is a profound and significant milestone, sometimes even a dangerous one. Never so profound, or dangerous though as in the brilliantly depicted future society shown to us here by Walter Jon Williams, where successfully Coming of Age makes the difference between having flesh and life—and being erased.

Walter Jon Williams was born in Minnesota and now lives in Albuquerque, New Mexico. His short fiction has appeared frequently in *Asimov's Science Fiction*, as well as in *The Magazine of Fantasy and Science Fiction, Wheel of Fortune, Global Dispatches, Alternate Outlaws*, and in other markets, and has been gathered in the collections *Facets* and *Frankensteins and Other Foreign Devils*. His novels include *Ambassador of Progress, Knight Moves, Hardwired, The Crown Jewels, Voice of the Whirlwind, House of Shards, Days of Atonement, Aristoi, Metropolitan, City on Fire*, a huge disaster thriller, *The Rift*, and a Star Trek novel, *Destiny's Way*. His most recent books are the first two novels in his acclaimed Modern Space Opera epic, "Dread Empire's Fall," *Dread Empire's Fall: The Praxis* and *Dread Empire's Fall: The Sundering*. Coming up are two new novels, *Orthodox War* and *Conventions of War*. He won a long-overdue Nebula Award in 2001 for his story "Daddy's World," and took the Nebula Award again in 2005 with "The Green Leopard Plague."

IT'S YOUR UNDERSTANDING and wisdom that makes me want to talk to you, Dr. Sam. About how Fritz met the Blue Lady, and what happened with Janis, and why her mother decided to kill her, and what became of all that. I need to get it sorted out, and for that I need a real friend. Which is you.

Janis is always making fun of me because I talk to an imaginary person. She makes even more fun of me because my imaginary friend is an English guy who died hundreds of years ago.

"You're wrong," I pointed out to her, "Dr. Samuel Johnson was a real person, so he's not imaginary. It's just my *conversations* with him that are imaginary."

I don't think Janis understands the distinction I'm trying to make.

But I know that *you* understand, Dr. Sam. You've understood me ever since we met in that Age of Reason class, and I realized that you not only said and did things that made you immortal, but that you said and did them while you were hanging around in taverns with actors and poets.

Which is about the perfect life, if you ask me.

In my opinion Janis could do with a Dr. Sam to talk to. She might be a lot less frustrated as an individual.

I mean, when I am totally stressed trying to comprehend the equations for electron paramagnetic resonance or something, so I just can't stand cramming another ounce of knowledge into my brain, I can always imagine my Dr. Sam—a big fat man (though I think the word they used back then was "corpulent")—a fat man with a silly wig on his head, who makes a magnificent gesture with one hand and says, with perfect wisdom and gravity, *All intellectual improvement, Miss Alison, arises from leisure.*

Who could put it better than that? Who else could be as sensible and wise? Who could understand me as well?

Certainly nobody *I* know.

(And have I mentioned how much I like the way you call me *Miss Allison?*)

We might as well begin with Fahd's Incarnation Day on Titan. It was the first incarnation among the Cadre of Glorious Destiny, so of course we were all present.

The celebration had been carefully planned to showcase the delights of Saturn's largest moon. First we were to be downloaded onto *Cassini Ranger*, the ship parked in Saturn orbit to service all the settlements on the various moons. Then we would be packed into individual descent pods and dropped into Titan's thick atmosphere. We'd be able to stunt through the air, dodging in and out of methane clouds as we chased each other across Titan's cloudy, photochemical sky. After that would be skiing on the Tomasko glacier, Fahd's dinner, and then skating on frozen methane ice.

We would all be wearing bodies suitable for Titan's low gravity and high-pressure atmosphere—sturdy, low to the ground, and furry, with six legs and a domelike head stuck onto the front between a pair of arms.

But my body would be one borrowed for the occasion, a body the resort kept for tourists. For Fahd it would be different. He would spend the next five or six years in orbit around Saturn, after which he would have the opportunity to move on to something else.

The six-legged body he inhabited would be his own, his first. He would be incarnated—a legal adult, and legally human despite his six legs and furry body. He would have his own money and possessions, a job, and a full set of human rights.

Unlike the rest of us.

After the dinner, where Fahd would be formally invested with adulthood and his citizenship, we would all go out for skating on the methane lake below the glacier. Then we'd be uploaded and head for home.

All of us but Fahd, who would begin his new life. The Cadre of Glorious Destiny would have given its first member to interplanetary civilization.

I envied Fahd his incarnation—his furry six-legged body, his independence, and even his job, which wasn't all that stellar if you ask me. After fourteen years of being a bunch of electrons buzzing around in a quantum matrix, I wanted a real life even if it meant having twelve dozen legs.

I suppose I should explain, because you were born in an era when electricity came from kites, that at the time of Fahd's Incarnation Day party I was not exactly a human being. Not legally, and especially not physically.

Back in the old days—back when people were establishing the first settlements beyond Mars, in the asteroid belt and on the moons of Jupiter and then Saturn—resources were scarce. Basics such as water and air had to be shipped in from other places, and that was very expensive. And of course the environment was extremely hazardous—the death rate in those early years was phenomenal.

It's lucky that people are basically stupid, otherwise no one would have gone.

Yet the settlements had to grow. They had to achieve self-sufficiency from the home worlds of Earth and Luna and Mars, which sooner or later were going to get tired of shipping resources to them, not to mention shipping replacements for all the people who died in stupid accidents. And a part of independence involved establishing growing, or at least stable, populations, and that meant having children.

But children suck up a lot of resources, which like I said were scarce. So the early settlers had to make do with virtual children.

It was probably hard in the beginning. If you were a parent you had to put on a headset and gloves and a body suit in order to cuddle your infant, whose objective existence consisted of about a skazillion lines of computer code anyway . . . well, let's just say you had to want that kid *really badly.*

Especially since you couldn't touch him in the flesh till he was grown up, when he would be downloaded into a body grown in a vat just for him. The theory being that there was no point in having anyone on your settlement who couldn't contribute to the economy and help pay for those scarce resources, so you'd only incarnate your offspring when he was already grown up and could get a job and help to pay for all that oxygen.

You might figure from this that it was a hard life, out there on the frontier.

Now it's a lot easier. People can move in and out of virtual worlds with nothing more than a click of a mental switch. You get detailed sensory input through various nanoscale computers implanted in your brain, so you don't have to put on oven mitts to feel your kid. You can dandle your offspring, and play with him, and teach him to talk, and feed him even. Life in the virtual realms claims to be 100 percent realistic, though in my opinion it's more like 95 percent, and only in the realms that *intend* to mimic reality, since some of them don't.

Certain elements of reality were left out, and there are advantages—at least if you're a parent. No drool, no messy diapers, no vomit. When the child trips and falls down, he'll feel pain—you *do* want to teach him not to fall down, or to bang his head on things—but on the other hand there won't be any concussions or broken bones. There won't be any fatal accidents involving fuel spills or vacuum.

There are other accidents that the parents have made certain we won't have to deal with. Accidental pregnancy, accidental drunkenness, accidental drug use.

Accidental gambling. Accidental vandalism. Accidental suicide. Accidentally acquiring someone else's property. Accidentally stealing someone's extra-vehicular unit and going for a joy ride among the asteroids.

Accidentally having fun. Because believe me, the way the adults arrange it here, all the fun is *planned ahead of time*.

Yep, Dr. Sam, life is pretty good if you're a grown-up. Your kids are healthy and smart and extremely well educated. They live in a safe, organized world filled with exciting educational opportunities, healthy team sports, family entertainment, and games that reward group effort, cooperation, and good citizenship.

It all makes me want to puke. If I *could* puke, that is, because I can't. (Did I mention there was no accidental bulimia, either?)

*Thy body is all vice, Miss Alison, and thy mind all virtue.*

Exactly, Dr. Sam. And it's the vice I'm hoping to find out about. Once I get a body, that is.

We knew that we weren't going to enjoy much vice on Fahd's Incarnation Day, but still everyone in the Cadre of Glorious Destiny was excited, and maybe a little jealous, about his finally getting to be an adult, and incarnating into the real world and having some real world fun for a change. Never mind that he'd got stuck in a dismal job as an electrical engineer on a frozen moon.

All jobs are pretty dismal from what I can tell, so he isn't any worse off than anyone else really.

For days before the party I had been sort of avoiding Fritz. Since we're electronic we can avoid each other easily, simply by not letting yourself be visible to the other person, and not answering any queries he sends to you, but I didn't want to be rude.

Fritz was cadre, after all.

So I tried to make sure I was too busy to deal with Fritz—too busy at school, or with my job for Dane, or working with one of the other cadre members on a project. But a few hours before our departure for Titan, when I was in a conference room with Bartolomeo and Parminder working on an assignment for our Artificial Intelligence class, Fritz knocked on our door, and Bartolomeo granted him access before Parminder and I could signal him not to.

So in comes Fritz. Since we're electronic we can appear to one another as whatever we like, for instance Mary Queen of Scots or a bunch of snowflakes or even *you*, Dr. Sam. We all experiment with what we look like. Right now I mostly use an avatar of a sort-of Picasso woman—he used to distort people in his paintings so that you had a kind of 360-degree view of them, or parts of them, and I think that's kind of interesting, because my whole aspect changes depending on what angle of me you're viewing.

For an avatar Fritz's used the image of a second-rate action star named Norman Isfahan. Who looks okay, at least if you can forget his lame videos, except that Fritz added an individual touch in the form of a balloon-shaped red hat. Which he thought made him look cool, but which only seemed ludicrous and a little sad.

Fritz stared at me for a moment, with a big goofy grin on his face, and Parminder sent me a little private electronic note of sympathy. In the last few months Fritz had become my pet, and he followed me around whenever he got the chance. Sometimes he'd be with me for hours without saying a word, sometimes he'd talk the entire time and not let me get a single word in.

I did my best with him, but I had a life to lead, too. And friends. And family. And I didn't want this person with me every minute, because even though I was sorry for him he was also very frustrating to be around.

*Friendship is not always the sequel of obligation.*

Alas, Dr. J., too true.

Fritz was the one member of our cadre who came out, well, wrong. They build us—us software—by reasoning backwards from reality, from our parents' DNA. They find a good mix of our parents' genes, and that implies certain things about *us*, and the sociologists get their say about what sort of person might be needful in the next generation, and everything's thrown together by a really smart artificial intelligence, and in the end you get a virtual child.

But sometimes despite all the intelligence of everyone and everything involved, mistakes are made. Fritz was one of these. He wasn't stupid exactly—he was as smart as anyone—but his mental reflexes just weren't in the right plane. When he was very young he would spend hours without talking or interacting with any of us. Fritz's parents, Jack and Hans, were both software engineers, and they were convinced the problem was fixable. So they complained and they or the AIs or somebody came up with a software patch, one that was supposed to fix his problem—and suddenly Fritz was active and angry, and he'd get into fights with people and sometimes he'd just scream for no reason at all and go on screaming for hours.

So Hans and Jack went to work with the code again, and there was a new software patch, and now Fritz was stealing things, except you can't really steal anything in sims, because the owner can find any virtual object just by sending it a little electronic ping.

That ended with Fritz getting fixed yet *again*, and this went on for years. So while it was true that none of us were exactly a person, Fritz was less a person than any of us.

We all did our best to help. We were cadre, after all, and cadres look after their own. But there was a limit to what any of us could do. We heard about unanticipated feedback loops and subsystem crashes and weird quantum transfers leading to fugue states. I think that the experts had no real idea what was going on. Neither did we.

There was a lot of question as to what would happen when Fritz incarnated. If his problems were all software glitches, would they disappear once he was meat and no longer software? Or would they short-circuit his brain?

A check on the histories of those with similar problems did not produce encouraging answers to these questions.

And then Fritz became *my* problem because he got really attached to me, and he followed me around.

"Hi, Alison," he said.

"Hi, Fritz."

I tried to look very busy with what I was doing, which is difficult to do if you're being Picasso Woman and rather abstract-looking to begin with.

"We're going to Titan in a little while," Fritz said.

"Uh-huh," I said.

"Would you like to play the shadowing game with me?" he asked.

Right then I was glad I was Picasso Woman and not incarnated, because I knew that if I had a real body I'd be blushing.

"Sure," I said. "If our capsules are anywhere near each other when we hit the atmosphere. We might be separated, though."

"I've been practicing in the simulations," Fritz said. "And I'm getting pretty good at the shadowing game."

"Fritz," Parminder said. "We're working on our AI project now, okay? Can we talk to you later, on Titan?"

"Sure."

And I sent a note of gratitude to Parminder, who was in on

the scheme with me and Janis, and who knew that Fritz couldn't be a part of it.

Shortly thereafter my electronic being was transmitted from Ceres by high-powered communications lasers and downloaded into an actual body, even if it was a body that had six legs and that didn't belong to me. The body was already in its vacuum suit, which was packed into the descent capsule—I mean nobody wanted us floating around in the *Cassini Ranger* in zero gravity in bodies we weren't used to—so there wasn't a lot I could do for entertainment.

Which was fine. It was the first time I'd been in a body, and I was absorbed in trying to work out all the little differences between reality and the sims I'd grown up in.

In reality, I thought, things seem a little quieter. In simulations there are always things competing for your attention, but right now there was nothing to do but listen to myself breathe.

And then there was a bang and a big shove, easily absorbed by foam padding, and I was launched into space, aimed at the orange ball that was Titan, and behind it the giant pale sphere of Saturn.

The view was sort of disappointing. Normally you see Saturn as an image with the colors electronically altered so as to heighten the subtle differences in detail. The reality of Saturn was more of a pasty blob, with faint brown stripes and a little red jagged scrawl of a storm in the southern hemisphere.

Unfortunately I couldn't get a very good view of the rings, because they were edge-on, like a straight silver knife-slash right across a painted canvas.

Besides Titan I could see at least a couple dozen moons. I could recognize Dione and Rhea, and Enceladus because it was so bright. Iapetus was obvious because it was half light and half dark. There were a lot of tiny lights that could have been Atlas or Pan or Prometheus or Pandora or maybe a score of others.

I didn't have enough time to puzzle out the identity of the other moons, because Titan kept getting bigger and bigger. It was a dull orange color, except on the very edge where the haze scatters blue light. Other than that arc of blue, Titan is orange the same way Mars is red, which is to say that it's orange all the way down, and when you get to the bottom there's still more orange.

It seemed like a pretty boring place for Fahd to spend his first years of adulthood.

I realized that if I were doing this trip in a sim, I'd fast-forward through this part. It would be just my luck if all reality turned out to be this dull.

Things livened up in a hurry when the capsule hit the atmosphere. There was a lot of noise, and the capsule rattled and jounced, and bright flames of ionizing radiation shot up past the view port. I could feel my heart speeding up, and my breath going fast. It was *my* body that was being bounced around, with *my* nerve impulses running along *my* spine. *This* was much more interesting. *This* was the difference between reality and a sim, even though I couldn't explain exactly what the difference was.

*It is the distinction, Miss Alison, between the undomesticated awe which one might feel at the sight of a noble wild prospect discovered in nature; and that which is produced by a vain tragedian on the stage, puffing and blowing in a transport of dismal fury as he tries to describe the same vision.*

Thank you, Dr. Sam.

*We that live to please must please to live.*

I could see nothing but fire for a while, and then there was a jolt and a *CrashBang* as the braking chute deployed, and I was left swaying frantically in the sudden silence, my heart beating fast as high-atmosphere winds fought for possession of the capsule. Far above I could just see the ionized streaks of some of the other cadre members heading my way.

It was then, after all I could see was the orange fog, that I remembered that I'd been so overwhelmed by the awe of what I'd been seeing that I forgot to *observe*. So I began to kick myself over that.

It isn't enough to stare when you want to be a visual artist, which is what I want more than anything. A noble wild prospect (as you'd call it, Dr. Sam) isn't simply a gorgeous scene, it's also a series of technical problems. Ratios, colors, textures. Media. Ideas. Frames. *Decisions*. I hadn't thought about any of that when I had the chance, and now it was too late.

I decided to start paying better attention, but there was nothing happening outside but acetylene sleet cooking off the hot exterior of the capsule. I checked my tracking display and my onboard map of Titan's surface. So I was prepared when a private message came from Janis.

"Alison. You ready to roll?"

"Sure. You bet."

"This is going to be *brilliant*."

I hoped so. But somewhere in my mind I kept hearing Dr. Sam's voice:

*Remember that all tricks are either knavish or childish.*

The trick I played on Fritz was both.

I had been doing some outside work for Dane, who was a communications tech, because outside work paid in real money, not the Citizenship Points we get paid in the sims. And Dane let me do some of the work on Fahd's Incarnation Day, so I was able to arrange which capsules everyone was going to be put into.

I put Fritz into the last capsule to be fired at Titan. And those of us involved in Janis' scheme—Janis, Parminder, Andy, and I— were fired first.

This basically meant that we were going to be on Titan five or six minutes ahead of Fritz, which meant it was unlikely that he'd be able to catch up to us. He would be someone else's problem for a while.

I promised myself that I'd be extra nice to him later, but it didn't stop me from feeling knavish and childish.

After we crashed into Titan's atmosphere, and after a certain amount of spinning and swaying we came to a break in the cloud, and I could finally look down at Titan's broken surface. Stark mountains, drifts of methane snow, shiny orange ethane lakes, the occasional crater. In the far distance, in the valley between a pair of lumpy mountains, was the smooth toboggan slide of the Tomasko glacier. And over to one side, on a plateau, were the blinking lights that marked our landing area.

And directly below was an ethane cloud, into which the capsule soon vanished. It was there that the chute let go, and there was a stomach-lurching drop before the airfoils deployed. I was not used to having my stomach lurch—recall if you will my earlier remarks on puking—so it was a few seconds before I was able to recover and take control of what was now a large and agile glider.

No, I hadn't piloted a glider before. But I'd spent the last several weeks working with simulations, and the technology was failsafed anyway. Both I and the onboard computer would have to screw up royally before I could damage myself or anyone else. I took command of the pod and headed for Janis' secret rendezvous.

There are various sorts of games you can play with the pods as they're dropping through the atmosphere. You can stack your airfoils in appealing and intricate formations. (I think this one's really stupid if you're trying to do it in the middle of thick clouds.) There's the game called "shadowing," the one that Fritz wanted to play with me, where you try to get right on top of another pod, above the airfoils where they can't see you, and you have to match every maneuver of the pod that's below you, which is both trying to evade you and to maneuver so as to get above you. There are races, where you try to reach some theoretical point in the sky ahead of the other person. And there's just swooping and dashing around the sky, which is probably as fun as anything.

But Janis had other plans. And Parminder and Andy and I, who were Janis' usual companions in her adventures, had elected to be a part of her scheme, as was our wont. (Do you like my use of the word "wont," Dr. Sam?) And a couple other members of the cadre, Mei and Bartolomeo, joined our group without knowing our secret purpose.

We disguised our plan as a game of shadowing, which I turned out to be very good at. It's not simply a game of flying, it's a game of spacial relationships, and that's what visual artists have to be good at understanding. I spent more time on top of one or more of the players than anyone else.

Though perhaps the others weren't concentrating on the game. Because although we were performing the intricate spiraling maneuvers of shadowing as a part of our cover, we were also paying very close attention to the way the winds were blowing at different altitudes—we had cloud-penetrating lasers for that, in addition to constant meteorological data from the ground—and we were using available winds as well as our maneuvers to slowly edge away from our assigned landing field, and toward our destined target.

I kept expecting to hear from Fritz, wanting to join our game. But I didn't. I supposed he had found his fun somewhere else.

All the while we were stunting around Janis was sending us course and altitude corrections, and thanks to her navigation we caught the edge of a low pressure area that boosted us toward our objective at nearly two hundred kilometers per hour. It was then that Mei swung her capsule around and began a descent toward the landing field.

"I just got the warning that we're on the edge of our flight zone," she reported.

"Roger," I said.

"Yeah," said Janis. "We know."

Mei swooped away, followed by Bartolomeo. The rest of us continued soaring along in the furious wind. We made little pretense by this point that we were still playing shadow, but instead tried for distance.

Ground Control on the landing area took longer to try to contact us than we'd expected.

"Capsules six, twenty-one, thirty," said a ground controller. She had one of those smooth, controlled voices that people use when trying to coax small children away from the candy and toward the spinach.

"You have exceeded the safe range from the landing zone. Turn at once to follow the landing beacon."

I waited for Janis to answer.

"It's easier to reach Tomasko from where we are," she said. "We'll just head for the glacier and meet the rest of you there."

"The flight plan prescribes a landing on Lake Southwood," the voice said. "Please lock on the landing beacon at once and engage your autopilots."

Janis' voice rose with impatience. "Check the flight plan I'm sending you! It's easier and quicker to reach Tomasko! We've got a wind shoving us along at a hundred eighty clicks!"

There was another two or three minutes of silence. When the voice came back, it was grudging.

"Permission granted to change flight plan."

I sagged with relief in my vac suit, because now I was spared a moral crisis. We had all sworn that we'd follow Janis' flight plan whether or not we got permission from Ground Control, but that didn't necessarily meant that we would have. Janis would have gone, of course, but I for one might have had second thoughts. I would have had an excuse if Fritz had been along, because I could have taken him to the assigned landing field—we didn't want him with us, because he might not have been able to handle the landing if it wasn't on an absolutely flat area.

I'd like to think I would have followed Janis, though. It isn't as if I hadn't before.

And honestly, that was about it. If this had been one of the adult-approved video dramas we grew up watching, something would have gone terribly wrong and there would have been a horrible crash. Parminder would have died, and Andy and I would have been trapped in a crevasse or buried under tons of methane ice, and Janis would have had to go to incredible, heroic efforts in order to rescue us. At the end Janis would have Learned an Important Life Lesson, about how following the Guidance of Our Wise, Experienced Elders is preferable to staging wild, disobedient stunts.

By comparison what actually happened was fairly uneventful. We let the front push us along till we were nearly at the glacier, and then we dove down into calmer weather. We spiraled to a soft landing in clean snow at the top of Tomasko glacier. The air-foils neatly folded themselves, atmospheric pressure inside the capsules equalized with that of the moon, and the hatches opened so we could walk in our vac suits onto the top of Titan.

I was flushed with joy. I had never set an actual foot on an actual world before, and as I bounded in sheer delight through the snow I rejoiced in all the little details I felt all around me.

The crunch of the frozen methane under my boots. The way the wind picked up long streamers of snow that made little spattering noises when they hit my windscreen. The suit heaters that failed to heat my body evenly, so that some parts were cool and others uncomfortably warm.

None of it had the immediacy of the simulations, but I didn't remember this level of detail either. Even the polyamide scent of the suit seals was sharper than the generic stuffy suit smell they put in the sim.

This was all real, and it was wonderful, and even if my body was borrowed I was already having the best time I'd ever had in my life.

I scuttled over to Janis on my six legs and crashed into her with affectionate joy. (Hugging wasn't easy with the vac suits on.) Then Parminder ran over and crashed into her from the other side.

"We're finally out of Plato's Cave!" she said, which is the sort of obscure reference you always get out of Parminder. (I looked it up, though, and she had a good point.)

The outfitters at the top of the glacier hadn't been expecting us for some time, so we had some free time to indulge in a snowball fight. I suppose snowball fights aren't that exciting if you're wearing full-body pressure suits, but this was the first real snowball fight any of us had ever had, so it was fun on that account anyway.

By the time we got our skis on, the shuttle holding the rest of the cadre and their pods was just arriving. We could see them looking at us from the yellow windows of the shuttle, and we just gave them a wave and zoomed off down the glacier, along with a

grown-up who decided to accompany us in case we tried anything else that wasn't in the regulation playbook.

Skiing isn't a terribly hazardous sport if you've got six legs on
a body slung low to the ground. The skis are short, not much
longer than skates, so they don't get tangled; and it's really hard
to fall over—the worst that happens is that you go into a spin
that might take some time to get out of. And we'd all been practicing on the simulators and nothing bad happened.

The most interesting part was the jumps that had been
molded at intervals onto the glacier. Titan's low gravity meant
that when you went off a jump, you went very high and you
stayed in the air for a long time. And Titan's heavy atmosphere
meant that if you spread your limbs apart like a skydiver, you
could catch enough of that thick air almost to hover, particularly
if the wind was cooperating and blowing uphill. That was wild
and thrilling, hanging in the air with the wind whistling around
the joints of your suit, the glossy orange snow coming up to
meet you, and the sound of your own joyful whoops echoing in
your ears.

*I am a great friend to public amusements, because they keep
people from vice.*

Well. Maybe. We'll see.

The best part of the skiing was that this time I didn't get so
carried away that I'd forgot to *observe*. I thought about ways to
render the dull orange sheen of the glacier, the wild scrawls made
in the snow by six skis spinning out of control beneath a single
squat body, the little crusty waves on the surface generated by the
constant wind.

Neither the glacier nor the lake is always solid. Sometimes
Titan generates a warm front that liquifies the topmost layer of
the glacier, and the liquid methane pours down the mountain to
form the lake. When that happens, the modular resort breaks
apart and creeps away on its treads. But sooner or later everything freezes over again, and the resort returns.

We were able to ski through a broad orange glassy chute
right onto the lake, and from there we could see the lights of the

resort in the distance. We skied into a big ballooning pressurized hangar made out of some kind of durable fabric, where the crew removed our pressure suits and gave us little felt booties to wear. I'd had an exhilarating time, but hours had passed and I was tired. The Incarnation Day banquet was just what I needed.

Babbling and laughing, we clustered around the snack tables, tasting a good many things I'd never got in a simulation. (They make us eat in the sims, to get us used to the idea so we don't accidentally starve ourselves once we're incarnated, and to teach us table manners, but the tastes tend to be a bit monotonous.)

"Great stuff!" Janis said, gobbling some kind of crunchy vat-grown treat that I'd sampled earlier and found disgusting. She held the bowl out to the rest of us. "Try this! You'll like it!"

I declined.

"Well," Janis said, "If you're afraid of new things . . ."

That was Janis for you—she insisted on sharing her existence with everyone around her, and got angry if you didn't find her life as exciting as she did.

About that time Andy and Parminder began to gag on the stuff Janis had made them eat, and Janis laughed again.

The other members of the cadre trailed in about an hour later, and the feast proper began. I looked around the long table—the forty-odd members of the Cadre of Glorious Destiny, all with their little heads on their furry multipede bodies, all crowded around the table cramming in the first real food they've tasted in their lives. In the old days, this would have been a scene from some kind of horror movie. Now it's just a slice of posthumanity, Earth's descendants partying on some frozen rock far from home.

But since all but Fahd were in borrowed bodies I'd never seen before, I couldn't tell one from the other. I had to ping a query off their implant communications units just to find out who I was talking to.

Fahd sat at the place of honor at the head of the table. The hair on his furry body was ash-blond, and he had a sort of widow's peak that gave his head a kind of geometrical look.

I liked Fahd. He was the one I had sex with, that time that Janis persuaded me to steal a sex sim from Dane, the guy I do outside programming for. (I should point out, Dr. Sam, that our simulated bodies have all the appropriate organs, it's just that the adults have made sure we can't actually use them for sex.)

I think there was something wrong with the simulation. What Fahd and I did wasn't wonderful, it wasn't ecstatic, it was just . . . strange. After a while we gave up and found something else to do.

Janis, of course, insisted she'd had a glorious time. She was our leader, and everything she did had to be totally fabulous. It was just like that horrid vat-grown snack-food product she'd tried—not only was it the best food she'd ever tasted, it was the best food *ever*, and we all had to share it with her.

I hope Janis actually *did* enjoy the sex sim, because she was the one caught with the program in her buffer—and after I *told* her to erase it. Sometimes I think she just wants to be found out.

During dinner those whose parents permitted it were allowed two measured doses of liquor to toast Fahd—something called Ring Ice, brewed locally. I think it gave my esophagus blisters.

After the Ring Ice things got louder and more lively. There was a lot more noise and hilarity when the resort crew discovered that several of the cadre had slipped off to a back room to find out what sex was like, now they had real bodies. It was when I was laughing over this that I looked at Janis and saw that she was quiet, her body motionless. She's normally louder and more demonstrative than anyone else, so I knew something was badly wrong. I sent her a private query through my implant. She sent a single-word reply.

*Mom . . .*

I sent her a glyph of sympathy while I wondered how had Janis' mom had found out about our little adventure so quickly. There was barely time for a lightspeed signal to bounce to Ceres and back.

Ground Control must have really been annoyed. Or maybe she and Janis' mom were Constant Soldiers in the Five Principles

Movement and were busy spying on everyone else—all for the greater good, of course.

Whatever the message was, Janis bounced back pretty quickly. Next thing I knew she was sidling up to me saying, "Look, you can loan me your vac suit, right?"

Something about the glint in her huge platter eyes made me cautious.

"Why would I want to do that?" I asked.

"Mom says I'm grounded. I'm not allowed to go skating with the rest of you. But nobody can tell these bodies apart—I figured if we switched places we could show her who's boss."

"And leave me stuck here by myself?"

"You'll be with the waiters—and some of them are kinda cute, if you like them hairy." Her tone turned serious. "It's solidarity time, Alison. We can't let Mom win this one."

I thought about it for a moment, then said, "Maybe you'd better ask someone else."

Anger flashed in her huge eyes. "I knew you'd say that! You've always been afraid to stand up to the grown-ups!"

"Janis," I sighed. "Think about it. Do you think your mom was the only one who got a signal from Ground Control? My parents are going to be looking into the records of this event *very closely*. So I think you should talk someone else into your scheme—and not Parminder or Andy, either."

Her whole hairy body sulked. I almost laughed.

"I guess you're right," she conceded.

"You know your mom is going to give you a big lecture when we get back."

"Oh yeah. I'm sure she's writing her speech right now, making sure she doesn't miss a single point."

"Maybe you'd better let me eavesdrop," I said. "Make sure you don't lose your cool."

She looked even more sulky. "Maybe you'd better."

We do this because we're cadre. Back in the old days, when the first poor kids were being raised in virtual, a lot of them cracked up once they got incarnated. They went crazy, or developed a lot of weird obsessions, or tried to kill themselves, or turned out to have a kind of autism where they could only relate to things through a computer interface.

So now parents don't raise their children by themselves. Most kids still have two parents, because it takes two to pay the citizenship points and taxes it takes to raise a kid, and sometimes if there aren't enough points to go around there are three parents, or four or five. Once the points are paid the poor moms and dads have to wait until there are enough applicants to fill a cadre. A whole bunch of virtual children are raised in one group, sharing their upbringing with their parents and creche staff. Older cadres often join their juniors and take part in their education, also.

The main point of the cadre is for us all to keep an eye on each other. Nobody's allowed to withdraw into their own little world. If anyone shows sign of going around the bend, we unite in our efforts to retrieve them.

Our parents created the little hell that we live in. It's our job to help each other survive it.

*A person used to vicissitudes is not easily dejected.*

Certainly Janis isn't, though despite cadre solidarity she never managed to talk anyone else into changing places with her. I felt only moderately sorry for her—she'd already had her triumph, after all—and I forgot all about her problems once I got back into my pressure suit and out onto the ice.

Skating isn't as thrilling as skiing, I suppose, but we still had fun. Playing crack-the-whip in the light gravity, the person on the end of the line could be fired a couple kilometers over the smooth methane ice.

After which it was time to return to the resort. We all showered while the resort crew cleaned and did maintenance on our suits, and then we got back in the suits so that the next set of tourists would find their rental bodies already armored up and ready for sport.

We popped open our helmets so that the scanners could be put on our heads. Quantum superconducting devices tickled our brain cells and recovered everything they found, and then our brains—our essences—were dumped into a buffer, then fired by communication laser back to Ceres and the sim in which we all lived.

The simulation seemed inadequate compared to the reality of Titan. But I didn't have time to work out the degree of difference, because I had to save Janis' butt.

That's us. That's the cadre. All for one and one for all.

And besides, Janis has been my best friend for practically ever.

Anna-Lee, Janis' mom, was of course waiting for her, sitting in the little common room outside Janis' bedroom. (Did I mention that we sleep, Dr. Sam? We don't sleep as long as incarnated people do, just a few hours, but our parents want us to get used to the idea so that when we're incarnated we know to sleep when we get tired instead of ignoring it and then passing out while doing something dangerous or important.

(The only difference between our dreams and yours is that we don't dream. I mean, what's the point, we're stuck in our parents' dream anyway.)

So I'm no sooner arrived in my own simulated body in my own simulated bedroom when Janis is screaming on the private channel.

"Mom is here! I need you *now*!"

So I press a few switches in my brain and there I am, right in Janis' head, getting much of the same sensor feed that she's receiving herself. And I look at her and I say, "Hey, you can't talk to Anna-Lee looking like *this*."

Janis is wearing her current avatar, which is something like a crazy person might draw with crayons. Stick-figure body, huge yellow shoes, round bobble head with crinkly red hair like wires.

"Get your quadbod on!" I tell her. "Now!"

So she switches, and now her avatar has four arms, two in the shoulders, two in the hip sockets. The hair is still bright red. Whatever her avatar looks like, Janis always keeps the red hair.

"Good," I say. "That's normal."

Which it is, for Ceres. Which is an asteroid without much gravity, so there really isn't a lot of point in having legs. In microgravity legs just drag around behind you and bump into things and get bruises and cuts. Whereas everyone can use an extra pair of arms, right? So most people who live in low- or zero-gravity environments use quadbods, which are much more practical than the two-legged model.

So Janis pushes off with her left set of arms and floats through the door into the lounge where her mom awaits. Anna-Lee wears a quadbod, too, except that hers isn't an avatar, but a three-dimensional holographic scan of her real body. And you can tell that she's really pissed—she's got tight lips and tight eyelids and a tight face, and both sets of arms are folded across her midsection with her fingers digging into her forearms as if she's repressing the urge to grab Janis and shake her.

"Hi, Mom," Janis said.

"You not only endangered yourself," Anna-Lee said, "but you chose to endanger others, too."

"Sit down before you answer," I murmured in Janis' inward ear. "Take your time."

I was faintly surprised that Janis actually followed my advice. She drifted into a chair, used her lower limbs to settle herself into it, and then spoke.

"Nobody was endangered," she said, quite reasonably.

Anna-Lee's nostrils narrowed.

"You diverted from the flight plan that was devised for your safety," she said.

"I made a new flight plan," Janis pointed out. "Ground Control accepted it. If it was dangerous, she wouldn't have done that."

Anna-Lee's voice got that flat quality that it gets when she's following her own internal logic. Sometimes I think she's the program, not us.

"You are not authorized to file flight plans!" she snapped.

"Ground Control accepted it," Janis repeated. Her voice had grown a little sharp, and I whispered at her to keep cool.

"And Ground Control immediately informed *me*! They were right on the edge of calling out a rescue shuttle!"

"But they didn't, because there was no problem!" Janis

snapped out, and then there was a pause while I told her to lower her voice.

"Ground Control accepted my revised plan," she said. "I landed according to the plan, and nobody was hurt."

"You planned this from the beginning!" All in that flat voice of hers. "This was a deliberate act of defiance!"

Which was true, of course.

"What harm did I do?" Janis asked.

("Look," I told Janis. "Just tell her that she's right and you were wrong and you'll never do it again.")

("I'm not going to lie!" Janis sent back on our private channel. "Whatever Mom does, she's never going to make me lie!")

All this while Anna-Lee was saying, "We must all work together for the greater good! Your act of defiance did nothing but divert people from their proper tasks! Titan Ground Control has better things to do than worry about you!"

There was no holding Janis back now. "You *wanted* me to learn navigation! So I learned it—because *you* wanted it! And now I've proved that I can use it, and you're angry about it!" She was waving her arms so furiously that she bounced up from her chair and began to sort of jerk around the room.

"And do you know why that is, Mom?" she demanded.

*"For God's sake shut up!"* I shouted at her. I knew where this was leading, but Janis was too far gone in her rage to listen to me now.

"It's because you're second-rate!" Janis shouted at her mother. "Dad went off to Barnard's Star, but *you* didn't make the cut! And I can do all the things you wanted to do, and do them better, and *you can't stand it!*"

*"Will you be quiet!"* I told Janis. "Remember that *she owns you!"*

"I accepted the decision of the committee!" Anna-Lee was shouting. "I am a Constant Soldier and I live a productive life, and I will *not* be responsible for producing a child who is a *burden* and a *drain on resources!*"

"Who says I'm going to be a burden?" Janis demanded.

"*You're* the only person who says that! If I incarnated tomorrow I could get a good job in ten minutes!"

"Not if you get a reputation for disobedience and anarchy!"

By this point it was clear that since Janis wasn't listening to me, and Anna-Lee *couldn't* listen, there was no longer any point in my involving myself in what had become a very predictable argument. So I closed the link and prepared my own excuses for my own inevitable meeting with my parents.

I changed from Picasso Woman to my own quadbod, which is what I use when I talk to my parents, at least when I want something from them. My quadbod avatar is a girl just a couple years younger than my actual age, wearing a school uniform with a Peter Pan collar and a white bow in her—my—hair. And my beautiful brown eyes are just slightly larger than eyes are in reality, because that's something called "neotony," which means you look more like a baby and babies are designed to be irresistible to grown-ups.

Let me tell you that it works. Sometimes I can blink those big eyes and get away with anything.

And at that point my father called, and told me that he and my mom wanted to talk to me about my adventures on Titan, so I popped over to my parents' place, where I appeared in holographic form in their living room.

My parents are pretty reasonable people. Of course I take care to *keep* them reasonable, insofar as I can. *Let me smile with the wise*, as Dr. Sam says, *and feed with the rich*. I will keep my opinions to myself, and try my best to avoid upsetting the people who have power over me.

Why did I soar off with Janis on her flight plan? my father wanted to know.

"Because I didn't think she should go alone," I said.

Didn't you try to talk her out of it? my mother asked.

"You can't talk Janis out of anything," I replied. Which, my parents knowing Janis, was an answer they understood.

So my parents told me to be careful, and that was more or less the whole conversation.

Which shows you that not all parents up here are crazy.

Mine are more sensible than most. I don't think many parents would think much of my ambition to get involved in the fine arts. That's just not *done* up here, let alone the sort of thing *I* want to do, which is to incarnate on Earth and apprentice myself to an actual painter, or maybe a sculptor. Up here they just use cameras, and their idea of original art is to take camera pictures or alter camera pictures or combine camera pictures with one another or process the camera pictures in some way.

I want to do it from scratch, with paint on canvas. And not with a computer-programmed spray gun either, but with a real brush and blobs of paint. Because if you ask me the *texture* of the thing is important, which is why I like oils. Or rather the *idea* of oils, because I've never actually had a chance to work with the real thing.

And besides, as Dr. Sam says, *A man who has not been in Italy, is always conscious of an inferiority, from his not having seen what is expected a man should see. The grand object of traveling is to see the shores of the Mediterranean.*

So when I told my parents what I wanted to do, they just sort of shrugged and made me promise to learn another skill as well, one just a little bit more practical. So while I minor in art I'm majoring in computer design and function and programming, which is pretty interesting because all our really complex programs are written by artificial intelligences who are smarter than we are, so getting them to do what you want is as much like voodoo as science.

So my parents and I worked out a compromise that suited everybody, which is why I think my parents are pretty neat actually.

About twenty minutes after my talk with my parents, Janis knocked on my door, and I made the door go away, and she walked in, and then I put the door back. (Handy things, sims.)

"Guess that didn't work out so good, huh?" she said.

"On your family's civility scale," I said, "I think that was about average."

Her eyes narrowed (she was so upset that she'd forgot to

change out of her quadbod, which is why she had the sort of eyes that could narrow).

"I'm going to get her," she said.

"I don't think that's very smart," I said.

Janis was smacking her fists into my walls, floor, and ceiling and shooting around the room, which was annoying even though the walls were virtual and she couldn't damage them or get fingerprints on them.

"Listen," I said. "All you have to do is keep the peace with your mom until you've finished your thesis, and then you'll be incarnated and she can't touch you. It's just *months*, Janis."

"My *thesis*!" A glorious grin of discovery spread across Janis' face. "I'm going to use my *thesis*! I'm going to stick it to Mom right where it hurts!"

I reached out and grabbed her and steadied her in front of me with all four arms.

"Look," I said. "You can't keep calling her bluff."

Her voice rang with triumph "Just watch me."

"Please," I said. "I'm begging you. *Don't do anything till you're incarnated!*"

I could see the visions of glory dancing before her eyes. She wasn't seeing or hearing me at all.

"She's going to have to admit that I am right and that she is wrong," she said. "I'm going to nail my thesis to her forehead like Karl Marx on the church door."

"That was Martin Luther actually." (Sometimes I can't help these things.)

She snorted. "Who cares?"

"I do." Changing the subject. "*Because I don't want you to die.*"

Janis snorted. "I'm not going to bow to her. I'm going to *crush her*. I'm going to show her how stupid and futile and second-rate she is."

And at that moment there was a signal at my door. I ignored it.

"The power of punishment is to silence, not to confute," I said.

Her face wrinkled as if she'd bit into something sour. "I can't *believe* you're quoting that old dead guy again."

*I have found you an argument*, I wanted to say with Dr. Sam, *but I am not obliged to find you an understanding.*

The signal at my door repeated, and this time it was attached to an electronic signal that meant *Emergency*! Out of sheer surprise I dissolved the door.

Mei was there in her quadbod, an expression of anger on her face.

"If you two are finished congratulating each other on your brilliant little prank," she said, "you might take time to notice that Fritz is missing."

"Missing?" I didn't understand how someone could be missing. "Didn't his program come back from Titan?"

If something happened to the transmission, they could reload Fritz from a backup.

Mei's expression was unreadable. "He never went. He met the Blue Lady."

And then she pushed off with two of her hands and drifted away, leaving us in a sudden, vast, terrible silence.

We didn't speak, but followed Mei into the common room. The other cadre members were all there, and they all watched us as we floated in.

When you're little, you first hear about the Blue Lady from the other kids in your cadre. Nobody knows for sure how we *all* find out about the Blue Lady—not just the cadres on Ceres, but the ones on Vesta, and Ganymede, and *everywhere*.

And we all know that sometimes you might see her, a kind smiling woman in a blue robe, and she'll reach out to you, and she seems so nice you'll let her take your hand.

Only then, when it's too late, you'll see that she has no eyes, but only an empty blackness filled with stars.

She'll take you away and your friends will never see you again.

And of course it's your parents who send the Blue Lady to find you when you're bad.

We all know that the Blue Lady doesn't truly exist, it's ordinary techs in ordinary rooms who give the orders to zero out your program along with all its backups, but we all believe in the Blue Lady really, and not just when we're little.

Which brings me to the point I made about incarnation earlier. Once you're incarnated, you are considered a human being, and you have human rights.

But *not until then*. Until you're incarnated, you're just a computer program that belongs to your parents, and if your parents think the program is flawed or corrupted and simply too awkward to deal with, they can have you zeroed.

Zeroed. Not killed. The grown-ups insist that there's a difference, but I don't see it myself.

Because the Blue Lady really comes for some people, as she came for Fritz when Jack and Hans finally gave up trying to fix him. Most cadres get by without a visit. Some have more than one. There was a cadre on Vesta who lost eight, and then there were suicides among the survivors once they incarnated, and it was a big scandal that all the grown-ups agreed never to talk about.

I have never for an instant believed that my parents would ever send the Blue Lady after me, but still it's always there in the back of my mind, which is why I think that the current situation is so horrible. It gives parents a power they should never have, and it breeds a fundamental distrust between kids and their parents.

The grown-ups' chief complaint about the cadre system is that their children bond with their peers and not their parents. Maybe it's because their peers can't kill them.

Everyone in the cadre got the official message about Fritz, that he was basically irreparable and that the chance of his making a successful incarnation was essentially zero. The message said that none of us were at fault for what had happened, and that everyone knew that we'd done our best for him.

This was in the same message queue as a message to me from Fritz, made just before he got zeroed out. There he was with his stupid hat, smiling at me.

"Thank you for saying you'd play the shadowing game with me," he said. "I really think you're wonderful." He laughed. "See you soon, on Titan!"

So then I cried a lot, and I erased the message so that I'd never be tempted to look at it again.

We all felt failure. It was our job to make Fritz right, and we hadn't done it. We had all grown up with him, and even though he was a trial he was a part of our world. I had spent the last few days avoiding him, and I felt horrible about it; but everyone else had done the same thing at one time or another.

We all missed him.

The cadre decided to wear mourning, and we got stuck in a stupid argument about whether to wear white, which is the traditional mourning color in Asia, or black, which is the color in old Europe.

"Wear blue," Janis said. So we did. Whatever avatars we wore from that point on had blue clothing, or used blue as a principal color somewhere in their composition.

If any of the parents noticed, or talked about it, or complained, I never heard it.

I started thinking a lot about how I related to incarnated people, and I thought that maybe I'm just a little more compliant and adorable and sweet-natured than I'd otherwise be, because I want to avoid the consequences of being otherwise. And Janis is perhaps more defiant than she'd be under other circumstances, because she wants to show she's not afraid. *Go ahead, Mom*, she says, *pull the trigger. I dare you.*

Underestimating Anna-Lee all the way. Because Anna-Lee is a Constant Soldier of the Five Principles Movement, and that means *serious*.

The First Principle of the Five Principles Movement states that *Humanity is a pattern of thought, not a side effect of taxonomy*, which means that you're human if you *think* like a human, whether you've got six legs or four arms or two legs like the folks on Earth and Mars.

And then so on to the Fifth Principle, we come to the statement that humanity in all its various forms is intended to occupy every possible ecosystem throughout the entire universe, or at least as much of it as we can reach. Which is why the Five Principles Movement has always been very big on genetic experimentation, and the various expeditions to nearby stars.

I have no problem with the Five Principles Movement, myself. It's rational compared with groups like the Children of Venus or the God's Menu people.

Besides, if there isn't something to the Five Principles, what are we doing out here in the first place?

My problem lies with the sort of people the Movement attracts, which is to say people like Anna-Lee. People who are obsessive, and humorless, and completely unable to see any other point of view. Nor only do they dedicate themselves heart and soul to whatever group they join, they insist everyone else has to join as well, and that anyone who isn't a part of it is a Bad Person.

So even though I pretty much agree with the Five Principles I don't think I'm going to join the movement. I'm going to keep in mind the wisdom of my good Dr. Sam: *Most schemes of political improvement are very laughable things.*

But to get back to Anna-Lee. Back in the day she married Carlos, who was also in the Movement, and together they worked for years to qualify for the expedition to Barnard's Star on the *True Destiny*. They created Janis together, because having children is all a part of occupying the universe and so on.

But Carlos got the offer to crew the ship, and Anna-Lee didn't. Carlos chose Barnard's Star over Anna-Lee, and now he's a couple light-months away. He and the rest of the settlers are in electronic form—no sense in spending the resources to ship a whole body to another star system when you can just ship the data and build the body once you arrive—and for the most part they're dormant, because there's nothing to do until they near their destination. But every week or so Carlos has himself awakened so that he can send an electronic postcard to his daughter.

The messages are all really boring, as you might expect from someone out in deep space where there's nothing to look at and nothing to do, and everyone's asleep anyway.

Janis sends him longer messages, mostly about her fights with Anna-Lee. Anna-Lee likewise sends Carlos long messages about Janis' transgressions. At two light-months out Carlos declines to mediate between them, which makes them both mad.

So Anna-Lee is mad because her husband left her, and she's mad at Janis for not being a perfect Five Principles Constant Soldier. Janis is mad at Carlos for not figuring out a way to take her along, and she's mad at Anna-Lee for not making the crew on the *True Destiny* and, failing that, not having the savvy to keep her husband in the picture.

And she's also mad at Anna-Lee for getting married again, this time to Rhee, a rich Movement guy who was able to swing the taxes to create *two new daughters*, both of whom are the stars of their particular cadres and are going to grow up to be perfect Five Principles Kids, destined to carry on the work of humanity in new habitats among distant stars.

Or so Anna-Lee claims, anyway.

Which is why I think that Janis underestimates her mother. I think the way Anna-Lee looks at it, she's got two new kids, who are everything she wants. And one older kid who gives her trouble, and who she can give to the Blue Lady without really losing anything, since she's lost Janis anyway. She's already given a husband to the stars, after all.

And all this is another reason why I want to incarnate on Earth, where a lot of people still have children the old-fashioned way. The parents make an embryo in a gene-splicer, and then the embryo is put in a vat, and nine months later you crack the vat open and you've got an actual baby, not a computer program. And even if the procedure is a lot more time-consuming and messy I still think it's superior.

So I was applying for work on Earth, both for jobs that could use computer skills, and also for apprenticeship programs in the fine arts. But there's a waiting list for pretty much any job you want on Earth, and also there's a big entry tax unless they *really* want you, so I wasn't holding my breath; and besides, I hadn't finished my thesis.

I figured on graduating from college along with most of my cadre, at the age of fourteen. I understand that in your day, Dr. Sam, people graduated from college a lot later. I figure there are several important reasons for the change: (1) we virtual kids don't sleep as much as you do, so we have more time for study; (2) there isn't that much else to do here anyway; and (3) we're really, really, *really* smart. Because if you were a parent, and you had a say in the makeup of your kid (along with the doctors and the sociologists and the hoodoo machines), would you say, *No thanks, I want mine stupid?*

No, I don't think so.

And the meat-brains that we incarnate into are pretty smart, too. Just in case you were wondering.

We could grow up faster, if we wanted. The computers we live in are so fast that we could go from inception to maturity in just two or three months. But we wouldn't get to interact with our parents, who being meat would be much slower, or with anyone else. So in order to have any kind of relationship with our elders, or any kind of socialization at all, we have to slow down to our parents' pace. I have to say that I agree with that.

In order to graduate I needed to do a thesis, and unfortunately I couldn't do the one I wanted, which was the way the paintings of Brueghel, etc., reflected the theology of the period. All the training with computers and systems, along with art and art history, had given me an idea of how abstract systems such as theology work, and how you can visually represent fairly abstract concepts on a flat canvas.

But I'd have to save that for maybe a postgraduate degree, because my major was still in the computer sciences, so I wrote a fairly boring thesis on systems interoperability—which, if you care, is the art of getting different machines and highly specialized operating systems to talk to each other, a job that is made more difficult if the machines in question happen to be a lot smarter than you are.

Actually it's a fairly interesting subject. It just wasn't interesting in my thesis.

While I was doing that I was also working outside contracts for Dane, who was from a cadre that had incarnated a few years ahead of us, and who I got to know when his group met with ours to help with our lessons and with our socialization skills (because they wanted us to be able to talk to people outside the cadre and our families, something we might not do if we didn't have practice).

Anyway, Dane had got a programming job in Ceres' communications center, and he was willing to pass on the more boring parts of his work to me in exchange for money. So I was getting a head start on paying that big Earth entry tax, or if I could evade the tax maybe living on Earth a while and learning to paint.

"You're just going to end up being Ceres' first interior decorator," Janis scoffed.

"And that would be a *bad* thing?" I asked. "Just *look* at this place!" Because it's all so functional and boring and you'd think they could find a more interesting color of paint than *grey*, for God's sake.

That was one of the few times I'd got to talk to Janis since our adventure on Titan. We were both working on our theses, and still going to school, and I had my outside contracts, and I think she was trying to avoid me, because she didn't want to tell me what she was doing because she didn't want me to tell her not to do it.

Which hurt, by the way. Since we'd been such loyal friends up to the point where I told her not to get killed, and then because I wanted to save her life she didn't want to talk to me anymore.

The times I mostly got to see Janis were Incarnation Day parties for other members of our cadre. So we got to see Ganymede, and Iapetus, and Titan again, and Rhea, and Pluto, Callisto, and

Io, and the antimatter generation ring between Venus and Mercury, and Titan again, and then Titan a fourth time.

Our cadre must have this weird affinity for orange, I don't know.

We went to Pallas, Juno, and Vesta. Though if you ask me, one asteroid settlement is pretty much like the next.

We went to Third Heaven, which is a habitat the God's Menu people built at L2. And they can *keep* a lot of the items on the menu, if you ask me.

We visited Luna (which you would call the Moon, Dr. Sam. As if there was only one). And we got to view *Everlasting Dynasty*, the starship being constructed in lunar orbit for the expedition to Tau Ceti, the settlement that Anna-Lee was trying her best to get Janis aboard.

We also got to visit Mars three times. So among other entertainments I looked down at the planet from the top of Olympus Mons, the largest mountain in the solar system, and I looked down from the edge of the solar system's largest canyon, and then I looked *up* from the bottom of the same canyon.

We all tried to wear blue if we could, in memory of the one of us who couldn't be present.

Aside from the sights, the Incarnation Day parties were great because all our incarnated cadre members turned up, in bodies they'd borrowed for the occasion. We were all still close, of course, and kept continually in touch, but our communication was limited by the speed of light and it wasn't anything like having Fahd and Chandra and Solange there in person, to pummel and to hug.

We didn't go to Earth. I was the only one of our cadre who had applied there, and I hadn't got an answer yet. I couldn't help fantasizing about what my Incarnation Day party would be like if I held it on Earth—where would I go? What would we look at? Rome? Mount Everest? The ocean habitats? The plans of Africa, where the human race began?

It was painful to think that the odds were high that I'd never see any of these places.

Janis never tried to organize any of her little rebellions on these trips. For one thing word had got out, and we were all pretty closely supervised. Her behavior was never less than what Anna-Lee would desire. But under it all I could tell she was planning something drastic.

I tried to talk to her about it. I talked about my thesis, and hoped it would lead to a discussion of *her* thesis. But no luck. She evaded the topic completely.

She was pretty busy with her project, though, whatever it was. Because she was always buzzing around the cadre asking people where to look for odd bits of knowledge.

I couldn't make sense of her questions, though. They seemed to cover too many fields. Sociology, statistics, minerology, criminology, economics, astronomy, spaceship design . . . The project seemed too huge.

The only thing I knew about Janis' thesis was that it was *supposed* to be about resource management. It was the field that Anna-Lee forced her into, because it was full of skills that would be useful on the Tau Ceti expedition. And if that didn't work, Anna-Lee made sure Janis minored in spaceship and shuttle piloting and navigation.

I finally finished my thesis, and then I sat back and waited for the job offers to roll in. The only offer I got came from someone who wanted me to run the garbage cyclers on Iapetus, which the guy should have known I wouldn't accept if he had bothered to read my application.

Maybe he was just neck-deep in garbage and desperate, I don't know.

And then the most astounding thing happened. Instead of a job in the computer field, I got an offer to study at the Pisan Academy.

Which is an art school. Which is in Italy, which is where the paintings come from mostly.

The acceptance committee said that my work showed a "naive but highly original fusion of social criticism with the formalities of the geometric order." I don't even *pretend* to know what they meant by that, but I suspect they just weren't used to the perspective of a student who had spent practically her entire live in a computer on Ceres.

I broadcast my shrieks of joy to everyone in the cadre, even those who had left Ceres and were probably wincing at their workstations when my screams reached them.

I bounced around the common room and everyone came out to congratulate me. Even Janis, who had taken to wearing an avatar that wasn't even remotely human, just a graphic of a big sledgehammer smashing a rock, over and over.

Subtlety had never been her strong point.

"Congratulations," she said. "You got what you wanted."

And then she broadcast something on a private channel. *You're going to be famous*, she said. *But I'm going to be a* legend.

I looked at her. And then I sent back, *Can we talk about this?*

*In a few days. When I deliver my thesis.*

*Don't*, I pleaded.

*Too late.*

The hammer hit its rock, and the shards flew out into the room and vanished.

I spent the next few days planning my Incarnation Day party, but my heart wasn't in it. I kept wondering if Janis was going to be alive to enjoy it.

I finally decided to have my party in Thailand because there were so many interesting environments in one place, as well as the Great Buddha. And I found a caterer that was supposed to be really good.

I decided what sort of body I wanted, and the incarnation specialists on Earth started cooking it up in one of their vats. Not the body of an Earth-born fourteen-year-old, but older, more like eighteen. Brown eyes, brown hair, and those big eyes that had always been so useful.

And two legs, of course. Which is what they all have down there.

I set the date. The cadre were alerted. We all practiced in the simulations and tried to get used to making do with only two arms. Everyone was prepared.

And then Janis finished her thesis. I downloaded a copy the second it was submitted to her committee and read it in one long sitting, and my sense of horror grew with every line.

What Janis had done was publish a comprehensive critique *of our entire society*! It was a piece of brilliance, and at the same time it was utter poison.

Posthuman society wrecks its children, Janis said, and this can be demonstrated by the percentage of neurotic and dysfunctional adults. The problems encountered by the first generation of children who spent their formative years as programs—the autism, the obsessions and compulsions, the addictions to electronic environments—hadn't gone away, they'd just been reduced to the point where they'd become a part of the background clutter, a part of our civilization so everyday that we never quite noticed it.

Janis had the data, too. The number of people who were under treatment for one thing or another. The percentage who had difficulty adjusting to their incarnations, or who didn't want to communicate with anyone outside their cadre, or who couldn't sleep unless they were immersed in a simulation. Or who committed suicide. Or who died in accidents—Janis questioned whether all those accidents were really the results of our harsh environments. Our machines and our settlements were much safer than they had been in the early days, but the rates of accidental death were still high. How many accidents were caused by distracted or unhappy operators, or for that matter were deliberate "suicide by machine"?

Janis went on to describe one of the victims of this ruthless type of upbringing. "Flat of emotional affect, offended by disorder and incapable of coping with obstruction, unable to function without adherence to a belief system as rigid as the artificial and constricted environments in which she was raised."

When I realized Janis was describing Anna-Lee I almost derezzed.

Janis offered a scheme to cure the problem, which was to get rid of the virtual environments and start out with real incarnated babies. She pulled out vast numbers of statistics demonstrating that places that did this—chiefly Earth—seemed to raise more successful adults. She also pointed out that the initial shortage of resources that had prompted the creation of virtual children in the first place had long since passed—plenty of water-ice coming in from the Kuyper Belt these days, and we were sitting on all the minerals we could want. The only reason the system continued was for the convenience of the adults. But genuine babies, as opposed to abstract computer programs, would help the adults, too. They would no longer be tempted to become little dictators with absolute power over their offspring. Janis said the chance would turn the grown-ups into better human beings.

All this was buttressed by colossal numbers of statistics, graphs, and other data. I realized when I'd finished it that the Cadre of Glorious Destiny had produced one true genius, and that this genius was Janis.

*The true genius is a mind of large general powers, accidentally determined to some particular direction.*

Anna-Lee determined her, all right, and the problem was that Janis probably didn't have that long to live. Aside from the fact that Janis had ruthlessly caricatured her, Anna-Lee couldn't help but notice that the whole work went smack up against the Five Principles Movement. According to the Movement people, all available resources had to be devoted to the expansion of the human race out of the solar system and into new environments. It didn't matter how many more resources were available now than in the past, it was clear against their principles to devote a greater share to the raising of children when it could be used to blast off into the universe.

And though the Five Principles people acknowledged our rather high death rate, they put it down to our settlements' hazardous environments. All we had to do was genetically modify people to better suit the environments and the problem would be solved.

I skipped the appendices and zoomed from my room across the common room to Janis' door, and hit the button to alert her to a visitor. The door vanished, and there was Janis—for the first time since her fight with Anna-Lee, she was using her quadbod avatar. She gave me a wicked grin.

"Great, isn't it?"

"It's *brilliant*! But you can't let Anna-Lee see it."

"Don't be silly. I sent Mom the file myself."

I was horrified. She had to have seen the way my Picasso-face gaped, and it made her laugh.

"She'll have you erased!" I said.

"If she does," Janis said. "She'll only prove my point." She put a consoling hand on my shoulder. "Sorry if it means missing your incarnation."

When Anna-Lee came storming in—which wasn't long after—Janis broadcast the whole confrontation on a one-way link to the whole cadre. We got to watch, but not to participate. She didn't want our advice any more than she wanted her mother's.

"You are unnatural!" Anna-Lee stormed. "You spread slanders! You have betrayed the highest truth!"

"I *told* the truth!" Janis said. "And you *know* it's the truth, otherwise you wouldn't be so insane right now."

Anna-Lee stiffened. "I am a Five Principles Constant Soldier. I know the truth, and I know my duty."

"Every time you say that, you prove my point."

"You will retract this thesis, and apologize to your committee for giving them such a vicious document."

Anna-Lee hadn't realized that the document was irretrievable, that Janis had given it to everyone she knew.

Janis laughed. "No way, Mom," she said.

Anna-Lee lost it. She waved her fists and screamed. "I know my duty! I will not allow such a slander to be seen by anyone!" She pointed at Janis. "You have three days to retract!"

Janis gave a snort of contempt.

"Or what?"

"Or I will decide that you're incorrigible and terminate your program."

Janis laughed. "Go right ahead, Mom. Do it *now*. Nothing spreads a new idea better than martyrdom." She spread her four arms. "*Do* it, Mom. I *hate* life in this hell. I'm ready."

*I will be conquered; I will not capitulate.*

Yes, Dr. Sam. That's it exactly.

"You have three days," Anna-Lee said, her voice all flat and menacing, and then her virtual image de-rezzed.

Janis looked at the space where her mom had been, and then a goofy grin spread across her face. She switched to the red-headed, stick-figure avatar, and began to do a little dance as she hovered in the air, moving like a badly animated cartoon.

"Hey!" she sang. "I get to go to Alison's party after all!"

I had been so caught up in the drama that I had forgot my in-carnation was going to happen in two days.

But it wasn't going to be a party now. It was going to be a wake.

"Dr. Sam," I said, "I've got to save Janis."

*The triumph of hope over experience.*

"Hope is what I've got," I said, and then I thought about it. "And maybe a little experience, too."

☙ ☙ ☙

My Incarnation Day went well. We came down by glider, as we had that first time on Titan, except that this time I told Ground Control to let my friends land wherever the hell they wanted. That gave us time to inspect the Great Buddha, a slim man with a knowing smile sitting cross-legged with knobs on his head. He's two and a half kilometers tall and packed with massively parallel quantum processors, all crunching vast amounts of data, thinking whatever profound thoughts are appropriate to an artificial intelli-gence built on such a scale, and repeating millions of sutras, which are scriptures for Buddhists, all at the speed of light.

It creeps along at two or three centimeters per day, and will enter the strait at the end of the Kra Peninsula many thousands of years from now.

After viewing the Buddha's serene expression from as many angles as suited us, we soared and swooped over many kilometers of brilliant green jungle and landed on the beach. And we all *did* land on the beach, which sort of surprised me. And then we all did our best to learn how to surf—and let me tell you from the start, the surfing simulators are *totally* inadequate. The longest I managed to stand my board was maybe twenty seconds.

I was amazed at all the sensations that crowded all around me. The breeze on my skin, the scents of the sea and the vegetation and the coal on which our banquet was being cooked. The hot sand under my bare feet. The salt taste of the ocean on my lips. The sting of the little jellyfish on my legs and arms, and the iodine smell of the thick strand of seaweed that got wrapped in my hair.

I mean, I had no *idea*. The simulators were totally inadequate to the Earth experience.

And this was just a *part* of the Earth, a small fraction of the environments available. I think I convinced a lot of the cadre that maybe they'd want to move to Earth as soon as they could raise the money and find a job.

After swimming and beach games we had my Incarnation Day dinner. The sensations provided by the food were really too intense—I couldn't eat much of it. If I was going to eat Earth food, I was going to have to start with something a lot more bland.

And there was my brown-eyed body at the head of the table, looking down at the members of the Cadre of Glorious Destiny who were toasting me with tropical drinks, the kind that have parasols in them.

Tears came to my eyes, and they were a lot wetter and hotter than tears in the sims. For some reason that fact made me cry even more.

My parents came to the dinner, because this was the first time they could actually hug me—hug me for real, that is, and not in a sim. They had downloaded into bodies that didn't look much like the four-armed quadbods they used back on Ceres, but that didn't matter. When my arms went around them, I began to cry again.

After the tears were wiped away we put on underwater gear and went for a swim on the reef, which is just amazing. More colors and shapes and textures than I could ever imagine—or imagine putting in a work of art.

*A work of art that embodies all but selects none is not art, but mere cant and recitation.*

Oh, wow. You're right. Thank you, Dr. Sam.

After the reef trip we paid a visit to one of the underwater settlements, one inhabited by people adapted to breathe water. The problems were was that we had to keep our underwater gear on, and that none of us were any good at the fluid sign language they all used as their preferred means of communication.

Then we rose from the ocean, dried out, and had a last round of hugs before being uploaded to our normal habitations. I gave Janis a particularly strong hug, and I whispered in her ear.

"Take care of yourself."

"Who?" she grinned. *"Me?"*

And then the little brown-haired body was left behind, looking very lonely, as everyone else put on the electrodes and uploaded back to their normal and very distant worlds.

As soon as I arrived on Ceres, I zapped an avatar of myself into my parents' quarters. They looked at me as if I were a ghost.

"What are *you* doing here?" my mother managed.

"I hate to tell you this," I said, "but I think you're going to have to hire a lawyer."

֎ ֎ ֎

It was surprisingly easy to do, really. Remember that I was assisting Dane, who was a communications tech, and in charge of uploading all of our little artificial brains to Earth. And also remember that I am a specialist in systems interoperability, which implies that I am also a specialist in systems *un*operability.

It was very easy to set a couple of artificial intelligences running amok in Dane's system just as he was working on our upload. And that so distracted him that he said yes when I said that I'd do the job for him.

And once I had access, it was the work of a moment to swap a couple of serial numbers.

The end result of which was that it was Janis who uploaded into my brown-haired body, and received all the toasts, and who hugged my parents with *my* arms. And who is now on Earth, incarnated, with a full set of human rights and safe from Anna-Lee.

I wish I could say the same for myself.

Anna-Lee couldn't have me killed, of course, since I don't belong to her. But she could sue my parents, who from her point of view permitted a piece of software belonging to *them* to prevent her from wreaking vengeance on some software that belonged to *her*.

And of course Anna-Lee went berserk the second she found out—which was more or less immediately, since Janis sent her a little radio taunt as soon as she downed her fourth or fifth celebratory umbrella drink.

Janis sent me a message, too.

"The least you could have done was make my hair red."

*My* hair. Sometimes I wonder why I bothered.

An unexpected side effect of this was that we all got famous. It turns out that this was an unprecedented legal situation, with lots of human interest and a colorful cast of characters. Janis became a media celebrity, and so did I, and so did Anna-Lee.

Celebrity didn't do Anna-Lee's cause any good. Her whole mental outlook was too rigid to stand the kind of scrutiny and questioning that any public figure has to put up with. As soon as she was challenged she lost control. She called one of the leading media interviewers a name that you, Dr. Sam, would not wish me to repeat.

Whatever the actual merits of her legal case, the sight of Anna-Lee screaming that I had deprived her of the inalienable right to kill her daughter failed to win her a lot of friends. Eventually the Five Principles people realized she wasn't doing their cause any good, and she was replaced by a Movement spokesperson who said as little as possible.

Janis did some talking, too, but not nearly as much as she would have liked, because she was under house arrest for coming to Earth without a visa and without paying the immigration tax. The cops showed up when she was sleeping off her hangover from all the umbrella drinks. It's probably lucky that she wasn't given the opportunity to talk much, because if she started on her rants she would have worn out her celebrity as quickly as Anna-Lee did.

Janis was scheduled to be deported back to Ceres, but shipping an actual incarnated human being is much more difficult than zapping a simulation by laser, and she had to wait for a ship that could carry passengers, and that would be months.

She offered to navigate the ship herself, since she had the training, but the offer was declined.

Lots of people read her thesis who wouldn't otherwise have heard of it. And millions discussed it whether they'd read it or not. There were those who said that Janis was right, and those that said that Janis was mostly right but that she exaggerated. There were those who said that the problem didn't really exist, except in the statistics.

There were those who thought the problem existed entirely in the software, that the system would work if the simulations were only made more like reality. I had to disagree, because I think the simulations *were* like reality, but only for certain people.

The problem is that human beings perceive reality in slightly different ways, even if they happen to be programs. A programmer could do his best to create an artificial reality that exactly mimicked the way he perceived reality, except that it wouldn't be as exact for another person, it would only be an approximation. It would be like fitting everyone's hand into the same-sized glove.

Eventually someone at the University of Adelaide read it and offered Janis a professorship in their sociology department. She accepted and was freed from house arrest.

Poor Australia, I thought.

I was on video quite a lot. I used my little-girl avatar, and I batted my big eyes a lot. I still wore blue, mourning for Fritz.

Why, I was asked, did I act to save Janis?

"Because we're cadre, and we're supposed to look after one another."

What did I think of Anna-Lee?

"I don't see why she's complaining. I've seen to it that Janis *just isn't her problem any more.*"

Wasn't what I did stealing?

"It's not stealing to free a slave."

And so on. It was the same sort of routine I'd been practicing on my parents all these years, and the practice paid off. Entire cadres—hundreds of them—signed petitions asking that the case be dismissed. Lots of adults did the same.

I hope that it helps, but the judge that hears the case isn't supposed to be swayed by public opinion, but only by the law.

And everyone forgets that it's my parents who will be on trial, not me, accused of letting their software steal Anna-Lee's software. And of course I, and therefore they, am completely guilty, so my parents are almost certainly going to be fined, and lose both money and Citizenship Points.

I'm sorry about that, but my parents seem not to be.

How the judge will put a value on a piece of stolen software that its owner fully intended to destroy is going to make an interesting ruling, however it turns out.

I don't know whether I'll ever set foot on Earth again. I can't take my place in Pisa because I'm not incarnated, and I don't know if they'll offer again.

And however things turn out, Fritz is still zeroed. And I still wear blue.

I don't have my outside job any longer. Dane won't speak to me, because his supervisor reprimanded him, and he's under suspicion for being my accomplice. And even those who are sympathetic to me aren't about to let me loose with their computers.

And even if I get a job somewhere, I can't be incarnated until the court case is over.

It seems to me that the only person who got away scot-free was Janis. Which is normal.

So right now my chief problem is boredom. I spent fourteen years in a rigid program intended to fill my hours with wholesome and intellectually useful activity, and now that's over.

And I can't get properly started on the non-wholesome thing until I get an incarnation somewhere.

*Everyone is, or hopes to be, an idler.*

Thank you, Dr. Sam.

I'm choosing to idle away my time making pictures. Maybe I can sell them and help pay the Earth tax.

I call them my "Dr. Johnson" series. *Sam. Johnson on Mars. Sam. Johnson Visits Neptune. Sam. Johnson Quizzing the Tomasko Glacier. Sam. Johnson Among the Asteroids.*

I have many more ideas along this line.

Dr. Sam, I trust you will approve.

# COMBAT SHOPPING

## by Elizabeth Moon

Going shopping at the mall can be an adventure even for today's teenagers—when you live amidst the icy wastes of the frozen moon Ganymede, however, the stakes can be a whole lot *higher* . . .

Elizabeth Moon has degrees in history and biology and served in the U.S. Marine Corps. Her novels include *Sheepfarmer's Daughter, Divided Allegiance, Oath of Gold, Sassinak* and *Generation Warriors* (written with Anne McCaffrey), *Surrender None, Liar's Oath, Planet Pirates* (with Jody Lynn Nye and Anne McCaffery), *Hunting Party, Sporting Chance, Winning Colors, Once a Hero, Rules of Engagement, Change of Command, Against the Odds, Trading in Danger, Marque and Reprisal,* and *Remnant Population.* Her short fiction has been collected in *Lunar Activity* and *Phases,* and she has edited the anthologies *Military SF 1* and *Military SF 2.* Her novel *The Speed of Dark* won a Nebula Award in 2004. Her most recent book is a new novel, *Engaging the Enemy.*

ANDI MURCHISON HEARD Mama call the first time, but she paid no attention. Mama always called four or five times and as long as she didn't wait until Mama's voice got that sort of squeak to it, nothing bad would happen. She had better things to do than come running when Mama called, anyway. This was the last chance she had to talk over tomorrow's plans with her friends at Base, friends she hadn't seen for five hundred boring days, the only friends she had.

On that day—the best day of her life so far—Mama had signed her up with a recreation group at Base Children's Park after her check-up at Base Clinic, and the recreation director had introduced her to a group of girls who came three days a week. She'd been a little daunted at first—they were all taller than she was—but they'd shown her how to play with the equipment, and soon she'd been shrieking and laughing with the rest. She'd been the first independent habitateur the others had ever met; they'd been the first Base children she'd seen since her trip out, when Mama and Pop had picked her up at the Creche.

Beth had been the first to find her on comm; since then Andi had talked to Beth or Vinnie almost every day even though Mama complained that her "chattering" had cost too much. Andi didn't care. It wasn't her fault she was there, and not someplace better; she hadn't asked to become a habitateur's adopted child, any more than the others had. She didn't care that only those two had stayed in contact, either. They told her all about the others, so she felt she still knew Terry, Hamilton, Lisa, Maddy, and even girls new to Base.

Tomorrow she would be back with them, back where she was sure she belonged. She would have five days there—some of it boring enough, following Mama around, but she'd been promised some time to spend with them. Combat shopping, Vinnie and Beth called it, when they had to find as much as they could in a hurry while spending as little as possible. She was still too young to stay at Base alone, but someday she'd be able to escape this—she looked around at the boring, too-familiar interior of the habitat.

"Andi! Now!" Mama's voice had taken on that dangerous edge. "Get off the comm, blast you!"

"Got to go. Parent trouble." She tapped that in and cleared the comm, not that anyone really needed it now. If only she lived on Earth, or MarZone, where everyone had personal communicators and a network of satellites meant anyone could talk to anyone. Here on Ganymede, as well as being stuck under a layer of ice in a closed habitat with nowhere to go and nothing to see, Jupiter's electromagnetic activity made such easy communications impossible.

When she came into the habitat's main living space, Mama

was hunched over the comm herself. That was a surprise; Mama mostly left the comm to Pop. The younger children—Gerry, Bird, and Damon—were already at the table, spooning up the same boring reconstituted slop that was all they had left in the last weeks before a trip to Base.

"Hurry up and eat," Mama said, without looking up. "You need to get the others packed."

Andi put a spoonful of the stuff—beige and lumpy and slightly gooey—into her bowl and tasted it. Bland. Boring. Then the meaning of Mama's words made it through her boredom.

"Others packed? What do you mean?" For one moment of blinding joy she imagined the others being sent away: Gerry the loud and exuberant, Bird the restless and fidgety, Damon with his inexplicable blank periods. But that couldn't be it; Mama and Pop would lose their subsidies.

Bird turned to her, face alight. "We're going to Base," she said softly. "Mama said so."

Andi's stomach clenched. "You're all going? There's not enough room—"

"It's Damon," Gerry said. "Mama's taking him to the Clinic at Base to see if they can fix him."

Andi glanced sideways at Damon, who was staring into his bowl, his spoon hovering above it. It was always hard to know if Damon noticed what anyone said. His blank periods came oftener now; he was falling behind in schoolwork, and he couldn't do even the simplest chores without supervision.

"Damon, eat your supper," she said. His spoon moved slowly, slowly, toward the bowl and stopped again. "Damon, spoon in—" she said. Then "Lift spoon" and "Eat it up!" Another bite went in his mouth.

"Andi, I said get them packed!" Mama said, sounding even more annoyed. "Gerry, you can get Damon fed. Bird, clean up."

Andi hastily gobbled the last few bites of supper and handed her bowl to Bird. "How many nights?" she asked Mama. "Two or three," Mama said, still staring at the comm screen. She tapped in something. "One each way traveling, one there, if we're unlucky. We'll stay on the shuttle; it costs too much to rent a room."

"But we were going to stay a week," Andi said. "You said—"

"I know what I said," Mama said, turning now to glare at her. "That's changed now. Damon needs a complete workup; he had another seizure this afternoon. That can't go on. If he can't work—" She left that unfinished. "We can't afford to waste the time or money just for you to have a joyride."

"It's not just a joyride," Andi said. "It's my exam—Pop said I could take the Class C exam—he *wants* me to take the Class C exam. And if I pass—when I pass—you said I could get some new clothes—I've been saving—"

"Jim wants a lot of things," Mama said, her mouth tightening to a hard line that spit the words out like stones. "We all want a lot of things we aren't going to get."

"But—I can still take the exam—" Even if she didn't get the new clothes, even if she didn't have a couple of days to shop and visit her friends, she could have that.

"It really doesn't matter if you take it now or the next trip," Mama said, turning back to the screen. "You're barely old enough to qualify. I need you to take care of Gerry and Bird while Damon and I are at the Clinic."

The next trip could be five hundred more days away, an impossible wait. Andi glanced at the table. Gerry, coaching Damon to eat, gave her a triumphant look of pure wickedness. She could just see trying to control Gerry—the way he'd shot up in the past few hundred days. Sure, he was younger, but he was smart and mischievous, and now he was taller than she was.

"They have child-minding services at Base," Andi said. "Last time, when I was there, remember? You put me in a recreation group—"

"It costs money!" Mama said. "We don't have money to waste on that when you're available."

Available. That's what she always was, right there handy, Handy-Andi as Gerry put it so nastily. Available, useful, labor-saving: that's what she was, and all she was, as far as Mama was

concerned. Andi stalked off to the boys' dorm, the single space
Gerry shared with Damon and Oscar, their older "brother."
Mama and Pop insisted they call each other brother and sister,
but none of them were gene-sibs. Like all the habitateurs' children, they were adoptees, children no one wanted back on Earth
or the inner colonies. Like the orphans once shipped out to farms
in the North American pioneer days.

Andi pulled a duffel out of the storage locker and stuffed it
with Damon's pajamas, Damon's spare jumpsuit, Damon's underwear, and two packets of Damon's pajama liners. He still wet
himself most nights. She put in Damon's night toy, a stuffed lamb
with the fleece worn almost off, and his favorite pillow. Both
smelled of Damon, but he liked it that way. Gerry's duffel was
easier—his underwear, his pajamas, his spare jumpsuit. She hesitated over his toolkit. Mama would say to leave it behind; Gerry
plus a toolkit, any kind of toolkit, was asking for trouble. And
the shuttle had its own set of tools. Still . . . it might keep him
more cooperative, if she included it. She stuffed it into the roll of
his underwear. Toiletries: the shuttle had waterless soap, but
they'd need toothbrushes, combs . . .

She brought both duffels out to the main room, just as Pop
and Oscar came in from the day's work. Gerry was still working
with Damon.

"What's this?" Pop said to Mama. "I thought it was just Andi
going this time."

"Damon's going into the Clinic for a full evaluation," Mama
said. Andi watched carefully. If Pop hadn't made the original decision, he might still overrule Mama.

"Are you sure that's necessary?" he asked. He glanced at Andi,
a warmer look than she ever got from Mama. "I promised her—"

"Yes," Mama said. "I queried the Clinic; they have an open
slot and they think it's urgent."

"Ennhuhhh!" Damon jerked back and fell out of his chair.
Oscar was there before Andi could move, cradling Damon's head,
making sure his airway was clear. Damon continued to grunt and
jerk about; it had scared Andi the first time she saw it, but now it

was just Damon. Gerry wiped up the spilled food and took Damon's bowl to Bird.

"All right," Pop said. "I can see he's getting worse. But it has to be covered by the agreement. We can't afford—"

"It is. They said so. It's impaired his functionality—Andi, why are you standing there like a stupid cow? Go pack for yourself and Bird."

Andi headed to the girls' dorm.

"And don't even try to get on comm!" Mama yelled after her. "Pack up and get right back out here."

Did that mean they were leaving tonight, like the original plan? That meant she would be at Base by early first shift, plenty of time to take the exam if only Mama hadn't said she couldn't. Andi pulled out two duffels and packed them both with the same pajamas, underwear, spare jumpsuit. She was so tired of cheap, practical gray.

Last time Beth had had a pink and white shirt and pink skirt; Vinnie's shirt and skirt had been yellow, the shirt with yellow flowers on a pale green background. All the other girls had worn colorful clothes, too. Now Vinnie had a new shirt, "the green of new leaves," she'd said. Beth had a blue one. They didn't wear jumpsuits, the Base kids. This year, Beth said, they were wearing loose pants, above knee length, and short full shirts. And shoes that had just come in from Earth, bright colored shoes. Even the boys.

The prices she quoted for these things had shocked Andi. Andi had saved her allowance and every credit she made by working overtime—Pop gave her a quarter of the profit for those hours—and it was enough for the exam and licensing fee, plus maybe one item, maybe two if she skimped on meals. Shirt? Short pants? Shoes?

But now—Andi slammed her own folded jumpsuit down into the duffel as if she could break it, and yanked the zipper closed. Now she wasn't even going to get any shopping at all. Or take the exam. And she'd forgotten the toiletries. She grabbed toothbrushes, combs, and glared at her image in the mirror. She looked like a child, still. She was short; her face was round as a baby's; her hair, cropped to a shiny black cap on her round head like some stupid doll. If she had cosmetics, would that help? A different hairstyle? Vinnie and Beth talked about how their faces and bodies had changed shape, how they had done things with their hair, how they stole chances to use their mothers' cosmetics.

She tried to imagine herself the way she might be as an adult—the adult she wanted to be. Tall, svelte, her black hair long and curling around her shoulders, actual cheekbones where she had those round cheeks. She would wear bright colors, clothes that rippled and flowed when she moved. She moved into the familiar fantasy . . . Andi Murchison, walking into a room where everyone turned to look, and she saw admiration and envy on all the faces . . . especially on the face of the old, dowdy, shrunken woman in the corner. Mama. She would come back and show Mama what Mama had never recognized—what a remarkable person she was—

"Andi! Stop wool-gathering and get out here!"

But not yet. Andi gathered up the two duffels and went back to the living space. Damon was sitting up now, looking dazed but not quite blank as Gerry helped him into one of the orange pressure suits. Damon was actually moving his arms and legs the right way. Mama already had her pressure suit on, her duffel at her side, and three more suits were laid out, waiting. Pop had an unhappy expression; his eyes looked sad, even pleading when he looked at Andi. She hated that look, which came more and more often; it made her uncomfortable when they were alone. Oscar was gone, probably cleaning up Damon's underwear.

"Get Bird suited," Mama ordered.

Andi put the suit on Bird, then wriggled into her own. It still fit easily; they had bought it a size large, expecting her to grow, and it was still a little loose. Better that than too tight. Gerry barely fit into his.

"I'll be back day after tomorrow, probably," Mama said to Pop. "At most the day after that. Try to keep things running—" She sounded as if she expected him to mess up.

He nodded. "Take care, Mama."

"I always do," Mama said. She started down the passage to the shuttle dock. Andi picked up her duffel and Bird's, and nudged Bird ahead of her down the passage.

After settling the younger children in their seats and making sure their safety harnesses were fastened correctly, Andi climbed through the hatch into the cockpit and settled into the right-hand seat. Mama, in the command seat, gave her a quick glance. "Checklist two," she said.

Andi helped work through the next two preflight lists. She had studied this; she had spent hours in the shuttle itself with the simulator running, first with Pop supervising her, then alone, every time the shuttle wasn't in use and she could find time from school, chores, work. She knew the lists backwards and forwards, knew the correct settings. Powering on, unhitching the umbilicals from the habitat, sealing the habitat so it wouldn't lose atmosphere, testing every circuit, every linkage.

"Preflight complete," Mama said finally. She was linked to Pop, back in the habitat's main room. "See you later."

The shuttle jerked away from the habitat. Andi was sure she could do better than that. In the last few weeks, her simulated launches had all been smoother than this. When they were level and on course to Base, Mama set the autopilot.

"Put the children down for sleep, Andi," Mama said.

Andi climbed back through the cockpit hatch. Gerry already had his seat flattened; she helped Damon and Bird flatten theirs, and made sure that Damon was positioned on his side, with his stuffed lamb and his pillow. She turned down the lights in that compartment, and pulled the cockpit hatch almost closed after climbing back through.

"You've got to learn to face facts, Andi," Mama said, when Andi clambered back into her seat. "I know you thought you were going to have a grand time at Base, hobnobbing with Base kids, wasting money on some kind of fancy something—probably clothes, the age you are—but that's not the kind of life you're going to have, and you might as well face up to it now."

Andi said nothing, but she felt a slow burn rising inside. She would have had a grand time, and she was going to have a good life, somehow, no matter what Mama said.

"It wouldn't have worked even if we'd had the time and money to stay," Mama went on. "They aren't your type, Andi. I knew plenty of that kind back on Earth. It's all right when you're a little kid, like you were last time. Their parents don't mind so much, and they get a glow out of feeling superior. But they won't ever be friends, real friends."

Andi stared out the window at the rumpled icy landscape below, the sky dominated by colorful Jupiter and its surrounding satellites, trying not to listen. So she was different—they were Base kids and maybe they had gene-parents. She was a habitateur, adopted. But why did that matter? They had come together so easily before . . . they had stayed in contact . . . they had shown no signs of getting tired of her. They were the only friends she'd ever had, and anyway they were the ones who suggested having lunch, going shopping. Mama just wanted her to stay isolated, have no friends. Mama didn't trust anyone.

"Andi! Are you even listening?"

"Yes, Mama." Andi looked over at Mama: the hard, lined face, the angry eyes, the tense, taut mouth. "You don't think they like me."

Mama's breath came out in an explosive gust. "It's more than that, girl. Children like that—they all go to school together, hang out together. They're a group, a . . . a clique. You've never been in a situation like that—"

"It's not my fault," Andi said. She could hear the sullenness in her own voice, and hated it, but she had imagined so many times how wonderful it would be to go to a real school, with other children, away from Mama for all those hours.

"No, it's not," Mama said. Now she was looking out the window, and her profile looked as much sad as angry. "Andi, the thing is, it's not fair. Nothing is. It's not your fault that you have to do schoolwork alone, but even if you were in school, in a regular class, it doesn't mean you'd enjoy it, that it would go well. If you're one of the children the other children don't like—there are always some—it's no fun at all."

"Vinnie and Beth like me," Andi said. "Why are you so sure the others wouldn't?"

"You're . . . different," Mama said. "Children don't like the different ones, not very long anyway. Just like you don't like Damon. You're short; you're not pretty—that's not an insult, it's the truth and you need to face up to it. And yet you're smart. Short, less than plain, and way too smart—the other children wouldn't put up with that. They might feel sorry for you, but like you? No."

Andi felt herself shrinking into the seat. She knew she was short. She knew she wasn't beautiful. But . . . less than plain? Did that mean ugly? Those times Mama had said *Get your ugly butt in here right this minute!*—was that only a plain description, not just Mama being angry? And *like Damon*? She wasn't anything like Damon.

"All you got going for you, Andi, is being smart and being able to work hard. That doesn't make an easy life, as I know well, but it's better than no life at all. That's what we're teaching you, me and Jim, how to work hard so you can be useful. Useful people survive; useless—" Her glance drifted past Andi to the compartment behind them.

Andi felt as if she'd been dipped in ice. What was that look? Mama's looks always meant something. Who was useless? Damon? Was he going to die? Was that what would happen at the Clinic? Panic and horror choked her; she turned quickly to stare at the instruments to her right.

"You'd better get some sleep," Mama said then. "I'll take first watch; I'll wake you later. You can have command until we're on approach to Base."

Andi reclined her seat, turned on her side away from Mama, and closed her eyes. She could not sleep; everything Mama said went around and around in her mind, especially that about useless people. What was going to happen to Damon? Mama was right about one thing: she didn't like Damon, really—and was that how ordinary kids would feel about her?—but she'd assumed the Clinic would fix him, make him well.

And what about her exam? She had to get it; she couldn't wait until the next trip, whenever that might be. A license was her one chance out. Pop had signed for her to take the exam this early, a hardship case; he wanted her to come out with him in the shuttle, prospecting, and whoever went with him had to have a license just in case. Now that Oscar could run the processing machinery, that gave Andi a chance for shuttle duty. She'd rather be in the shuttle with Pop than in the habitat with Mama, but more than that, a shuttle license, even a Class C, was her one chance to get out of the trap she felt closing around her.

Finally she fell asleep, and then Mama was shaking her by the shoulder. She woke up, yawning, then sat staring at the window while Mama snored in the other seat, until the autopilot binged, telling them to contact Base Traffic Control. During those hours, she came up with what might be a plan, if she could get Gerry to agree, if Mama didn't suspect. She was already on the list for the exam; they would be at Base in plenty of time. If she could sneak off and take the exam . . . Mama would be furious later, but too late. To do that, she'd have to keep Gerry and Bird from tattling. Gerry would be the worst . . . Gerry didn't do anything without a payoff, and all she had to bribe him with was her savings, what she'd planned to spend on food and shopping. Bird was usually biddable, and Andi could save back enough to promise her a treat. It was Bird's first trip to Base since her adoption; anything would do. She hoped. If Mama found out . . . she didn't want to think about that.

Ahead, she could now see the huge low dome of Base sticking up above the icy plain, the shuttle docking bays around its perimeter. Base was mostly underground—under-ice, anyway—level after level, Vinnie and Beth had told her. They lived twelve stories down.

Mama made the docking connection competently enough; Andi mentally critiqued every move. She'd have applied the lateral thrusters two seconds earlier, at less power, and that would have brought them to zero motion relative more smoothly. But Mama was within parameters. Base Traffic Control congratulated her on a safe docking, and authorized the hookup of ship's umbilicals.

"I've made appointments for all of you to get your physicals," Mama said when she'd turned off the comm. "Saves a trip and you're overdue anyway. Get the others awake and cleaned up; we'll eat ship rations for breakfast. Oh—I almost forgot. Here's a pill you should take." She fished a bubble-pack of pills out of her pocket and tore off one for Andi.

"What is it?" Andi asked, as she had before without getting an answer.

"Just take it," Mama said, as she had.

Andi nodded, and went back to wake the others. Typical of Mama to come up with something else unpleasant for her to do, something else that got in the way of her own plans. Last time her Clinic evaluation had taken just under an hour . . . if it didn't last any longer this time, she might still make it to the exam. In the process of getting the other children up, handing out food bars and water, supervising bathroom visits and toothbrushing, and revising her original plan to adapt to Clinic checkups, she forgot the pill she'd tucked into her front pocket.

Then it was time to go to the Clinic, and Mama led them at a brisk pace out of the docking area and along sloping passages. Andi pointed out the wall maps to Gerry and Bird. Even here, there were more people around, enough that Bird's small hand in hers grew wet with tension.

"How many people are on Base?" Gerry asked, looking around.

"Too many," Mama said. "And none of them trustworthy. Keep that in mind, all of you."

"They're all bad?" Gerry asked.

"They try to trick us into spending more money than we have; they hope we can't pay fees and they can seize the shuttle or even our habitats, make us employees, not independents. Company serfs. And don't forget the workforce pirates. If you think you have a hard life now—" Mama looked directly at Andi as she said this, "it's nothing to what the workforce pirates do to children. Company serfs at least get paid; pirate slaves get nothing."

Gerry looked thoughtful but not subdued.

When they arrived at the Clinic, Mama checked them all in. "I'm going to be with Damon for his workup," she said. "Andi, you're in charge of Gerry and Beth. All three of you will get your checkup, and then wait for me—"

Andi had already planned for this. She looked around the waiting area as if seriously considering its possibilities, then shook her head. "Mama, you know how restless Bird is. There's nothing here for her to play with. Can't I take them to the playground and let her enjoy that? With me along, it shouldn't cost anything."

Mama looked at Bird, who was already shifting from foot to foot, and then back at Andi. "You don't fool me," she said. Andi's heart sank. "You just want to play yourself, and you're hoping to meet those girls. But—" Another look at Bird and then Gerry. Andi tried not to show anything on her face. "I suppose it can't hurt," Mama said. "And you have money, if it does cost— it was your idea; you can spend your own money on it. We'll be here through lunch, anyway, and you have to eat somewhere. Is there a place near the playground? Or you could go to Boone Concourse if you're really careful and stay together. You won't get lost, will you?"

"I won't get lost, Mama," Andi said. "I know how to read the maps on the walls. And Bird will enjoy the playground." She was careful not to catch Gerry's eye; he would know she was up to something, but he wouldn't know what. She hoped. And he wouldn't tell Mama anything until he was sure it was worth telling.

Andi and Bird were called in while Mama was still waiting. The medical exam was as annoying and embarrassing as always.

"You're twelve?" the woman in the flowered smock asked, looking up from the record.

"Yes," Andi said. "And I'm short and yes, it's in my gene scan, and no, it's not associated with any developmental problems."

The woman flushed. "I didn't say—"

"You were going to ask. They always do."

"Touchy about it, aren't you?" the woman asked.

"You would be too, if people thought you were years younger than you are," Andi said.

"I can see that," the woman said. "Your other metrics all look good, though. How do you feel about adolescence?"

Andi stared at her. "Feel about it? How am I *supposed* to feel about it? It's going to happen no matter what I do, and I'm still going to be stuck on a subsistence habitat with—" she glanced at Bird, who was staring at her, mouth open, and moderated what she'd almost said. "Legally, I must stay with my family-of-record until I'm sixteen," she said. "There's nobody at the habitat my age, and we haven't been to Base for the past five hundred days. I don't have any friends—"

"So you resent it?"

"*And* I'm short and not exactly a raving beauty. Not that it matters, since there aren't any boys except my brothers in my habitat anyway."

"I sense hostility," the woman said.

Andi laughed. "Hostility? None at all. Why would I be hostile? I'm one of the luckiest kids in the universe. I'm a space pioneer on Ganymede and someday they'll write stories about us. *Little Habitat in Ice* or something."

"It's a good thing you've got a sense of humor," the woman said. "Well, we have your blood sample now, and we'll contact your mother if there are any problems."

For the first time, Andi remembered the pill in her pocket. Should she ask about it? Would this woman know? But if Mama found out she'd asked, she'd be really mad . . . better be safe.

"Bird, will you be all right while I use the toilet?" she asked. Bird had already had her blood drawn, and all that remained was the eye test and the hearing test, Andi was sure. Bird nodded, and Andi cocked an eyebrow at the woman in the smock.

"Sure—out in the hall, three down on the left," the woman said. "You'll come right back here?"

"Yes, ma'am," Andi said. "Straight back."

In the toilet, Andi locked the door and called Vinnie on her phone.

"I have to bring my little brother and sister along to lunch," she said. "Mama insisted on dragging them along and I have to take care of them. I couldn't tell you before; it all happened after she made me get off the comm yesterday—"

"Hamilton and Lisa aren't going to like that," Vinnie said. Andi remembered them more from the stories Vinnie and Beth told about them than from that one whirlwind day of fun. "Hamilton said we should all go to the matinee to see the new shows, but they're rated for twelve and over. She's kind of bossy. Can't you drop them at the playground? The recreation supervisor can take care of them."

"I can't," Andi said. "Mama didn't give me enough money, and anyway if she found out she'd kill me."

"Oh, well," Vinnie said, sounding faintly disgusted. "I guess we can hang around with you, Beth and me. Maybe Terry will, too. It's just—it'd be more fun if we were all together. But we can go to the theater any time."

"Thanks," Andi said, feeling anything but grateful. "I should be out of the exam in time to meet you in Boone Concourse for lunch at noon."

"We'll be there," Vinnie said. "Just don't be late."

Now to collect Bird and Gerry, and convince them to cooperate. Bird was still in the exam room, just finishing the hearing test. Andi smiled at the woman in the smock, and took Bird by the hand when the exam was over. Out in the waiting area, a scowling Gerry was being watched by another woman in a different colored smock, who looked relieved as Andi approached.

"You're the sister? Good. Your mother said to be back here by the end of second shift, no later. She said you had a phone, but not to call unless it's an emergency. Do you understand?"

"Yes, ma'am," Andi said. She eyed Gerry. "We'll be careful," she said, hoping that would make the woman go away, but she stood there watching as Andi led the other two out into the passage. Gerry opened his mouth, but Andi spoke quickly and softly.

"Listen, both of you. There's time—we have all day—I can take my certification exam and get my license if you just don't tell Mama. That's all I'm asking: just don't tell Mama."

"And what're you offering?" Gerry asked.

"Fifty," Andi said. She was willing to go to eighty, but Gerry had to think he was forcing her, or it wouldn't work.

"Fifty! That's not near enough." His eyes narrowed. "I know you've been saving up for this—"

"I have to have enough for the exam and licensing fee, and to buy lunch for you and Bird," Andi said, trying to sound reasonable and grown up. "And I need a new shipsuit—"

"Girls and clothes," Gerry said, rolling his eyes. "I don't care if you wear an old shipsuit! You haven't grown; it's mine that doesn't fit."

"If I don't have enough for the license, then I can't take the exam, and there's no reason for you not to tell Mama whatever you want." Andy kept them moving; adults would notice if they stood still arguing.

"Sixty," Gerry said. "Why do I care if you get a license or not?"

"If something happens to Mama or Pop, you'll care," Andi said. Playing the guilt card rarely worked with Gerry, but it was worth a try.

"It hasn't happened yet," Gerry said. "Sixty or nothing."

Sixty wasn't as bad as she'd feared. She'd have gone without lunch herself, without anything, as long as she got that license. But she couldn't let him know that.

"I don't know what you could find to spend sixty on, plus your own allowance," she said, forcing a grumble when she felt more like cheering. "But all right. After we leave—" The corridor around them still had too many people in the smocks and jackets of medical personnel, people that might tattle to Mama.

Once they were out of the Clinic, into the swirl of traffic, Gerry pulled her aside and stopped short. "Now," Gerry said.

Andi fished in her pouch, carefully not letting him see how much money she really had, and handed him three 20-credit strips. "There you are."

"This'll do," Gerry said. "Now—where do we meet?"

"Wait—you have to help me with Bird, at least until I get to the exam. Anyone along here might be going to the Clinic, might happen to speak to Mama."

"Oh, all right." Gerry shrugged and started off again.

"Then I'll show you where to go in Boone Concourse," Andi said.

A wall map gave them the most direct route to the Testing Center; Bird trotted along without complaint, though Andi could feel that she was getting confused and tired. Good. That meant she might stay where she was put while Andi took the exam.

"The thing you have to watch for is the workforce pirates," Andi said to Gerry, over Bird's head. "They're looking for unattached kids old enough to be useful—and you are, now."

"I know, I know. Mama said. But nobody's gonna catch me," Gerry said.

"Gerry, listen. They have tricks. You mustn't eat or drink anything anyone gives you—don't let anyone pay for your food at a kiosk, either. Sometimes they have accomplices there. Base Stores kids go around in groups too big to snatch, or with an adult."

"So I'll join up with some other kids—"

"No! Some of them are workforce bait." Maybe it wasn't the brightest idea to let Gerry off by himself. She'd told him before about the workforce pirates that snatched unattached children, but he didn't seem worried enough. "What you do is act like you know where you're going, on an errand for some adult. If anyone asks, say you're going to TeacherSource for tapes your teacher ordered—they'll think someone will be looking for you if you don't come back on time."

"What's TeacherSource?"

"The education store. It's just off Boone Concourse on the Green axis."

"Boring," Gerry said. "I'm not going there, that's for sure."

"Gerry, if you just hang around looking idle, like a habitat tourist, they'll grab you—"

"I can take care of myself," he said, too cockily. Andi's second thoughts became third thoughts, but it was too late to change plans now; there ahead was the Testing Center, and Gerry had already let go of Bird's hand and turned away.

"Gerry—!"

He waved, and turned back the way they had come. And they didn't have a rendezvous. "Boone Concourse—the food stands," she called, hoping no workforce pirate was nearby. Surely they wouldn't hang around the Testing Center.

At the intake desk, she gave her name, showed her ID card with its proof of age.

"You're the youngest applicant we've had in a long time," the intake clerk said. "Hardship case, I see. And who's that with you? She's clearly too young."

"My little sister," Andi said.

"Well, she can't go in with you," the clerk said. "There's a waiting room for family members; she can wait there. Your test starts in fifteen minutes. Remember that you cannot take any communications device into the test area. The rental lockers are over there, half-cred for the duration of the exam. Here's your examination plate; give it to the examiner." He handed her the silvery rectangle that would—if she passed—become her third-class license.

Andi took Bird into the waiting room. Here were no toys for children, just rows of hard seats, about half occupied by adults, and two cube readers, both in use. Her heart sank. Bird never sat still for ten minutes, even with plenty of toys around. And there was nothing for her to do.

She had come this far; she wasn't going to stop now. "Bird, you sit here until I come back. Do not talk to anyone. Do not go anywhere."

"Don't leave me, Andi!" Bird's face turned red.

"I'm not going far, Bird. I have to take a test—you know, like back home when it's schooltime. Remember? I'm just going in another room to take the test. I'll be back."

"Andi, don't go!" But it was calculation, not panic, in her eyes.

"I'll give you a present when I come back, if you're right here, Bird."

"What present?" Bird asked. Andi tried to think what might be a big enough promise, and yet affordable when she deducted the cost of lunches for them.

"A surprise," she said finally, spreading her hands. "A big, big surprise. And meantime you can hold my phone while I take the test. Just don't call anyone; it'll cost too much."

"I'll stay," Bird said. "I won't call."

"Promise?" Bird might be flighty as her name, but she kept promises the way only a nine-year-old could.

"Promise."

"I'll be back," Andi said.

The written exam, graded automatically as she took it, was supposed to last an hour. Andi finished it in thirty-seven minutes, with a perfect score. She had no time to feel triumphant; she went to check on Bird.

"I stayed," Bird said proudly. "What's my surprise?"

"The exam's not over," Andi said. "I just get a break in the middle. I can take you to the toilets—"

"You said *a* test, not *two* tests. You said there'd be a surprise."

"And there will be, soon as I finish. Come on, Bird, there's just time."

Bird had her lower lip stuck out a little, but she came along to the toilets, and when Andi brought her back, sat down where Andi told her.

"Next time I come out, I'll be finished," Andi said. "Just wait here for me." Bird nodded; Andi went back into the testing area.

This time it was the simulator test, and it lasted the full hour, plus five minutes as the examiner tried to talk her out of actually getting the license even though she had passed. "You're too young," he kept saying. "You could wait a year; your scores are good but your judgment can't be mature."

Finally, he signed off on her score, and gave that and her blank license to the clerk. Andi kept trying to see around the corner to the waiting room—Bird would be about ready to explode, having to wait so long—but the clerk had more questions for her to answer and she had to give a DNA sample. At last the engraving machine spit out her license, with its embedded circuitry and indelible surface engraving, and she had it in her hand.

"Thanks," she said, feeling a good half-meter taller. Her very own license. She hurried to the waiting room where . . . Bird wasn't.

Where nobody was. No adults, no children, and most especially no nine-year-old with a stubborn jaw and sea-green eyes.

"Bird?" The word came out in a gasp. She started to look under the chairs, but that was ridiculous. Bird wasn't hiding under a chair. Bird was gone.

"The toilets," she said aloud. "She must've gone to the toilet again."

She stopped at the intake desk anyway. "Did you see a little girl—she came in with me?"

"No," the clerk said, not looking up.

"Black hair, green eyes, so tall?"

The clerk glanced up briefly. "I told you she can't go in with—oh . . . haven't you finished yet?"

Andi flung away from the desk. Across the corridor, down past a row of offices, to the public toilets. Inside, faced with rows of shut doors, and a woman's voice coaxing a toddler from inside one of them. "Now sweetie, you know you need to—"

"BIRD!" Andi yelled. "Bird, are you in here?"

A door banged open on the other side; an angry middle-aged woman in some kind of uniform—dark green with patches and silver braid—stalked around the divider. She had a pilot's silver rocket-shaped pin on her collar. "Stop that yelling! Didn't anyone teach you manners, you kids?"

"I—I'm sorry," Andi said. "I'm looking for my little sister—" The woman towered over her.

"There's no need to yell," the woman said coldly. She put her hands in the cleanser unit and went right on talking. "I should report you and your parents as well. You're far too young to be left in charge of a smaller child."

"I am not too young," Andi said. "I'm just short for my age."

"Well, you look about eight," the woman said. "And clearly you're irresponsible, or you wouldn't have lost her. I suppose you were larking about and not paying attention—"

Andi opened her mouth to say she had been taking a test, not larking about, but actually—she hadn't been paying attention to Bird. And arguing with someone in uniform was dangerous. Mama and Pop had both said that, over and over. Always smile, always say ma'am and sir a lot.

"Sorry—ma'am," she said, backing out of the area. "I'll just go—"

"You'd better find her," the woman said, without looking at her. "This is a dangerous place for small children." Then she glanced down at Andi and her face softened. "Look—I can tell you're not from Base. If you need help—"

"No, ma'am, no, thank you," Andi said. "I can find her myself."

"Here's my card—" The woman held out a datastrip. "If you don't find her, if you need to contact the authorities, you can use my name."

She had to take it; if she didn't, the woman might be angrier, might insist on reporting her.

"Thank you, ma'am," she said again, taking the strip and stuffing in her belt-pouch. "I don't think I'll need to, but thank you."

The woman shook her head, as if she was going to argue some more, but something in her pocket buzzed. She turned away, shrugging, and walked off, fishing what must be a phone out of her uniform.

Andi stared after her. Panic bubbled; she fought it down. Bird was nine. Nine wasn't like a toddler. Of course Bird could read and use a wall map. So where would she have gone? Off to Boone Concourse to meet Gerry? Back to the Clinic to tell Mama that Andi had made her sit by herself? Or somewhere else?

If Bird had gone to the Clinic, no telling how much head start she had, and probably Mama already knew. Unless Bird sat herself down in the waiting area, which—in the mood she was probably in—she wouldn't. If Mama already knew, the best thing would be to stay far away and hope Mama's anger wore off. At least she wouldn't be punished until she went back. If Mama didn't know, going to the Clinic would only alert her. Either way, going back to the Clinic was a bad idea.

Andi glanced at the nearest map, and headed for Boone Concourse. Most likely Bird had gone to find Gerry; she wouldn't have wanted to meet Mama and spend the rest of the day stuck in a Clinic waiting room. Most likely she and Gerry would be spending Andi's money at a snack kiosk.

At last Boone Concourse opened ahead of her, centered by the hanging garden that went right up to the apex of the dome, surrounded by brightly lit shops, crowded with hurrying people. Last time she'd been here, she'd been so excited she'd bounced up and down: all that *space*. All those people. Colors, lights, noise, music, smells . . . someplace to be other than the same crowded, boring habitat.

Now, looking around for a glimpse of Gerry or Bird (or, she hoped, both) she found the space and people mere confusion. There were children of various sizes, but none in dull gray jumpsuits. Adults brushed past her, scowling down at her. She had to walk close to the shops and kiosks to see who was there; she had to check out all sides of the central garden column. She barely noticed the proud banner that announced Base now had a population of 23,548, except that Gerry had asked how many people were on Base and she would remember to tell him.

No sign of Gerry or Bird in any of the food shops or near the snack kiosks. No sign of them in the game booths. The very smell

of food made Andi's stomach turn as panic crawled up her
throat. She wanted to be angry with Gerry—why hadn't he
stayed where she told him to? Bird was little enough to make
mistakes; Gerry was only a year younger than she was; he knew
better.

But that anger ebbed quickly into a cold bottomless pit of
fear. It wasn't Gerry's fault, or Bird's fault. It was her own fault,
for leaving them alone, and if they were captured by workforce
pirates . . . that, too, would be her fault. Had that already happened? Her imagination was all too eager to make up horrific
scenes: a dull-eyed Gerry drugged into obedience; a terrified Bird
loomed over by an angry spacer.

She was not going to let that happen. She set her jaw and
headed for TeacherSource. Gerry had said he wouldn't go there,
but maybe he'd thought it over. He liked books; she might find
him browsing the shelves. She'd told him, when she came home
last time, about the chip player the store let children use to read
some of the titles.

"Andi! Over here!"

Andi whirled, but realized even as she moved that it wasn't
Gerry's voice or Bird's. She'd completely forgotten her friends,
and there they were, waving at her from one of the food stalls.
She recognized Vinnie and Beth—but they were so much taller,
so . . . so grown-up looking. And the girls with them—those
must be Lisa, Hamilton, and Terry. They too had grown; she
knew Hamilton only by her silvery blonde hair.

"You're late," Vinnie said as Andi came nearer. Then she
blinked. "You haven't grown a centimeter; you *still* look like
you're eight years old. Where are the kids? Didn't you say you'd
be dragging your kid brother and sister along?"

"Is that the same old jumpsuit you were wearing last time?"
Hamilton asked, her lip curling. "It makes you look like a grade-
schooler as well as a habber. We have to do something about that
in a hurry; I can't be seen hanging out with a baby habber." She
lifted a shoulder and turned on Vinnie. "*You* said she was cute
and fun; *you* said she was worth skipping out for. I'm not at all

sure clothes will make that much difference. She's so *short*." The tone made "short" sound like a disease. Vinnie flinched and looked down.

Andi felt like someone had hit her in the face. Was this what Mama had been talking about? Was Mama right about outsiders after all? No: she was not going to believe it. Whatever Hamilton thought, Vinnie and Beth were her friends. "I am a habber kid," Andi said. "And yes, I'm short. So what? It's not like I asked for it."

"Well, of course you didn't want to be a little round-faced babydoll," Hamilton said, drawling the words. "Who would? At least you have that much sense. But you can't expect us to ignore it, now can you?"

Vinnie and Beth said nothing, standing there with their mouths open. Andi felt hollow inside; why didn't they defend her? That was what friends in books did. Lisa broke in as Hamilton turned her perfect profile to Andi and looked off across the Concourse. "Where *are* the brats? Did you manage to dump them somewhere, I hope?"

Andi had momentarily forgotten Gerry and Bird, in the rush of anger and shame from Hamilton's attack. Now her mind snapped back to that problem. "No, I—"

Before she could explain, Beth moved over and gave her a quick hug. "I'm so glad to see you," Beth said, grinning. She at least had no edge to her voice. "So—did you pass? I thought you'd run all the way here to tell us; I was afraid you'd been stopped by a proctor for running in the corridors."

"Yes, I passed, but I have a problem," Andi said. This was not how she'd planned the meeting with her friends. If they were her friends. Beth felt like a friend, at least. "I've lost Gerry and Bird. I have to find them."

"Oh, Gerry'll take care of Bird," Vinnie said, shrugging. She was eyeing Hamilton, Andi noticed. "He's what—eleven?—this year."

"Yes, but I don't think he can take care of her," Andi said.

"I'm not even sure she's with him. Listen: I'm in big trouble." Quickly, she explained the whole miserable day so far.

"You weren't supposed to take the test?" Vinnie sounded shocked. "And you went anyway?"

"I had to," Andi said. "I couldn't wait until next time—"

"But you lost Bird," Vinnie said in exactly the tone Mama might have used.

"I didn't mean to lose Bird," Andi said. "If she'd only stayed where I told her to—"

"But you knew she couldn't sit still that long," Vinnie said. "You've told us how restless she is." Andi had noticed before that Vinnie was a bit of a prig, but this was too much.

"You're not helping," Andi said. She could feel her temper rising. "I've got to find them; I don't need scolding."

"But you shouldn't have—" Vinnie began. Beth interrupted.

"Vinnie, stop it! Andi, I'm sure we can help you. Tell us what they look like, what they're wearing. Do they have their own phones? What's their code?"

"If Mama hadn't insisted on no pictures by comm, you'd already know," Andi said. "And Bird's got my phone—I left it with her while I took the test—but Gerry doesn't have one. Gerry's about this tall—" she gestured a couple of centimeters over her own head. "And he's got brown hair and eyes and skin about the color of that biscuit. He's wearing a gray jumpsuit just like mine." She noticed that the other girls weren't paying attention; Hamilton was staring across the concourse as if this whole conversation had nothing to do with her. Lisa and Terry were watching Hamilton.

Hamilton turned suddenly, avoiding Andi's gaze and looking at all the other girls. "Look, are you coming to the matinee or not?" she said. "I'm not going to waste my afternoon skipping school on a bunch of runty habber scabs."

"Me, either," said Lisa quickly, and Terry nodded.

"I—" Vinnie looked at Andi, then at Beth. "I guess—"

"We can help," Beth said again, firmly. She reached out and

touched Vinnie's arm, pulling her closer. "We can see a matinee anytime. Andi's our friend—"

"Yours, maybe. Not mine," Hamilton said. "Come on, let's go." She stalked off, Lisa and Terry trailing. Vinnie took a step that direction, looked at Beth, and stayed where she was, heaving a big sigh.

"You know what she's like," Vinnie said to Beth. "She'll be impossible tomorrow." Beth shrugged. Vinnie turned back to Andi. "Dressed like you, then," she said. "Basic habbers' issue." Her lip curled delicately. Andi felt her cheeks burning.

"I can't help what Mama picked out for us. I was going to buy some clothes as soon as I could." Though she didn't have the money now that she'd bribed Gerry. And what difference did it make what clothes she had on, when Gerry and Bird were missing?

"All in gray," Beth said, squinting a little. "Vin, didn't we see a little boy in gray about the time we got here, before the others arrived? He jumped up from one of those benches, remember, and started walking really fast—I noticed because he was following a man with a little girl dressed the same way. I thought they were a family, he and the girl and the man. How tall is Bird, Andi?"

"This high," Andi said. "Black hair, all curly, and green eyes."

"I didn't see her eyes," Beth said. "Black hair, though. Remember, Vinnie? The naughty girl?"

"Naughty?" Andi said. "Bird's not naughty!"

"She was with this man—I thought he was her father or something—and she was kind of dragging back. She didn't yell, though. Then he picked her up."

Bird wouldn't yell. When she got scared, she went quiet, even if she struggled. None of them were yellers, not even Gerry. Mama didn't like noisy kids. This had to be worst-case. Workforce pirates.

"Which way did they go? How long ago?"

"That way—" Beth pointed. "If that was Bird, it wasn't your father?"

"No," Andi said. "I told you; Pop's back at the habitat. It has to be workforce pirates." She started in the direction Beth pointed, slowing to glance into each storefront.

"Wait—you don't know where they went!" Vinnie said.

"And I won't, if I stay here jabbering," Andi said. "Are you coming, or not?"

"You don't have to be so bossy," Vinnie said, but she followed Beth, who had already caught up to Andi.

"Don't you think we ought to contact the Base proctors?" Beth asked as Andi hurried along, breaking stride only to look into each storefront they passed. "What if we run into them? Pirates, I mean?"

"No! Mama said never talk to Base officials if we don't have to."

"But if someone's lost, that's what you're supposed to do," Beth said.

"Don't they have taggers on?" Vinnie asked. "Little kids on Base wear taggers. We could rent a locator—"

"No," Andi said. "Taggers cost money. Mama expected me—"

"Oh." Vinnie's smug look had vanished. Away from the other girls she seemed friendlier, more like the Vinnie on the comm. "This is really serious, isn't it? Your mother's going to be so mad—"

"Yes," Andi said. She didn't want to think about how mad Mama was going to be. "But what matters is Bird and Gerry."

"If it was workforce pirates, they didn't have Gerry," Beth said. "He was following; maybe the man didn't notice him, and he can get Bird back."

"Come on, Bethie," Vinnie said. "An eleven-year-old kid get another kid back from the pirates? They're more likely to get him too."

"I was just trying to cheer her up," Beth said, with a sidelong glance at Andi.

"I am cheered up," Andi said. Her voice didn't sound cheerful even to her. "At least I have someone with me." She looked around. The corridor they'd started along was narrowing as it slanted gently upward; it had changed from retail outlets to blank-fronted residential units with numbers by the entrances. "If this was a book," she said, "Gerry would've figured out a way to leave a trail we could follow. They could've gone into any one of these." There were no bread crumbs, no obvious bits of clothing, no cryptic chalk marks on the walls, or . . . or whatever else Gerry might've thought to try. She thought of the branching corridors they'd passed, most leading downward, and wondered if she'd picked the right way to go.

"Would Gerry follow Bird and the man through a door like this, if he hadn't been caught?" Vinnie asked, pointing to one of the numbered entrances.

"I don't think so," Andi said. "I think he'd wait outside or something. Call me, maybe." She shook her head. "But he can't, because Bird has my phone. If she didn't lose it somewhere."

"He could call your mother," Vinnie said. "Or the proctors."

"He wouldn't do that," Andi said. Even as she said it, she thought it might be a good idea if Gerry ignored the promise he'd made. But she knew he wouldn't. He was as stubborn as she was. He would think of something else.

"Let's go on," Beth said. "If he's not been caught, and he's waiting near where someone took Bird, we can find him—"

Andi nodded. "We can't waste time knocking on all these doors, that's for sure."

Another ten minutes took them from the residential zone to a busier area where cargo 'bots moved along magnetic lines on the floor and adults in various uniforms stared at them as they passed one open bay after another.

"We really shouldn't be here," Vinnie said. "We're almost up to dock level. This is the kind of place my parents said—"

"Nothing will happen while we're all together," Beth said. "We'll be fine." She sounded almost cheerful.

Andi was less certain. She felt hostility in the glances, the closed, unfriendly faces. All but one, anyway. A woman in a blue smock smiled at them from a kiosk set a meter out from the wall near the entrance to what looked like a cafe. The name on the kiosk and the entrance both was the same: Paddy's Wagon. Andi decided it would be safe to speak to the smiling woman. They had to find out somehow if this was the way Gerry had come.

"Excuse me," Andi said, approaching the kiosk. "Did you see a boy about this tall—" she gestured. "Wearing a gray jumpsuit?"

"Honey, you should be in school this time of day," the woman said. She had a pleasant, drawling voice. "Are you on a field trip? Where's your teacher?"

"I'm looking for my little brother," Andi said.

The woman's gaze shifted to Vinnie and Beth. "You're Base children, aren't you? Why aren't *you* in class?"

"It's a holiday—" Beth said.

"We got permission—" Vinnie said. They looked at each other and turned red.

"You're truants," the woman said, with no doubt in her voice. She grinned, a grin that made Andi shiver. "Old enough to know better, and I'll bet you dragged *her* along—" she nodded at Andi, "—because she's off one of those habitats and too young to know the rules."

"I'm as old as they are!" Andi said, putting together what Hamilton had said and this woman said . . . Beth and Vinnie and the others had skipped school to meet her? They must be friends, then, even if Hamilton didn't act like it.

"Sweetie, it's not nice to tell stories," the woman said, coming out from behind the kiosk and patting Andi on the head, a pat that turned into a stroke of her hair. Andi shivered again. "You girls are lucky you ran into me," the woman said. "Some of these men around here are—you know—not very nice." She chuckled. "Why don't we go in here, have a nice cup of something, and I'll get in touch with your parents—"

"No!" Vinnie and Beth said together.

"No?" The woman's eyebrows went up in a movement so obviously fake that Andi wanted to run right then. "You don't want me to call your parents and make sure you get home safely? Or call yourself? I'm sure you all have personal phones. No?" She chuckled. "Still after adventure, are you?"

"Not . . . exactly," Beth said. "But I'm not supposed to go into . . . into places like this without my parents."

"I want to find my little brother," Andi said. The woman barely glanced at her before focusing on Beth.

"Y'know, hon, if you don't want me to call your parents or the proctors, you're going to have to give me a little tit for tat."

Beth looked confused; Vinnie's chin went up. "Come on, Beth, Andi. We're leaving."

"Oh, I don't think so," the woman said. Andi looked over her shoulder. Three men blocked the passage behind them. "Let's see . . . Beth?" Beth looked at her. "So you're Beth, you must be Andi—" She touched Andi's hair again. "And what's your name, Miss Priss?"

"Vinnie," said Vinnie sullenly. "Tell those men to go away. I want to go home."

"Vinnie, let me give you some advice. Don't sass me and don't try to order me around. It won't work. Now—what's your full name?"

"Virginia Lowes Pillar," Vinnie said. Her chin had come up. "My father works in Central Administration; you'd better not do anything to me—"

"Vinnie, I told you. Don't tell me what to do; I'm in charge here." The woman's smile now wasn't at all friendly. Andi tried to look around without seeming to. With the woman's attention focused on Vinnie, maybe she could slip away. But . . . could she leave Vinnie and Beth in trouble? In all the stories, friends stuck together. They had come with her, in spite of Hamilton; it was her own fault that they were in danger now. So she should stay with them. But on the other hand, Gerry and Bird—

She was still caught in this dilemma when the situation went even more sour. The men behind closed in silently and the woman in blue reached out and caught hold of Vinnie's arm.

Vinnie yanked back, right into the grip of one of the men. Andi ducked sideways and tried to get her back to a wall, but too late—she felt strong hands grabbing her arms, and the tricks that had worked against Oscar did not work now. The prick of a needle came as no surprise, and her last thought before falling into darkness was *You are so stupid!*

◈◈◈

Andi woke up slowly; feeling her way through misty cobwebs was what it seemed like. She was stiff; when she tried to move, she couldn't. Panic woke her the rest of the way—where was she? What had happened? She got her eyes open; they felt gummy and she wanted to rub them, but her hands were bound behind her.

Gerry was in front of her, sideways—no, they were both on a floor. He had a bruise on his jaw; as she looked, he opened his eyes, blinking several times. Then he focused on her face and grinned.

Behind him was a gray lump that must be Bird. She lifted her head, fighting off dizziness. Bird's eyes were closed; she looked asleep. Andi tried to look around. They were on the floor, or deck between two rows of seats. She could see an opening that looked a lot like a shuttle hatch, with brighter light on the other side of it. Then she heard voices, men's voices, somewhere the other side of that door or hatch.

"Three habber kids, two Base—not a bad catch."

"Base'll be annoyed. Good families, those two; not worth the trouble it'll cause. No special skills."

"They're out cold now. We'll can memory-dope 'em, drop 'em back near Boone, let 'em explain to their parents. They never got a look at our faces; the drug'll eat the last ten minutes before the knockout, so they won't be able to ID Lil. But the habber brats have potential. One of 'em's got a brand-new Class C license."

"Well, then. Take care of the Base kids—don't maul 'em up too bad—"

"—and make sure they don't wake up until late second shift. I know."

Gerry stared into Andi's eyes, then glanced at Bird, who was still unconscious. He opened his mouth, but she shook her head at him and he nodded.

"We've still got cargo to load before we take off. Not more'n twenty minutes and I'll be out of here. Let me just check—"

Andi closed her eyes and let all her muscles slack, trying to think herself asleep, as she heard someone's footsteps clicking on metal, coming nearer. She hoped Gerry had the sense to do the same. Someone's breathing, someone's clothes rustling a little . . . she didn't know if it was one person or two, and she tried not to think about it, to think sleepy thoughts instead. A hard finger prodded her ribs; she grunted a little and burrowed into a tighter coil the way Bird and Damon did when they didn't want to get up in the morning.

"Hmph," came a murmur from overhead; she couldn't tell if it was someone talking to himself, or to a companion. "Small as they are, that probably was enough—"

She heard the footsteps shuffling away, then the boots-on-metal sound again, and the soft thud of a hatch closing, and the multiple snicks of a lock. Was it safe to open her eyes? Had all the men gone, or was one sitting quietly, watching, as in the story-tapes? She listened, hearing mostly her own heartbeat, and finally opened an eye to find Gerry staring at her.

The compartment was empty, except for the three of them. But surely it was monitored; she looked around cautiously, not yet moving more than her eyes. Anything might hide a spy-eye; anything might hide a microphone.

"Andi?" Gerry's voice was low. She moved her head slightly, *No.* He subsided, but looked around as she did, then wriggled a little and showed her one hand, unbound.

Andi grinned at him, giving a very slight nod. She didn't know how he'd done it, but if he had one hand loose . . . he pulled the other out from under Bird. Andi struggled with her own bonds, but whatever they'd used cut into her wrists. Stiff plastic, it felt like.

Gerry put a finger to his lips, then moved slowly, soundlessly, first sitting up then scrunching forward. He had what looked like a fastener in his hand, something with a broad head and a strip of stiff material sticking out. He reached over Andi and did something—she couldn't tell what—and the bonds on her wrists fell open.

She hugged Gerry, and felt much better, for as long as it took to remind herself that Bird was still out cold and they were still locked in a compartment of—of what? Clearly some kind of vehicle, but it could be a compartment in anything from a surface-traversing hopper to a space-going tradeship. And it didn't matter, because those men were coming back, and would take them somewhere Andi did not want to go.

"I know where they put my toolkit. Maybe I can trick the lock," Gerry said in her ear, very softly.

Andi looked around. She had been lying more or less facing a hatch, the one the men had gone out by, on the side of the cylinder, but there was another hatch in the flat end behind her head. She didn't want to go where the men had gone—one of them might be right outside—but the other direction might offer another exit.

"That one," she said to Gerry. "And I'm going to try to wake Bird."

"Let her sleep," Gerry advised. "She'll make noise." He looked into an open locker and pulled out his toolkit with a grin. In moments he was at work on the second hatch. Andi watched, her stomach knotting tighter every moment.

With a final clunk, the lock released, and the hatch slid sideways into its recess. Andi stared past Gerry's head at the control panels of a shuttle cockpit.

"Wow!" Gerry said, too loudly, and pulled himself forward. Andi grabbed his leg.

"Quiet!" she said. "Stay down, in case—" but he had already ducked back.

"It's outside of Base," he said. "I can see the outside of the dome, and the sky—"

No escape that way, then, unless there was a covered access passage for the pilot.

"Let me get up there." Andi shoved at Gerry, who was still blocking the way.

"What're you—you can't fly this—"

"If I can find my license—" Andi felt in all her pockets. Nothing. But the license wouldn't work for anyone else; it had her biometrics locked into it. They wouldn't have wanted it too far away from her, she hoped, though the man who snatched her could have put it in his own pocket for safekeeping. She stood, still dizzy from the drug, and looked at the compartment more closely. Something banged loudly, outside; she flinched and almost dropped to the floor—the deck, rather. But the banging was aft, probably in a cargo compartment. Loading cargo, the men had said. Twenty minutes—how long had they been lying there or struggling with the hatch? How much time did they have left?

Above the floor where they'd been dumped and the seats, storage lockers of various sizes lined the bulkheads, most with keys in them. Andi opened one; it was empty.

"Look in those," she said to Gerry, nodding at the other side of the shuttle. "My license may be in one of them." She kept trying the ones on her side. Nothing in the first, the second, the third. The fourth on her side was locked, with no key. "Gerry—come open this. Quietly."

He fiddled with the lock. Nothing. Tried a key from one of the other lockers. Nothing. Tried again with something from his toolkit, and got it open. Inside was her license; she picked it up with relief so strong she felt dizzy all over again. She clambered through the hatch and looked out the windows.

Outside the shuttle, she saw no moving figures at all. The icy plain, stained dull orange by the light of the planet, was empty of all she could recognize as life. Far away, the ice heaped up in rough lumps on the horizon, the rugged terrain they had flown across coming to Base. On the Base side, she saw only the slight curve of the dome ahead; no other shuttle was docked within her view.

Sure for the moment that no one was walking around outside

looking in the cockpit windows, she settled into the pilot's seat and took another look at the shuttle controls. It was not the same model as her family's. The onboard schematic showed it to be a third smaller. It had only three compartments: the one in which they'd been left, and two aft compartments. The cockpit spy-eye viewer showed her both interior and exterior of both of those: the aft-most with its big hatch open, and someone—three someones—loading cargo. Outside, the man who had first grabbed her, now holding some kind of weapon. No exit out the hatch they'd come through, then. She'd expected that.

"Can you fly this kind?" Gerry asked. He was crouched beside her on the deck.

"I—don't know." She had trained for the family's shuttle, the most stable, staid kind of transportation in the region. As close to idiot-proof, one of the training guides said, as a craft could be. This was something else. True, the panels were all familiar—the attitude indicators, the delta vee indicators, the indicators for fuel, the navigational suite. But the parameters were far beyond what the family shuttle could manage. She could go faster, maneuver more sharply . . . crash more thoroughly.

"Andi—" Gerry began.

She could at least lock the doors. Really lock the doors. SECURE HATCHES was in the same place here. If she did that, the man couldn't get back in without shooting holes in the shuttle, and maybe not then. Would he try to destroy it? Would he even notice? It would give her time, maybe . . .

She looked for the selection under SECURE HATCHES and found CREW COMPARTMENT. She touched it. Nothing happened.

"It didn't work," Gerry said unnecessarily. "I wonder why—"

"My license." She had to insert her license into the command slot, look into retinal scan and put her thumb on the plate to prove that the person in the pilot's chair was actually the license holder. She did so; the command slot sucked her license in; lights blinked across the panels, and the license popped partway out.

"Ready to receive commands," said a pleasant female voice. Andi jumped and looked around. "Welcome, Captain Murchison. Please be advised that Class C license holders may not access advanced features of this craft. Please be sure that you understand the limitations as laid out in the operating manual—"

Andi closed her mouth with an effort—Captain Murchison? Her?—and pushed the SECURE HATCH combination for the crew compartment again. This time a yellow light under "crew compartment hatch" turned green.

"Crew compartment hatch secured," the voice said. "Continue to prepare for undocking?"

"One thing at a time," Andi muttered to herself. The family shuttle didn't have a voice interactive A.I.; she wasn't used to a machine paying attention to her talk.

"Pardon?"

On the spy-eye viewer, Andi saw someone jump down from the aft cargo compartment, lower that hatch, and touch it with what must be a control unit; the hatch's icon now showed yellow on the control panel. That man walked up to the one with the weapon, and both turned to the hatch to the crew compartment. One of them touched the control unit to the hatch, pulled it back, shook it, and touched again.

"Oh, frangos!" Andi said. "They'll figure it out in two seconds." She touched the SECURE HATCH ALL control, and all the hatch icons turned green. "We've got to undock now."

"Understand command *Undock Now*," the voice said. "Initiating release of life support umbilicals; initiating release of docking clamps. Clearance from Base Traffic?"

Banging came from behind them; on the spy-eye the man with the weapon was using it to hammer on the hatch.

"No clearance necessary," Andi said firmly, fastening the safety webbing around herself with shaking fingers. "Emergency." And to Gerry, "Get into that seat and buckle up." Bird would have to take her chances; anything would be better than being stolen away to the pirates' factories. Gerry scrambled to obey.

"Warning," the A.I.'s pleasant voice went on. "Failure to obtain clearance may cause damage to dockside facilities, personal injury to persons dockside, and result in legal consequences including possible fines, confiscation of property, loss of license, and confinement in a correctional institution."

"Understood." Andi watched the play of indicators on the panels. "Initiate power supply main engine."

The shuttle came alive with a steady thrum. She watched the output climb. If the pirates had any sense, they had already retreated down dockside and sealed off the bay . . . but in the spy-eye she saw one of them—the one she thought of as the worst, struggling into a pressure suit, reaching for a helmet.

"Power-up complete," the voice announced. "Undock sequence complete."

"Confirm," Andi said. The figures she had studied so carefully, the calculations she'd done on the test earlier that day, all seemed tangled in her head. What was the correct vector? Given the mass of this shuttle and the power output of its engines, what initial acceleration should she choose?

"Recommended options displayed," the A.I. said, as if it understood. "Please indicate choice . . ." That simplified things: she had only three choices. The A.I. unit would allow her to take off vertically, forward low-ascent, or forward medium-ascent.

"Two," Andi said. Forward low-ascent sounded safest.

"Option two confirmed," the voice said. "Initiating—" The shuttle shivered, then lurched a little to the left as air gusted out of the docking passage when the collar seal broke. It steadied, then, and lifted smoothly. She had an instant of unalloyed glee: free, with her own ship. She could go anywhere, anywhere at all!

"Course?" the voice asked. Andi opened her mouth to answer when another voice, not at all pleasant, snarled out of a different speaker.

"Shuttlecraft PR-275N! This is Traffic Control! Return to dock immediately! You are in violation of regulations. You are being targeted by our defense weapons and if you do not respond and return, you will be fired upon."

"They sound mad," Gerry said. He sounded scared.

"They probably are." Andi hunted around for the comm controls, and finally found the transmit key. "Here—you talk to them."

"Me? What am I supposed to say?"

"It doesn't matter. Sound young and scared; we don't want them to shoot us."

Gerry shook his head, but spoke into the pickup. "Traffic Control? We have a problem—" His voice squeaked; he did sound young and scared.

"Shuttle PR-275N, is that you? Who are you? Who's in command?" At least the voice wasn't talking about shooting them this instant.

"My . . . my sister. They tried to kidnap us—"

"Your *sister*? Who is this? How old are you?"

"I'm eleven," Gerry said. He paused and put on a tone of sweet reasonableness. "I don't want to tell you who I am because you'll tell Mama, and Mama will be really really mad at us."

"How old is your sister? Let us talk to her." Now the voice sounded as much worried as angry.

"I don't think she should talk to you," Gerry said, still in the voice of a child being very reasonable. "She's flying the shuttle and she needs to concentrate. She waves her hands when she talks."

"I do not!" Andi said. The shuttle was flying itself at the moment, heading away from Base on a course that would take them far away from anything she knew. Andi had found the volume control for the voice of the shuttle's flight computer, and was able to discuss possible courses with it. What would it take to get to the habitat? Back to Base?

"Tell your sister to turn the shuttle around and come back to Base," Traffic Control said. "Does she know how to turn it around?"

"I don't know," Gerry said. He turned to Andi, and, with the pickup still on, said, "Do you know how to go back?"

"I think so," Andi said. "But I'm not sure it's safe. If those men shoot at us . . ."

"Men shot at you?" Traffic Control said. "What men?"

"There were men who grabbed my other sister, the little one," Gerry said. "Then they grabbed me when I tried to rescue her. Then Andi—that's the sister flying the shuttle—came to rescue us and they grabbed her, too. They gave all of us shots. But they put us in the shuttle and thought we were asleep, only we woke up and got into the controls—"

"How old is your sister?"

Gerry looked at Andi; she nodded at him.

"Twelve."

"You're in a shuttle with an unlicensed pilot?!" Now it was the adult's voice that sounded squeaky. "How'd you do that?"

"Not exactly," Gerry said.

"Listen, I have to talk to her. We want you to be safe—"

"I can talk now," Andi said. The shuttle was behaving perfectly; she trusted the A.I. to do what she told it.

"Look, the first thing is to get you kids back to safety—now you need to tell me your name."

"Why?" Andi asked.

"So we can notify your parents; they must be worried sick."

"If they don't know, they won't worry," Andi said. "And besides, I need to tell you what happened, so you won't shoot at us."

"You need to come back here and get safely docked at Base. Look, you can let us take control of the shuttle, and we can bring it in for you—"

"No, thank you," Andi said. "I don't need salvage—"

"Listen, you can't land that thing safely. Even with autopilot enabled."

Andi said, "I'm not going back to the same place; the bad men are still there." Suddenly she thought of Vinnie and Beth. "And they have two other girls—you'd better find them."

"Other girls? On the shuttle with you?"

"No. On Base. They were going to give them a drug so they'd have no memory, and then leave them somewhere near Boone Concourse. They were supposed to be held until late second shift." What time was it now? Andi looked at the shuttle's clock, which was probably set to Base time.

"Do you know who they are?"

Vinnie and Beth wouldn't thank her for getting them in trouble with their parents . . . but could she really trust the pirates not to hurt them? "They're Base residents," she said. "Vinnie Pillar and Beth Cowan. They . . . skipped class to meet me for lunch today. There's a woman named Lil, near someplace called Paddy's Wagon; she helped catch us and she may know where they are now."

"You still haven't told us who you are," Traffic Control said.

"I'll tell you when I get back," Andi said. "But you need to find them."

"We will. But listen . . . here's a pilot who will talk to you and help you get down safely."

"Hello there," a woman's voice said. "This is Senior Pilot Gallagher. Understand you have a little problem—"

Andi's mouth went dry. She recognized that voice. That was the woman in uniform who had scolded her in the restroom. She said nothing, but fished the woman's card out of her pocket to check. Yes. Gallagher, Naomi L.

Would the woman recognize her? Would it be better or worse if she did?

"I'm fine," she said, in what she hoped was a deeper, grown-up voice.

"You are now," the woman—Gallagher said. "But let's keep you that way. I gather you're in the pilot's seat, right? I want you to look at the control boards in front of you. There should be a row of lighted buttons right at the bottom. Can you tell me what color they are?"

"They're all green," Andi said. "And I know what they—"

"Fine," Gallagher said. "And above them, do you see the—"

"Excuse me," Andi said. She was not going to sit through a boring, slow-motion tour of instruments she knew better than her own fingerprints. "Please, ma'am. I have a Class C license."

A moment's silence. "You do." Not a question, but a sort of stunned statement.

"I do. I passed my test today." Best to come clean about the rest, too. She wouldn't be able to keep her name a secret now; too easy to check with the Testing Center records. "Er . . . I met you. In the restroom. You gave me your card."

"In the—*you*? You were that youngster who—"

"Yes, ma'am." Now was the time for calm reasonableness. She hoped.

"You'd better tell me your name," Gallagher said. "And put the visual on."

Andi switched on the visual. Gallagher's intent expression changed to a rueful smile.

"Good heavens, it is you . . . and you still look about eight. What's your name?"

"Andi Murchison," Andi said. "My Mama's at the Clinic with Damon, my littlest brother. He's been really sick, so please don't bother her. It's not just that she'll be mad at me—she can be mad at me later. She doesn't need to be bothered right now."

"I see," Gallagher said. "Well, be that as it may, we need to get you and—who's on the shuttle with you?"

"Gerry and Bird," Andi said. "Gerry was on the radio; Bird's still unconscious from whatever they gave her."

"We need to get you and Gerry and Bird home safe," Gallagher said. "Let's see if you deserve that license. Take your ship off autopilot and execute a turn to the following heading." She gave the figures slowly enough that Andi had no problem catching them.

Andi tapped the control; the A.I.'s voice murmured "Captain Murchison resumes active control." Andi entered the commands for a right turn to the correct heading and the A.I. repeated them in the same mellow, pleasant tone.

"Excellent," Gallagher said. "Now, I want to bring you in about sixty degrees around Base from where you were, slot 37. Start a slow descent to 500 meters; tell me what your rate will be . . . you do have a voice-active A.I. on that shuttle, right?"

"Yes, ma'am," Andi said. "Do you want me to turn up the volume?"

"No, that's fine. You don't want to confuse our voices."

"Descent options?" Andi said to the A.I.

"Descent options now displayed," the A.I. said. "Please state final altitude desired."

"Five hundred meters."

"Is this in preparation for landing?" the A.I. asked.

"Yes."

"Is Traffic Control authorizing this landing?" The A.I.'s tone was almost prim, though still pleasant.

"Yes," Andi said. She looked at the descent options, all quite conservative, and chose the slowest.

"Confirming descent at one-five-zero meters per min-utes . . ." the A.I. said.

Andi passed this information to Gallagher and looked over at Gerry. He looked happy, though the bruise on his chin was darker now. "Go check on Bird," she said. "See if there's any way to put something under her head; if she's waking up, get her into a seat and strapped in."

"Yes, ma'am, Captain Murchison ma'am," Gerry said, grinning as he unbuckled his safety harness. "I guess I *am* glad you got your license today." Then, as he clambered around to go through the hatch to the passenger compartment, "Of course, we wouldn't be in this mess if you'd done what Mama told you."

Andi reached over and smacked his backside just as he went through. "Or if you and Bird had done what I told you. Just how did you get caught, anyway?"

"She's still unconscious," Gerry said, without answering that. "But I can lift her . . . just a second." Various creaks and clunks. "I've got one of the seats flattened out."

"I don't know if you should lift her," Andi said. "What if her neck's broken or something?"

"Andi!" That was Gallagher. "Are you talking about your lit-tle sister? Is she still unconscious?"

"Yes," Andi said. "Gerry's flattened out one of the seats; he was going to move her up there and strap her in for landing."

"Tell him not to move her; I'll get a medic in here to give you advice."

Andi turned to the hatch. "Did you hear that, Gerry? They said don't move her until they talk to a medic."

"I heard. You know, Andi, these seats are really fancy. You can lower them almost to the floor by pushing a button."

"Don't play with the seats, Gerry," Andi said. "I still want to know—"

"Captain Murchison, let's talk about your landing protocol." That was Gallagher again. Andi blinked. The older woman had called her Andi before, like an adult talking to a child. Why was she being formal now?

"Yes, ma'am?" she said, trying to read the expression on that older face. Beside her now on the screen were two other faces, a young man in a coat like those she'd seen at the Clinic, and an older man in the same green uniform as Gallagher's.

"As you know, the autopilot function can safely land a shuttle in an emergency situation in vertical mode, but cannot bring it to dock. If you choose to let the autopilot land your craft, it must be at least 500 meters from Base, and you will then require a tow vehicle to bring you dockside—"

"But I can bring it in myself!" Andi said.

"That is true. You have a license; the shuttle has accepted you as its commander. You have every legal right to land and dock the shuttle yourself. And—since I've now seen your scores on your exam—you probably have the skills to bring your family shuttle—the one you trained in—into dock very neatly."

A pause, during which Andi stared at the screen, wondering what was coming, and Gallagher stared back. The man in green turned to Gallagher. "Are you crazy, Naomi? Look at her! She's barely out of the cradle and this is her first actual flight, and it's not even the model she knows! You can't be thinking of letting her try it, even if she didn't have an injured child aboard! You've got to exercise prime authority."

Gallagher raised a hand, and the man fell silent, his mouth

shutting like a trap. "It's my choice, Sam. You gave me this job. She's obviously bright, with plenty of initiative, and besides—it's her legal right."

He snorted, but said nothing more. Gallagher looked at Andi. "Captain Murchison, let me express my concern about your landing that particular shuttle. It's not the shuttle you trained in. Every craft is a little different in its responses. I believe that even so you are capable of landing it safely enough—I believe the probability of your doing so is quite high, perhaps as high as 92 percent. The landing might be a tad rough without doing you or the craft any harm. But we do not know the condition of your little sister. If in fact she has other injuries than drug-induced unconsciousness—injury to her neck or spine, for instance—then the slightest jolt on landing could do her permanent damage or even kill her."

"How—how smooth is an autopilot landing?" Andi asked, her mouth dry.

"It depends on the quality of the A.I.-autopilot interface. Frankly, I would not care to trust it in this instance, since I can't personally examine that interface. There is another possibility."

"What?" Andi asked.

"Through this communications link, I can remotely control your craft and bring it to dock myself, if you relinquish command to me and certify that with your A.I. Naturally you would do this only if you thought I could do better. I know I can do it; you don't yet, but I brought Sam along to back up my claim to be a very experienced pilot, including in remote-control situations."

"I . . ."

"Captain Murchison, it is your decision. I will not take control of your ship without your permission—I could do so but I won't, not unless your maneuvers risk injury to the Dome. Under law, you get to make the choice."

"You want me to let you bring us in," Andi said. She could feel herself drooping, imagining them brought in by someone else, like helpless babies.

"It's an option," Gallagher said. There was no urgency in her voice, no anger, nothing for Andi to take hold of and resent.

"I thought maybe—" Andi stopped. She had had a flash of inspiration minutes back, but hadn't really thought it out yet. In law, citizens who helped capture criminals could claim part of whatever the criminals had when they were captured. Like, for instance, this shuttle, because surely workforce pirates were criminals. Even with all that had gone wrong, she felt a river of joy right under the surface; she and this shuttle belonged together. She *was* Captain Murchison; the ship didn't care if she was short and ugly. With her own ship, she could be free, she could go anywhere. She glanced up to the sky, full as it was of deadly danger and immense opportunity.

"I wondered about . . . about salvage," she said. She hated the wavering, pleading tone in her voice. "It says in the law—"

Gallagher actually grinned. "You little monkey! You never stop thinking, do you?" Her voice changed back to the steady, reasonable tone of the earlier conversation. "Captain Murchison, on my word as a senior pilot, I will not put in a salvage claim for any assistance rendered, and you can see my two witnesses right here."

"Naomi, this is ridiculous!" the man in green said.

"Sam, quit judging her by her size. That's a born pilot adventurer, or I'm a backhills miner. Now speak up and confirm what I said."

Andi's mood lifted; she felt two meters tall. A born pilot adventurer? Someone else saw that in her?

"All right. Er . . . Captain Murchison, I stand witness that Senior Pilot Gallagher has renounced any claim for salvage as a result of any assistance given you in docking at Base."

"And I, Medic First Class Patel," the other man said. "I heard and confirm what Senior Pilot Gallagher said. But please, Captain, do consider what is best for the child who is not conscious. If I may—?" He looked at Gallagher, who nodded. "Is there anyone aboard who knows how to take a pulse, without moving the child's head?"

"I . . . don't know," Andi said. "I'll ask." Gerry had helped Mama with Damon—they all had—but she didn't know if that translated into taking pulses. Gerry, when she asked, shook his head. He was sitting beside Bird, on the deck. "No," she told the medic. "I'm sorry . . ."

"But she is breathing?"

"Oh, yes."

"Do you have anything, any pillows or blankets or anything, that could be put so her head won't wobble around if there's a bump?"

Again, Andi asked Gerry, who found nothing but a jacket wadded up in one of the lockers. The medic explained how it should be placed, and suggested that Gerry sit with her and try to hold her head still "without pushing on it at all!"

So . . . Gerry and Bird would be unrestrained, not safely strapped in, when the shuttle landed. Andi didn't like that. She looked at the altimeter and the rate-of-descent indicator. The A.I. was bringing them smoothly down, exactly as ordered. Another few minutes and they would be at 500 meters, and then . . . then it would be time to make a landing. One way or another.

"You really need to listen to Naomi," the other man—Sam somebody—said. "She's an outstanding pilot; I've been on expeditions with her; she was senior pilot on the Io—"

"Ma'am," Andi said to Gallagher. "Can I ask you a question?"

"Of course, Captain Murchison," Gallagher said.

"So far this shuttle hasn't felt that different. The A.I. told me because I had only a Class C license, there were functions I couldn't access. From what I can tell, it just means I have to go slower and pick more conservative maneuvers."

Gallagher nodded. "Most high-performance craft do have safeguards like that."

"So . . . is there anything I'm likely to need, in landing, that would be blocked? If there were an . . . an emergency? You don't do anything . . . anything extreme in landing, ever, I thought."

"That's true," Gallagher said. "The only thing I can think of that might cause such a problem would be a serious drive malfunction, requiring some fairly extreme uses of steering jets. Very unlikely, I'd think."

"But it could happen?"

"Yes, it could. I'm sorry, but I can't tell exactly what functions are blocked without getting into your system." She said nothing more. What she might have said spoke up in Andi's mind as if telepathy were real. *Unlikely or not, something can always go wrong. Are you willing to risk your little sister's life just so you can show off?*

"Mama says never ask for help," Andi muttered to herself.

Gallagher clearly heard that. "Your family's very independent; that's probably what made you such a self-starter."

Andi struggled to understand what she was feeling. She wanted to land the ship herself; she wanted to go away—far away from Base and her family—somewhere with the ship and . . . and do something, she couldn't think what. She wanted to please Gallagher—which was probably letting Gallagher land the shuttle. But Gallagher wasn't pushing her, wasn't making clear what she wanted. "Pilot adventurer" warred with "just a child" and her worry about Bird and her other worry about Beth and Vinnie, and yet other worries about Damon and Mama and what Mama was going to do to her when she found out . . .

"I think," she said, and stopped. Gallagher waited. Then it came out in a rush, as if someone else were speaking. "I want to do it myself; I think I can do it myself. But I'm not sure, and Bird and Gerry aren't strapped in and even if they were they're—well Bird is—just a kid. It's not fair. Mama says nothing's fair and don't trust anybody and I can't ever have what I want and she didn't want me to take the test, so it's my fault, because I did anyway, and . . . I think I *can* do it. But . . . I think you *should* do it. But not because I'm scared to try."

Gallagher nodded. "I will do my best, Captain Murchison, to bring you in without jarring your sister at all. Here's what you need to do." She explained the sequence of commands that would slave the A.I. to her master pilot's certificate. "Now, Captain, I'd like you to remain on the bridge—er, in the cockpit—and observe closely. We will be in constant contact, so if you see anything that concerns you, be sure to tell me. You're my copilot. I may need to hand over some specific tasks. It's just a bit trickier to fly one of these things remotely."

Andi had expected *Now just sit back and don't worry.* "Th-thank you," she managed.

Then she gave the A.I. the commands and that pleasant voice said, "Command change logged: Captain Murchison relinquishes command to Base senior pilot Gallagher. Welcome, Captain Gallagher."

Gallagher took them out of the slow descent and made a circuit to the left that ended with the shuttle approaching Base directly. "Now what we're going to do," Gallagher said to Andi, "is try for a zero-relative-motion touchdown. Given the medical concerns, and your sister's position on the floor—I have access to the compartment visuals now—Medic Patel says a vertical will be best. What I want you to do is monitor any sideways drift— there's often a little current coming off the side of the dome, or a little bleed from the dock seals. Can you do that?"

"Yes, Captain Gallagher," Andi said, returning courtesy for courtesy.

"Excellent. Barring emergencies, you are now authorized as my copilot, under my license, and all functions are available to you."

Andi watched the view outside until Gallagher brought the shuttle to a hover. Then she looked only at the readouts: the nav lasers, locked onto the shuttle pad X below, gave their position more accurately than she'd be able to see.

"We're going down," she said to Gerry. "Don't move."

"I think Bird's waking up."

"Well, talk to her or something. Don't let her move." From the corner of her right eye, she could see the shape of the dome moving upward. She forced her eyes back to the controls. The shuttle was coming down perfectly centered in the landing zone as steadily as a bead sliding down a string. Then the side of Base filled the windows on that side, and she felt the first shudder, the first tendency to tip and skid away as the downblast came off the Base wall to the side as well as the landing pad itself.

Her hands countered it with the steering jets almost as the shuttle moved, and brought it back to center. It didn't take much—but it was pure pride now that held her, pride more than fear. She could do it; she could show them.

And then they were down, the shuttle safely grounded so gently that Andi didn't know herself when the skids touched.

"We have a medical team standing by in the docking area, Captain Murchison," Gallagher said. "You have control of your ship now. Do you need help with the hatches? The ground crew says the forward one appears to have been dented."

"One of the men did that," Andi said. She touched the A.I. control and informed the pleasant voice that they needed to complete docking procedures and open the passenger compartment hatch.

"Life support and electrical umbilical hookup complete," the A.I. told her a moment or two later, as the outside spy-eye flicked on and she saw a small crowd waiting. Medics in obvious medical clothing. Men and women in uniform. Andi looked for Gallagher but didn't see her. "Passenger hatch open. Open cargo hatches?"

"Not now," Andi said. She could hear the people outside. Who would they be? Where was Gallagher? And what was she supposed to do? Captains stayed with their ship, but Gerry and Bird would need her. She unbuckled her harness and twisted around to look into the passenger compartment.

A man and a woman who looked like medics were just climbing aboard. The man met Andi's gaze. "Hi," he said. "I'm Ron and this is Claire. We're here to take care of Bird—" The woman went down on one knee; Andi couldn't see what she was doing from there. She spoke into a shoulder mike, but Andi couldn't hear what she said. Then the woman turned and smiled at Andi.

"She's alive and I don't think she has any broken bones," Claire said. "We're going to take her to the clinic to be sure and to help her wake up."

"Should I come with her?" Andi asked.

"Senior pilot Gallagher is coming to see you," Claire said.

"And someone should stay with the shuttle, for legal reasons. What about you, though, Gerry? Why don't you come along?"

Gerry gave Andi a frantic look. "I want us to stay together," he said. The cocky assurance of that morning seemed to have melted away in the last hour or so.

"If I have to stay here, Bird needs someone with her she knows," Andi said. "Please do it, Gerry. You were a big help—"

He put his head back into the cockpit. "You were great, Andi. Whatever happens. I thought when they grabbed me I was done for; I hoped you'd figure it out but I never thought you'd be smart enough to get put in with us."

She didn't have time to tell him that had nothing to do with being smart before the medics had Bird out of the ship and onto a litter, and called Gerry to follow. Two men in gray-blue uniforms, who said they were Base proctors, came aboard then.

"Pop the aft hatches," one of them said. "We need to inspect the cargo."

"Yes, sir," Andi said. The A.I. unlocked the hatches on her command and one of the men climbed back out. The other poked around the passenger compartment, opening and shutting all the locker doors.

"What are you looking for?" Andi asked.

"Whatever's here," the man said. "Look, kid, I'm not supposed to talk to you; you'll have to make a statement to the chief investigating officer later."

"A statement?"

"What happened. Start to finish. Now just let me finish this inventory."

Andi felt shaky. Now that it was all over, she was hungry, thirsty, and she really could use the bathroom, if that man would ever leave her alone.

She heard a familiar voice outside and glanced at the external view: Mama, arguing with a man in uniform at the other end of the docking area. She boosted the external pickup.

"I don't care; she's my daughter and you have to let me see

her. How do I know she's all right? The other two went to the Clinic? I have a right to see her; she's my daughter."

Andi wanted to sink through the cockpit all the way through Base to the center of Ganymede. Mama was in what Pop called a spittin' rage, and she could tell from the man's posture that he was going to cave in and let Mama come to the shuttle. She was trapped again, this time strapped in as well. She fumbled with the buckles but before she got them all undone, Mama was at the hatch.

"You get out of there and let my child alone!" Mama said.

"Excuse me?" the proctor said. "Who are you?"

"I'm her mama, and we don't need any of your interference," Mama said. Andi yanked the last buckle loose and turned around.

"He's not interfering," she said. "He's investigating."

"Don't give me any of your sass, girl," Mama said. "You have well and truly done it this time. You didn't take that pill, did you?"

Of all the accusations Mama might have made, that was the last of them, and for a moment Andi couldn't think what Mama was talking about. "Pill?"

"I gave you that pill this morning. You hid it, didn't you? Just to get me in trouble!"

"I don't know what—oh!"

"*Oh* is right! You know perfectly well what you did; it was all part of your plan!"

"I just forgot, Mama," Andi said. "Really I did."

Mama pushed past the astonished proctor, reached through the hatch, grabbed Andi by the shoulder, yanked her out of the chair and onto the deck. Andi was too surprised to resist, let alone fight back, and besides, Mama in a rage had the strength of two or three. "You are the most stubborn, disobedient, ungrateful child I ever knew! We take you brats in, we feed you, we clothe you, we work ourselves to the bone for you, and this—this is how you repay us! Running around behind my back, telling people I mistreated you!"

"I didn't—" Andi said. Mama smacked her across the face, then grabbed a hank of her hair and shook her.

"Liar. I hope they lock you up for years, you sneak, you thief, you liar! You broke so many laws they ought to throw you out the airlock!"

"Listen, lady, you can't do that—" the proctor said from behind Mama, reaching out to grab her arm. She rounded on him, catching him square in the face; he staggered back.

"You!" Mama had turned on Andi again. She was in full rage now, eyes glittering, spittle flying. "I *told* you not to take that test. I *told* you to watch them kids. And I *told* you to take that pill and not say nothin' to nobody 'bout family business. It was nobody's business if you had them pills every day or not. It didn't do you harm to be short." A blow for each *told*. Andi's ears rang; she felt dizzy and sick.

"Stop that now." A voice she knew, a voice now as cold as the icy surface outside. Mama let go her hair. Time seemed to pause; Andi could not have said how long she was huddled on the floor.

"You gonna make me?" Mama said. Andi looked up; Mama had turned half around, and Andi could see men in blue uniforms and one woman—Gallagher—in green. Gallagher smiled at Mama.

"Don't tempt me," she said.

"This is my child," Mama said. "I got a right to discipline her when she's done wrong. And she's done a whole lot of wrong today."

"You don't have a right to beat up on her," Gallagher said.

"Madam," one of the proctors said in a stiff, formal voice. "You have assaulted an officer of the law. That is an offense. You will step over here and be placed under arrest."

"No, I won't!" Mama said.

Andi's thoughts caught up again. "What was that about the pill?"

"Never mind," Mama said. "You should've taken it, but I explained how you forget all the time and don't like to take it, and that's why your blood test didn't show it." She smiled, a ghastly fake smile. "You can tell them, Andi, that I did my best to get you to take your medicine."

Gallagher and Mama were both looking at her, as if they expected an answer. Andi tried to get up, but she felt dizzy again; she pushed herself up until she could lean onto one of the seats and tried to scoot back a little, away from Mama.

"How often did you take your medicine?" Gallagher asked. "Was it always the same pill?"

"I don't need medicine," Andi said. "I'm healthy. The only time Mama gave me a pill was when we visited the Clinic."

"What's this about a pill?" one of the proctors asked. "We have a more important problem here—"

"Andi, do you have the pill you forgot to take, or was it lost later?"

"I don't know." Andi felt in her jumpsuit pocket and found the little round, hard pill still in its plastic blister. "Here it is."

Mama snatched at it, but Gallagher caught Mama's arm in a grip that Mama couldn't break and swung her around, away from Andi. "Get her away from the—from Andi," Gallagher said. The proctors moved in. Mama struggled for a moment, but there were too many of them; they bound her hands and then she stood hunched and submissive.

"Give the pill to the proctor, Andi," Gallagher said. "It's evidence."

"Evidence of what?" the proctor said. "What's going on here?"

"You'll need to take that to the Clinic. Andi was supposed to be getting daily medications to enhance her growth. Sometimes the treatment fails, so failure to grow isn't proof of no medication. But not finding it in her blood-work is. Apparently her mother gave it to her just before a scheduled exam, but this time Andi didn't take the pill. So it showed up as a flag on her medical record."

"But I thought required medications for such conditions were provided, part of the adoptive stipend," the proctor said.

"We've got a couple ourselves, and we get all the medications provided."

"They are provided," Gallagher said. "They were provided for Andi and all her siblings. But her mother found another use for them . . . sold them on the black market, I expect."

"I did it for her," Mama said. "I did it for all of them. Things is hard enough out there, never enough money, the Company charges for everything and cheats us on sales. Times we'd all have gone hungry if I hadn't had somethin' to sell. What difference did it make if she stayed short? Being tall wasn't gonna make her pretty, or rich."

"I could have been tall?" Andi said. "You had pills to make me grow tall and you *sold* them?"

"We needed the money more'n you needed to be tall," Mama said.

"And what about the others?" Andi said. "What about Bird and Gerry and Damon? Were they supposed to get medicine, and did you sell that?"

Mama didn't answer aloud, but her expression made it clear. Andi's rage swelled until she thought she would burst with it. "How could anyone do that to a child? To their child?"

"You never were my child," Mama said. "Not really. The law said we had to have you brats if we wanted land, so we took you in." Her face flushed again. "And now look what you've done! Bird and Gerry in the Clinic, my life and your Pop's ruined, all because of you."

"Get her out of here," Gallagher said. The proctors led Mama away, steadying her down the steps to the dockspace floor.

Mama looked back once. "I hope you rot in a prison cell."

Andi blinked back tears. She was not going to cry, no matter what, not in front of Gallagher.

"We need to get the medics for you," Gallagher said, stooping down to look at her. "Bruises, cuts—"

"No," Andi said. "I'm all right, really."

"Well, you can't stay on the deck—let me help you up, get

you cleaned up a little, then we can tell—by the way, when did you eat last?"

"A ship rat bar early this morning," Andi said after a moment's thought. So that hollow feeling was from more than the day's events and a few smacks from Mama.

"Food, then, after a chance to wash your face," Gallagher said.

"I'm fine," Andi said again, as she struggled to rise. Gallagher helped her up; Andi's head spun for a moment, but then she was able to walk to the shuttle's small toilet space.

Later, during a meal of foods she had never tasted before, she felt her wits coming back to her, enough to worry about what would happen next. Her face hurt now, but not badly; she certainly didn't need to go to the Clinic for a few bruises and a cut lip.

"We need to have a chat," Gallagher said.

Andi knew what "have a chat" meant. Her appetite vanished. "I'm in trouble, I know—" she began.

Gallagher's eyebrows went up. "You? Hardly. Oh, there are some irregularities, sure, but on the whole you're not the one in trouble. Thanks to you, we have a team of child thieves in custody, a highly illegal cargo has been seized, and your two friends—both from influential families—are alive and unharmed." Gallagher's grinned. "You've had quite a day, and a lot of people want to thank you for it. I thought you needed some quiet time before you had to deal with all that excitement."

Andi's appetite returned, and she ate a bite of something brown and crispy. "Yes, ma'am. What is all this?"

Gallagher cocked her head. "I hope it doesn't make you sick; I should have thought about that. Do you grow any of your own food, in your habitat?"

"No. I asked one time and Mama said it took too much time and cost too much. We have those tubs of staples and packets of additives. You put them in the processor and add water, and if there's any flavor packets left—"

"Ah. Well, you may have a stomachache later, though I hope

the enzyme additives in the sauces will prevent that. Sometimes peoples' bodies react to any change of food."

"I feel fine," Andi said. She ate the last of the brown crispy things and put her fork down.

"Ready to talk? And listen?"

Now it would come; Andi tried to stay relaxed. The warm, comfortable feeling in her stomach helped with that. "Yes, ma'am."

"Several things happened today, some that you don't know about. First, you and your family went to the Clinic early this morning for checkups, right? And your littlest brother was sick?"

"Yes, ma'am."

"You had a blood test as part of your checkup. You already know about that: they found no growth hormone, and it's in your record that you were supposed to be given it daily. But there were other results of the exams you and your siblings took, and the youngest child's condition, which led them to the conclusion that medical neglect and perhaps abuse was going on. I don't know all the details—"

"The others, too?"

"Yes. And evidence as well of misappropriation of medications supplied—"

"Misappropriation? What's that?"

"Stealing, basically. Your mother—or both parents, probably—were selling medications provided for you and your siblings."

"What did Bird and Gerry need medicines for?" Andi asked. But even as she asked, she thought of Bird's nervousness, her inability to sit still and work steadily on anything.

"I don't know," Gallagher said. "But it was in their records. Then, there's the matter of your Class C exam. Yes, the law says twelve-year-olds can apply for a hardship license, and your father had signed for you to do that. But records show there are three licensed pilots at your habitat: your two parents and your older brother. Why did they need you as well?"

"Pop said Oscar was big enough to run the processor-packer," Andi said. "And that way I could go out on prospecting trips with him, even overnight."

"Did you want to do that?" Gallagher asked.

"I wanted the license," Andi said. "I wanted to get away—away from Mama, and really—away from all of it. Someday—" All she had dreamed tangled in her throat and she couldn't get it out.

"What is it you want in your life, Andi?" Gallagher asked gently.

Andi felt tears pricking her eyes again and blinked them back. She was not going to cry. Not when someone was actually listening. "I want to get *away*. But not just get away, I want to get to—to find new places. When I was doing simulations in our shuttle, it was the only time I could see out, see the sky. And—and there it is, the whole universe. There's the planet—well, we can't go there, it would kill us, but all the other moons. The outer planets. And I don't even get to see the other side of Ganymede except when we come to Base and then we're underground again."

"Do you ever think of going back to Earth, or MarZone?"

"Not really," Andi said. "Earth sent us out here, all us kids, because they didn't want us. I don't want to go where I'm not wanted. I want to find a place where . . . where people want me, or where there's no one. One or the other."

Gallagher nodded. "So you weren't forced to take shuttle training or the exam early?"

"No," Andi said. "And anyway, I'm good at it."

"That you are," Gallagher agreed. "Your test scores were . . . remarkable. We've also accessed your school records. Your parents have only provided basic schooling, right?"

"Basic?"

"Andi, colonial law requires that parents provide a basic education to all their children for a minimum of eight years, but they can go beyond that if they want."

"I thought only kids in real schools could get things like that," Andi said. "Mama said—"

Gallagher's mouth twisted for a moment. "Teaching modules are equally available to homeschoolers and classrooms." She cleared her throat. "The thing is, Andi, with the evidence of medical neglect—amounting to abuse in some cases—and misappropriation of medication and attempt to defraud—and concern about your taking the exam as a hardship case—an emergency meeting was held this afternoon and determined that all you children should be removed from parental custody. Your parents are facing serious charges—"

So Mama was right about that at least. The family was destroyed because of Andi.

"It's not you," Gallagher said, as if reading her mind. "Your parents chose to withhold medication you and the others needed; they chose to conceal that from the Clinic by medicating you before exams; they chose to sell the medications illegally."

"But—what happens to us? Where will we go? And . . . will I ever grow?"

"You think of that as a serious problem?"

"Well, yeah," Andi said. "How would you like being called a runt, having everybody think you're a baby?"

"I didn't like being called a giraffe or a flagpole because I was tall and skinny," Gallagher said. "My mother's hair went white really early, when she was in her twenties; she didn't like being called an old lady. We survived it."

"Yeah, but people grew up to you, didn't they? They grow past me."

Gallagher looked at her. "Andi, you say you want to go out to the frontiers and explore, right?"

The change of topic broke the tempo of her thoughts for a moment. "Yes, why?"

"There's more than one frontier. One of them is inside. If you want to go forward, you have to leave things behind. Not saying it's easy . . ."

"Like . . . Mama?"

"Like the Andi who hates being short, when being short isn't

something you can change. Do you know what the height re-
quirement is for that new expedition to the outer planets?"

"No—what new expedition?"

"Planning stages. Supposed to leave in three or four years,
about the time you'll be eligible to apply as junior crew. I'm too
tall for it. They won't take anyone over 1.6 meters."

"What's the minimum?" Andi tried not to let herself hope
that she might have a chance of getting on that crew.

"There isn't one." Gallagher paused to let that sink in, then
went on. "Andi, you want to explore, you said. Be with people
who want you. See new things. Being short won't stop you. Only
*you* can stop you."

"You really think so?" Andi asked.

"I know so," Gallagher said. "Someday I'll tell you why, but
right now we're going to meet some people who are very interested in your future. I hope you are."

☻☻☻

Andi was having the best day in her life, hanging out in Boone
Concourse with her friends after school. New clothes, a pixie
haircut that looked so much less babyish than the old style,
matching colors and designs on her fingers and toes, a crowd of
other girls vying for her attention . . . no more gray jumpsuit, no
more of Mama's depressing predictions. All the children had new
homes, new families. Beth's parents had been so grateful for her
information, information that led to the capture of the workforce
pirates and finding Beth and Vinnie safe, that they had agreed to
become her new guardians. Beth had taken Andi to the best
shops, to style consultants, and her parents had agreed that "cul-
tural opportunities" includes fashion as well as classes in music
appreciation and art.

Captain Gallagher, the first time she'd seen the new Andi,
complete with the silver and emerald-green nails and matching
silver and green hair ornament, had shaken her head. "You are *so*
twelve," she'd said, grinning. "Enjoy it while it lasts, Andi. It
won't all be easy."

Andi had figured that out. Right now she was a novelty, on the edge of celebrity. Girl pilot-adventurer outwits wicked workforce pirates. That wouldn't last. Nor would the teachers' fascination with her untapped potential, that brilliance the assessment tests said she possessed.

But this was now, and now was a new life. Someday she might qualify for an expedition to the outer planets—though she wasn't sure she wanted to spend long months in another windowless habitat. She might explore more in the Jovian system, maybe even with Captain Gallagher. Or she might do something else—anything else that didn't involve being stuck where she had been stuck. She would work hard in school—she had already found the classwork in Beth and Vinnie's class ridiculously easy while haughty Hamilton, who'd ignored her, barely passed. The teacher had even threatened to call Hamilton's parents to the school for a conference. And she, Andi, would succeed at something, whether it was exploration or not.

But for now, right this minute, it was enough to be sitting with a crowd of friends in one of the booths of Dave's Desserts, spooning up yet another delicious food she'd never had before, after an hour of shopping. She had an allowance from her own money, a trust fund established from the sale of the pirates' shuttle and cargo. Her new friends were teaching her about sales and loss leaders and clothing exchanges—ways to get more for less, what they called combat shopping. So the new green sandals that went so well with her nails, and the green and silver dress cape they all agreed she needed, plus a little music player and a stack of required tapes for music appreciation—all fit into her new budget.

Hamilton strolled into the shop, trailing Terri and Lisa as if they were part of her costume. She looked at Andi with utter contempt.

"You may be famous, and you may have new clothes, but you're still short," she said, as nastily as ever. "And ugly." Silence fell around them. Andi felt herself going red; she felt even shorter for a moment, then a gust of laughter moved through her. She scrunched down in her seat, making herself even smaller, and grinned straight into that haughty face.

"You may be beautiful, but you're still rude," she said, in the sweetest, most childlike voice she could produce. "And stupid and lazy, wasn't that what the teacher said?" The others laughed.

Hamilton flushed red this time, turned on her heel, and stalked off. Lisa and Terry just stood there, looking embarrassed and nervous. Andi sat up straight, smiled at them.

"You can join us if you want," she said. "I don't mind." Two other girls scooted over to make room, and the two sat down.

She still didn't like being short and round-faced and, well, plain, but it mattered a lot less when she had other good things going on. Maybe she'd never be the tall, svelte Andi of her fantasies, but she would be something equally interesting, equally successful. And she didn't care if Mama ever knew it or not.

# THE MARS GIRL

## by Joe Haldeman

The whole point of exploration is to find new things, things you never expected were there. As the fascinating story that follows points out, though, sometimes to find new things, you need new *eyes* to look for them . . .

Born in Oklahoma City, Oklahoma, Joe Haldeman took a B.S. degree in physics and astronomy from the University of Maryland, and did postgraduate work in mathematics and computer science. But his plans for a career in science were cut short by the U.S. Army, which sent him to Vietnam in 1968 as a combat engineer. Seriously wounded in action, Haldeman returned home in 1969 and began to write. He sold his first story to *Galaxy* in 1969, and by 1976 had garnered both the Nebula Award and the Hugo Award for his famous novel *The Forever War*, one of the landmark books of the '70s. He took another Hugo Award in 1977 for his story "Tricentennial," won the Rhysling Award in 1983 for the best science fiction poem of the year (although usually thought of primarily as a "hard-science" writer, Haldeman is, in fact, also an accomplished poet, and has sold poetry to most of the major professional markets in the genre), and won both the Nebula and the Hugo awards in 1991 for the novella version of "The Hemingway Hoax." His story "None So Blind" won the Hugo Award in 1995. His other books include a mainstream novel, *War Year*, the SF novels *Mindbridge*, *All My Sins Remembered*, *There Is No Darkness* (written with his brother, SF writer Jack C. Haldeman II), *Worlds*, *Worlds Apart*, *Worlds Enough and Time*, *Buying Time*, *The Hemingway Hoax*, *Tools of the Trade*, *The Coming*, the mainstream novel *1968*, and *Camouflage*, which won the prestigious James Tiptree, Jr. Award. His short work has been gathered in the collections *Infinite Dreams, Dealing in Futures, Vietnam and Other Alien Worlds,* and *None So Blind.* As editor, he has produced the anthologies *Study War No More, Cosmic Laughter,* and *Nebula Award Stories: 17.* His most recent book is a new science fiction novel, *Old Twentieth.* Haldeman lives part of the year in Boston, where he teaches writing at the Massachusetts Institute of Technology, and the rest of the year in Florida, where he and his wife, Gay, make their home.

## 1. GOODBYE, COOL WORLD

THE SPACE ELEVATOR is the only elevator in the world with barf bags. My brother Card pointed that out. He notices things like that; I noticed the bathroom. One bathroom, for forty-some people. Locked in an elevator for two weeks. It's not as big as it looks in the advertisements.

It wasn't too bad, actually, once we started going up. Nothing like the old-fashioned way of getting into orbit, strapped to a million pounds of high explosive. We lost weight slowly during the week it took us to get to the Orbit Hilton, where we were weightless. We dropped off a dozen or so rich tourists there (and spent a couple of hours and no money, looking around) and then continued crawling up the Elevator for another week, to where our Mars ship the *John Carter* was parked, waiting.

The newsies called it "Kids in Space," hand me a barf bag. The Mars colony had like seventy-five people, aged from the early thirties to the late sixties, and they wanted to add some young people. They set up a lottery among scientists and engineers with children age nine and older, and my parents were among the nine couples chosen, so they dragged me (Carmen Dula) and Card along.

Card thought it was wonderful, and I'll admit I thought it was spec, too, at the time. So Card and I got to spend a year of Saturday mornings training to take the test—just us; there was no test for parents. Adults make it or they don't, depending on things like education. Our parents have enough education for any dozen normal people.

These tests were basically to make *us* seem normal, or at least normal enough not to go detroit locked up in a sardine can with twenty-nine other people for six months.

So here's the billion-dollar question: Did any of the kids aboard pass the tests just because they actually were normal? Or did all of them also give up a year of Saturdays so they could learn how to hide their homicidal tendencies from the testers?

And the trillion-dollar question is "What was I *thinking*?" We had to stay on Mars a minimum of five years. I would be twenty-one, having pissed away my precious teenage years on a rusty airless rock.

So anyhow. Going aboard the good ship *John Carter* were seven boys and seven girls, along with their eighteen parents and one sort of attractive pilot, Paul Santos, not quite twice my age.

I just turned sixteen but am starting college. Which I'll attend by virtual reality and email. No wicked fraternity parties, no experimenting with drugs and sex and finding out how much beer you can hold before overflowing. Maybe this whole Mars thing was a ruse my parents made up to keep me off campus. My education was going to be so incomplete!

The living area of the *John Carter* was huge, compared to the Elevator. We had separate areas for study and exercise and meals, and a sleeping floor away from the parents, as long as we behaved. I roomed with my best friends aboard, Elspeth and Kaimei, from Israel and California.

We spent the first couple of hours strapped in, up in the lander on top of the ship. Most of the speed we needed for getting to Mars was "free"—when we left the high orbit at the end of the Space Elevator, we were like a stone thrown from an old-fashioned sling, or a bit of mud flung from a bicycle tire. Two weeks of relatively slow crawling built up into one big boost, from the orbit of Earth to the orbit of Mars.

We started out strapped in because there were course corrections, all automatic. The ship studied our progress and then pointed in different directions and made small bursts of thrust, which Paul studied but didn't correct. Then we unstrapped and floated back to the artificial gravity of the rotating living area.

It would take six months to get to Mars, most of it school-work and exercising. I started class at the University of Maryland in the second week.

I was not the most popular girl in my classes—I wasn't *in* class at all, of course, except as a face in a cube. As we moved away from Earth and the time delay grew longer, it became im-possible for me to respond in real time to what was going on. So if I had questions to ask, I had to time it so I was asking them at the beginning of class the next day.

That's a prescription for making yourself a tiresome know-it-all bitch. I had all day to think about the questions and look stuff up. So I was always thoughtful and relevant and a tiresome know-it-all bitch. Of course it didn't help at all that I was younger than everybody else and a brave pioneer headed for an-other planet. The novelty of that wore off real fast.

Card wasn't having any such problems. But he already knew most of his classmates, some of them since grade school, and was more social anyhow. I've always been the youngest in my class, and the brain.

It's not as if anybody had forced me into the situation. I was bored as hell in grade school and middle school, and when I was given the option of testing out of a grade and skipping ahead, I did it, three times. Not a big problem when you're eight and ten and twelve. It *is* a problem when you're barely sixteen and every-body else is "college age," at least by the calendar.

I'm also a little behind them socially, or a lot behind. I had male friends but didn't date much. Still a virgin, technically, and when I'm around older kids feel like I'm wearing a sign pro-claiming that fact.

That raised an interesting possibility. I never could see myself still a virgin at twenty-one. I might wind up being the first girl to lose it on Mars—or on any other planet at all. Maybe some day they'd put up a plaque: "In this storage room on such-and-such a date . . ."

About a month out, we developed a little problem, that we hoped wouldn't kill everybody more or less slowly. The ship started losing air, slowly but surely. We found out it was leaking out of the lander, but couldn't find the leak. So we just closed the airlock between the lander and the living quarters.

Paul was not happy about that, having to run things away from his pilot's console, using a laptop. But it wasn't like he had to steer around asteroids or anything.

The six months actually went by pretty fast. You might think that being locked up in a space ship would drive people crazy, but in fact it seemed to drive them sane, even the youngest. The idea of "Spaceship Earth" is such an old cliché that Granddad makes a face at it. But being constantly aware that we were isolated, surrounded by space, did seem to make us more considerate of one another. So if Earth is just a bigger ship, why couldn't they learn to be as virtuous as we are? Maybe they don't choose their crew carefully enough.

Anyhow, Mars became the brightest star, and then a little circle, and then a planet. We pumped air back into the lander and left our home there in orbit. Some people took pills as they strapped in. I wasn't that smart.

## 2. DOWN TO MARS

Someday, maybe before I'm dead, Mars will have its own Space Elevator, but until then people have to get down there the old-fashioned way, in space-shuttle mode. It's like the difference between taking an elevator from the top floor of a building, or jumping off with an umbrella and a prayer. Fast and terrifying.

We'd lived with the lander as part of our home for weeks, and then as a mysterious kind of threatening presence, airless and waiting. Most of us weren't eager to go into it.

Before we'd made our second orbit of Mars, Paul opened the inner door, prepared to crack the airlock, and said, "Let's go."

We'd been warned, so we were bundled up against the sudden temperature drop when the airlock opened, and were not surprised that our ears popped painfully. But then we had to take our little metal suitcases and float through the airlock to go strap into our assigned seats, and try not to shit while we dropped like a rock to our doom.

From my studies I knew that the lander loses velocity by essentially trading speed for heat—hitting the thin Martian atmosphere at a drastic angle so the ship heats up to cherry red. What the diagrams in the physical science book don't show is the tooth-rattling vibration, the bucking and gut-wrenching wobble. If I'm never that scared again in my life I'll be really happy.

All of the violence stopped abruptly when the lander decided to become a glider, I guess a few hundred miles from the landing strip. I wished we had windows like a regular airplane, but then realized that might be asking for a heart attack. It was scary enough just to squint at Paul's two-foot-wide screen as the ground rose up to meet us, too steep and fast to believe.

We landed on skis, grating and rumbling along the rocky ground. They'd moved all the big rocks out of our way, but we felt every one of the small ones. Paul had warned us to keep our tongues away from our teeth, which was a good thing. It could be awkward, starting out life on a new planet unable to speak because you've bitten off your tongue.

We hadn't put on the Mars suits for the flight down; they were too bulky to fit in the close-ranked seats—and I guess there wasn't any disaster scenario where we would still be alive and need them. So the first order of the day was to get dressed for our new planet.

We'd tested them several times, but Paul wanted to be super-cautious the first time they were actually exposed to the Martian near-vacuum. The airlock would only hold two people at once, so we went out one at a time, with Paul observing us, ready to toss us back inside if trouble developed.

We unpacked the suits from storage under the deck and

sorted them out. One for each person and two blobby general-purpose ones.

We were to leave in reverse alphabetical order, which was no fun, since it made our family dead last. The lander had never felt particularly claustrophobic before, but now it was like a tiny tin can, the sardines slowly exiting one by one.

At least we could see out, via the pilot's screen. He'd set the camera on the base, where all seventy-five people had gathered to watch us land, or crash. That led to some morbid speculation on Card's part. What if we'd crash-landed *into* them? I guess we'd be just as likely to crash into the base behind them. I'd rather be standing outside with a space suit on, too.

We'd seen pictures of the base a million times, not to mention endless diagrams and descriptions of how everything worked, but it was kind of exciting to see it in real time, to actually be here. The farm part looked bigger than I'd pictured it, I guess because the people standing around gave it scale. Of course the people lived underneath, staying out of the radiation.

It was interesting to have actual gravity. I said it felt different and Mom agreed, with a scientific explanation. Residual centripetal blah blah blah. I'll just call it real gravity, as opposed to the manufactured kind. Organic gravity.

A lot of people undressed on the spot and got into their Mars suits. I didn't see any point in standing around for an hour in the thing. I'm also a little shy, in a selective way. I waited until Paul was on the other side of the airlock before I revealed my unvoluptuous figure and barely necessary bra. Which I'd have to take off anyhow, for the skinsuit part of the Mars suit.

That part was like a lightweight body stocking. It fastened up the front with a gecko strip and then you pushed a button on your wrist and something electrical happened and it clasped your body like a big rubber glove. It could be sexy-looking if your body was. Most people looked like big gray cartoons, the men with a little more detail than I wanted to see.

The outer part of the Mars suit was more like lightweight armor, kind of loose and clanky when you put it on, but it also did an electrical thing when you zipped up, and fit more closely. Then clumsy boots and gloves and a helmet, all airtight. The joints would sigh when you moved your arms or legs or bent at the waist.

Card's suit had a place for an extension at the waist, since he could grow as much as a foot taller while we were here. Mine didn't have any such refinement, though the chest part was optimistically roomy.

Since we did follow strict anti-alphabetical order, Card got the distinction of being the last one out, and I was next to last. I got in the airlock with Paul, and he checked my oxygen tanks and the seals on my helmet, gloves, and boots. Then he pumped most of the air out, watching the clock, and asked me to count even numbers backward from thirty. (I asked him whether he had an obsession with backward lists.) He smiled at me through the helmet and kept his hand on my shoulder as the rest of the air pumped out and the door silently swung open.

The sky was brighter than I'd expected, and the ground darker. "Welcome to Mars," Paul said on the suit radio, sounding really far away.

We walked down a metal ramp to the sandy rock-strewn ground. I stepped onto another planet.

How many people had ever done that?

Everything was suddenly different. This was the most real thing I'd ever done.

They could talk until they were blue in the face about how special this was, brave new frontier, leaving the cradle of Earth, whatever, and it's finally just words. When I felt the crunch of Martian soil under my boot it was suddenly all very plain and wonderful. I remembered an old cube—a movie—of one of the first guys on the Moon, jumping around like a little kid, and I jumped myself, and again, way high.

"Careful!" came Paul's voice over the radio. "Get used to it first."

"Okay, okay." While I walked, feather light, toward the

other airlock, I tried to figure out how many people had actually done it, set foot on another world. A little more than a hundred, in all of history. And me one of them, now.

There were four people waiting at the airlock door; everyone else had gone inside. I looked around at the rusty desert and stifled the urge to run off and explore—I mean, for more than three months we hadn't been able to go more than a few dozen feet in any direction, and here was a whole new world. But there would be time. Soon!

Mother was blinking away tears, unable to touch her face behind the helmet, crying with happiness. The dream of her lifetime. I hugged her, which felt strange, both of us swaddled in insulation. Our helmets clicked together and for a moment I heard her laugh.

While Paul went back to get Card, I just looked around. I'd spent hours there in virtual, of course, but that was fake. This was hard-edged and strange, even fearsome in a way. A desert with rocks. Yellow sky of air so thin it would kill you in a breath.

When Card got to the ground, he jumped higher than I had. Paul grabbed him by the arm and walked him over.

The airlock held four people. Paul and the two strangers gestured for us to go in when the door opened. It closed automatically behind us and a red light throbbed for about a minute. I could hear the muffled clicking of a pump. Then a green light and the inside door sighed open.

We stepped into the greenhouse, a dense couple of acres of grain and vegetables and dwarf fruit trees. A woman in shorts and a T-shirt motioned for us to take off our helmets.

She introduced herself as Emily. "I keep track of the airlock and suits," she said. "Follow me and we'll get you square."

Feeling overdressed, we clanked down a metal spiral stair to a room full of shelves and boxes, the walls unpainted rock. One block of metal shelves was obviously for our crew, names written on bright new tape under shelves that held folded Mars suits and the titanium suitcases.

"Just come on through to the mess hall after you're dressed," she said. "Place isn't big enough to get lost. Not yet." They planned to more than double the underground living area while we were here.

I helped Mother out of her suit and she helped me. I needed a shower and some clean clothes. My jumpsuit was wrinkled and damp with old sweat, fear sweat from the landing. I didn't smell like a petunia myself. But we were all in the same boat.

Paul and the two other men in Mars suits were rattling down the stairs as we headed for the mess hall. The top half of the corridor was smooth plastic that radiated uniform dim light, like the tubes that had linked the Space Elevator to the Hilton and the *John Carter*. The bottom half was numbered storage drawers.

I knew what to expect of the mess hall and the other rooms; the colony was a series of inflated half-cylinders inside a large irregular tunnel, a natural pipe through an ancient lava flow. Someday the whole thing would be closed off and filled with air like the part we'd just left, but for the time being everyone lived and worked in the reinforced balloons.

It all seemed pretty huge after living in a space ship. I don't suppose it would be that imposing if you went there directly from a town or a city on Earth.

The mess hall wasn't designed for everyone to crowd in there at once. Most of the colonists were standing around at the far end. There were two dining tables with plenty of empty chairs for us new people. We sat down, I guess all of us feeling a little awkward. Everybody sort of staring and nodding. We hadn't seen a stranger since the Hilton—but then none of these Martians had seen a new person since the last ship, fifteen months before.

I looked through the crowd and immediately picked out Oz. He gave me a little wave and I returned it.

The room had two large false windows, like the ones on the ship, looking out onto the desert. I assumed they were real-time. Nothing was moving, but then all the life on the planet was presumably right here.

You could see our lander sitting at the end of a mile-long

plowed groove. I wondered whether Paul had cut it too close, stopping a couple of hundred feet away. He'd said the landing was mostly automatic, but I didn't see him let go of the joystick.

There was a carafe of water on the table, and some glasses. I poured half a glass, careful not to spill any, feeling everybody's eyes on me. Water was precious here, at least for the time being.

When Paul and the other two came into the room, an older woman stepped forward. Like many of them, men and women, she was wearing a belted robe made of some filmy material. She was pale and bony.

"Welcome to Mars. Of course I've spoken with most of you. I'm Dargo Solingen, current general administrator.

"The first couple of ares"—Martian days—"you are here, just settle in and get used to your new home. Explore and ask questions. We've assigned temporary living and working spaces to everyone, a compromise between the wish list you sent a couple of weeks ago and . . . reality." She shrugged. "It will be a little tight until the new module is in place. We will start on that as soon as the ship is unloaded."

She almost smiled, though it looked like she didn't have much practice with it. "It is strange to see children. It will be an interesting social experiment."

"One you don't quite approve of?" Dr. Jefferson said.

"You may as well know that I don't. But I was not consulted."

"Dr. Solingen," a woman behind her said in a tone of warning.

"I guess none of you were," he said. "It was an Earth decision."

Oz stepped forward. "We were polled. Most of us were very much in favor."

The woman who had cautioned Solingen joined him. "A hundred percent of the permanent party. Those of us who are not returning to Earth." She was either pregnant or the only fat person in the room. Looking more carefully, I saw one other woman who appeared to be pregnant.

You'd think that would have been on the news. Maybe it was,

and I missed it, not likely. Mother and I exchanged significant
glances. Something was going on.


## 3. MOVING IN

It turned out to be nothing more mysterious than a desire for pri-
vacy on the women's part, and everybody's desire to keep Earth
out of their hair. When the first child was born, the Earth press
would be all over them. Until then, there was no need for anyone
to know the blessed event was nigh. So they asked that we not
mention the pregnancies when writing or talking to home.

I shared a small room with Elspeth and Kaimei—an air mattress on the floor and a bunk bed. We agreed to rotate, so everyone would have an actual bed two-thirds of the time.

There was only one desk, with a small screen and a clunky
keyboard and an old VR helmet with a big dent on the side. The
timing for that worked out okay, since Elspeth had classes seven
hours before Eastern time, and Kaimei three hours later. We drew
up a chart and taped it to the wall. The only conflict was my
physical science class versus Kaimei's History of Tao and Bud-
dhism. Mine was mostly equations on the board, so I used the
screen and let her have the helmet.

Our lives were pretty regimented the first couple of weeks,
because we had to coordinate classes with the work roster here,
and leave a little time for eating and sleeping.

Everybody was impatient to get the new module set up, but it
wasn't just a matter of unloading and inflating it. First there was
a light exoskeleton of spindly metal rods that became rigid when
they were all pulled together. Then floorboards to bear the
weight of the things and people inside. Then the connection to
the existing base, through an improvised airlock until they were
sure the module wouldn't leak.

I enjoyed working on that, at first outdoors, unloading the
ship and sorting and pre-assembling some parts; then later, down
in the lava cave, attaching the new to the old. I got used to working in the Mars suit and using the "dog," a wheeled machine

about the size of a large dog. It carried backup oxygen and power.

About half the time, though, my work roster put me inside, helping the younger ones do their lessons and avoid boredom. "Mentoring," they called it, to make it sound more important than babysitting.

One day, though, while I was just getting off work detail, Paul came up and asked whether I'd like to go exploring with him. What, skip math? I got fresh oxygen and helped him check out one of the dogs and we went for a walk.

The surface of Mars might look pretty boring to an outsider, but it's not at all. It must be the same if you live in a desert on Earth: you pretty much have the space around your home memorized, every little mound and rock—and when you venture out it's "Wow! A different rock!"

He took me off to the left of Telegraph Hill, walking at a pretty good pace. The base was below the horizon in less than ten minutes. We were still in radio contact as long as we could see the antenna on top of the hill, and if we wanted to go farther, the dog had a collapsible booster antenna that went up ten meters, which we could leave behind as a relay.

We didn't need it for that, but Paul clicked it up into place when we came to the edge of a somewhat deep crater he wanted to climb into.

"Be really careful," he said. "We have to leave the dog behind. If we both were to fall and be injured, we'd be in deep shit."

I followed him, watching carefully as we picked our way to the top. Once there, he turned around and pointed.

It's hard to really say how strange the sight was. We weren't that high up, but you could see the curvature of the horizon. To the right of Telegraph Hill, the gleam of the greenhouse roof. The dog behind us looked tiny but unnaturally clear, in the near vacuum.

Paul was carrying a white bag, now a little rust-streaked from the dust. He pulled out a photo-map of the crater, unfolded it, and showed it to me. There were about twenty X's, starting on the top of the crater rim, where we must have been standing, then down the incline, and across the crater floor to its central peak.

"Dust collecting," he said. "How's your oxygen?"

I chinned the readout button. "Three hours forty minutes."

"That should be plenty. Now you don't have to go down if you—"

"I do! Let's go!"

"Okay. Follow me." I didn't tell him that my impatience wasn't all excitement, but partly anxiety at having to talk and pee at the same time. Peeing standing up, into a diaper, trying desperately not to fart. "Funny as a fart in a space suit" probably goes back to the beginning of space flight, but there's nothing real funny about it in reality. I'd taken two anti-gas tablets before I came out, and they seemed to still be working.

Keeping your footing was a little harder, going downhill. Paul had the map folded over so it only showed the path down the crater wall; every thirty or forty steps he would fish through the bag and take out a pre-labeled plastic vial, and scrape a sample of dirt into it.

On the floor of the crater I felt a little shiver of fear at our isolation. Looking back the way we'd come, though, I could see the tip of the dog's antenna.

The dust was deeper than I'd seen anyplace else, I guess because the crater walls kept out the wind. Paul took two samples as we walked toward the central peak.

"You better stay down here, Carmen. I won't be long." The peak was steep, and he scrambled up it like a monkey. I wanted to yell "Be careful," but kept my mouth shut.

Looking up at him, the sun behind me, I could see Earth gleaming blue in the ochre sky. How long had it been since I thought of Earth, other than "the place where school is"? I guess I hadn't been here long enough to feel homesickness. Nostalgia for Earth—crowded place with lots of gravity and heat.

It might be the first time I seriously thought about staying. In five years I'd be twenty-one and Paul would still be under forty. I didn't feel romantic about him, but I liked him and he was funny. That would put us way ahead of a lot of marriages I'd observed.

Romance was for movies and books, anyhow. When actual people you know started acting that way, they were so ridiculous.

But then how did I really feel about Paul? Up there being heroic and competent and, admit it, sexy.

Turn down the heat, girl. He's only twelve years younger than your father, Probably sterile from radiation, too. I didn't think I wanted children, but it would be nice to have the option.

He collected his samples and tossed the bag down. It drifted slowly, rotating, and landed about ten feet away. I was enough of a Martian to be surprised to hear a click when it landed, the soles of my boots picking the noise up, conducted through the rock of the crater floor.

He worked his way down slowly, which was a relief. I was holding the sample bag; he took it and I followed him back the way we had come.

At the top of the crater wall, he stopped and looked back. "Can't see it from here," he said. "I'll show you."

"What?"

"My greatest triumph," he said, and started down. "You'll be impressed."

He didn't offer any further explanation on the ground. He picked up the dog's handle and proceeded to walk around to the other side of the crater.

It was a dumbo, an unpiloted supply vehicle. Its rear end was tilted up, the nose down in a small crater.

"I brought her in like that. I was not the most popular man on Mars." As we approached it, I could see the ragged hole someone had cut in the side with a torch or a laser. "Landed it right on the bay door, too."

"Wow. I'm glad you weren't hurt."

He laughed. "It was remote control; I landed it from a console inside the base. Harder than being aboard, actually." We turned around and headed back to the base.

"It was a judgment call. There was a lot of variable wind, and it was yawing back and forth." He made a hand motion like a fish swimming. "I was sort of trying not to hit the base or Telegraph Hill. But I overdid it."

"People could understand that."

"Understanding isn't forgiving. Everybody had to stop their science and become pack animals." I could see the expression on Solingen's face, having to do labor, and smiled.

She really had something against me. I had to do twice as much babysitting as Elspeth or Kaimei—and when I suggested that the boys ought to do it, too, she said that "personnel allocation" was *her* job, thank you. And when my person got allocated to an outside job, it would be something boring and repetitive, like taking inventory of supplies. (That was especially useful, in case there were Martians sneaking in at night to steal nuts and bolts.)

When we got back, I went straight to the console and found a blinking note from the Dragon herself, noting that I had missed math class, saying she wanted a copy of my homework. Did she monitor anybody else's VR attendance?

I'd had the class recorded, of course, the super-exciting chain rule for differentiation. I fell asleep twice, hard to do in VR, and had to start over. Then I had a problem set with fifty chains to differentiate. Wrap me in chains and throw me in the differential dungeon, but I had to sleep. I got the air mattress partly inflated and flopped onto it without undressing.

❧ ❧ ❧

Not delivering my homework like a good little girl got me into a special corner of Dargo Hell. I had to turn over my notes and homework in maths every day to Ana Sitral, who obviously didn't have time for checking it. She must have done something to piss off the Dragon herself.

Then I had to take on over half of the mentoring hours that Kaimei and Elspeth had been covering, and was not allowed any outside time. I had been selfish, Dargo said, tiring myself out on a silly lark, using up resources that might be needed for real work. So I had the temerity to suggest that part of my real work was getting to know Mars, and she really blew up about that. It was not up to me to make up my own training schedule.

Okay, part of it was that she didn't like kids. But part was also that she didn't like *me*, and wouldn't if I was a hundred years old. She didn't bother to hide that from anybody. I complained to Mother and she didn't disagree, but said I had to learn to work with people like that. Especially here, where there wasn't much choice.

I didn't bother complaining to Dad. He would make a Growth Experience out of it. I should try to see the world her way. Sorry, Dad. If I saw the world her way and thought about Carmen Dula, wouldn't that be self-loathing? That would not be a positive growth experience.

## 4. FISH OUT OF WATER

After a month, I was able to put a Mars suit on again, but I didn't go up to the surface. There was plenty of work down below, inside the lava tube that protected the base from cosmic and solar radiation.

There's plenty of water on Mars, but most of it is in the wrong place. If it was on or near the surface, it had to be at the north or south pole. We couldn't put bases there, because they were in total darkness a lot of the time, and we needed solar power.

But there was a huge lake hidden more than a kilometer below the base. It was the easiest one to get to on all of Mars, we learned from some kind of satellite radar, which was why the base was put here. One of the things we'd brought on the *John Carter* was a drilling system designed to tap it. (The drills that came with the first ship and the third broke, though, the famous Mars Luck.)

I worked with the team that set the drill up, nothing more challenging than fetch-and-carry, but a lot better than trying to mentor kids when you wanted to slap them instead.

For a while we could hear the drill, a faint sandpapery sound that was conducted through the rock. Then it was quiet, and most of us forgot about it. A few weeks later, though, it was Sagan 12th, which from then on would be Water Day.

We put on Mars suits and then walked down between the wall of the lava tube and the base's exterior wall. It was kind of creepy, just suit lights, less than a meter between the cold rock and the inflated plastic you weren't supposed to touch.

Then there was light ahead, and we came out into swirling madness—it was a blizzard! The drill had struck water and sent it up under pressure, several liters a minute. When it hit the cold vacuum it exploded into snow.

It was ankle-deep in places, but of course it wouldn't last; the vacuum would evaporate it eventually. But people were already working with lengths of pipe, getting ready to fill the waiting tanks up in the hydroponics farm. One of them had already been dubbed the swimming pool. And that's how the trouble started.

I got on the work detail that hooked the water supply up to the new pump. That was to go in two stages: emergency and "maintenance."

The emergency stage worked on the reasonable assumption that the pump wasn't going to last very long. So we wanted to save every drop of water we could, while it still did work.

This was the "water boy" stage. We had collapsible insulated water containers that held fifty liters each. That's 110 pounds on Earth, about my own weight, awkward but not too heavy to handle on Mars.

All ten of the older kids spent a couple of hours on duty, a couple off, doing water boy. We had wheelbarrows, three of them, so it wasn't too tiring. You fill the thing with water, which takes eight minutes, then turn off the valve and get away fast, so not too much pressure builds up before the next person takes over. Then trundle the wheelbarrow around to the airlock, leave it there, and carry or drag the water bag across the farm to the storage tanks. Dump in the water—a slurry of ice by then—and go back to the pump with your wheelbarrow.

The work was boring as dust, and would drive you insane if you didn't have music. I started out being virtuous, listening to classical pieces that went along with a book on the history of music. But as the days droned by, I listened to more and more city and even sag.

You didn't have to be a math whiz to see that it was going to take three weeks at this rate to fill the first tank, which was two meters tall and eight meters wide, bigger than some backyard pools in Florida.

The water didn't stay icy; they warmed it up to above room temperature. We all must have fantasized about diving in there and paddling around. Elspeth and Kaimei and I even planned for it.

There was no sense in asking permission from the Dragon. What we were going to do was coordinate our showers so we'd all be squeaky clean—so nobody could say we were contaminating the water supply—and come in the same time, off shift, and see whether we could get away with a little skinny-dip. Or see how long we could do it before somebody stopped us.

At two weeks, the engineers sort of forced our hand. They'd been working on a direct link from the pump to this tank and the other two.

Jordan Westling, Barry's inventor dad, seemed to be in charge of that team. We always got along pretty well. He was old but always had a twinkle in his eye.

He and I were alone by the tank while he fiddled with some tubing and gauges. I lifted the water bag with a groan and poured it in.

"This ought to be the last day you have to do that," he said. "We should be on line in a few hours."

"Wow." I stepped up on a box and looked at the water level. It was more than half full, with a little layer of red sediment at the bottom. "Dr. Westling . . . what would happen if somebody went swimming in this?"

He didn't look up from the gauge. "I suppose if somebody washed up first and didn't pee in the pool, nobody would have to know. It's not exactly distilled water. Not that I would endorse such an activity."

When I went back to the water point I touched helmets with Kaimei—that way you can talk without using the suit radio, which is probably monitored—and we agreed we'd do it at 02:15, just after the end of the next shift. She'd pass the word on to Elspeth, who came on at midnight. That would give her time to have a quick shower and smuggle a towel up to the tank.

I got off at 10 and VR'ed a class on Spinoza, better than any sleeping pill. I barely stayed awake long enough to set the alarm for 1:30.

Two and a half hours' sleep was plenty. I awoke with eager anticipation and, alone in the room, put on a robe and slippers and quietly made my way to the shower.

Kaimei had already bathed, and was sitting outside the shower with a reader. I took my two-liter shower and, while I was drying, Elspeth came in from work, wearing skinsuit and socks.

After she showered, the three of us tiptoed past the work/study area—a couple of people were working there, but a hanging partition kept them from being distracted by passersby.

The mess hall was deserted. We went up through the changing room and the airlock foyer and slipped into the farm.

There were only dim maintenance lights at this hour. We padded our way to the swimming pool tank—and heard whispered voices!

Oscar Jefferson, Barry Westling, and my idiot brother had beat us to it!

"Hey girls," Oscar said. "Look—we're out of a job." A faucet in the side was gurgling out a narrow stream.

"My father said we could quit," Barry said, "so we thought we'd take a swim to celebrate."

"You didn't tell him," I said.

"Do we look like idiots?" No, they looked like naked boys. "Come on in. The water's not too cold."

I looked at the other two girls and they shrugged okay. Space ships and Mars bases don't give you a lot of room for modesty.

I sort of liked the way Barry looked at me anyhow, when I stepped out of my robe and slippers. When Kaimei undressed, his look might have been a little more intense.

I stepped up on the box and had one leg over the edge of the tank when the lights snapped on full.

"Caught you!" Dargo Solingen marched down the aisle between the tomatoes and the squash. "I *knew* you'd do this." She looked at me, one foot on the box and the other dangling in space. "And I know exactly who the ringleader is."

She stood with her hands on her hips, studying. Elspeth was only half undressed, but the rest of us were obviously ready for some teenaged sex orgy. "Get out, now. Get dressed and come to my office at 0800. We will have a disciplinary hearing." She stomped back to the door and snapped off the bright lights on her way out.

"I'll tell her it wasn't you," Card said. "We just kind of all decided when Barry's dad said the thing was working."

"She won't believe you," I said, stepping down. "She's been after my ass all along."

"Who wouldn't be?" Barry said, studying the subject. He was such a born romantic.

❧ ❧ ❧

All of our parents were crowded into the Dragon's office at 0800. That was not good. My parents both were working the shift from 2100 to 0400, and needed their sleep. The parents were on one side of the room, and we were on the other, separated by a large video screen.

Without any preamble, Dargo Solingin made the charge: "Last night your children went for a swim in the new Water Tank

One. Tests on the water reveal traces of coliform bacteria, so it cannot be used for human consumption without boiling or some other form of sterilization."

"It was only going to be used for hydroponics," Dr. Westling said.

"You can't say that for certain. At any rate, it was an act of extreme irresponsibility, and one that you encouraged." She pointed a hand control at the video screen and clicked. I saw myself talking to him.

"What would happen if somebody went swimming in this?" He answered that nobody would have to know—not that he would endorse such a thing. He was restraining a smile.

"You're secretly recording me?" he said incredulously.

"Not you. Her."

"She didn't do it!" Card blurted out. "It was my idea."

"You will speak when spoken to," she said coldly. "Your loyalty to your sister is touching, but misplaced." She clicked again, and there was a picture of me and Kaimei at the water point, touching helmets.

"Tonight has to be skinny-dipping night. Dr. Westling says they'll be on line in a few hours. Let's make it 0215, right after Elspeth gets off." You could hear Kaimei's faint agreement.

"You had my daughter's suit bugged?" my father said.

"Not really. I just disabled the OFF switch on her suit communicator."

"That is so . . . so illegal. On Earth they'd throw you out of court and then—"

"This isn't Earth. And on Mars, there is nothing more important than water. As you would appreciate if you had lived here as long as I have." Oh, sure. I think you could live longer without water than without air.

"Besides, it was improper for the boys and girls to be together naked. Even if they hadn't planned any sexual misbehavior—"

"Oh, please," I said. "Excuse me for speaking out of turn, Dr. Solingen, but there was nothing like that. We didn't even know the boys would be there."

"Really. The timing was remarkable, then. And you weren't acting surprised about them when I turned on the lights. Nor modest." Card was squirming, and put up his hand, but the Dragon ignored it. She turned to the parents. "I want to discuss with you what punishment might be appropriate."

"Twenty laps a day in the pool," Dr. Westling said, almost snarling. He didn't like her anyhow, I'd noticed, and spying on him apparently had been the straw that broke the camel's back. "They're just kids, for Chris'sake."

"You're going to say they didn't mean any harm. They have to learn that Mars doesn't recognize that as an excuse.

"An appropriate punishment, I think, would start with not allowing them to bathe for a month. I would also reduce the amount of water they be allowed to drink, but that is difficult to control. And I wouldn't want to endanger their health." God, she is so All Heart.

"For that month, I would also deny them recreational use of the cube and VR, and no exploring on the surface. Double that for the instigator, Ms. Dula"—and she turned back to face us—"and her brother as well, if he insists on sharing the responsibility."

"I do!" he snapped.

"Very well. Two months for both of you."

"It seems harsh," Kaimei's father said. "Kaimei told me that the girls did take the precaution of showering before entering the water."

"Intent means nothing. The bacteria are there."

"Harmless to plants," Dr. Westling repeated.

She looked at him for a long second. "Your dissent is noted. Are there any other objections to this punishment?"

"Not the punishment," my mother said, "but Dr. Dula and I both object to the means of acquiring evidence."

"I am perfectly willing to stand on review for that." The old-timers would probably go along with her. The new ones might still be infected by the Bill of Rights, or the laws of Russia and France and Israel.

There were no other objections, so she reminded the parents

that they would be responsible for monitoring our VR and cube use, but even more, she would rely on our sense of honor.

What were we supposed to be "honoring," though? The now old-fashioned sanctity of water? Her right to spy on us? In fact, her unlimited authority?

I would find a way to get back at her.

## 5. NIGHTWALK

After one day of steaming over it, I'd had enough. I don't know when I made the decision, or whether it even *was* a decision, rather than a kind of sleepwalking. It was sometime before three in the morning. I was still feeling so angry and embarrassed I couldn't get to sleep.

So I got up and started down the corridor to the mess hall, nibble on something. But I walked on past.

It looked like no one else was up. Just dim safety lights. I wound up in the dressing room and realized what I was doing.

Paul had shown me how to prop a pencil in the inner door so that the airlock chime wouldn't go off. With that disabled, a person could actually go outside alone, undetected. I could just be by myself for an hour or two, then sneak back in.

And did I ever want to be by myself.

I went through the dress-up procedure as quietly as possible. Then before I took a step toward the airlock, I visualized myself doing a safety check on another person and did it methodically on myself. It would be so pathetic to die out there, breaking the rules.

I went up the stairs silently as a thief. Well, I *was* a thief. What could they do, deport me?

For safety's sake, I decided to take a dog, even though it would slow me down a bit. I actually hesitated, and tested carrying two extra oxygen bottles by themselves, but that was awkward. *Better safe than sorry*, I said to myself in Mother's voice, and ground my teeth while saying it. But going out without a dog and dying would be pathetic. Arch-criminals are evil, not pathetic.

The evacuating pump sounded loud, though I knew you could hardly hear it in the changing room. It rattled off into silence, then the red light glowed green and the door swung open into darkness.

I stepped out, pulling the dog, and the door slid shut behind it.

I decided not to turn on the suit light, and stood there for several minutes while my eyes adjusted. Walking at night just by starlight—you couldn't do that any other place I've lived. It wouldn't be dangerous if I was careful. Besides, if I turned on a light, someone could see me from the mess hall window.

The nearby rocks gave me my bearings, and I started out toward Telegraph Hill. On the other side I'd be invisible from the base, and vice versa—alone for the first time in almost a year. Earth year.

Seeing the familiar rock field in this ghostly half-light brought back some of the mystery and excitement of the first couple of days. The landing and my first excursion with Paul.

If he knew I was doing this—well, he might approve, secretly. He wasn't much of a rule guy, except for safety.

Thinking that, my foot turned on a small rock and I staggered, getting my balance back. Keep your eyes on the ground while you're walking. It would be, what is the word I'm looking for, *pathetic* to trip and break your helmet out here.

It took me less than a half hour to get to the base of Telegraph Hill. It wasn't all that steep, but the dog's traction wasn't really up to it. A truly adventurous person would leave the dog behind and climb to the top with her suit air alone, and although I do like adventure, I'm also afflicted with pathetico-phobia. The dog and I could go around the mountain rather than over it. I decided to walk in a straight line for one hour, see how far I could get, and walk back.

That was my big mistake. One of them, anyhow. If I'd just gone to the top, taken a picture, and headed straight back, I might have gotten away with it.

I wasn't totally stupid. I didn't go into the hill's "radio shadow," and I cranked the dog's radio antenna up all the way, since I was headed for the horizon, and knew that any small depression in the ground could hide me from the colony's radio transceiver.

The wind picked up a little. I couldn't feel or hear it, of course, but the sky showed it. Jupiter was just rising, and its bright pale yellow light had a halo, and was slightly dimmed, by the dust in the air. I remembered Dad pointing out Jupiter, and then Mars, the morning we left Florida, and had a delicious shiver at the thought that I was standing on that little point of light now.

The area immediately around the colony was as well explored as any place on Mars, but I knew from rock-hounding with Paul that you could find new stuff just a couple hundred meters from the airlock door. I went four or five kilometers, and found something really new.

I had been going for 57 minutes, about to turn back, and was looking for a soft rock that I could mark with an X or something—maybe scratch SURRENDER, PUNY EARTHLINGS on it, though I suspected people would figure out who had done it.

There was no noise. Just a suddenly weightless feeling, and I was falling through a hole in the ground—I'd broken through something like a thin sheet of ice. But there was nothing underneath it!

I was able to turn on the suit light as I tumbled down, but all I saw was a glimpse of the dog spinning around beside and then above me.

It seemed like a long time, but I guess I didn't fall for more than a few seconds. I hit hard on my left foot and heard the sickening sound of a bone cracking, just an instant before the pain me.

I lay still, bright red sparks fading from my vision while the pain amped up and up. Trying to think, not scream.

My ankle was probably broken, and at least one rib on the left side. I breathed deeply, listening—Paul told me about how he had broken a rib in a car wreck, and he could tell by the sound that it had punctured his lung. This did hurt, but didn't sound different—and then I realized I was lucky to be breathing at all. The helmet and suit were intact.

But would I be able to keep breathing long enough to be rescued?

The suit light was out. I clicked the switch over and over, and nothing happened. If I could find the dog, and if it was intact, I'd have an extra sixteen hours of oxygen. Otherwise, I probably had two, two and a half hours.

I didn't suppose the radio would do any good, underground, but I tried it anyway. Yelled into it for a minute and then listened. Nothing.

These suits ought to have some sort of beeper to trace people with. But then I guess nobody else ever wandered off and disappeared.

It was about four. How long before someone woke up and noticed I was gone? How long before someone got worried enough to check, and see that the suit and dog were missing?

I tried to stand and it wasn't possible. The pain was intolerable and the bone made an ominous sound. I couldn't help crying but stopped after a minute. Pathetic.

Had to find the dog, with its oxygen and power. I stretched out and patted the ground back and forth, and scrabbled around in a circle, feeling for it.

It wasn't anywhere nearby. But how far could it have rolled after it hit?

I had to be careful, not just crawl off in some random direction and get lost. I remembered feeling a large, kind of pointy, rock off to my left—good thing I hadn't landed on it—and could use it as a reference point.

I found it and moved up so my feet were touching it. Visualizing an old-fashioned clock with me as the hour hand, I went off in the 12:00 direction, measuring four body lengths inchworm style. Then crawled back to the pointy rock and did the same thing in the opposite, 6:00, direction. Nothing there, nor at 9:00 or 3:00, and I tried not to panic.

In my mind's eye I could see the areas where I hadn't been able to reach, the angles midway between 12:00 and 3:00, 3:00 and 6:00, and so on. I went back to the pointy rock and started over. On the second try, my hand touched one of the dog's wheels, and I smiled in spite of my situation.

It was lying on its side. I uprighted it and felt for the switch that would turn on its light. When it came on, I was looking straight into it and it dazzled me blind.

Facing away from it, after a couple of minutes I could see some of where I was. I'd fallen into a large underground cavern, maybe shaped like a dome, though I couldn't see as far as the top. I guessed it was part of a lava tube that was almost open to the surface, worn so thin that it couldn't support my weight.

Maybe it joined up with the lava tube that we lived in! But even if it did, and even if I knew which direction to go, I couldn't crawl the four kilometers back. I tried to ignore the pain and do the math, anyhow—sixteen hours of oxygen, four kilometers, that means creeping 250 meters per hour, dragging the dog along behind me . . . no way. Better to hope they would track me down here.

What were the chances of that? Maybe the dog's tracks, or my boot prints? Only in dusty places, if the wind didn't cover them up before dawn.

If they searched at night, the dog's light might help. How close would a person have to come to the hole, to see it? Close enough to crash through and join me?

And would the dog's power supply last long enough to shine all night and again tomorrow night? It wouldn't have to last any longer than that.

The ankle was hurting less, but that was because of numbness. My hands and feet were getting cold. Was that a suit malfunction, or just because I was stretched out on this cold cave floor. Where the sun had never shined.

With a start, I realized the coldness could mean that my suit was losing power—it should automatically warm up the gloves and boots. I opened my mouth wide and with my chin pressed the switch that ought to project a technical readout in front of my eyes, with "power remaining," and nothing came up.

Well, the dog obviously had power to spare. I unreeled the recharge cable and plugged its jack into my LSU.

Nothing happened.

I chinned the switch over and over. Nothing.

Maybe it was just the readout display that was broken; I was getting power but it wasn't registering. Trying not to panic, I wiggled the jack, unplugged and replugged it. Still nothing.

I was breathing, though; that part worked. I unrolled the umbilical hose from the dog and pushed the fitting into the bottom of the LSU. It made a loud pop and a sudden breeze of cold oxygen blew around my neck and chin.

So at least I wouldn't die of that. I would be frozen solid before I ran out of air; how comforting. Acid rush of panic in my throat; I choked it back and sucked on the water tube until the nausea was gone.

Which made me think about the other end, and I clamped up. I was not going to fill the suit's emergency diaper with shit and piss before I died. Though the people who deal with dead people probably have seen that before. And it would be frozen solid, so what's the difference. Inside the body or outside.

I stopped crying long enough to turn on the radio and say goodbye to people, and apologize for my stupidity. Though it's unlikely that anyone would ever hear it. Unless there was some kind of secret recorder in the suit, thanks to the Dragon, and someone stumbled on it years from now.

I wished I had Dad's zen. If Dad were in this situation he would just accept it, and wait to leave his body.

I tipped the dog up on end, so its light shone directly up toward the hole I'd fallen through, still too high up to see.

I couldn't feel my feet or hands anymore and was growing heavy-lidded. I'd read that freezing to death was the least painful way to go, and one of my last coherent thoughts was "Who came back to tell them?"

Then I hallucinated an angel, wearing red, surrounded by an ethereal bubble. He was incredibly ugly.

## 6. ANGEL IN HELL

I woke up in some pain, ankle throbbing and hands and feet burning. I was lying on a huge inflated pillow. The air was thick and muggy and it was dark. A yellow light was bobbing toward me, growing brighter. I heard lots of feet.

It was a flashlight, or rather a lightstick like you wear night-dancing, and the person holding it . . . wasn't a person. It was the red angel from my dream.

Maybe I was still dreaming. I was naked, which sometimes happens in my dreams. The dog was sitting a few feet away. My broken ankle was splinted between two pieces of what felt like wood. On Mars?

This angel had too many legs, like four, sticking out from under the red tunic thing. His head, if that's what it was, looked like a potato that had gone really bad. Soft and wrinkled and covered with eyes. Maybe they *were* eyes, lots of them, or antennae. Like fat hairs that moved around. He was almost as big as a small horse. He seemed to have two regular-sized arms and two little ones. For an angel, he smelled a lot like tuna fish.

I should have been terrified, naked in front of this monster, but he definitely was the one who had saved me from freezing to death. Or he was dressed like that one.

"Are you real?" I said. "Or am I still dreaming, or dead?"

He made some kind of noise, sort of like a bullfrog with teeth chattering. Then he whistled and the lights came on, dim but enough to see around. The unreality of it made me dizzy.

I was taking it far too calmly, maybe because I couldn't think of a thing to do. Either I was in the middle of some complicated dream, or this is what happens to you after you die, or I was completely insane, or, least likely of all, I'd been rescued by a Martian.

But a Martian wouldn't breathe oxygen, not this thick. He wouldn't have wood for making splints. Though this one might know something about ankles, having so many of them.

"You don't speak English, do you?"

He responded with a long speech that sounded kind of threatening. Maybe it was about food animals not being allowed to talk.

I was in a circular room, a little too small for both me and Big Red, with a round wall that seemed to be several layers of plastic sheeting. He had come in through slits in the plastic. The polished stone floor was warm. The high ceiling looked like the floor, but there were four bluish lights imbedded in it, that looked like cheap plastic decorations.

It felt like a hospital room, and maybe it was one. The pillow was big enough for one like him to lie down on it.

On a stone pedestal over by the dog was a pitcher and a glass made of something that looked like obsidian. He poured me a glass of something and brought it over.

His hand, also potato-brown, had four long fingers without nails, and lots of little joints. The fingers were all the same length and it looked like any one of them could be the thumb. The small hands were miniature versions of the big ones.

The stuff in the glass didn't smell like anything and tasted like water, so I drank it down in a couple of greedy gulps.

He took the glass back and refilled it. When he handed it to me, he pointed into it with a small hand, and said, "Ar." Sort of like a pirate.

I pointed and said, "Water?" He answered with a sound like "war," with a lot of extra R's.

He set down the glass and brought me a plate with something that looked remarkably like a mushroom. No, thanks. I read that story.

(For a mad moment I wondered whether that could be it—I *had* eaten, or ingested, something that caused all this, and it was one big dope dream. But the pain was too real.)

He picked the thing up delicately and a mouth opened up in his neck, broad black teeth set in grisly red. He took a small nibble and replaced it on the plate. I shook my head no, though that could mean yes in Martian. Or some mortal insult.

How long could I go without eating? A week, I supposed, but my stomach growled at the thought.

He heard the growling and pointed helpfully to a hole in the floor. That took care of one question, but not quite yet, pal. We've hardly been introduced, and I don't even let my *brother* watch me do that.

I touched my chest and said "Carmen." Then I pointed at his chest, if that's what it was.

He touched his chest and said "Harn." Well, that was a start.

"No." I took his hand—dry, raspy skin—and brought it over to touch my chest. "Car-men," I said slowly. Me Jane, you Tarzan. Or Mr. Potato Head.

"Harn," he repeated, which wasn't a bad Carmen if you couldn't pronounce C or M. Then he took my hand gently and placed it between his two small arms and made a sputtering sound no human could do, at least with the mouth. He let go but I kept my hand there and said, "Red. I'll call you Red."

"Reh," he said, and repeated it. It gave me a shiver. I was communicating with an alien. Someone put up a plaque! But he turned abruptly and left.

I took advantage of being alone and hopped over to the hole and used it, not as easy as that sounds. I needed to find something to use as a crutch. This wasn't exactly Wal-Mart, though. I drank some water and hopped back to the pillow and flopped down.

My hands and feet hurt a little less. They were red, like bad sunburn, which I supposed was the first stage of frostbite. I could have lost some fingers and toes—not that it would matter much to me, with lungs full of ice.

I looked around. Was I inside of Mars or was this some kind of a space ship? You wouldn't make a space ship out of stone. We had to be underground, but this stone didn't look at all like the petrified lava of the colony's tunnel. And it was warm, which had to be electrical or something. The lights and plastic sheets looked pretty high-tech, but everything else was kind of basic—a hole in the floor? (I hoped it wasn't somebody else's ceiling!)

I mentally reviewed why there can't be higher forms of life

on Mars, least of all technological life: No artifacts—we've mapped every inch of it, and anything that looked artificial turned out to be natural. Of course there's nothing to breathe, though I seemed to be breathing. Same thing with water. And temperature.

There are plenty of microscopic organisms living underground, but how could they evolve into big bozos like Red? What is there on Mars for a big animal to eat? Rocks?

Red was coming back with his lightstick, followed by someone only half his size, wearing bright lime green. Smoother skin, like a more fresh potato. I decided she was female and called her Green. Just for the time being; I might have it backward. They had seen me naked, but I hadn't seen them—and wasn't eager to, actually. They were scary enough this way.

Green was carrying a plastic bag with things inside that clicked softly together. She set the bag down carefully and exchanged a few noises with Red.

First she took out a dish that looked like pottery, and from a plastic bag shook out something that looked like an herb, or pot. It started smoking immediately, and she thrust it toward me. I sniffed it; it was pleasant, like mint or menthol. She made a gesture with her two small hands, a kind of shooing motion, that I interpreted to mean "breathe more deeply," and I did.

She took the dish away and brought two transparent disks, like big lenses, out of the bag and handed one to me. While I held it, she pressed the other one against my forehead, then chest, then the side of my leg. She gently lifted up the foot with the broken ankle, and pressed it against the sole. Then she did the other foot. She put the lenses back in her bag and stood motionless, staring at me like a doctor or scientist.

I thought, okay, this is where the alien sticks a tube up your ass, but she must have left her tube back at the office.

She and Red conferred for a while, making gestures with their small arms while they made noises like porpoises and machinery. Then she reached into the bag and pulled out a small metal tube, which caused me to cringe away, but she gave it a snap with her wrist and it ratcheted out to about six feet long. She mimicked using it as a cane, which looked really strange, like a spider missing four legs, and handed it to me, saying "Harn."

Guess that was my name now. The stick felt lighter than aluminum, but when I used it to lever myself up, it was rigid and strong.

She reached into her bag of tricks and brought out a thing like her tunic, somewhat thicker and softer and colored gray. There was a hole in it for my head, but no sleeves or other complications. I put it on gratefully and draped it around so I could use the stick. It was agreeably warm.

Red stepped ahead and, with a rippling gesture of all four hands, indicated "Follow me." I did, with Green coming behind me.

It was a strange sensation, going through the slits in those plastic sheets, or whatever they were. It was like they were alive, millions of feathery fingers clasping you and then letting go all at once, to close behind you with a snap.

When I went through the first one, it was noticeably cooler, and cooler still after the second one, and my ears popped. After the fourth one, it felt close to freezing, though the floor was still warm, and the air was noticeably thin; I was almost panting, and could see my breath.

We stepped into a huge dark cavern. Rows of dim lights at about knee level marked off paths. The lights were all blue, but each path had its own kind of blue, different in shade or intensity. Meet me at the corner of bright turquoise and dim aquamarine.

I tried to remember our route, left at this shade and then right at *this* one, but I was not sure how useful the knowledge would be. What, I was going to escape? Hold my breath and run back to the base?

We went through a single sheet into a large area, at least as well lit as my hospital room, and almost as warm. It had a kind of barnyard smell, not unpleasant. There were things that had to be plants all around, like broccoli but brown and gray with some yellow, sitting in water that you could hear was flowing. A little mist hung near the ground, and my face felt damp. It was a hydroponic farm like ours, but without greens or the bright colors of tomatoes and peppers and citrus fruits.

Green leaned over and picked something that looked like a cigar, or something less polite, and offered it to me. I waved it away; she broke it in two and gave half to Red.

I couldn't tell how big the place was, probably acres. So where were all the people it was set up to feed?

I got a partial answer when we passed through another sheet, into a brighter room about the size of the new pod we'd brought on the *John Carter*. There were about twenty of the aliens arranged along two walls, standing at tables or in front of things like data screens, but made of metal rather than plastic. There weren't any chairs; I supposed quadrupeds don't need them.

They all began to move toward me, making strange noises, of course. If I'd brought one of them into a room, humans would have done the same thing, but nevertheless I felt frightened and helpless. When I shrank back, Red put a protective arm in front of me and said a couple of bullfrog syllables. They all stopped about ten feet away.

Green talked to them more softly, gesturing toward me. Then they stepped forward in an orderly way, by colors—two in tan, three in green, two in blue, and so forth—each standing quietly in front of me for a few seconds. I wondered if the color signified rank. None of the others wore red, and none were as big as Big Red. Maybe he was the alpha male, or the only female, like bees.

What were they doing? Just getting a closer look, or taking turns trying to destroy me with thought waves?

After that presentation, Red gestured for me to come over and look at the largest metal screen.

Interesting. It was a panorama of our greenhouse and the other parts of the colony that were above ground. The picture might have been from the top of Telegraph Hill. Just as I noticed that there were a lot of people standing around—too many for a normal work party—the *John Carter* came sliding into view, a rooster tail of red dust fountaining out behind her. A lot of the people jumped up and down and waved.

Then the screen went black for a few seconds, and a green rectangle opened slowly . . . it was the airlock light at night, as the door slid open. I was looking at myself, just a little while ago, coming out and pulling the dog behind me.

The camera must have been like those flying bugs that Homeland Security spies use. I certainly hadn't seen anything.

When the door closed, the picture changed to a ghostly blue, like moonlight on Earth. It followed me for a minute or so. Stumbling and then staring at the ground as I walked more cautiously.

Then it switched to another location, and I knew what was coming. The ground collapsed and the dog and I disappeared in a cloud of dust, which the wind swept away in an instant.

The bug, or whatever it was, drifted down through the hole to hover over me as I writhed around in pain. A row of glowing symbols appeared at the bottom of the screen. There was a burst of white light when I found the dog and switched it on.

Then Big Red floated down—this was obviously the speeded-up version—wearing several layers of that wall plastic, it seemed; riding a thing that looked like a metal sawhorse with two side-cars. He put me in one and the dog in the other. Then he floated back up.

Then they skipped all the way to me lying on that pillow, naked and unlovely, in an embarrassing posture—I blushed, as if any of them cared—and then moved in close to my ankle, which was blue and swollen. Then a solid holo of a human skeleton, obviously mine, in the same position. The image moved in the same way as before. The fracture line glowed red, and then my foot, below the break, shifted slightly. The line glowed blue and disappeared.

Just then I noticed it wasn't hurting anymore.

Green stepped over and gently took the staff away from me. I put weight on the foot and it felt as good as new.

"How could you do that?" I said, not expecting an answer.

No matter how good they were at healing themselves, how could they apply that to a human skeleton?

Well, a human vet could treat a broken bone in an animal she'd never seen before. But it wouldn't heal in a matter of hours.

Two of the amber ones brought out my skinsuit and Mars suit, and put them at my feet.

Red pointed at me and then tapped on the screen, which again showed the surface parts of the colony. You could hardly see them for the dust, though; there was a strong storm blowing.

He made an up-and-down gesture with his small arms, and then his large ones, obviously meaning "Get dressed."

So with about a million potato eyes watching, I took off the tunic and got into the skinsuit. The diaper was missing, which made it feel kind of baggy. They must have thrown it away—or analyzed it, ugh.

The creatures stared in silence while I zipped that up and then climbed and wiggled into the Mars suit. I secured the boots and gloves and then clamped the helmet into place, and automatically chinned the switch for an oxygen and power readout, but of course it was still broken. I guess that would be asking too much—you fixed my ankle but you can't fix a foogly space suit? What kind of Martians *are* you?"

It was obvious I wasn't getting any air from the backpack, though. I'd need the dog's backup supply.

I unshipped the helmet and faced Green, and made an exaggerated pantomime of breathing in and out. She didn't react. Hell, they probably breathed by osmosis or something.

I turned to Red and crouched over, patting the air at the level of the dog. "Dog," I said, and pointed back the way we'd come.

He leaned over and mimicked my gesture, and said, "Nog." Pretty close. Then he turned to the crowd and croaked out a speech, which I think had both "Harn" and "nog" in it.

He must have understood, at least partly, because he made that four-armed "come along" motion at me, and went back to the place where we'd entered. I went through the plastic and looked back. Green was leading four others, it looked like one of each color, following us.

Red leading us, we all went back along what seemed the same path we'd used coming over. I counted my steps, so that when I told people about it I'd have at least one actual concrete number. The hydroponic room, or at least the part we cut through, was 185 steps wide; then it was another 204 steps from there to the "hospital" room. I get about 80 centimeters to a step, so the trip covered more than 300 meters, allowing for a little dog-leg in the middle. Of course it might go on for miles in every direction, but at least it was no smaller than that.

We went into the little room and they watched while I un-reeled the umbilical and plugged it in. The cool air coming through the neck fitting was more than a relief. I put my helmet back on. Green stepped forward and did a pretty good imitation of my breathing pantomime.

I sort of didn't want to go. I was looking forward to coming back, and learning how to communicate with Red and Green. We had other people more qualified, though. I should have listened to Mother when she got after me to take a language in school. If I'd known this was going to happen, I would have taken Chinese and Latin and Body Noises.

The others stood away from the plastic and Red gestured for me to follow. I pulled the dog along through the four plastic lay-ers; this time we turned sharply to the right and started walking up a gently sloping ramp.

After a few minutes I could look down and get a sense of how large this place was. There was the edge of a lake—an immense amount of water even if it was only a few inches deep. From above, the buildings looked like domes of clay, or just dirt, with no win-dows, just the pale blue light that filtered through the door layers.

There were squares of different sizes and shades that were probably crops like the mushrooms and cigars, and one large square had trees that looked like six-foot-tall broccoli, which could explain the wooden splints.

We came to a level place, brightly lit, that had shelves full of bundles of the plastic stuff. Red walked straight to one shelf and pulled off a bundle. It was his Mars suit. Bending over at a strange angle, bobbing, he slid his feet into four opaque things like thick socks. His two large arms went into sleeves, ending in mittens. Then the whole thing seemed to come alive, and ripple up and over him, sealing together and then inflating. It didn't have anything that looked like an oxygen tank, but air was coming from somewhere.

He gestured for me to follow and we went toward a dark corner. He hesitated there, and held out his hand to me. I took it, and we staggered slowly through dozens of layers of the stuff, toward a dim light.

It was obviously like a gradual airlock. We stopped at another flat area, which had one of the blue lights, and rested for a few minutes. Then he led me through another long series of layers, where it became completely dark—without him leading me, I might have gotten turned around—and then it lightened slightly, the light pink this time.

When we came out, we were on the floor of a cave; the light was coming from a circle of Martian sky. When my eyes adjusted, I could see there was a smooth ramp leading uphill to the cave entrance.

I'd never seen the sky that color. We were looking up through a serious dust storm.

Red pulled a dust-covered sheet off his sawhorse-shaped vehicle. I helped him put the dog into one of the bowl-like sidecars, and I got in the other. There were two things like stubby handlebars in front, but no other controls that I could see.

He backed onto the thing, straddling it, and we rose off the ground a foot or so, and smoothly started forward.

The glide up the ramp was smooth. I expected to be buffeted around by the dust storm, but as impressive as it looked, it didn't have much power. My umbilical tube did flap around in the wind, which made me nervous. If it snapped, a failsafe would close off the tube so I wouldn't immediately die. But I'd use up the air in the suit pretty fast.

I couldn't see more than ten or twenty feet in any direction, but Red, I hoped, could see farther. He was moving very fast. Of course, he was unlikely to hit another vehicle, or a tree.

I settled down into the bowl—there wasn't anything to see— and was fairly comfortable. I amused myself by imagining the re-action of Dargo Solingen and Mother and Dad when I showed up with an actual Martian.

It felt like an hour or more before he slowed down and we hit the ground and skidded to a stop. He got off his perch labori-ously and came around to the dog's side. I got out to help him lift it and was knocked off balance by a gust. Four legs were a defi-nite advantage here.

He watched while I got the umbilical untangled and then pointed me in the direction we were headed. Then he made a shooing motion.

"You have to come with me," I said, uselessly, and tried to translate it into arm motions. He pointed and shooed again, and then backed on to the sawhorse and took off in a slow U-turn.

I started to panic. What if I went in the wrong direction? I could miss the base by twenty feet and just keep walking on into the desert.

I took a few deep breaths. The dog was pointed in the right direction. I picked up its handle and looked straight ahead as far as I could see, through the swirling gloom. I saw a rock, directly ahead, and walked to it. Then another rock, maybe ten feet away. After the fourth rock, I looked up and saw I'd almost run into the airlock door. I leaned on the big red button and the door slid open immediately. It closed behind the dog and the red light on the ceiling started blinking. It turned green and the inside door opened on a wide-eyed Emily.

"Carmen! You found your way back!"

"Well, um . . . not really . . ."

"Got to call the search party!" She bounded down the stairs yelling for Howard.

I wondered how long they'd been searching for me. I would be in shit up to my chin.

I put the dog back in its place—there was only one other parked there, so three were out looking for me. Or my body.

Card came running in when I was half out of my skinsuit. "Sis!" He grabbed me and hugged me, which was moderately embarrassing. "We thought you were—"

"Yeah, okay. Let me get dressed? Before the shit hits the fan?" He let me turn around and step out of the skinsuit and into my coverall.

"What, you went out for a walk and got lost in that dust storm?"

For a long moment, I thought of saying yes. Who was going to believe my story? I looked at the clock and saw that it was 1900. If it was the same day, seventeen hours had passed. I *could* have wandered around that long without running out of air.

"How long have I been gone?"

"You can't remember? All foogly day, man. Were you derilious?"

"Delirious." I kneaded my brow and rubbed my face hard with both hands. "Let me wait and tell it all when Mother and Dad get here."

"That'll be hours! They're out looking for you."

"Oh, that's great. Who else?"

"I think it was Paul the pilot."

"Well," said a voice behind me. "You decided to come back after all."

It was Dargo Solingen. There was a quaver of emotion in her voice that I'd never heard. I think anger.

"I'm sorry," I said. "I don't know what I was thinking."

"I don't think you were thinking at *all*. You were being a foolish *girl*, and you put more lives than your own into danger."

About a dozen people were behind her. "Dargo," Dr. Jefferson said. "She's back, she's alive. Let's give her a little rest."

"Has she given *us* any rest?" she barked.

"I'm *sorry*! I'll do anything—"

"You will? Isn't that pretty. What do you propose to do?"

Dr. Estrada put a hand on her shoulder. "Please let me talk to her." Oh, good, a shrink. I needed a xenologist. But she would listen better than Solingen.

"Oh . . . do what you want. I'll deal with her later." She turned and walked through the small crowd.

Some people gathered around me and I tried not to cry. I wouldn't want *her* to think she had made me cry. But there were plenty of shoulders and arms for me to hide my eyes in.

"Carmen." Dr. Estrada touched my forearm. "We ought to talk before your parents get back."

"Okay." A dress rehearsal. I followed her down to the middle of A.

She had a large room to herself, but it was her office as well as quarters. "Lie down here," she indicated her single bunk, "and just try to relax. Begin at the beginning."

"The beginning isn't very interesting. Dargo Solingen embarrassed me in front of everybody. Not the first time, either. Sometimes I feel like I'm her little project. Let's drive Carmen crazy."

"So in going outside like that, you were getting back at her? Getting even in some way?"

"I didn't think of it that way. I just had to get out, and that was the only way."

"Maybe not, Carmen. We can work on ways to get away without physically leaving."

"Like Dad's zen thing, okay. But what I did, or why, isn't really important. It's what I *found*!"

"So what did you find?"

"Life. Intelligent life. They saved me." I could hear my voice and even I didn't believe it.

"Hmm," she said. "Go on."

"I'd walked four kilometers or so and was about to turn around and go back. But I stepped on a place that wouldn't support my weight. Me and the dog. We fell through. At least ten meters, maybe twenty."

"And you weren't hurt?"

"I *was*! I heard my ankle break. I broke a rib, maybe more than one, here."

She pressed the area, gently. "But you're walking."

"They fixed . . . I'm getting ahead of myself."

"So you fell through and broke your ankle?"

"Then I spent a long time finding the dog. My suit light went out when I hit the ground. But finally I found it, found the dog, and got my umbilical plugged in."

"So you had plenty of oxygen."

"But I was freezing. The circuit to my gloves and boots wasn't working. I really thought that was it."

"But you survived."

"I was rescued. I was passing out and this, uh, this *Martian* came floating down, I saw him in the dog's light. Then everything went black and I woke up—"

"Carmen! You have to see that this was a dream. A hallucination."

"Then how did I get here?"

Her mouth set in a stubborn line. "You were very lucky. You wandered around in the storm and came back here."

"But there *was* no storm when I left! Just a little wind. The storm came up while I was . . . well, I was underground. Where the Martians live."

"You've been through so much, Carmen . . ."

"This was *not* a dream!" I tried to stay calm. "Look. You can check the air left in the tanks. My suit and the dog. There will be *hours* unaccounted for. I was breathing the Martians' air."

"Carmen . . . be reasonable . . ."

"No, *you* be reasonable. I'm not saying anything more until—" There was one knock on the door and Mother burst in, followed by Dad.

"My baby," she said. When did she ever call me that? She hugged me so hard I could barely breathe. "You found your way back."

"Mother . . . I was just telling Dr. Estrada . . . I didn't find my way back. I was brought."

"She had a dream about Martians. A hallucination."

"*No*! Would you just listen?"

Dad sat down cross-legged, looking up at me. "Start at the beginning, honey."

I did. I took a deep breath and started with taking the suit and the dog and going out to be alone. Falling and breaking my ankle. Waking up in the little hospital room. Red and Green and the others. Seeing the base on their screen. Being healed and brought back.

There was an uncomfortable silence after I finished. "If it wasn't for the dust storm," Dad said, "it would be easy to verify your . . . your account. Nobody could see you from here, though, and the satellites won't show anything, either."

"Maybe that's why he was in a rush to bring me back. If they'd waited for the storm to clear, they'd be exposed."

"Why would they be afraid of that?" Dr. Estrada asked.

"Well, I don't know. But I guess it's obvious that they don't want anything to do with us—"

"Except to rescue a lost girl," Mother said.

"Is that so hard to believe? I mean, I couldn't say three words to them, but I could tell they were good-hearted."

"It just sounds so fantastic," Dad said. "How would you feel in our position? By far the easiest explanation is that you were under extreme stress and—"

"*No*! Dad, do you really think I would do that? Come up with some elaborate lie?" I could see on his face that he did indeed. Maybe not a lie, but a fantasy. "There's objective proof. Look at the dog. It has a huge dent where it hit the ground in the cave."

"Maybe so; I haven't seen it," he said. "But being devil's advocate, aren't there many other ways that could have happened?"

"What about the *air*? The air in the dog! I didn't use enough of it to have been out so long."

He nodded. "That would be compelling. Did you dock it?"

Oh hell. "Yes. I wasn't thinking I'd have to *prove* anything." When you dock the dog it automatically starts to refill air and power. "There must be a record. How much oxygen a dog takes on when it recharges."

They all looked at each other. "Not that I know of," Dad said. "But you don't need that. Let's just do an MRI of your ankle. That'll tell if it was recently broken."

"But they *fixed* it. The break might not show."

"It will show," Dr. Estrada said. "Unless there was some kind of . . . magic involved."

Mother's face was getting red. "Would you both leave? I need to talk to Carmen alone." They both nodded and went out.

Mother watched the door close. "I know you aren't lying. You've never been good at that."

"Thanks," I said. Thanks for nothing.

"But it was a stupid thing to do, going off like that, and you know it."

"I do, I *do*! And I'm sorry for all the trouble I—"

"But look. I'm a scientist, and so is your dad, after a fashion, and so is almost everybody else who's going to hear this story today. You see what I'm saying?"

"Yeah, I think so. They're going to be skeptical."

"Of course they are. They don't get paid for believing things. They get paid for questioning them."

"And you, Mother. Do you believe me?"

She stared at me with a fierce intensity I'd never seen before in my life. "Look. Whatever happened to you, I believe one hundred percent that you're telling the truth. You're telling the truth about what you remember, what you believe happened."

"But I might be nuts."

"Well, wouldn't you say so? If I came in with your story? You'd say 'Mom's getting old.' Wouldn't you?"

"Yeah, maybe I would."

"And to prove that I wasn't crazy, I would take you out and

show you something that couldn't be explained any other way. You know what they say about extraordinary claims?"

"They require extraordinary evidence."

"That's right. Once the storm calms down, you and I are going out to where you say . . . to where you fell through to the cave." She put her hand on the back of my head and rubbed my hair. "I so much want to believe you. For my sake as well as yours. To find life here."


## 7. THE DRAGON LADY

Mother wanted to call a general assembly, so I could tell everybody the complete story, all at once, but Dargo Solingen wouldn't allow it. She said that children do stunts like this to draw attention to themselves, and she wasn't going to reward me with an audience. Of course she's an expert about children, never having had any herself. Good thing. They'd be monsters.

So it was like the whisper game, where you sit in a circle and whisper a sentence to the person next to you, and she whispers it to the next, and so on. When it gets back to you, it's all wrong, sometimes in a funny way.

This was not particularly funny. People would ask if I was really going around on the surface without a Mars suit, or think the Martians stripped me naked and interrogated me, or they broke my ankle on purpose. I put a detailed account on my website, but a lot of people would rather talk than read.

The MRI didn't help much, except for people who wanted to believe I was lying. Dr. Jefferson said it looked like an old childhood injury, long ago healed. Mother was with me at the time, and she told him she was absolutely sure I'd never broken that ankle. To people like Dargo Solingen that was a big shrug; so I'd lied about that, too. I think we won Dr. Jefferson over, though he was inclined to believe me, anyhow. So did most of the people who came over on the *John Carter* with us. They were willing to believe in Martians before they'd believe I would make up something like that.

Dad didn't want to talk about it, but Mother was fascinated. I went to talk with her at the lab after dinner (she and two others were keeping a 24-hour watch on an experiment). "I don't see how they could be actual Martians," she said, "in the sense that we're Earthlings. I mean, if they evolved here as oxygen-water creatures similar to us, then that was three billion years ago. And, as you said, a large animal isn't going to evolve alone, without any other animals. Nor will it suddenly appear, without smaller, simpler animals preceding it. So they must be like us."

"From Earth?"

She laughed. "I don't think so. None of the eight-limbed creatures on Earth has very high technology. I think they have to have come from yet another planet. Unless we're completely wrong about areology, about the history of conditions on this planet, they can't have come from here."

"What if they used to live on the surface?" I said. "Then moved underground as the planet dried up and lost its air?"

She shook her head. "The time scale. No species more complicated than a bacterium has survived for billions of years."

"None on Earth," I said.

"Touché," she laughed. A bell chimed and she went to the other side of the room and looked inside an aquarium, or terrarium. Or ares-arium, here, I suppose. She looked at the things growing inside and typed some numbers onto her clipboard.

"So they went underground three billion years ago with the technology to duplicate what sounds like a high-altitude Earth environment. And stayed that way for three billion years." She shook her head. "It's not likely. And I still want to know where the fossils are. Maybe they dug them all up and destroyed them, just to confuse us?"

"But it's not like we've looked everywhere. Paul says it may be that life wasn't distributed uniformly, and we just haven't found any of the islands where things lived. The dinosaurs or whatever."

"Well, you know it didn't work that way on Earth. Fossils everywhere, from the bottom of the sea to the top of the Himalayas. Crocodile fossils in Antarctica."

"Okay. That's Earth."

"It's all we have. Coffee?" I said no and she poured herself half a cup. "You're right that it's weak to generalize from one example. Paul could very well be right, too; there's no evidence one way or the other.

"But look. We know all about one form of life on Mars: you and me and the others. We have to live in an artificial bubble that contains an alien environment, maintained by high technology, because we *are* the aliens here. So you stumble on eight-legged potato people who also live in a bubble that contains an alien environment, evidently maintained by high technology. The simplest explanation is that they're aliens, too. Alien to Mars."

"Yeah, I don't disagree. I know about Occam's Razor."

She smiled at that. "What's fascinating to me, one of many things, is that you spent hours in that environment and felt no ill effects. Their planet's very earthlike."

"What if it *was* Earth?"

That stopped her. "Wouldn't we have noticed?"

"I mean a long time ago. What if they lived only on mountain tops, and developed high technology thousands and thousands of years ago. Then they all left."

"It's an idea," she said. "But it's hard to believe that every one of them would be willing and able to leave—and that there would be no trace of their civilization, ten or even a hundred thousand years later. And where are their genetic precursors? The eight-legged equivalent of apes?"

"You don't really believe me."

"Well, I do; I do," she said seriously. "I just don't think there's an easy explanation."

"Like Dargo Solingen's? The Figment of Imagination Theory?"

"Especially that. People don't have complex consistent hallucinations; they're *called* hallucinations because they're fantastic, dreamlike.

"Besides, I saw the dog; you couldn't have put that dent in it

with a lead-lined baseball bat. And she can't explain the damage
to your Mars suit, either, without positing that you leaped off the
side of a cliff just to give yourself an alibi." She was getting
worked up. "And I'm your *mother*, even if I'm not a model one. I
would goddamn remember if you had ever broken your ankle!
That healed hairline fracture is enough proof for me—and for Dr.
Jefferson and Dr. Milius and anybody else in this goddamned
hole who didn't convict you before you opened your mouth."

"You've been a good mother," I said.

She suddenly sat up and hugged me across the table. "Not so
good. Or you wouldn't have done this."

She sat down and rubbed my hand. "But if you hadn't done
it—" She laughed. "—how long would it have been before we
stumbled on these aliens? They're watching us, but don't seem
eager to have us see them."

The window on the wall was a greenboard of differential
equations. She clicked on her clipboard and it became a real-time
window. The storm was still blowing, but it had thinned out
enough so I could see a vague outline of Telegraph Hill.

"Maybe tomorrow we'll be able to go out and take a look. If
Paul's free, he'd probably like to come along; nobody knows the
local real estate better than him."

I stood up. "I can hardly wait. But I *will* wait, promise."

"Good. Once is enough." She smiled up at me. "Get some
rest. Probably a long day tomorrow."

Actually, I was up past midnight catching up on schoolwork,
or not quite catching up. My brain wouldn't settle down enough
to worry about Kant and his Categorical Imperative. Not with
aliens out there waiting to be contacted.


## 8.  BAD  COUGH

Paul was free until 1400, so right after breakfast we suited up
and equipped a dog with extra oxygen and climbing gear. He'd
done a lot of climbing and caving on both Earth and Mars. If we

found the hole—*when* we found the hole—he was going to approach it roped up, so if he broke through the way I did, he
wouldn't fall far or fast.

I'd awakened early with a slight cough, but felt okay. I got
some cough suppressant pills from the first-aid locker, chewed
one and put two in my helmet's tongue-operated pill cache.

We went through the airlock and weren't surprised to see
that the storm had covered all my tracks, and everyone else's—
including Red's; I was hoping that his sawhorse thing might have
gouged out a distinctive mark when it stopped.

We still had a good chance of finding the hole, thanks to the
MPS built into the suit and its inertial compass. I'd started counting steps, going west, when I set out from Telegraph Hill, and
was close to five thousand when I fell through. That's about four
kilometers, maybe an hour's walk in the daytime.

"So we're probably being watched," Mother said, and waved
to the invisible camera. "Hey there, Mr. Red! Hello, Dr. Green!
We're bringing back your patient with the insurance forms."

I waved, too, both arms. Paul put up both his hands palm
out, showing he wasn't armed. Though what it would mean to a
four-armed creature, I wasn't sure.

No welcoming party appeared, so we went to the right of
Telegraph Hill and started walking and counting. A lot of the terrain looked familiar. Several times I had us move to the left or
right when I was sure I had been closer to a given formation.

We walked a half-kilometer or so past Paul's wrecked
dumbo. I hadn't seen it in the dark.

Suddenly I noticed something. "Wait! Paul! I think it's just
ahead of you." I hadn't realized it, walking in the dark, but what
seemed to be a simple rise in the ground was actually rounded,
like an overturned shallow bowl.

"Like a little lava dome, maybe," he said. "That's where
you fell through." He pointed at something I couldn't quite see
from my angle and height. "Big enough for you and the dog,
anyhow."

He unloaded his mountaineering stuff from the dog, then took a hammer and pounded into the ground a long piton, which is like a spearpoint with a hole for the rope. Then he did another one about a foot away. He passed an end of the rope through both of them and tied it off.

He pulled on the rope with all his weight. "Carmen, Laura, help me test this." We did and it still held. He looped most of the rope over his shoulder and took a couple of turns under his arms, and then clamped it through a metal thing he called a crab. It's supposed to keep you from falling too fast, even if you let go.

"This probably isn't all necessary," he said, "since I'm just taking a look down. But better safe than dead." He backed up the slight incline, checking over his shoulder, and then got on his knees to approach the hole.

I held my breath as he took out a big flashlight and leaned over the edge. I didn't hear mother breathing, either.

"Okay!" he said. "There's the side reflector that broke off your dog. I've got a good picture."

"Good," I tried to say, but it came out as a cough. Then another cough, and then several, harder and harder. I felt faint and sat down and tried to stay calm. Eyes closed, shallow breathing.

When I opened my eyes, I saw specks of blood on the inside of my helmet. I could taste it inside my mouth and on my lips. "Mother, I'm sick."

She saw the blood and kneeled down next to me. "Breathe. Can you breathe?"

"Yes. I don't think it's the suit." She was checking the oxygen fitting and meter on the back.

"How long have you felt sick?"

"Not long . . . well, *now* I do. I had a little cough this morning."

"And didn't tell anybody."

"No, I took a pill and it was all right."

"I can see how all right it was. Do you think you can stand?"

I nodded and got to my feet, wobbling a little. She held on to my arm. Then Paul came up and held the other.

"I can just see the antenna on Telegraph Hill," he said. "I'll call for the jeep."

"No, don't," I pleaded. "I don't want to give the Dragon the satisfaction."

Mother gave a nervous laugh. "This is way beyond that, sweetheart. Blood in your lungs? What if I let you walk back and you dropped dead?"

"I'm not going to *die*." But saying that gave me a horrible chill. Then I coughed a bright red string onto my faceplate. Mother eased me back down, and awkwardly sat with my helmet in her lap while Paul shouted "Mayday!" over the radio.

"Where did they come up with that word?" I asked Mother.

"Easy to understand on a radio, I guess. 'Mo' dough' would work just as well." I heard the click as her glove touched my helmet. Trying to smooth my hair.

I didn't cry. Embarrassing to admit, but I guess I felt kind of important, dying and all. Dargo Solingen would feel like shit for doubting me. Though the cause-and-effect link there wasn't too clear.

I lay there trying not to cough for maybe twenty minutes before the jeep pulled up, driven by Dad. One big happy family. He and mother lifted me into the back and Paul took over the driving, leaving the dog and his climbing stuff behind.

It was a fast and rough ride back. I got into another coughing spasm and spattered more blood and goop on the faceplate.

Mother and Dad carried me into the airlock like a sack of grain or something, and then were all over each other trying to get me out of the Mars suit. At least they left the skinsuit on while they hurried me through the corridor and mess area to Dr. Jefferson's aid station.

He asked my parents to step outside, set me on the examination table, and stripped off the top of the skinsuit, to listen to my breathing with a stethoscope. He shook his head.

"Carmen, it sure sounds as if you've got something in your

lungs. But when I heard you were coming in with this, I looked at the whole-body MRI we took yesterday, and there's nothing there." He clicked on his clipboard and asked the window for my MRI, and there I was in all my transparent glory.

"Better take another one." He pulled the top up over my shoulders. "You don't have to take anything off; just lie down here." The act of lying down made me cough sharply, but I caught it in my palm.

He took a tissue and gently wiped my hand, and looked at the blood. "Damn," he said quietly. "You aren't a smoker. I mean on Earth."

"Just twice. Once tobacco and once pot. Just one time each."

He nodded. "Now take a really deep breath and try to hold it." He took the MRI wand and passed it back and forth over my upper body. "Okay. You can breathe now.

"New picture," he said to the window. Then he was quiet for too long.

"Oh my. What . . . what could that be?"

I looked, and there were black shapes in both of my lungs, about the size of golf balls. "What is . . . what are they?"

He shook his head. "Not cancer, not an infection, this fast. Bronchitis wouldn't show up black, anyhow. Better call Earth." He looked at me with concern and something else, maybe puzzlement. "Let's get you into bed in the next room, and I'll give you a sedative. Stop the coughing. And then maybe I'll take a look inside."

"Inside?"

"Brachioscopy, put a little camera down there. You won't feel anything."

❦ ❦ ❦

In fact, I didn't feel anything until I woke up several hours later. Mother was sitting by the bed, her hand on my forehead.

"My nose . . . the inside of my nose feels funny."

"That's where the tube went in. The brachioscope."

"Oh, yuck. Did he find anything?"

She hesitated. "It's . . . not from Earth. They snipped off some of it and took it to the lab. It's not . . . it doesn't have DNA."

"I've got a Martian disease?"

"Mars, or wherever your potato people are from. Not Earth, anyhow; everything alive on Earth has DNA."

I prodded where it ached, under my ribs. "It's not organic?"

"Well, it is. Carbon, hydrogen, oxygen. Nitrogen, phosphorus, sulfur—it has amino acids and proteins and even something like RNA. But that's as far as it goes."

That sounded bad enough. "So they're going to have to operate? On both of my lungs?"

She made a little noise and I looked up and saw her wiping her eyes. "What is it? Mother?"

"It's not that simple. The little piece they snipped off, it had to go straight into the glove box, the environmental isolation unit. That's the procedure we have for any Martian life we discover, because we don't know what effect it might have on human life. In your case . . ."

"In my case, it's already attacked a human."

"That's right. And they can't operate on you in the glove box."

"So they're just going to leave it there?"

"No. But Dr. Jefferson can't operate until he can work in a place that's environmentally isolated from the rest of the base. They're working on it now, turning the far end of Unit B into a little self-contained hospital. You'll move in there tomorrow or the next day, and he'll take out the stuff. Two operations."

"Two?"

"The first lung has to be working before he opens the second. On Earth, he could put you on a heart/lung machine, I guess, and work on both. But not here."

I felt suddenly cold and clammy and I must have turned pale. "It's not that bad," Mother said quickly. "He doesn't have to open you up; he'll be working through a small hole in your side. It's called thorascopy. Like when I had my knee operated on, and

I was just in and out. And he'll have the best surgeons on Earth looking over his shoulder, advising him."

With a half-hour delay, I thought. What if their advice was "No—don't do *that*!" Oops.

I thought of an old bad joke: Politicians cover their mistakes with money; cooks cover their mistakes with mayonnaise; doctors cover theirs with dirt. I could be the first person ever buried on Mars, what an honor.

"Wait," I said. "Maybe *they* could help."

"The Earth doctors? Sure—"

"No! I mean the aliens."

"Honey, they couldn't—"

"They fixed my ankle just like that, didn't they?"

"Well, evidently they did. But that's sort of a mechanical thing. They wouldn't have to know any internal medicine . . ."

"But it wasn't medicine at all, not like we know it. Those big lenses, the smoking herbs. It was kind of mumbo-jumbo, but it worked!"

There was one loud rap on the door, and Dr. Jefferson opened it and stepped inside, looking agitated. "Laura, Carmen—things have gone from bad to worse. The Parienza kids started coughing blood; they've got it. So I put my boy through the MRI, and he's got a mass in one of his lungs, too.

"Look, I have to operate on the Parienzas first; they're young and this is hitting them harder . . ."

"That's okay," I said. By all means, get some practice on someone else first.

"Laura, I want you to assist me in the surgery along with Selene." Dr. Milius. "So far, this is only infecting the children. If it gets into the general population, if *I* get it—"

"Alf! I'm not a surgeon—I'm not even a doctor!"

"If Selene and I get this and die, you are a doctor. You are *the* doctor. You at least know how to use a scalpel."

"Cutting up animals that are already dead!"

"Just . . . calm down. The machine's not that complicated. It's a standard waldo interface, and you have real-time MRI to show you where you're going."

"Can you hear yourself talking, Alphonzo? I'm just a biologist."

There was a long moment of silence while he looked at her. "Just come and pay attention. You might have to do Carmen."

"All right," Mother said. She looked grim. "Now?"

He nodded. "Selene's preparing them. I'm going to operate on Murray while she watches and assists; then she'll do Roberta while I observe. Maybe an hour and a half each."

"What can I do?" I said.

"Just stay put and try to rest," he said. "We'll get to you in three or four hours. Don't worry . . . you won't feel anything." Then he and mother were gone.

Won't feel anything? I was already feeling pretty crappy. I get pissed off and go for a walk and bring back the Plague from Outer Space?

I touched the window and said "Window outside." It was almost completely dark, just a faint line of red showing the horizon. The dust storm was over.

The whole plan crystallized then. I guess I'd been thinking of parts of it since I knew I'd be alone for a while.

I just zipped up my skinsuit and walked. The main corridor was almost deserted, people running along on urgent errands. Nobody was thinking of going outside—no one but me.

If the aliens had had a picture of me leaving the base at two in the morning, before, then they probably were watching us all the time. I could signal them. Send a message to Red.

I searched around for pencil to disable the airlock buzzer. Even while I was doing it, I wondered whether I was acting sanely. Was I just trying to escape being operated on? Mother used to say "Do something, even if it's wrong." There didn't seem to be anything else to do other than sit around and watch things go from bad to worse.

If the aliens were watching, I could make Red understand how serious it was. Whether he and Green could do anything, I didn't know. But what else was there? Things were happening too fast.

I didn't run into anyone until I was almost there. Then I nearly collided with Card as he stepped out of the Pod A bathroom. "What you doing over here?" he said. "I thought you were supposed to be in sick bay."

"No, I'm just—" Of course I started coughing. "Let me by, all right?"

"No! What are you up to?"

"Look, microbe. I don't have time to explain." I pushed by him. "Every second counts."

"You're going outside again! What are you, crazy?"

"Look, look, look—for once in your life, don't be a . . ." I had a moment of desperate inspiration, and grabbed him by the shoulders. "Card, listen. I need you. You have to trust me."

"What, this is about your crazy Martian story?"

"I can prove it's not crazy, but you have to come help me."

"Help you with what?"

"Just suit up and step outside with me. I think they'll come if I signal them, and they might be able to help us."

He was hesitant. I knew he only half believed me—but at least he did half believe me. "What? What do you want me to do outside?"

"I just want you to stand in the door, so the airlock can't close. That way no grown-up can come out and froog the deal."

That did make him smile. "So what you want is for me to be in as deep shit as you are."

"Exactly! Are you up for it?"

"You are so easy to see through, you know? You could be a window."

"Yeah, yeah. Are you with me?"

He glanced toward the changing room, and then back down the hall. "Let's go."

We must have gotten me into my suit in ninety seconds flat. It took him an extra minute because he had to strip and wiggle into the skinsuit first. I kept my eye on the changing room door, but I didn't have any idea what I would say if someone walked in. We're playing doctor?

My faceplate was still spattered with dried blood, which was part of the vague plan: I assumed they would know that the blood meant trouble, and their bug camera, or whatever it was, would be on me as soon as I stepped outside. I had a powerful flashlight, and would turn that on my face, with no other lights. Then wave my arms, jump around, whatever.

We rushed through the safety check and I put two fresh oxygen bottles into the dog I'd bashed up. Disabled the buzzer, and we crowded into the airlock, closed it and cycled it.

We'd agreed not to use the radio. Card signaled for me to touch helmets. "How long?"

"An hour, anyhow." I could walk past Telegraph Hill by then.

"Okay. Watch where you step, clumsy." I hit his arm.

The door opened and I stepped out into the darkness. Card put one foot out on the sand and leaned back against the door. He pantomimed looking at his watch.

I closed my eyes and pointed the light at my face. Bright red through my eyelids; I knew I'd be dazzled blind for a while after I stopped. So after I'd given them a minute of the bloody faceplate I just stood in one place and shined the light out over the plain, waving it around in fast circles, which I hoped would mean "Help!"

I wasn't sure how long it had taken Red to bring me from their habitat level to the cave where he was parked, and then on to here. Maybe two hours? I hadn't been tracking too well. Without a dust storm it might be faster. I pulled on the dog and headed toward the right of Telegraph Hill.

The last thing I expected to happen was this: I hadn't walked twenty yards when Red came zooming up on his weird vehicle and stopped in a great spray of dust.

Card broke radio silence with a justifiable "*Holy shit!*"

Red helped me put the dog on one side and I got into the other and we were off. I looked back and waved at Card, and he waved back. The base shrank really fast and slipped under the horizon.

I looked forward for a moment and then turned away. It was

just a little too scary, screaming along a few inches over the ground, missing boulders by a hair. The steering must have been automatic. Or maybe Red had inhuman reflexes. Nothing else about him was all that human.

Except the need to come back and help. He must have been waiting nearby.

It seemed no more than ten or twelve minutes before the thing slowed down and drifted into the slanted cave I remembered. Maybe he had taken a roundabout way before, to hide the fact that they were so close.

We got out the dog and I followed him back down the way we had come a couple of days before. I had to stop twice with coughing fits, and by the time we got to the place where he shed his Mars suit, there was a scary amount of blood.

An odd thing to think, but I wondered whether he would take my body back if I died here. Why should I care?

We went on down, and at the level where the lake was visible, Green was waiting, along with two small ones dressed in white. We went together down to the dark floor and followed blue lines back to what seemed to be the same hospital room where I'd first awakened after the accident.

I slumped down on the pillow, feeling completely drained and about to barf. I unshipped my helmet and took a cautious breath. It smelled like a cold mushroom farm, exactly what I expected.

Red handed me a glass of water and I took it gratefully. Then he picked up my helmet with his two large arms and did a curiously human thing with a small one: he wiped a bit of blood off the inside with one finger, and then lifted it to his mouth to taste it.

"Wait!" I said. "That could be poison to you!"

He set the helmet down. "How nice of you to be concerned," he said, in a voice like a British cube actor.

I just shook my head. After a few seconds I was able to say "What?"

"Many of us can speak English," Green said, "or other of your languages. We've been listening to your radio, television, and cube for two hundred years."

"But . . . before . . . you . . ."

"That was to protect ourselves," Red said. "When we saw you had hurt yourself and I had to bring you here, it was decided that no one would speak a human language in your presence. We are not ready to make contact with humans. You are a dangerous violent race that tends to destroy what it doesn't understand."

"Not all of us," I said.

"We know that. We were considering various courses of action when we found out you were ill."

"We monitor your colony's communications with Earth," one of the white ones said, "and saw immediately what was happening to you. We all have that breathing fungus soon after we're born. But with us it isn't serious. We have an herb that cures it permanently."

"So . . . you can fix it?"

Red spread out all four hands. "We are so different from you, in chemistry and biology. The treatment might help you. It might kill you."

"But this crap is sure to kill me if we don't do anything!"

The other white-clad one spoke up. "We don't know. I am called Rezlan, and I am . . . of a class that studies your people. A scientist, or philosopher.

"The fungus would certainly kill you if it continued to grow. It would fill up your lungs and you couldn't breathe. But we don't know; it never happens to us. Your body may learn to adapt to it, and it would be . . . illegal? Immoral, improper . . . for us to experiment on you. If you were to die . . . I don't know how to say it. Impossible."

"The cure for your ankle was different," Green said. "There was no risk to your life."

I coughed and stared at the spatter of blood on my palm. "But if you don't treat me, and I die? Won't that be the same thing?"

All four of them made a strange buzzing sound. Red patted my shoulder. "Carmen, that's a wonderful joke. 'The same thing.'" He buzzed again, and so did the others.

"Wait," I said, "I'm going to *die* and it's funny?"

"No no no," Green said. "Dying itself isn't funny." Red put his large hands on his potato head and waggled it back and forth, and the others buzzed.

Red tapped his head three times, which set them off again. A natural comedian. "If you have to explain a joke, it isn't funny."

I started to cry, and he took my hand in his small scaly one and patted it. "We are so different. What is funny . . . is how we here are caught. We don't have a choice. We have to treat you even though we don't know what the outcome will be." He buzzed softly. "But that's not funny to you."

"*No!*" I tried not to wail. "I can see this part. There's a paradox. You might kill me, trying to help me."

"And that's not funny to you?"

"No, not really. Not at all, really."

"Would it be funny if it was somebody else?"

"Funny? *No!*"

"What if it was your worst enemy. Would that make you smile?"

"No. I don't have any enemies that bad."

He said something that made the others buzz. I gritted my teeth and tried not to cry. My whole chest hurt, like both lungs held a burning ton of crud, and here I was trying not to barf in front of a bunch of potato-head aliens. "Red. Even if I don't get the joke. Could you do the treatment before I foogly die?"

"Oh, Carmen. It's being prepared. This is . . . it's a way of dealing with difficult things. We joke. You would say laughing instead of crying." He turned around, evidently looking back the way we had come, though it's hard to tell which way a potato is looking. "It is taking too long, which is part of why we have to laugh. When we have children, it's all at one time, and so they all need the treatment at the same time, a few hundred days later, after they bud. We're trying to grow . . . it's like trying to find a vegetable out of season? We have to make it grow when it doesn't want to. And make enough for the other younglings in your colony."

"The adults don't get it?"

He did a kind of shrug. "We don't. Or rather, we only get it once, as children. Do you know about whooping cough and measles?"

"What-sels?"

"Measels and whooping cough used to be diseases humans got as children. Before your parents' parents were born. We heard about them on the radio, and they reminded us of this."

A new green-clad small one came through the plastic sheets, holding a stone bowl. She and Red exchanged a few whistles and scrapes. "If you are like us when we are small," he said, "this will make you excrete in every way. So you may want to undress."

How wonderful. Here comes Carmen, the shitting pissing farting burping barfing human sideshow. Don't forget snot and earwax. I got out of the Mars suit and unzipped the skinsuit and stepped out of that. I was cold, and every orifice clenched up tight. "Okay. Let's go."

Red held my right arm with his two large ones, and Green did the same on the left. Not a good sign. The new green one spit into the bowl, and it started to smoke.

She brought the smoking herb under my nose and I tried to get away, but Red and Green held me fast. It was the worst-smelling crap you could ever imagine. I barfed through mouth and nose and then started retching and coughing explosively, horribly, like a cat with a hairball. It did bring up the two fungus things, like furry rotten fruit. I would've barfed again if there had been anything left in my stomach, but I decided to pass out instead.

### 9. INVASION FROM EARTH

I half woke up, I don't know how much later, with Red tugging gently on my arm. "Carmen," he said, "do you live now? There is a problem."

I grunted something that meant yes, I am alive, but no, I'm

not sure I want to be. My throat felt like someone had pulled something scratchy and dead up through it. "Sleep," I said, but he picked me up and started carrying me like a child.

"There are humans from Earth here," he said, speeding up to a run. "They do not understand. They're wrecking everything." He blew through the plastic sheets into the dark hall.

"Red . . . it's hard to breathe here." He didn't respond, just ran faster, a rippling horse gait. His own breath was coming hard, like sheets of paper being ripped. "Red. I need . . . suit. Oxygen."

"As we do." We were suddenly in the middle of a crowd— hundreds of them in various sizes and colors—surging up the ramp toward the surface. He said three short words over and over, very loud, and the crowd stopped moving and parted to let us through.

When we went through the next set of doors I could hear air whistling out. On the other side my ears popped with a painful *crack* and I felt cold, colder than I ever had been. "What's happening?"

"Your . . . humans . . . have a . . . thing." He was wheezing before each word. "A tool . . . that . . . tears . . . through."

He set me down gently on the cold rock floor. I shuddered out of control, teeth chattering. No air. Lungs full of nothing but pain. The world was going white. I was starting to die but instead of praying or something I just noticed that the hairs in my nose had frozen and were making a crinkly sound when I tried to breathe.

Red was putting on the plastic layers that made up his Mars suit. He picked me up and I cried out in startled pain—the skin on my right forearm and breast and hip had frozen to the rock— and he held me close with three arms while the fourth did something to seal the plastic. Then he held me with all four arms and crooned something reassuring to weird creatures from another planet. He smelled like a mushroom you wouldn't eat, but I could breathe again.

I was bleeding some from the ripped skin and my lungs and

throat still didn't want to work, and I was being hugged to death by a nightmarish singing monster, so rather than put up with it all my body just passed out again.

I woke up to my father fighting with Red, with me in between. Red was trying to hold on to me with his small arms while my father was going after him with some sort of pipe, and he was defending himself with the large arms. "No!" I screamed. "Dad! No!"

Of course he couldn't hear anything in the vacuum, but I guess anyone can lip-read the word "no." He stepped back with an expression on his face that I had never seen. Anguish, I suppose, or rage. Well, here was his daughter, naked and bleeding, in the many arms of a gruesome alien, looking way too much like a movie poster from a century ago.

Taka Wu and Mike Silverman were carrying a spalling laser. "Red," I said, "watch out for the guys with the machine."

"I know," he said, "We've seen you use it underground. That's how they tore up the first set of doors. We can't let them use it again."

It was an interesting standoff. Four big aliens in their plastic-wrap suits. My father and mother and nine other humans in Mars suits, armed with tomato stakes and shovels and one laser, the humans looking kind of pissed off and frightened. The Martians probably were, too. A good thing we hadn't brought any guns to this planet.

Red whispered. "Can you make them leave the machine and follow us?"

"I don't know . . . they're scared." I mouthed "Mother, Dad," and pointed back the way we had come. "Fol-low us," I said with slow exaggeration. Confined as I was, I couldn't make any sweeping gestures, but I jabbed one forefinger back the way we had come.

Dad stepped forward slowly, his hands palm out. Mother started to follow him. Red shifted me around and held out his hand and my father took it, and held his other one out for mother. She took it and we went crabwise through the dark layers of the second airlock. Then the third and the fourth, and we were on the slope overlooking the lake.

The crowd of aliens we'd left behind was still there, perhaps a daunting sight for mother and Dad. But they held on, and the crowd parted to let us through.

I noticed ice was forming on the edge of the lake. Were we going to kill them all?

"Pardon," Red muttered, and held me so hard I couldn't breathe, while he wiggled out of his suit and left it on the ground, then set me down gently.

It was like walking on ice—on *dry* ice—and my breath came out in plumes. But he and I walked together along the blue line paths, followed by my parents, down to the sanctuary of the white room. Green was waiting there with my skinsuit. I gratefully pulled it on and zipped up. "Boots?"

"Boots," she said, and went back the way we'd come.

"Are you all right?" Red asked.

My father had his helmet off. "These things speak English?"

Red sort of shrugged. "And Chinese, in my case. We've been eavesdropping on you since you discovered radio."

My father fainted dead away.

☙ ☙ ☙

Green produced this thing that looked like a gray cabbage and held it by Dad's face. I had a vague memory of it being used on me, sort of like an oxygen source. He came around in a minute or so.

"Are you actually Martians?" Mother said. "You can't be."

Red nodded in a jerky way. "We are Martians only the same way you are. We live here. But we came from somewhere else."

"Where?" Dad croaked.

"No time for that. You have to talk to your people. We're losing air and heat, and have to repair the door. Then we have to treat your children. Carmen was near death."

Dad got to his knees and stood up, then stooped to pick up his helmet. "You know how to fix it? The laser damage."

"It knows how to repair itself. But it's like a wound in the body. We have to use stitches or glue to close the hole. Then it grows back."

"So you just need for us to not interfere."

"And help, by showing where the damage is."

He started to put his helmet on. "What about Carmen?"

"Yeah. Where's my suit?"

Red faced me. I realized you could tell that by the little black mouth slit. "You're very weak. You should stay here."

"But—"

"No time to argue. Stay here till we return." All of them but Green went bustling through the airlock.

"So," I said to her. "I guess I'm a hostage."

"My English no good," she said. "Parlez-vous Français?" I said no. "Nihongo hanasu koto ga dekimasu?"

Probably Japanese, or maybe Martian. "No, sorry." I sat down and waited for the air to run out.


## 10. ZEN FOR MORONS

Green put a kind of black fibrous poultice on the places where my skin had burned off from the icy ground, and the pain stopped immediately. That raised a big question I couldn't ask, having neglected both French and Japanese in school. But help was on its way.

While I was getting dressed after Green had finished her poulticing, another green one showed up.

"Hello," it said. "I was asked here because I know English. Some English."

"I—I'm glad to meet you. I'm Carmen."

"I know. And you want me to say my name. But you couldn't say it yourself. So give me a name."

"Um . . . Robin Hood?"

"I am Robin Hood, then. I am pleased to meet you."

I couldn't think of any pleasantries, so I dove right in: "How come your medicine works for us? My mother says we're unrelated at the most basic level, DNA."

"Am I 'DNA' now? I thought I was Robin Hood."

This was not going to be easy. "No. Yes. You're Robin Hood. Why does your medicine work on humans?"

"I don't understand. Why shouldn't it? It's medicine."

So much for the Enigmatic Superior Aliens theory. "Look. You know what a molecule is?"

"I know the word. Very small. Too small to see." He took his big head in two large-arm hands and wiggled it, the way Red did when he was agitated. "Forgive me. Science is not my . . . there is no word. I can't know science. I don't think any of us can, really. But especially not me."

I gestured at everything. "Then where did *this* all come from? It didn't just *happen*."

"That's right. It didn't happen. It's always been this way."

I needed a scientist and they sent me a philosopher. Not too bright, either. "Can you ask her?" I pointed to Green. "How can her medicine work, when we're chemically so different?"

"She's not a 'her.' Sometimes she is, and sometimes she's a 'he.' Right now she's a 'what.'"

"Okay. Would you please ask it?"

They exchanged a long series of wheedly-poot-rasp sounds.

"It's something like this," Robin Hood said. "Curing takes intelligence. With Earth humans, the intelligence comes along with the doctor, or scientists. With us, it's in the medicine." He touched the stuff on my breast, which made me jump. "It knows you are different, and works on you differently. It works on the very smallest level."

"Nanotechnology," I said.

"Maybe smaller than that," he said. "As small as chemistry. Intelligent molecules."

"You do know about nanotechnology?"

"Only from TV and the cube." He spidered over to the bed. "Please sit. You make me nervous, balanced there on two legs."

I obliged him. "This is how different we are, Carmen. You know when nanotechnology was discovered."

"End of the twentieth century sometime."

"There's no such knowledge for us. This medicine has always been. Like the living doors that keep the air in. Like the things that make the air, concentrate the oxygen. Somebody made them, but that was so long ago, it was before history. Before we came to Mars."

"Where *did* you come from? When?"

"We would call it Earth, though it's not your Earth, of course. Really far away, really long ago." He paused. "More than ten thousand ares."

A hundred centuries before the Pyramids. "But that's not long enough ago for Mars to be inhabitable. Mars was Mars a million ares ago."

He made an almost human gesture, all four hands palms up. "It could be much longer. At ten thousand ares, history becomes mystery. Our faraway Earth could be a myth. There aren't any space ships lying around.

"What deepens the mystery is that we could never live on Mars, on the surface, but we *could* live on Earth, your Earth. So why were we brought many light years and left on the wrong planet?"

I thought about what Red had said. "Maybe because we're too dangerous."

"That's a theory. Or it might have been dinosaurs. They looked pretty dangerous."


## 11. SUFFER THE LITTLE CHILDREN

The damage from the laser was repaired in a few hours, and I was bundled back to the colony to be rayed and poked and prodded and interviewed by doctors and scientists. They couldn't find anything wrong with me, human or alien in origin.

"The treatment they gave you sounds like primitive arm-waving," Dr. Jefferson said. "The fact that they don't know why it works is scary."

"They don't know why *anything* works over there. It sounds like it's all hand-me-down science from thousands of years ago."

He nodded and frowned. "You're the only data point we have. If the disease were less serious, I'd introduce it to the kids one at a time, and monitor their progress. But there's no time."

Rather than try to take a bunch of sick children over there, they invited the aliens to come to us. It was Red and Green, logically, with Robin Hood and an amber one following closely behind. I was outside, waiting for them, and escorted Red through the airlock.

Half the adults in the colony seemed crowded into the changing room for a first look at the aliens. There was a lot of whispered conversation while Red worked his way out of his suit.

"It's hot," he said. "The oxygen makes me dizzy. This is less than Earth, though?"

"Slightly less," Dr. Jefferson said. He was in the front of the crowd. "Like living on a mountain."

"It smells strange. But not bad. I can smell your hydroponics."

"Where are children?" Green said as soon as she was out of the suit. "No time talk." She held out her bag of herbs and chemicals and shook it.

The children had been prepared with the idea that these "Martians" were our friends, and had a way to cure them. There were pictures of them and their cave. But a picture of an eight-legged potato-head monstrosity isn't nearly as distressing as the real thing—especially to a room full of children who are terribly ill with something no one can explain (but which they suspect is Martian in origin). So their reaction when Dr. Jefferson walked in with Dargo Solingen and Green was predictable—screaming and crying and, from the ambulatory ones, escape attempts. Of course the doors were locked, with people like me spying in through the windows, looking in on the chaos.

Everybody loves Dr. Jefferson, and almost everybody is afraid of Dargo Solingen, and eventually the combination worked. Green just quietly stood there like Exhibit A, which helped. It takes a while not to think of giant spiders when you see them walk.

They had talked about the possibility of sedating the children, to make the experience less traumatic, but the only data they had about the treatment was my description, and they were afraid that if the children were too relaxed, they wouldn't cough forcefully enough to expel all the crap. Without sedation, the experience might haunt them for the rest of their lives, but at least they would *have* lives.

They wanted to keep the children isolated, and both adults would have to stay in there for a while after the treatment, to make sure they hadn't caught it, unlikely as that seemed.

So the only thing between the child being treated and the ones who were waiting for it was a sheet suspended from the ceiling, and after the first one, they all had heard what they were in for. It was done in age order, youngest to oldest, and at first there was some undignified running around, grabbing the victims and dragging them behind the sheet, where they volubly did the hairball performance.

But the children all seemed to sleep peacefully after the thing was over, which calmed most of the others—if they were like me, they hadn't been sleeping much. Card, one of the oldest, who had to wait the longest, pretended to be unconcerned and sleep before the treatment. I know how brave that was of him; he doesn't handle being sick well. As if I did.

The rest of us were mostly crowded into the mess hall, talking with Red and Robin Hood. The other one asked that we call him Fly in Amber, and said that it was his job to remember, so he wouldn't be saying much.

Red said that his job, his function, was hard to describe in human terms. He was sort of like a mayor, a local leader or organizer. He also did things that called for a lot of strength.

Robin Hood said he was being modest; for forty ares he had been a respected leader. When their surveillance device showed that I was in danger of dying, they all looked to Red to make the decision and then act on it.

"It was not a hard decision," he said. "Ever since you landed, we knew that a confrontation was inevitable. I took this opportunity to initiate it, so it would be on our terms. I couldn't know that Carmen would catch this thing, which you call a disease, and bring it back home with her."

"You don't call it a disease?" one of the scientists asked.

"No . . . I guess in your terms it might be called a 'phase,' a developmental phase. You go from being a young child to being an older child. For us, it's unpleasant but not life-threatening."

"It doesn't make sense," the xenologist Howard Jain said. "It's like a human teenager who has acne, transmitting it to a trout. Or even more extreme than that—the trout at least has DNA."

"And you and the trout have a common ancestor," Robin Hood said. "We have no idea what we might have evolved from."

"Did you get the idea of evolution from us?" he asked.

"No, not as a practical matter. We've been cross-breeding plants for a long time. But Darwinism, yes, from you. From your television programs back in the twentieth century."

"Wait," my father said. "How did you build a television receiver in the first place?"

There was a pause, and then Red spoke: "We didn't. It's always been there."

"What?"

"It's a room full of metal spheres, about as tall as I am. They started making noises in the early twentieth century . . ."

"Those like me remembered them all," Fly in Amber said, "though they were just noises at first."

". . . and we knew the signals were from Earth, because we only got them when Earth was in the sky. Then the spheres started showing pictures in mid-century, which gave us visual clues for decoding human language. Then when the cube was developed, they started displaying in three dimensions."

"How long is 'always'?" Howard Jain asked. "How far back does your history go?"

"We don't have history in your sense," Fly in Amber said. "Your history is a record of conflict and change. We have neither, in the normal course of things. A meteorite damaged an outlying area of our home 4,359 ares ago. Otherwise, not much has happened until your radio started talking."

"You have explored Mars more than we have," Robin Hood said, "with your satellites and rovers, and much of what we know about the planet, we got from you. You put your base in this area because of the large frozen lake underground; we assume that's why we were put here, too. But that memory is long gone."

"Some of us have a theory," Red said, "that the memory was somehow suppressed, deliberately erased. What you don't know you can't tell."

"You can't erase a memory," Fly in Amber said.

"*We* can't. The ones who put us here obviously could do many things we can't do."

"You are not a memory expert. I am."

Red's complexion changed slightly, darkening. It probably wasn't the first time they'd had this argument. "One thing I do remember is the 1950s, when television started."

"You're that old!" Jain said.

"Yes, though I was young then. That was during the war between Russia and the United States, the Cold War."

"You have told us this before," Robin Hood said. "Not all of us agree."

Red pushed on. "The United States had an electronic network it called the 'Distant Early Warning System,' set up so they would know ahead of time, if Russian bombers were on their way." He paused. "I think that's what we are."

"Warning whom?" Jain said.

"Whoever put us here. We're on Mars instead of Earth because they didn't want you to know about us until you had space flight."

"Until we posed a threat to them," Dad said.

"That's a very human thought." Red paused. "Not to be insulting. But it could also be that they didn't want to influence your development too early. Or it could be that there was no profit in contacting you until you had evolved to this point."

"We wouldn't be any threat to them," Jain said. "If they could come here and set up the underground city we saw, thousands and thousands of years ago, it's hard to imagine what they could do now."

The uncomfortable silence was broken by Maria Rodriguez, who came down from the quarantine area. "They're done now. It looks like all the kids are okay." She looked around at all the serious faces. "I said they're okay. Crisis over."

Actually, it had just begun.

## 12. THE MARS GIRL

Which is how I became an ambassador to the Martians. Everybody knows they didn't evolve on Mars, but what else are you going to call them?

Red, whose real name is Twenty-one Leader Leader Lifter Leader, suggested that I would be a natural choice as a go-between. I was the first human to meet them, and the fact that they risked exposure by saving my life would help humans accept their good intentions.

On Earth, there was a crash program to orbit a space station, Little Mars, that duplicated the living conditions they were used to. Before my five-year residence on Mars was over, I was taken back there with Red and three other Martians, along with Howard Jain, who would be coordinating research.

Nobody wanted to bring them all the way down to Earth quite yet. A worldwide epidemic of the lung crap wouldn't improve relations, and nobody could say whether they might harbor something even more unpleasant.

So I'm sort of a lab animal, under quarantine and constant medical monitoring, maybe for life. But I'm also an ambassador, the human sidekick for Red and the others. Leaders come up from Earth to make symbolic gestures of friendship, even though it's obviously more about fear than brotherhood. When the Others show up, we want to have a good report card from the Martians.

That will be decades or centuries or even millennia—unless

they've figured a way around the speed-of-light speed limit. I'm pretty confident they have. So I might meet them.

A couple of days a week, the Elevator comes up and I meet all kinds of presidents and secretariats and so forth, though there's always a pane of glass between us. More interesting is talking with the scientists and other thinkers who vie for one-week residences here, in the five Spartan rooms the Mars Institute maintains. Sometimes rich people come over from the Hilton to gawk. They pay.

The rest of the time, I spend with Red and the others, trying to learn their language—me, who chickened out of French—and teach them about humans. Meanwhile exercise two hours a day in the thin cold air and Martian gravity, and study for my degrees in xenology. I'll be writing the book some day. Not "a" book. The book.

Every now and then some silly tabloid magazine or show will do the "poor little Mars Girl" routine, about how isolated I am in this goldfish bowl hovering over the Earth, never to have anything like a normal life.

But everybody on Mars is under the same quarantine as I am; everybody who's been exposed to the Martians. I could go back some day and kick Dargo Solingen out of office. Marry some old space pilot.

Who wants a normal life, anyhow?